DON'T LET OUT THE
MAGIC
SMOKE

I: THREE ON A MATCH

G. L. NOBLE

❦

Special Thanks to:
Commodore for the Amiga
Rick Stiles for UEdit
Grasshopper LLC for PageStream
and
Sawyer Brown for the Music

❦

ISBN   1-442-17981-3
EAN-13 978-1-442-17981-3

http://www.magicsmoke.info

Cover design by Nisse B. Noble

Printed in the United States of America

PREFACE

One night, out of boredom, I opened the portal. I fluttered through, soaring and diving through the night sky. I quickly tired, and looking about for a place to catch my breath, I noted a small Air Force jet. Since thoughts have the advantage of being invisible, I hitched a ride on the shoulder of the pilot.

It might have been my presence that attracted the alien. Perhaps it was the alien that attracted me. It matters not, however, to the events that followed: the saga of two ordinary pilots, stumbling through a universe they don't quite understand, attempting with varying levels of success to help contain the magic smoke.

I have tried in my humble way to record faithfully what I witnessed. And as I write this, I also hope, for all concerned, that my footsteps through the universe do not let out the magic smoke.

– GLN

Contents

1

For Here, Or To Go?

"But Dervish, you know that is a no-contact world. We have not received Mother's permission to proceed," the interface computer argued in a soft feminine voice.

"She hasn't caught us so far. Shut off autologging, Love, and let's go!"

They winked in just above atmosphere over the Pacific. From there, they headed east and descended toward the Nevada desert. Dervish glanced out at the blackness below. "If he's out tonight I want to get up close. See if we can make friends."

Dervish would have sworn that Love sighed as she began scanning. Only a few moments went by before she reported, "Dervish, the pilot you are interested in is within range now."

Dervish grinned as the small jet registered on the equipment. "Okay, Love, down we go!"

"I do not consider this advisable," Love replied, as she slowly descended toward the approaching jet.

"Why not? It's too dark to see us, and I'll jam their equipment so they won't pick us up below."

"But I am unable to predict how his craft will respond to the turbulence we will create."

Dervish thought a moment. "He's a good pilot. It shouldn't cause him any trouble." As his Bird neared the fighter, Dervish began to merge with the jet's computer. He attempted to analyze the circuitry in order to mask his presence from the equipment. As he played with the logic, the jet became unstable and attempted to stall. He quickly withdrew from the computer. "Damn! That thing's so primitive you mask one thing and the rest won't work."

Angel leveled the little fighter as it started to shimmy, then checked the gauges and readouts to be sure they added up to something logical. He eased her back into a slow climb, but she balked and tried to stall.

"Shit," Angel grumbled. The readouts were fluctuating wildly and the CRT display was a kaleidoscope of random garbage; then, as he watched, the readouts stabilized. "Damn computer musta barfed," he mumbled, glancing out at the slate-black Nevada sky. "Tower, this is Angel. I'd like to bring her in. The computer's really screwing up. I'm down to twelve thousand feet. Am I clear at this altitude?"

"Angel, tower here. You're clear to proceed at present altitude. Attempting to clear permission to land."

"Thanks." He glanced around at the grey boxes that held the flight computers. "Fucking retards," he grumbled. "Nothing works in this piece of crap." He reached over and flicked on the See-Night equipment. *A set of fog lights would do more good*, he thought, as the screen remained black. "Damned experimental junk," he sputtered. He hit the black metal box with his fist, and it obediently came to life, indicating the presence of something above him. He frowned and dropped the fighter a few hundred feet for clearance, then rekeyed the mike. "Hey," he snapped, while attempting to level his jet, "why the hell didn't you tell me I had company up here?"

"The pilot has detected us on his equipment and has reported that fact to those below," Love informed Dervish. "He is also descending to avoid us. I recommend that we leave."

"No, I want to meet him. He really does sound upset, though." Dervish glanced longingly at the receding jet. "Let's just get out of tracking range and wait until he cools down."

"Angel, tower. What are you talking about?"

"What do you mean, 'what am I talking about'? The other *fucking* blip on your radar. Or are you blind, too?" Angel sassed. As the jet lurched sideways, stubbornly determined to keep its nose pointing downward, the tracking equipment began to beep.

"The only blip I have is you ... hang on ... just confirmed a reading off your transponder. What the ... no, still nothing showing on radar. Can you ID it?"

"Negative. Whatever it is ain't in the IFF database."

"Then it's not ours. Hang on ..."

"Look, if *you* aren't seeing anything, it's probably just another blown chip. I got problems here. This piece of ... this thing is falling apart."

"Angel, the colonel just requested you check it out. Falcon says it'll be a couple of minutes before they get the phased array pointed this way."

"Sure thing," Angel shot back, "but I doubt this baby can take much more altitude. I think one of the squirrels musta died or something."

"Angel, Hollister here. That is controlled air space. If there's something up there, I want to know what it is, got that? If you can't fly 'em, put in for a transfer to infantry."

"No disrespect meant, sir, but this thing is shimmying so bad you could mix daiquiris up here ... and she keeps trying to stall. Can't you scramble someone else?"

"Dammit, Angel!" Hollister barked. The tone of voice and the long pause that followed only tightened the knot in Angel's gut. "Okay, bring it home. But, so help me, if it checks out okay, you're gonna be driving a tram at Disneyland."

Angel grimaced as he released the mike button. "Up yours," he muttered, then flicked it back on. "Sorry; can't make out what you're saying over the damned beeps." He flipped a switch. "There, that's better. What were you saying, Colonel?"

"Angel, turn the transponder back on and get your butt back here now."

"Transponder? Oh. Right. I thought that was the door ajar warning."

"Angel."

"Sir?"

"When you land, report to Major Ehrlich. Class A uniform."

Angel wrinkled his nose in disgust. "Yes, sir." He gave a one-fingered salute to the radio and began a slow turn to head for base.

"I believe we are being scanned by phased radar," Love informed Dervish. "Invoking jammers and gaining altitude."

Angel took a deep breath as the readouts once again went wild. The beeping became a solid tone, then silenced as a strong turbulence enveloped the craft. The jet twisted and fought the controls, then stalled, the air currents flinging it about violently as he tried to recover. It dipped slightly, then veered off into a flat spin. The sudden g's slammed him sideways into the seat. He blacked out.

"Drop the jammers. You're creaming his flight computer." Dervish winced as he watched the small jet spin off. "Oh, crap! Get a tow beam on him."

"Locked on. I do not think he will be pleased with us."

"Maybe we better introduce ourselves some other night." Dervish sighed. "Man, if there's a way to fuck something up, I can find it."

"I think you and that pilot will be very good friends," Love stated. "You appear to have a lot in common."

Angel regained consciousness to find himself gliding silently only a few hundred feet above a highway. *Shit, I'm either dead or dreaming*, he thought. He tried to gather his wits about him, but his mind refused to function. He took a deep breath and eased her down onto the pavement. He sat there a few minutes while the blood returned to his brain and the reality of his position soaked in. He started the engine, taxied down the highway into a truck stop, walked in shakily and ordered a cup of coffee.

✦ ✦ ✦

Major Richardson sat at his desk reviewing a file labelled Captain Ryan Eugene Douglas. The more he read, the more he felt Douglas was right for the new project.

He glanced up at his associate and nodded. "I agree, he's ideal. Where did you find his file?"

The other psychiatrist rubbed his nose. "An Air Force JAG brought it in. It seems his commander has recommended court martial."

"For what?"

"Screwing around."

Richardson wrinkled his brow. "Most pilots do. What happened?"

"He landed on the highway."

"Mmmm ... so what does the attorney want from us?"

The other man shrugged. "He's looking for confirmation that it was a reasonable option after pulling out of a flat spin. The commander claims that if Douglas hadn't simply been screwing around he wouldn't have lost control."

"Perhaps. But why court martial?"

"Apparently, Douglas taxied into a truck stop and ordered a couple of cheeseburgers to go before flying the jet back to base."

"Oh." Richardson smiled. He studied the file a moment, then chuckled. "I'll handle this, if you don't mind. I'd like to talk with this guy anyway; make sure he'll fit the project."

"No problem. I wasn't looking forward to travelling to Nevada."

✦ ✦ ✦

Richardson looked up as Angel shuffled into the room: tall, lanky, gawky as a grizzly, his hands stuffed in his back pockets. His deep blue eyes stared back at Richardson as he approached the desk. Richardson motioned for him to be seated.

Angel plopped himself into the chair and leaned back, causing the front legs of the chair to lose contact with the floor. "Mornin', sir," he drawled.

Richardson nodded. "Yes it is, Captain."

Angel smiled. "You're okay, doc."

"Are you?" Richardson asked slowly.

Angel straightened his shoulders and eyed Richardson suspiciously. "Oh. So now Hollister's claiming I'm not just a fuckoff – I'm a crazy fuckoff, huh?"

Richardson smiled. "No. He claims you're irresponsible, not crazy."

Angel shrugged. "So then why am I here?"

Richardson gazed down at the folder. He looked back at Angel. "I have to know what really happened up there to prevent you from being court martialed."

Angel wrinkled his nose. "You got the file. I can't tell you anything that ain't already in there."

Richardson glanced back down at the papers. "The report states that you requested permission to land due to equipment malfunction. You were in a slow descent when the jet went into a flat spin. You landed on the highway, taxied to a truck stop, ordered two cheeseburgers and fries to go, and then brought the jet back. Is that about right?"

Angel nodded.

"How did you manage to land the jet?"

Angel diverted his gaze to the floor. "Don't rightly know, sir."

"Would you describe for me everything that took place from the time you received permission to bring her in until you returned to base?"

Angel shrugged. "Not much to tell." He glanced back at Richardson, then seemed to focus just beyond him. "I brought her around and started a descent. Hit some turbulence. She balked, went into a flat spin."

Richardson attempted to catch Angel's eye. "What happened then?"

"I'm not exactly sure, but somehow I got her leveled off about a hundred feet over the highway. I just didn't feel much like flying any more at the moment, so I set her down. Taxied her into a truck stop."

When it became apparent that Angel was not going to say anything further, Richardson motioned for him to continue. "And?"

"And I just sat and drank coffee for about fifteen minutes, trying to figure out how come I was still alive. Then I brought her back."

"Are you aware that the recorder registered a flameout at eleven thousand feet?"

"It's possible. I told you, I was in a flat spin. I was a little disoriented."

Richardson squinted hard at Angel. "It's pretty hard to forget a restart."

Angel shrugged noncommittally.

"Were you unconscious?"

"Do you think she would have leveled herself?"

"Autopilot, maybe?"

"Nope. Not equipped. Besides, no idiot box can get you out of a flat spin."

"Then how did you manage it?"

"Like I said, I just don't know."

Richardson nodded. "Why the cheeseburgers and fries?"

"I either had to eat something or barf."

Richardson swiveled his chair slightly to rest his elbow on the desk. "What was up there with you?" he asked casually.

"Huh?"

"Your transponder was tracking something a few hundred feet above you until you landed on the highway."

Angel frowned disgustedly. "That thing was completely scrambled. Read the maintenance report. It's amazing she made it back to base."

"Falcon reported two blips until you dropped below tracking altitude."

"I doubt that was real. Tower only had me."

Richardson reflected a moment. Concluding that Angel wasn't going to talk about the incident further, he continued. "Would you be interested in a highly classified and equally dangerous assignment?"

"I might. Especially if it includes a transfer."

"It does." Richardson smiled and closed the folder. "Due to the nature of the assignment, I'll have to interview your friends, relatives and associates. If you qualify for top clearance, I can proceed with the transfer. Do I have your permission?"

Angel frowned. "Since when does the Air Force need permission to check anything?"

"I don't *need* it," Richardson replied lightly. "But I would like your coöperation and trust. I won't do anything that you don't know about. I expect you to return the favor."

Angel smiled. "You got it, doc." He bit his lip a moment. "Umm ... I don't have any friends ... and my only relative is my aunt." He shifted his weight uncomfortably in the chair. "Well, my mother is probably still somewhere in Colorado. I haven't talked to her since I was nine. Marilyn might have her address."

"Marilyn?"

"My aunt."

Richardson nodded. "I guess that's all I need for now. I'll get back to you in a few days."

Angel dropped the front legs of the chair back to the floor, picked himself up and started slowly for the door. He half turned as he walked out. "Doc?"

"Yes?"

"Would you have bothered to clear things up with Hollister if you weren't interested in me for this project?"

"No."

Angel's eyes twinkled. "We're gonna get along just fine, doc."

Richardson chuckled. "I believe we will."

Richardson drove up the long driveway to the front of the ranch. He glanced at the papers he had spread out on the passenger seat. "Must be the place," he said as he got out.

A large black dog bounded up to him, wagging its tail.

"You're not much of a watchdog," he chided as he scratched the dog behind the ears.

The dog danced around delightedly at his feet as Richardson made his way to the door and knocked. After a while, he knocked again. "Looks like no one's home," he informed the dog.

The dog glanced out across the field and barked once softly. Richardson followed the dog's gaze to a large berry patch. "Oh, someone's out there. Well, come on, pup. Let's have a look."

She had her back to him, picking berries. He liked what he saw. She was robust; not fat, but well proportioned. Her long honey-blond hair fell in tangles down her back. He had to remind himself that he was here on business.

The dog raced ahead of him and skidded to a stop by her feet. He heard her giggle as she put down the basket of berries to ruff up the dog's fur.

Richardson stepped forward and picked up the basket. "Please, allow me," he mumbled self-consciously.

She looked up, smiled, then noted his uniform. Her face lost all expression as her skin paled. "Ryan ..." she stuttered.

"He's fine," Richardson blurted, realizing what she must be thinking. "I'm sorry; I shouldn't have worn my uniform. Thoughtless of me."

She took a deep breath and attempted to compose herself. "No ... no. I really did overreact, didn't I?"

Richardson smiled at her warmly. "A logical conclusion, considering military practice." He realized from her reaction that Angel had not informed her he was going to call. That served to convince him that he had picked the right person. "I'm Major Richardson. I gather that you are Marilyn ... Ryan's aunt. I truly assumed that he would have informed you I'd be dropping by."

She flushed slightly under his easy smile. "No," she admitted, nodding toward the house. "Ahh ... Major, would you mind coming into the house? I'm afraid I need to sit down."

"Not at all," he replied quickly. He walked next to her, marveling that someone so graceful could be related to someone as awkward as Angel.

Richardson made himself comfortable in one of the large chairs in the living room as Marilyn went to get some coffee. He was pleased to note nothing that supported his sudden fear that she might be married. She wasn't wearing a ring, and Angel hadn't mentioned an uncle. He smiled as she handed him a cup and helped himself to the cream and sugar she had placed on the table. "Ryan is being considered for a special project. I just need to check on a few things concerning his childhood."

She shrugged her shoulders. "He was a good boy, if that's what you mean. Did well in school, too."

"I'm mostly concerned with his standoffish nature and apparent ... dislike of his mother."

Marilyn's eyes narrowed. She set down her cup and studied Richardson a moment. "Ryan is shy," she stated defensively, "not standoffish. And his mother is ... well, why don't you visit her yourself?"

"No need. From what I've gathered, he spent very little time with her, so she really won't be able to tell me much of anything about him." He paused while he set down his cup. "How would you describe Ryan? His commander feels that he's a bit ... wild."

Marilyn frowned. "Wild? That commander has a thing or two to learn about Texans. Ryan's a fine young man. He spends most of his leave mending fences here on the ranch. Sends me all his pay, too."

Richardson grinned. "That would tend to limit his activities some." He glanced out the window at the miles and miles of nothing. "What can you tell me of his childhood?"

Marilyn pursed her lips and settled back into her chair. "I'll tell you what I know, but you gotta remember I'm probably a little biased."

"I would hope so."

Something in his manner made Marilyn decide she liked him. She took a sip of her coffee and gazed out the window. The dog bounded over and snuggled up against her feet. She unconsciously reached down and stroked his fur as she spoke. "Ryan's mom had a job with a big company. It paid real good, but she traveled a lot." She gazed over at Richardson, noted his nod, and continued. "My folks owned the ranch just over the hill back yonder. His dad ... my brother Henry ... well, he was pretty busy trying to run this place, so Ryan stayed with us quite a bit when she was gone. Got to where he spent more time with us than at home, even when she was in town."

"Your mother raised him?"

"No, mostly I took care of him."

"Did he seem to resent that?"

"Not as near as I can figure. He was ... well, he didn't seem all that close to his mother ... never cried or nothing. She'd come over sometimes when she was in the area but she never took him anywhere."

"He said he hasn't spoken to her since he was nine. What happened back then?"

Marilyn glanced at Richardson, then down at the dog. "It was ... just before his ninth birthday. She just came and got him one day. Didn't say nothing to my folks. Took him with her to Colorado. Seems she filed for a divorce and moved in with her boss."

"So he stopped talking to her?"

"He's never spoke about it much." She looked back at Richardson and held his gaze. "I don't pry."

"But I do."

She smiled despite herself. "I guess you need to know all this, huh?"

"It would help a great deal."

"Well, he wasn't very happy. He called here a few times crying ... he wanted to come home. But his mom hired all them fancy lawyers and we couldn't afford none, so she got custody."

"He graduated from high school here. How did he ... escape his mother?"

Marilyn wrinkled her brow. "He ran away. Flagged down a rig with Texas plates and asked the trucker to take him to his daddy."

"Didn't his mother demand he be returned?"

"Our dad got the judge to give custody to my brother."

"Really?"

"Well, Ryan had run away two other times. See, the man his mother was living with beat him. And his mother had lied to him, saying we didn't want him. Since the divorce wasn't final, she was just plain living in sin. The judge figured that wasn't a good way to bring up a kid."

"Did Ryan stay with your parents after that?"

She shook her head. "According to the custody papers, Ryan had to stay here at my brother's ranch, so I moved in to help take care of him."

"How old were you then?"

"Nineteen."

"Didn't you resent having to take care of a child when you were ..."

Marilyn stiffened. "Do you really need *my* life story, too?"

"No, but I *am* interested. If you don't mind me saying so, you're quite an attractive woman. I find it hard to believe that there weren't a large number of young men pounding on the door."

Marilyn blushed. "Henry won the marksmanship trophy in this county every year as long as he lived," she teased. "Actually, I guess I sort of felt like Ryan was my kid, too. Hell, I raised him. Besides, I never took a fancy to any of the ones that did come calling."

Richardson smiled, then gazed out the window. "How did Ryan handle the death of his father?"

Marilyn bit her lip. "Henry got cancer. Ryan was sixteen when he died. He was angry ... bitter. But you got to understand he was still just a kid."

"Those are very normal feelings." Richardson tried to catch her eye. "I can assure you that Ryan has the assignment if he wants it. I would feel better, however, if you let me take you to dinner."

She smiled wickedly. "I would be right pleased to join you. Providing you don't try to pry any more information out of me," she added.

"Perhaps a gentle nudge or two, but I promise not to pry."

Colonel Hollister looked up and sighed. The one thing that could ruin an otherwise beautiful day was now standing at his door.

Major Richardson brushed off his jacket. He straightened his badge and made sure his flight surgeon wings showed plainly enough to be imposing. Assuring himself that Hollister had seen him, he deliberately knocked on the door.

"Oh, come in!" Hollister shouted. *Why does the Air Force insist on calling a goddam shrink a surgeon*, he grumbled to himself.

"Thank you, sir," Richardson replied quietly as he slipped into the office. He seated himself, placed a folder on his lap, and casually crossed his legs. "I've been reviewing Douglas' file, and ..."

"Douglas?"

Richardson sat up straight and eyed the colonel over the rims of his glasses. "Captain. Ryan. Eugene. Douglas," he stated, pronouncing each word slowly and carefully.

Hollister's mind raced, but was a bit slow dropping into gear. "Uhhh ... who?"

"Angel?" Richardson prompted.

"Oh, yeah. Angel," Hollister mumbled. "So?"

Richardson smiled smugly. "So?" he stated airily. "I believe you've just demonstrated the heart of the problem."

Hollister closed his eyes and thumped his knuckles on the grey steel desk. "What in blazes are you talking about?"

"You have completely failed to notice your pilots as individuals," Richardson pointed out methodically. "You don't even recognize Douglas by name. How do you expect him to act responsibly if you only think of him as Angel ... a handle he earned, I believe, for his daredevil stunts?"

Hollister pursed his lips, flared his nostrils and gave Richardson a cold stare. "I'm not running a therapy group, I'm attempting to test weapons systems here!"

"To test fighters, you need test pilots. Douglas is one of your best. He won't be flying if he's court martialed."

"You think he shouldn't be? He's been busted, grounded, and docked enough to fall below the poverty line. Landing on the fucking highway is just one stunt too many."

Richardson gazed down at the file folder on his lap. He slowly opened it and leisurely browsed the contents.

Hollister grunted. "Well?"

Richardson gazed up. "As I started to explain, I have been looking over Douglas' file and I came across something quite interesting."

Hollister cleared his throat. "And what was that?"

Richardson ran his finger across the paper and stopped about a third of the way down. "Here. The tower reported that they lost contact with him when he went into a flat spin. Something happened out there that he's refusing to talk about."

"Yeah. He was fucking around again. He lost it and went into a dive."

Richardson stiffened as he peered over his glasses. "The data recovered from the black box confirms Ryan's report. Flameout at eleven thousand, flat spin to within a few hundred feet, and then a slow descent."

Hollister groaned. "So?" he grumbled.

"Douglas somehow managed to pull out of a flat spin while unconscious. I don't believe that has ever been done before."

Hollister eyed Richardson. "Unconscious? No goddam way."

"And the engine was not restarted until the altimeter registered ground level."

"I'm not saying he isn't good. But he's goddam dangerous!"

Richardson shook his head slowly. "If you will allow me to proceed?"

Hollister knew he wasn't going to get Richardson to leave until he heard him out. *Shrinks are crazy by definition*, he thought. "Go on," he mumbled.

"I think he should be sent to Eglin," Richardson stated.

"He should be locked up," Hollister replied. He hated to admit it when Richardson knew more than he did, but Eglin didn't ring a bell. Curiosity won the battle with his pride. "Ummm ... what's going on at Eglin?"

Richardson took off his glasses and blew on them. He took his handkerchief from his pocket and began to clean the lenses. "The Pentagon requested I recommend two pilots for project Chevron," he finally said.

"How'd those groundpounders get you involved with Chevron?"

"Security. I'm looking over seventeen possible candidates. I am, after all, well respected in my field," Richardson stated, pausing for effect. "The pilots' psychological profiles, of course, must show they are not ... reachable."

Hollister lit a cigar, mostly because he knew how much the smoke bothered Richardson. He puffed on it for a while, studying the psychiatrist. "It's obvious no one can reach Angel," he admitted.

Richardson returned his handkerchief to his pocket. "I feel Douglas is ideal for the project," he said as he slowly put his glasses back on. "I plan on letting him cool his heels there by himself for ... about six weeks. Then I'll send in the other pilot. One he'll take a liking to. Once they ..."

"Angel *like* someone? You've gotta be joking!"

"Douglas will form an attachment to the right person. He would have to be a very good pilot, and younger. I've found a couple of potential candidates. Once they become close friends, Douglas may open up and tell him what really happened out there."

"And they'll get married and live happily ever after. Now, get out of my office!"

Richardson cleared his throat. "I suppose I might discuss this with Major General Detrum. Since he also comes from Texas, he might ..."

"You do that," Hollister challenged. "I have enough shit on Angel to send him away for fifty years. Let's see what that does to his clearances!"

Richardson slowly closed the file and thumped his finger against it. "Actually, I've been wanting to talk to Detrum anyway," he added quietly as he stood up. "I ran across some statistics that I think he would find quite interesting."

Hollister sighed. "What have you discovered?"

"Are you aware that not one pilot under your command has ever reenlisted? I believe that sets a new record."

"Do you really?" Hollister bellowed, as he crushed out his cigar. He let out a mouthful of air and turned a bit purple around the edges. "All right. Gimme those goddam transfer papers!"

"Yes, sir," Richardson said. He took a stack of forms from his folder and put them on the desk. "Once you sign these, I expect I'll be far too busy finding the other candidate to talk to Detrum."

Hollister studied the doctor a few moments. "Did they teach you those tactics in shrink school?" he asked sourly.

"No," Richardson replied. "Officer training."

Richardson landed his Learjet and taxied to the far end of the large field. The jet was the only toy he had allowed himself; he didn't think it proper or wise to broadcast his independent wealth. He looked around and smiled. He'd always liked Williams. Perhaps it was its location in Arizona; more likely it was because his uncle Don was base commander. He strolled leisurely toward the group of buildings where Colonel Tellik was to meet him.

He gazed skyward. It was odd seeing nothing in the air but a few T-38s. Just two days ago, the sky had been cluttered with F-5s and F-16s from Luke, all of them screeching and diving as the Israelis challenged the Americans for supremacy. It seemed to him that the Israelis needed very little training. Why they were stationed at Williams for that purpose he could not guess, but he was glad that his uncle had invited him to watch the fun. He'd never have considered Charlie if he hadn't seen him fly.

He thought back to his conversation with Charlie's parents. His father had not said one word the whole time. Charlie's mother had even answered the questions that he had directed specifically to the father.

That confirmed the comments of the sergeant that had recruited Charlie. Charlie had hung around the recruiting office since grade school. Shy, perhaps even more so than Angel; soft spoken, easy going, likable, but very hard to really know. Charlie wanted very much to fly, but his mother was determined that her son would become a doctor. The sergeant said it had taken three weeks to convince Charlie's father to sign the enlistment papers when Charlie graduated high school a couple of years early. Now, would Charlie be able to make friends with Angel?

He stopped outside the building to thumb through the personnel folder. Captain, five-six, blond hair, green eyes, twenty-one years old. *Hmmm*, he thought, *that would make him ... five years younger than Angel. Well, I'll have to chance that. Charles Lewis Raychovsky ... sheesh, what a name to give a kid. His mother must have named him.*

It was obvious that Charlie was Tellik's favorite, especially now that he was the only one to have scored against the Israelis. He wasn't too sure how he would convince Tellik to reassign him. *Well, worse come to worst, I'll just have to ask Uncle Don for a favor*, he thought, as he opened the door and walked into the building.

After half an hour of humoring Tellik by going over the other possible candidates, Richardson scratched his head and flipped the folder open. "Nope, this is the one. Raychovsky."

Tellik shook his head firmly. "No, no, *no*," he stated. "You're not sending one of my best pilots to babysit some screwball from Nellis. Did you see those touch-and-goes he did? Hawk has more potential ..."

"And Douglas will make him even better," Richardson cut in.

Tellik glared at the doctor as the skin in the corners of his mouth tried to remember how to wrinkle into a smile. "The ground crew likes Hawk. The maintenance guys like Hawk. All the pilots like him. Even *I* like him," he said emphatically. "Find yourself another candidate."

Richardson smiled back. "I'll concede that he probably likes to be called Hawk better than Raychovsky." He placed the transfer papers on the desk, nodded slightly, then slowly left the room.

✦   ✦   ✦

Hawk walked across the dirt field. He studied the man sitting by the hangar; he looked odd for a test pilot; a bit too tall, too thin, and his rusty blond hair a smidgen too long. Even from a few feet away, the man's bright blue eyes challenged Hawk's right to approach. "Douglas?" he asked tentatively.

Angel propped his feet on the hangar door and kicked back his chair. He studied the new arrival, then nodded. "Pretty dull place, ain't it?" he offered in his easy Texas drawl. "They call me Angel. I don't think it started out as a compliment, but I've kinda come to like it."

The other pilot extended a hand. "I'm Hawk."

"Make yourself at home, kid," Angel stated, pointing at another chair. "You're liable to be here a long time."

Hawk shrugged, put his hand down and flopped into the chair. He stared out at the damp, scruffy ground around the runway and sighed. He missed the tall old redwoods and the fresh snap in the air back home. The musty smell around this place reminded him of a rotting sock. "What's the schedule like?" he asked, mainly to break the uncomfortable silence. "No one told me when we're supposed to take them things up."

"It's posted over there somewhere," Angel drawled, pointing inside the hangar, "but no one ever looks at it. Want a Pepsi? I'd offer you a beer, but I'm in enough trouble already."

"You too?"

"About the only way you end up on assignments like this," Angel chuckled. "What did *you* do to piss 'em off?"

"A little bit of touch and go between hangars ... how about you?"

"I was having a little trouble with a prototype. Landed her on this highway, right? Taxied into a truck stop. I ordered me a couple cheeseburgers and fries to go. You should have seen the look on the guy's face. The truckers were cool, though."

"C.O. probably blew it, huh?"

"Wasn't as bad as I thought it was gonna be. That part didn't end up on my record, just that I ditched on the highway. The base general being from Texas probably helped some. But it wasn't long after that I got transferred here."

Hawk chuckled. "I'd tell 'em to stuff it, but then I couldn't fly."

"Probably how come you're a test pilot," Angel replied, taking a swig of soda while swatting at a fly. "It's not all bad, though. You don't get leaned on too much. They must know we're the only ones that'll fly them critters before the bugs are out."

Hawk shrugged. "I thought we were gonna be at the main base. Damn, that's a big place. Took me almost two days to find out I was supposed to be at Epler, and then nobody knew where it was. This must really be the armpit of the Air Force."

"Naw, actually it's pretty mellow out here. This strip is supposed to be inactive. I kinda like it. Only thing you gotta watch out for is the mosquitoes. They're bigger than the planes."

"How do those handle?" Hawk asked, gazing across the field at the little black fighters. Their angular, box-like shape looked awesome. "I got a few hours in the simulator, but that isn't the same. All they said was 'take 'em out and shake 'em down; and be careful, they got live weapons on 'em'."

"The weapons aren't too bad; I even hit a target yesterday!" Angel replied. "Actually, those are pretty sweet little buggers."

"If you say so," Hawk replied skeptically. "Last prototype I played with handled like a pig ... stalled out doing a double flip."

"Wanna go check 'em out?" Angel said, grabbing his helmet and standing up. "I'll show you what these suckers can do."

"Love it. Ahhh ... can we just do that?"

"Sure," Angel replied as they walked across the field. "As long as we clear it with Tower."

Angel ran Hawk through the preflight, then boarded his jet and strapped on the harness. Informing Tower of their intention to take off, he started the engines. He watched Hawk accelerate smoothly down the runway, kick in the afterburners and take off. The tiny craft was airborne a bit over halfway down the runway. *Not bad*, Angel thought; *with a little coaching, he'll do all right.*

He listened to the pitch of the engine as his mind wandered back to the can of soda he left sitting in the hangar. He half wondered if he might find a Seven-Eleven somewhere within their flight path. He doubted it; there weren't many of them in the middle of the ocean.

He revved the jet to full throttle and sent her shooting down the runway. He lit the burners and had her airborne a third of the way down the strip. The powerful machines always gave him a confidence he never experienced anywhere else. *These babies are sure somethin' else*, he thought. *Damn, I wish I never had to land. I just don't think straight on the ground*. As he broke through the clouds he made radio contact with Hawk. "So, what do you think of her?"

"All right, I guess," Hawk came back. "She responds quick enough, but I haven't pushed her yet."

"If you're worried, we can skim the water," Angel responded with a chuckle. "Not so far to fall."

"Angel, Tower. Maintain normal operating altitude."

"Party pooper," Angel shot back. "You guys get any more annoying and I might just head over there and use that tower for target practice."

"Your record is bad enough Angel, you don't have to add to it."

"What's your opinion, Hawk?" Angel called. "Wanna get your wings wet?"

"Can I take the fifth?"

"Only if you offer me some," Angel quipped.

"Better switch to echo," Hawk came back. "Don't want these droll comments played back to us at a court martial."

"ANGEL, TOWER. RADIO CONTACT MUST BE MAIN...."

Angel grinned as he turned off the long range radio. He switched to short range and drawled, "Ten-four, good buddy. No smokeys in sight, so lets get truckin'." Hawk's responding chuckle assured him he had a good wingman.

"I love doing that to 'em," Angel admitted. "They never know whether to believe me or not."

They climbed to cruising altitude, then headed south out over the Gulf. They exchanged idle conversation, dirty jokes, and aerial stunts for the next twenty-five minutes. Then the equipment gave warning, as a single blip appeared on the radar display. The blip became two blips and the tracking equipment identified the culprits.

"Shit, MiG-21s. I make 'em at about nineteen miles," Angel hollered. "Must be out of Cuba. What are they doin' here? We'd better call 'em in." He flipped the radio back to long range. "Tower, Angel. Spotted two MiG-21s out here. Requesting permission to remind 'em whose air space they're in."

"Angel, dammit, we've been calling you. We're tracking four 21s ... and a possible bogey way above you. Intercept is already en route from Homestead. Get back here with those things."

"Roger that. Coming in," Angel replied. He dipped a wing tip in Hawk's direction as the two jets veered off toward home. "Damn, looks like they're following," he muttered.

The pilots swooped down into the cover of the low hanging fog. As the MiGs dived after them, the little jets soared skyward again.

"Hey," Hawk shouted, "one of 'em got lock on me. What are they up to?"

His question was answered by Angel. "Christ, he fired. Get the fuck out of there."

Hawk dropped three flares as he reefed high and right. A few seconds later, the missile veered off sharply and neatly destroyed one of them.

"What's with those jerks?" Angel yelled. "Fuck, there's the rest of 'em. Check your four o'clock! They're hot on our trail!"

"Got 'em," Hawk called.

A strange voice filtered though the radio. "Sorry. I think it was my fault. They were following me. You cannot outrun their missiles. Dive!"

"Jesus H. Christ," Angel exclaimed, catching the readout on the latest blip. "We got one above us! No ID. Recognize the accent?"

"Negative on the accent," Hawk replied. "Hey, stranger, move it ... these guys are serious."

"No, I will deal with them," the strange voice insisted. "Dive now! Steeply! You will be dead if you do not."

"Dammit, mister, move it," Angel yelled. "Hawk! Dive for the fog! Port! They got lock again!"

"I'm with ya," Hawk replied.

As both pilots dived, the air behind them exploded. The shock wave that followed propelled the tiny jets faster than anticipated; it took some tricky flying to pull them up before they plummeted into the waves. Then, as if by mutual agreement, both jets went screaming skyward again.

"I ... I don't fucking believe this," Angel stammered, watching his screen,

A dry chuckle crackled over the radio. "I apologize for this. I was playing with them. I think it must have made them nervous."

"There's nothin' left of 'em at all," Hawk gasped.

A few more chuckles drifted across the ether. "I am sorry I disturbed the air currents. I had to take them all at once. If I scratched my Bird, she would not talk to me for a long time!"

Angel's jaw dropped when he circled back and saw the sleek gray fighter. "Shit, I thought this was the hottest thing we had. Never seen nothing like that!"

"Me neither," agreed Hawk, looping back to form up. As he looked over the craft, he noticed that it bore no markings; that bothered him, as did the pilot's strange manner of speech. "Where you stationed?"

"Let me just say that I am not from around here."

"Hey, good buddy," Angel called to their benefactor, "thanks a heap. I didn't catch your handle in all the commotion."

"You can call me Dervish," he replied. "Let me ask, what are you going to say happened up here?"

"Well, Dervish," said Angel with a grin, "nothing personal, but if I tell them what I saw and heard, I'd spend the rest of my life debriefing. I'm mighty glad you're on our side, though."

"I have always enjoyed dirty jokes and clean fights," Dervish replied. "They will not have seen much of this Bird on long-range radar. You should have little explaining to do."

"Okay; we'll think of something," Hawk said with obvious relief. "Space junk, maybe."

"I did not need to hear that," Dervish's strange voice replied with a bit of a chuckle. "I must go now. Mother is calling; I have been radio silent too long. I hope I will see you again."

"We owe you one," Hawk shot back. "I'm not too sure what we could help you with, but keep it in mind."

"I will do that," Dervish responded.

"Thanks again, pardner," Angel added.

As they watched, Dervish's strange craft began a dead vertical climb. Twenty-seven seconds later, the tracking equipment lost him at an altitude of eleven miles.

"Damn, he wasn't kidding when he said he wasn't from around here!" Hawk stated numbly. "We haven't got anything like that, do we?"

"Nope. Well, not that I know of anyway."

"Ummm ... what are we gonna tell 'em when we land?"

"I dunno ... didn't look like no flying saucer to me," Angel mused.

"Think we'll ever see him again?"

"I think so, yeah. At least I hope so," Angel replied. "Sure would like to fly me one of them suckers!"

"Nice guy. Good thing he liked your jokes!"

"Got a few more I can tell you on the way back. Let's land these babies and sneak off base for a beer."

"I think we better have that beer on base," Hawk said with a laugh. "Bet we'll be watched for a while!"

"You're probably right," Angel agreed, as he set course for home.

2

Graduation Day

Richardson sighed as he gazed up at the two CIA agents. "Douglas has been missing for three weeks and you're just now getting around to informing me?"

He was bothered that Marilyn hadn't called to tell him, either. *Okay,* he thought, *so I only took her to dinner a few times. But she did go flying with me to the Grand Ole Opry. And she seemed to have a good time. Damn. I was hoping she liked me.*

Noting that Richardson appeared to be lost in thought, the older of the two agents cleared his throat. "It was impossible to pull the black box until they got the fighter off the ice floe. You practically have to take the thing apart to get at it. It wasn't until then we concluded he might still be alive."

Richardson rose slowly from his desk and walked to his file cabinet. He pulled open one of the drawers and thumbed through the charts.

"Wouldn't it be easier if you kept that stuff on computer?" the younger agent asked.

"For you, yes, Mr. Frankel," Richardson replied, as he pulled out a folder. "Then you would already have what you were looking for last night when you went through my office." He walked back to his desk, sat down and glared at the agents.

"Invasion of privacy is still against the law," he informed them dryly. "I suppose you decided it would take too long to break the code these notes are written in."

Frankel bit his lip while agent Yablanski glared back at the doctor. "We gave you the subpoena," he grumbled. "What more do you want?"

"Look, dammit, I'm a doctor," Richardson replied. "This information is privileged. There are some things I won't divulge. If you tell me what you're looking for though, I might be able to determine whether there's anything relevant in here."

The room was silent as Yablanski thought for a few minutes. "Okay, Doc. There was another voice on the log tape. Male, strange accent, stiff English, no contractions. Maybe it would be better if I played it for you."

Richardson nodded. "Inflections in a voice can often provide a clue," he said. "Do you have a copy with you?"

"Yeah," Frankel replied. "We just came from trying for a voice print. No luck." He pulled a small recorder from his pocket and hit the play button. Static and hiss sputtered out of the small speaker. Under the noise, voices could be heard.

"Angel," the strange voice called. "Did you get the landing coördinates?"

"Are you crazy?" Angel replied. "There's nothing but water and ice down there!"

"And a friend waiting to see you."

"I don't know any talking seals." There was a long pause. "Dervish?"

"Yes. It is I."

"Hey, I got you on radar now ... who's your friend?"

"It is on ... automatic."

"I can't land there! That's just an ice floe."

"It is okay. I have locked a tractor beam on you."

"I'm gonna be pissed if I take a bath," Angel muttered. "Okay, here goes!"

The hissing and crackling continued for about another thirty seconds.

"Hey," Angel called. "We did it. With a good thirty feet to spare! Shit, just like Clint Eastwood! Cutting power."

The crackling stopped and only background hiss continued. Frankel turned off the recorder. "When the base in Greenland noticed the fighter losing altitude, they put in a call. When Douglas didn't respond, they scrambled some fighters. The pilots sighted the plane on an ice floe, but no sign of Douglas. The helicopters arrived and landed. Couldn't find him anywhere. That's when we got called in."

Yablanski looked at Richardson hopefully. "We didn't find a body, and nothing was missing from the plane. No boats or subs were sighted in the area. We put a man on his aunt's ranch, we've got holds on his bank accounts and credit cards, we've sent his picture out to all law enforcement. Checked all records for a lead on this Dervish guy. Nothing has turned up. We've run into a brick wall. Where do you think he went?"

Richardson thought a moment. "Have you spoken with his aunt?"

The agent shook his head. "No. We figured it would be best to keep this quiet until we find out what really happened."

Richardson relaxed back into his chair. If Marilyn didn't know, there was no reason for her to have called. Relieved, he reran the conversation in his head. "Hmmm ... the one that Douglas was talking to said 'tractor beam', right? And a second ... something on automatic. Look, maybe that tape was a hoax. Did the radar boys pick up anything?"

"They said the main tracking equipment experienced a failure just a few seconds before Angel lost altitude," Frankel replied. "Satellite reception of the area was completely snowed ... nothing but garbage."

Richardson's mind raced as he scanned Douglas' file. "Seems like more than a coincidence," he mused. *Tractor beam*, he thought. *That could explain how Angel pulled out of a flat spin. And whatever was using that beam might have accidentally caused Angel to lose control of the jet in the first place.* He thought back to Hawk's odd question a few months ago and chided himself for not having put it together then. He got up and pulled Hawk's file, glancing at it for a few moments. "Hmmm ... yes, here it is." He walked back to his desk as he read from the file. "Do you know of anything we have that can fly vertically? I don't mean VTOL, I mean vertical flight."

Yablanski cleared his throat; Frankel shrugged his shoulders. Richardson glanced up at the agents, who were staring blankly at him. "Gentlemen, I don't have the slightest idea where an alien would take him."

"Very funny, Doc," Yablanski pointed out stiffly.

"I'm not joking," Richardson stated. "Are you saying that someone on this planet has tractor beams? Planes that fly vertically? Equipment that jams satellites as well as radar?"

Frankel blew out a puff of air and started to pace around the room. "We don't know what to think," he blurted. "That's why we're here."

Richardson jotted something down, then flipped the file closed. "Have you contacted Captain Raychovsky?"

"Who?"

Richardson shook his head slowly. "The pilot he flew with for almost six months."

"Huh?"

"They were stationed together in Florida," Richardson said. "I believe they became quite close. You boys haven't done your homework."

The two agents looked at Richardson blankly.

Richardson sighed. "Does the name Hawk ring a bell?"

"Hawk!" Franklin stammered. "That's the guy who tried to get in touch with Douglas last week!"

"And what was he told?"

Yablanski grimaced. "Only that he couldn't talk to Douglas at the moment. Security reasons."

Richardson thought for a few seconds, his brow in a slight furrow. "I don't think Douglas will go anywhere without him. I'd put a tail on Raychovsky if I were you."

"Shouldn't we question him?"

"If Douglas calls him, Raychovsky will mention that first thing, especially if you tell him not to. That's simple human nature. And they are the best of friends. He's going to believe Douglas, not you."

"Ahhh ... can we use your secure line?"

"Be my guest," Richardson said. "Uncle Sam pays the bill."

Frankel glared at him as Yablanski picked up the phone. "Do you have the number where he's stationed?"

Richardson handed him the note he had just written. He got up and walked back to his cabinet, filing away the folders as Yablanski made his call.

"They're putting a couple APs on him. He's requested a six hour pass for tonight," Yablanski stated as he hung up the phone. "They're two hours ahead of us. That gives us ... six hours to get there and get organized."

Richardson puckered his lips and furrowed his brow. "If Douglas does show up, don't approach him. If you scare him off, he might never return."

"Isn't it amazing how everybody suddenly becomes an expert in field work?" Yablanski grumbled.

Richardson sighed and shook his head. "I know my pilots."

The two agents looked at each other a moment, then quickly left the office.

Richardson walked back to his chair. He studied the small crystal unicorn that stood on the corner of his desk. "Tractor beams ... it has to be aliens. Angel would never defect. Not willingly." He gazed about the room and sighed. *I really must talk to Marilyn about this*, he thought. *I think Angel will contact her first. She can advise him that the CIA is watching Hawk. I don't want those clowns hurting either of my boys.* He glanced back at the unicorn. "I wonder what it's like to fly off into the stars ... it really is what Angel always wanted," he told it. "I just wish he would have taken me along."

The unicorn did not reply.

✦   ✦   ✦

The four APs stopped when they saw Hawk enter the bar. They walked back to the alley and turned in. "Why don't you two keep an eye on the back entrance," one of the APs said.

The other two walked a bit further into the alley and stopped to call in their location.

"If you see Angel, nab him," Yablanski responded. "Use force if you have to, but don't kill him; we need some answers. We're organizing a tight net around the general area."

"Got it," the AP answered, then turned off the two-way. He turned to the other AP and grinned. "Watch, Hawk's just there to meet some chick."

"And just think, Jake, old Uncle Sam's blowing a few thousand of our tax dollars just to make sure he has a trouble-free evening," the other man replied.

"Couldn't be spent on a nicer guy," Jake commented, resting his back against a telephone pole. "Harry ... do you really think he's here to meet Angel?"

"They *were* pretty close," Harry responded, lighting a cigarette and dropping his walkie-talkie in its holder. "But you know Hawk. He likes everybody."

"Probably the only friend Angel ever had."

"Or will have," Harry grumbled. "Strange son-of-a-gun. Never seemed to like anyone very much."

"I wonder what kind of a mess he got himself into this time."

"Must be a real doozey. CIA agents and all."

Jake looked around. "But he's a smart one. I think we better blend with the shadows. He'll vanish if he spots us."

"He won't get very far with all those agents around."

"They don't know Angel," Jake chuckled as they moved back into the alleyway. He leaned against the side of the building and stretched. "It's liable to be a long night."

"Nope," Harry replied, putting out his cigarette. He pointed down the block. "Looks like we got lucky! There's our boy now. Bet we'll get a promotion for pulling this off."

"Hmmm ... he's got someone with him," Jake whispered. "Call it in quick."

"Other one looks kinda small," Harry mumbled. "Don't see any weapons. Probably won't be too much hassle."

They waited until the two men passed, then stepped out behind them. "Angel," Harry called. "Come on back here."

Angel stopped walking and half turned to look at them. "Shit," he muttered. "You wouldn't happen to have a stun gun on ya?" he asked the little man next to him.

Dervish wrinkled his nose and shook his head. He turned and looked at the two men. Noting that one of them was talking into a radio, he reached out with his mind. Merging with the walkie-talkie, he altered its frequency drastically. "I blocked their transmission. That might slow them down a little. We should attempt to convince them that they wish to go home."

Angel shrugged and started back toward the APs. "What's up?" he asked nonchalantly.

"Got a mess of CIA agents that want to talk to you," Harry informed him. "Why don't you just come along nice like. I don't want to get Hawk in trouble too."

Angel grabbed Harry's shirt and pulled him close. "What have you done to Hawk?" he growled.

Dervish sidestepped quickly, moving between Harry and Jake. He grinned at Jake as he shifted his balance slightly.

"N-nothing," Harry choked, attempting to break free.

Jake no sooner drew his gun than Dervish kicked it from his hand, whirled around and kicked Jake again, then knocked Harry unconscious with a blow to the side of the head.

Jake dived for the gun. Dervish took a flying leap, landing on top of him. Dervish grabbed the gun and flung it further down the alley. As he did, Jake tried to sink his teeth into Dervish's arm.

The noise brought the other two APs from around the corner. Angel shoved Harry into one and laid the other out with a quick right hook.

Dervish growled as he knocked Jake unconscious.

Angel pounced on the remaining AP as the man attempted to crawl out from under Harry. Dervish came up and placed a neat chop to the side of his neck. The man became limp, so Angel let loose and stood up.

"Let's find Hawk and get outta here before the whole friggin' army arrives," Angel muttered.

Dervish nodded as they made their way quickly into the bar.

✦   ✦   ✦

Hawk sat nursing a beer while occasionally glancing at his watch. He felt uncomfortable sitting in a bar by himself. He was also curious; there were so many unanswered questions about this strange reunion. Early this morning, Angel had called. All he had said was: "Meet me at Keegan's tonight at nineteen hundred. Gotta go." They used to come here after a particularly nasty day of flying, but what was Angel doing here now?

They had become close during the six months they flew together. He figured he knew Angel pretty well, but this had him stumped. With Angel, there had never been a dull moment, from their first flight together, where they barely talked their way out of getting court martialed, to their last, which had resulted in Angel's transfer to Greenland. Still, they had managed to keep in touch. But the last time he tried to call, he got a real runaround. Never did get to speak to Angel; security reasons, they had stated.

"Sorry I'm late," drawled a familiar voice, "but we ran into some trouble. Nothing we couldn't handle, but this isn't the nicest part of town, ya know!"

"Angel! What the hell happened?" Hawk asked as he embraced the slightly bedraggled pilot. "And who's your friend?" he added, nodding toward the small man standing next to Angel.

The man was rubbing a nasty bruise on his right arm. He was dressed in a gray t-shirt about two sizes too large, long gray bell-bottom jeans, tennis shoes and a brown knit ski cap which was pulled down over his ears. He looked nervously from Angel to Hawk.

Angel looked at the door, then back at Hawk. "Let's get outta here," he mumbled, heading toward the back entrance. "I'll tell ya on the way."

Hawk shrugged, reluctantly put his beer on the bar and followed the two out the door. Angel walked halfway down the alley at a brisk pace, then stopped.

Hawk glanced at Angel, then at the odd little man who was holding out his arm in an attempt to shake hands.

"Hawk, meet Dervish," Angel intoned in a semi-serious voice.

Hawk froze in the middle of shaking the little man's hand. "You mean ...?" he started to stammer.

"Yup," drawled Angel. "Ready to go?"

Hawk was still staring speechlessly at Angel when Dervish took a small communication device from his pocket. "Go? What is this, I'm being shanghaied?"

"You got it," Angel drawled, amused by Hawk's reaction. "Beam us aboard, Scotty!"

Hawk felt very strange for a moment as the whole world seemed to turn into swirling sparkles of color. As his vision cleared, he was no longer in an alley; he was on a sort of triangular platform in a room that resembled a large bubble. The air held a pungent, medicated smell.

"Decontamination chamber," Dervish explained. "Never know what one can pick up on underdeveloped worlds." His grin implied that his statement could apply to Hawk as well as to any microscopic organism that happened to have hitched a ride.

As the door of the bubble slowly opened, Dervish gestured grandly for them to exit. Noting the frozen expression on Hawk's face, he grinned and gestured again while he announced with mock seriousness, "welcome to my parlor, said the spider to the fly ... and please be kind enough to wipe your feet."

Hawk decided then and there that he really liked Dervish. Following him down a wide corridor, Hawk kept expecting to hear a page for Captain Kirk, or to see Spock walk toward them. Instead, he saw a few other strange men, dressed as casually as Dervish, that seemed to be loitering around just to gawk back at him.

"Some of the other Fliers," Dervish explained when he noticed Hawk looking at the other men. "They are a very tight group; they do not feel that underdeveloped worlds have much to offer." Dervish studied Hawk a moment, then grinned. "But you are pretty good," he added, "pulling out of a nose dive as you did ... and in a primitive plane at that. It will not be long before you can show them a few things. I think they will accept you very soon." He opened a door to his left and motioned for them to enter.

The room was small, containing only a bed and two chairs. Dervish flopped down on the bed. "Have a seat," he said. "The commander is now putting your clearance into the computer. Then I can show you around."

"What's this all about?" Hawk asked him, not at all sure that he was going to like the answer.

"We are Fliers for Interstellar Defense," Dervish explained. "It is a freelance group; we try to keep the advanced races from bothering anyone. We also defend some planetary systems on a contract basis."

"They're real nice guys," Angel drawled, "but I guess you're wondering what all this has to do with us."

"No shit."

"Three are required to form a group at my old station," Dervish started to explain. "I am only one, and ..."

"Maybe this oughta wait 'til after he's eaten," Angel interrupted. "He's always a bear on an empty stomach. Besides, I think I can explain it better."

Hawk growled at Angel, but sat down. He expected to feel some acceleration, or at least a sense of movement, but he felt nothing. Neither Angel nor Dervish seemed inclined to continue the conversation at the moment, and Hawk was not too sure that he wished to push them.

Colonel Rendal scratched his ear a moment, then set coördinates for a short punch to just outside the solar system. Normally he'd have made a Flier wait the few hours it was going to take to punch to his destination, but Dervish couldn't get his new friend onto the flight deck unless Mother had approved his clearances. And there was no way he could enter the security information into Mother during a punch.

He thought about the way his Fliers were responding to having Dervish on board, and it bothered him. Even the comms officer had made a snide comment. When he'd called him on it, the man merely shrugged, stammered something about Alderians making him nervous, then quickly found some excuse to leave the room. As soon as Dervish was off the ship, he intended to knock their collective heads together.

He got up and walked across the room, seated himself in the soft chair in front of comms and waited. The base ship winked back into real space and the ready light flashed on. He pondered it a moment, then put in a call to Nathan.

"Colonel Rendal?" Threenica's voice brought his attention back to the matter at hand.

"Uhhh ... yes. Is Nathan around?"

"Yes," Threenica replied. "Nathan ... Colonel Rendal calling."

Rendal pictured tall and lanky Threenica, his head a bit too large for his body, leaning out of the room and shouting down the hall at Fliers' headquarters. *Will that crazy bean counter ever grow up?* he wondered.

"Rendal," Nathan's voice called. "Any problems picking up that Earth kid?"

"No. I just finished entering his data into Mother. I just wanted to ... check with you."

"What do you think of them?" Nathan asked.

"I spent a little time with the first one ... Angel, I believe. He seems a bit rough around the edges, but a good pilot. I haven't met the other one yet."

"Oh." Nathan sounded disappointed. "Ummm ... could you call me back with your evaluation? It will be a while before I can meet them."

"Sure. You know, Nathan, I'm a bit surprised that you consented to this."

Nathan was silent for a few moments. "I wasn't too sure myself," he admitted. "Dervish was so insistent on it though, I finally relented. He's been so ... so ..."

"Isolated," Rendal finished for him. "I still say that's Sparks' fault. He should have let Dervish join a squad when he first became a Flier."

"I don't know," Nathan countered. "Sparks wanted to coach him for a while. He was going to place him with Chakler's squad, before he lost all of them over Falkner."

"I remember. That was a bad one."

"He took it real hard. Come to think of it, he never mentioned placing Dervish after that, and somehow I just let it slip through the cracks; he was hopping about so much handling all the trouble spots, and Dervish was a great help to him."

Rendal rubbed his eye and slowly licked his lips. "I know," he grumbled. "But the kid's so shy. Keeping him isolated for so many years has put a wedge in that isn't shaking loose. Damn, I wish you'd have let him stay with me."

Nathan was slow to reply. "If I had it to do over, I suppose I'd side with you. Sparks was adamantly against it. Said he needed Dervish's abilities with what he was doing."

"Well, he made a freak out of him," Rendal blurted. "Dervish is more withdrawn than ever. It's gotten so the other Fliers won't speak to him. I'm very concerned."

"So am I," Nathan assured him, "That's why I finally agreed to let him pick up those Earth kids."

"Why don't you station them with me for a while. I really think I could ..."

"No," Nathan cut him off. "He wants to return to his old station as soon as the kids are initiated."

"You think on it," Rendal replied. "Kids don't always know what's best for them."

Nathan chuckled. "Some of us older ones haven't figured it out either."

Rendal cracked a smile. "I'll talk to you later. I want to go meet this guy before Dervish takes off with him."

Hawk sat for a while trying to convince himself it was all a dream ... brought on, no doubt, by eating one of his mother's cookies. A voice came from a speaker somewhere in the ceiling, but Hawk didn't understand the language. When the voice stopped talking, Dervish stood up. "You are cleared," he said.

Angel guided a sullen Hawk out the door, following Dervish down the hall and into an elevator. The doors opened to another set of hallways identical to the ones they had just left. Hawk followed Angel and Dervish across the hall through a set of double doors that opened into a sort of cafeteria. As they sat down at a table, the few groups of men scattered around the room casually glanced their way, but their expressions did not seem friendly.

"I will go get some coffee and stuff to eat," Dervish said as he wandered off to the other side of the room.

"You sure it's safe here?" Hawk asked, glancing back at the men staring at them.

"They're harmless," Angel teased. "Not terribly friendly, but I haven't been attacked yet."

"How long have you ... been here?"

Angel rubbed his nose a moment. "About three weeks."

Dervish returned with the coffee and something that looked and tasted vaguely like cheese and crackers.

"Is this milk?" Hawk asked as he poured the white liquid into his coffee.

"It comes from the same creature that this comes from," Dervish offered, pointing at the stuff next to the crackers. He looked up and saw a man approaching. "It is ... ahhh, Hawk, this is Colonel Rendal," he began in English, then switched to Common. "Colonel, this is Hawk."

Hawk looked up. The man was dressed in the same casual manner as the rest of the men he had seen, but bore the unmistakable air of command. He was much taller than Dervish, and he definitely looked alien. His tawny hair was streaked with glittering silver, his eyes were closer together than the humans of Earth, and his nose was almost flat. Dervish nodded smartly to the man; his face held a sassy grin, but his eyes betrayed a great deal of respect for the man.

The man looked Hawk over, taking in each nuance of his persona and analyzing it. Hawk felt like an amoeba under a microscope. The man nodded, said something to Dervish, then walked away.

Dervish looked relieved. "The colonel likes you," he stated. "That is probably a good thing. He might have thrown us out an airlock if he was not pleased."

Hawk winced. "So ... just what's really going on here?"

"Let's see," Angel replied nonchalantly. "We're cruising in a base ship with a pack of crazy alien beings, heading out into the deep blackness of outer space ... I'm not sure of our exact location ... while eating ..."

"Yeah, fine," Hawk interrupted. "As strange as it may seem, I actually figured out that much all by myself. What I want to know is *why*!"

Angel shrugged. "Remember we said we'd help him out if we could?"

"Yeah."

"Now's our chance."

"How?" Hawk asked suspiciously.

"Well, see," Angel began, "Dervish wants to transfer back to his old space station. He's not really happy here in the boonies. Unfortunately, they only assign squads to the bigger stations, and none of the squads here want to go."

"Ummm ... okay. So?" Hawk asked, mainly to stall for time while he came to grips with the reality of the situation.

"Well, Dervish says he'll train us on those nifty fighters," Angel hedged, "if we'd sort of enlist 'til he gets us transferred. He figures that once he gets back there, one of the squads there will let him join."

Dervish looked at Hawk hopefully.

Hawk diverted his gaze and looked at Angel. "Then what?"

Angel glanced down. "Then ... you can go home, if you want," he mumbled. "I figure on staying. I don't think I'd be too welcome back there anyway."

"Why? What happened?"

"Well, ummm, when Dervish picked me up I left my 15 floating on a chunk of ice. The APes we ran into didn't seem overjoyed with that."

The word APes rang Hawk's bell. "Hey, I gotta get back *now*; I can't just disappear. What would I say? Well, umm ... I know it sounds strange, but I was walking down this alley and ..."

Angel wrinkled his nose. "Look, it takes six to make a full squad. At least three for flight duty. If you won't do it, Dervish is gonna be stuck out here. You can always tell 'em you had amnesia. Besides, what have you got to go back for, your mother?"

Hawk rolled his eyes. "She's a good reason for leaving. All she ever does is nag. But my *stuff*; I gotta get my stuff."

"Umm ... we can't just turn around, y'know?" Angel mumbled. "Besides, it's past curfew and they wouldn't let ya back out."

"But ... my books, my pictures, my CDs, my camera, my laptop and ... damn! All my stuff!"

"So, you can buy other stuff," Angel offered. "And there's no WiFi around here anyway."

Hawk sat there a moment, then shrugged. "Well, yeah, I guess ... shit, couldn't they just beam me down to my room real quick to ... grab a few things?"

"Only large freighters and base ships like this one can beam things," Dervish stated. "And they have to be quite close. We are far away from Earth now."

"Hell ... I guess I don't need that stuff anyway."

"Then you will stay?" Dervish asked.

Hawk felt rotten. He probably wouldn't be alive if it wasn't for this strange little man, but the thought of leaving home bothered him. He stewed about it a few minutes, guilt finally winning the battle over emotional ties. "Yeah, I guess," he mumbled.

Dervish's face lit up. "Thank you. Come, I will take you to the flight deck and show you the Birds."

"They're wild!" Angel babbled excitedly as he got up to follow. "Man, punching is a feeling you'll never believe until you do it.

Hawk downed the rest of his coffee, more than half wishing this was some strange dream and he would wake up any moment safe in his bunk on base.

Dervish looked at him and bit his lip. "If you are not happy, I will take you home," he said quietly.

Hawk shook his head. "I'm fine," he lied, in what he hoped was a convincing voice. Much of his mind was already wondering how those little fighters handled.

Dervish studied Hawk and raised an eyebrow. "It is okay," he said assuringly. "I will take you back. I understand; you should not stay if you are unhappy."

Hell, Hawk thought. *I've always wanted to fly off into the stars.* He looked back at Dervish and smiled. "No. I want to stay," he said firmly, and this time he really meant it.

Dervish grinned. "I will take you to the Birds," he said as they walked across the hall to the elevators. "Then we will go to the space station where we live."

Hawk looked at Angel, hoping for more information.

Angel read Hawk's look easily. "We sorta wheedled the colonel into picking you up. See, with me it was easy. I was out there over the ice floes. Dervish just brought down two Birds, one running in auto-pilot, and we took off from there. Didn't want to chance that so close to civilization."

Hawk pursed his lips. "Angel," he said quietly, "why did you *really* come back for me?"

"Like I said, it takes three to fly. Besides ... I kinda missed you."

The elevator stopped and the doors opened into a strange crossgrid of bars. "Those are the scanning devices," Dervish explained. "If the computer does not have your biological print on file, it will not open the doors leading to the flight deck."

"Mmm," Hawk said. He was still trying to decide whether Angel was telling him the whole truth. "What took you so long to decide to come get me?" he asked, glancing at Angel.

"We had to wait for a base ship," Angel explained. "They rarely come out this way. This one wasn't too far out, so we flagged it down."

Hawk nodded as they walked down the stairs to the lower deck. His eyes went wide as he stared at the fighters up close; they were the sexiest things he had ever seen.

"Ain't they something," Angel said as they neared three of the fighters. "They can talk to you, too! And they really think."

Hawk looked to Dervish for confirmation; *he* wasn't from Texas.

Dervish shrugged. "The interface computer is a neural network. It transfers your commands to the navigation system, made up of five parallel processors serving three redundant neural networks. I have modified the interface computer to have a ... personality." He glanced down at his feet as he spoke. "I was lonely," he continued. "It does not affect the way they fly, though."

Angel nudged Hawk with his elbow. "Cutest goddam voice you ever did hear," he snickered. "Makes you want to find the nearest female and ..."

Dervish cleared his throat. "I brought you a flight suit and helmet. My apologies if they do not fit perfectly. We can exchange them when we reach the station. We must leave now. They are eager to proceed to their destination."

"Is that why they're so hostile?" Hawk asked, nodding toward the group of six strange looking men standing near some other fighters. They glared back at him. He gave them a friendly wave, the kind you give twenty Hell's Angels when passing them in a dark alley. They seemed about as amused as the bikers would have been.

Dervish looked down. "They do not like me," he stated quietly.

Hawk felt a flash of anger. He didn't really know Dervish, but he liked him. Nothing about him had set off those feelings that always informed him when he should be wary of someone. He glanced back at the men with a disgusted frown.

Angel approached one of the fighters and a ramp began to lower to allow him to enter. "Bunch of jerks," he snapped as he climbed up.

The men turned their backs on Hawk almost as a unit, but one, a bit to the left of the group, took his hand out of his pocket and flashed Hawk a thumbs up. Hawk smiled; then, noting the six fingers, wondered if that sign meant the same thing around here.

Dervish looked up at Angel. "They are very good Fliers," he countered. "Do not judge them."

Angel pretended not to hear the comment as the stairs lifted and the hatch closed behind him with a reassuring thud.

Dervish pointed to the other fighter. "That is your Bird. She has been programmed with your language and biological patterns and will accept your orders now. She is capable of executing the launch and punch maneuvers without your assistance. Enjoy the ride, okay?"

Hawk nodded and climbed up the stairs. He peered into the cockpit and whistled; all the readouts were gibberish. He climbed in and picked up the flight suit that was lying on the seat. *Well,* he thought, *at least something's familiar.* The helmet was a bit big, but comfortable. He sat down and looked at the various lights that blinked occasionally. He heard the hatch close and felt his heart begin to pound. "Whoa," he mumbled to himself. "Wonder what this sucker can do?"

"Please strap on the safety harness, Hawk," an alluring voice requested. "We have been cleared to launch."

Hawk looked at what he assumed was the flight computer, as that was where the voice was coming from. "Ahhh ... thanks," he stammered. "Is there something else I'm supposed to do?"

"I have been programmed to execute all maneuvers without assistance," the computer answered. "However, if you prefer, I can guide you through them."

"Yeah. Thanks. What do I do first?"

"Lock in the coördinates that are flashing on the screen."

"Ummm ... how do I do that?"

"Touch the capture button and then the hold button, Hawk," the computer answered.

"Which one is which?" Hawk mumbled. "I'm really farmisht."

"I am sorry, Farmisht," the computer responded. "The data I received identified you as Hawk. The capture button is on your left, top row, third from the right. The hold button is also on your left, second row, first button."

"Thanks, Gracie," he replied, locking in the coördinates. "I *am* called Hawk. Farmisht is ... ummm ... a state of mind that means I don't understand what is going on."

"Gracie?" the computer questioned.

"Yeah. I'd like to call you Gracie, if that's okay. You remind me of someone I was very fond of; that was her name."

"I am pleased that I remind you of someone you liked," Gracie replied. "I will respond to that name from now on."

The fighter started gliding toward a large set of doors near the hull of the ship. Another fighter was already in the docking bay and Gracie moved in alarmingly close to it.

"Ahhh ... Gracie. Is that Dervish or Angel next to us?"

"Neither," Gracie replied in a disgusted tone. "That is Love, Dervish's fighter. Dervish is inside of her."

"That's what I meant. I was asking who was in the fighter. I'm not entirely dim, you know."

"I will not make a judgement on that until I have known you for a longer period of time," Gracie replied, as the bay doors closed behind them.

Hawk watched as the doors in front of him opened. The darkness about him was broken only by a few stars. Gracie activated the infrared sensors and the cabin seemed to become transparent. "Whoa," Hawk exclaimed as Gracie glided out into space. "My God, it's beautiful!"

"Got your ears on, pardner?" Angel's voice intruded.

Hawk glanced up at the speaker. "Gracie, how do I activate the radio?"

"Communications are coming in on the short-range receiver," Gracie informed him. "To respond, push the button all the way to your right, bottom row."

"Then what?"

"Then you have to speak," Gracie replied dryly.

Hawk pushed the button. "I think so."

Angel chuckled. "Takes a little getting used to. First few days I kept looking for a mike. You got the coördinates locked in?"

"I did what Gracie here told me to do."

"Gracie, huh?" Angel replied, then thought a moment. "Wouldn't be thinking of Gracie Allen by any chance?"

Hawk just laughed.

"I named this one Goldie. Okay, push the punch button over the display."

"Look, clown," Hawk retorted. "There's lots of buttons over the display. Which one?"

"The punch button should have a green back light, signifying that valid coördinates have been locked in," Gracie told him. "It is in the third row, fifth from your left."

Hawk glanced over at the computer. "Thanks, Gracie. It's nice one of us knows what we're doing. I'd be completely lost without you."

"You shouldn't have said that," Angel shot back. "It'll go to her head!"

"Thank you, Hawk," Gracie replied. "I am pleased that you are my Flier. I am sure you will have everything memorized shortly."

"That is good," Dervish's voice added. "She likes you, Hawk. You two will make a team. Push the punch button ... we must go now."

"Radio's dead in a punch," Angel remembered quickly, "so don't panic. It'll be about thirty minutes ... talk to you then."

Hawk watched Goldie wink out, then looked in the direction of Dervish's fighter. Love was still there.

"I will wait for you to go," Dervish informed him.

Hawk let out a mouthful of air and touched the button lightly. The universe about him winked out. He expected to feel some extreme acceleration, but instead he felt almost weightless. He sat there in silence watching the light show before him; the sight was breathtaking. Swirls of sparkling colors sprayed out in all directions, forming intricate geometrical patterns that reminded him of a kaleidoscope.

"Are you all right?" Gracie asked; her voice almost sounded concerned. "You have not spoken in ten minutes, and your heart and respiration rates appear to be elevated."

"Ahhh ... yeah, I'm fine," he stammered. "It's just so beautiful out there."

"I am pleased that you find it enjoyable," she replied. "Some Fliers do not like the sensation."

"Why?"

"Apparently, it is related to the way they perceive things," she informed him. "All beings develop differently; the perception of beauty is therefore different."

"I hadn't really thought about that. Do you store all that information inside this fighter?"

"No. I can access a vast network of computers that is collectively called Mother. Mother maintains all such data and also keeps track of the last reported position of each fighter."

"Oh," Hawk replied, then lapsed into silence, thinking about everything that had happened since Angel kidnapped him. He also thought about what the Air Force would do when he failed to report back. Angel had said that he and Dervish ran into some APs; Intel would probably attribute his disappearance to whatever they had concluded Angel was up to. What would they tell his mother? He could almost hear her whining voice: 'Why do you have to waste your life flying around? If God had meant you to fly, he'd have given you wings. You should marry a nice Jewish girl and settle down with a family. I am still waiting for grandchildren. Is this asking so much? ... '

Shit, I don't want to go back, he thought. *At least not until she thinks I'm dead.* He pondered what he was going to do for the rest of his life. Dervish had said they were contract defense. *Well, the guys I saw looked happy; I guess they ... we .... get paid ... I'm going to have to get more information about all of this.* "Is there anything else I should know?" he finally asked.

"I am not sure what information would be relevant," Gracie replied. "Perhaps you should ask Dervish."

"Okay," Hawk replied with some disappointment.

"If you have any specific questions, I will answer them for you."

"What will we be doing most of the time?"

"Dervish will spend considerable time training you with regard to controlling this fighter and its weapons systems. When you are comfortable with it, you will be assigned a sweep shift along with Dervish and Angel. Four squads fly a shift, each patrolling a quadrant of the guarded sectors."

"What's a sector?"

"The explored universe was divided into sectors over a thousand of your years ago," Gracie replied. "Sectors were not made the same size; the number of freighters that used an area and the number of habitable planets contained in a given area determined how much space became a sector. A galaxy is most commonly divided into eight sectors, but there are some galaxies that consist of as few as one or as many as five hundred sectors."

"Ummm ... how do I know what sector I'm in?"

"You can ask me, or you can bring up the display and it will show the sector number along with any pertinent data concerning the planets or vessels in the area."

"How do I bring up the display?"

"Touch the button on the bottom row, third from your left. At the present time, it will display information on the sector we are punching to."

Hawk touched the button and smiled as the display came to life. "Wonderful," he mumbled. "Unfortunately, I can't read any of this stuff."

"I am sorry. I am converting the display to English. Can you read it now?"

"Yeah! Thanks!" Hawk found he could get more information on a specific part of the display by touching that point on the screen. He became so involved in playing with his new toy that he failed to notice the universe wink back in.

"Hawk! You okay?" Angel called. "You're awful quiet."

Hawk reached over and pushed the short range radio button.

"The radio was on, Hawk," Gracie reminded him. "You just turned it off."

"Thanks, Gracie," he mumbled as he turned it back on. "Yeah, I'm fine. I got distracted playing with the display."

"The station's just a few minutes from here," Angel said. "Follow us in."

Hawk made a face. "Actually, as long as we're in the neighborhood, I thought I'd pop in and see my Aunt Sadie."

"The closest habitable planet is Tarsis," Gracie responded. "However, I do not think your aunt would be on that planet; the inhabitants are reputed to eat all other life forms."

"You don't know my aunt. They'd get indigestion," Hawk replied. "How about if you follow them, Gracie. I don't know where we're going."

"Receiving permission to dock," Gracie informed him. "The display will indicate the bay to which you have been assigned."

"Real useful," Hawk mumbled. "It says ... yepths eths."

"Translating."

"Hmmm ... now it says bay six," Hawk commented. "Which one is bay six?"

"The one we're entering," Angel answered. "You get a beep when you're near the correct bay."

"I feel like a complete idiot," Hawk grumbled.

"Shit, man," Angel countered, "no one can catch on instantly."

A soft beep sounded as Gracie approached the open doors and moved far into the bay. The infrared sensors shut down and the cabin lost its transparency. The doors behind him shut tight, and moments later the doors opened in front of him. Gracie glided onto the flight deck and maneuvered to a position close to another fighter.

Hawk sat in silence as the hatch popped open and the stairs lowered and latched into place. He got up slowly and started to climb down. "Thanks, Gracie. See you later."

"You are welcome, Hawk."

Hawk stepped down onto the flight deck and looked around. There were at least fifty fighters spaced out in groups of five to six across the deck. He noticed some men working on the fighters, others just standing around talking; no one seemed the least bit interested in his arrival. They were a bit too far off to get a good look at them. He wondered how different they would look up close. Dervish motioned for Hawk to follow.

The deck had a spongy feel to it, vaguely like walking on a trampoline. Hawk wondered if it had any bounce, but refrained from indulging his curiosity. They walked silently off the deck.

"Do you like your Bird?" Dervish asked hesitatingly as the door opened and they entered the elevator.

Hawk nodded. "She's great," he replied as the elevator shot upward. "I got to spend some time getting to know her, though. Ahhh ... where's Angel?"

"He went to get us dinner," Dervish replied. "Our floor," he added as the elevator stopped and the doors opened.

As they started down the hallway, Dervish pointed behind them. "The bathrooms are down there, all the way to the end. Your room is over here." He opened a door on the right and Hawk looked in.

It was bigger than the room he'd had in the Air Force, and he wouldn't have to share this one. The walls were light gray. A large comfortable-looking bed took up most of one wall with a small table next to it. The other wall was covered with shelves. On the far side was a desk and chair. He set his helmet down on the table and started taking off his flight suit.

"Do those fit?" Dervish asked.

"Yeah. The helmet seemed a bit big, but it feels okay."

Dervish smiled. "I will get you other clothes and ... things. Uniforms are not usually required." He walked out the door and disappeared down the hall.

Hawk flopped himself down on the bed and stifled a yawn. He closed his eyes, just to rest them, but was fast asleep by the time Angel arrived with dinner.

Seven hours later he opened his eyes and slowly gazed about the room. It took him a few moments to remember he wasn't on Earth. The thought was sobering. He got up and noted that Dervish had left a few towels, a change of sheets and an extra blanket along with the clothes and underwear. He put the things away, took a change of clothes and a towel and headed to the bathroom.

He finished showering and was combing his hair when another man walked in undressed, carrying a towel. The thought of walking around naked bothered Hawk and he wondered if this was common practice. The man was about Angel's height, but broader. His skin was chestnut; long, dark, red-brown hair hung past his shoulders. His eyes appeared to be dark brown, but the light in the bathroom was not adjusted for accurate observation.

The man looked at Hawk, took a double take, then said something. Hawk shrugged. "Sorry. I don't understand."

The man smiled and pointed to his own hair, then to Hawk's. It dawned on Hawk that all the Fliers he had seen so far had worn their hair on the longish side. His was long for the Air Force, but semi-shaved compared to these guys. He wondered how many languages he would have to learn.

"On Earth they made us cut it," he said, knowing the guy couldn't understand, but feeling compelled to say something.

The man then pointed to himself. "Pepper." He then pointed to Hawk.

Hawk pointed to himself. "Hawk."

Pepper smiled and walked back to the showers. Hawk started out of the bathroom, only to jump back to keep from being trampled by two squads of Fliers conducting a foot race down the hall. *Shit*, he thought, *pilots are the same throughout the universe.* He felt odd not being able to communicate and was relieved to see Angel waiting by his room. "Sorry about falling asleep," he said as he approached.

Angel chuckled. "It's okay, pardner. Thought you might want to grab a bite before we go out."

"Yeah. Uhhh ... where's Dervish?"

"He's tinkering with the Birds. Grab your flight gear and I'll take you to the cafeteria."

"I met a guy in the bathroom," Hawk said as they walked down the hall. "I think his name is Pepper."

Angel shook his head. "They've all sorta been avoiding me," he mumbled. He was silent until they entered the cafeteria, then turned and looked at Hawk with a devilish twinkle in his eyes. "Maybe it's my Kermit the Frog skivvies."

Hawk gave him a friendly shove. "Nahh," he teased. "It's your pink Minnie Mouse slippers. You look darling in them, though."

Gracie skimmed sideways, swooped up into a half roll, then glided to a stop. "Phhhhffffffffttttttt!" Hawk commented.

"You were doing good 'til ya stopped," Angel shot back.

"I didn't mean to stop!" Hawk muttered. "I wanted her to go up ... I mean sideways ... vertical ... shit, I can't get used to this internal reference on gravity. It's like I go right, but instead the universe turns left."

"It's just like a video game," Angel responded. "Well, you never played them much either."

"You'd think I could get my act together in four fucking days!"

Angel pondered that for a moment. "Why don't you stay and work on it? Dervish and I can make the munchie run."

"Might as well," Hawk sighed. "See if you can pick up some fruit juice or something."

"Sure thing, pardner. See what I can do."

Hawk watched as Love and Goldie winked out and then looked back at the display. "Gracie, I think I'm hopeless."

"Perhaps it is because you have decided that the controls are relevant to a fixed position instead of any position you are in," Gracie responded. "Let me take you through a few maneuvers with gravity at an external location, then again with gravity referenced to the cockpit floor. I believe you will actually find the second more intuitive once you become used to it."

"Why not," Hawk replied slowly. "I don't have anything else to do."

"Gravity now at fixed position," Gracie replied. She then executed some rather sharp turns and dives, sending Hawk slamming against the harness a few times. "Maneuvers like that are always rough," she informed him as he rubbed his sore shoulder.

As Gracie went into a sharp turn, the tracking equipment sounded its alert. Another Bird swooped down at him out of nowhere. Hawk's instinctive reactions took over. He broke the roll, taking Gracie parallel to the oncoming Bird and under it. He flipped her over in front of the other Bird; the tracking equipment locked.

A vaguely familiar voice came from the radio, but he didn't understand it.

"Gracie, who's that, and what's he saying?"

"The Flier is Pepper. He is informing you that your response was superb."

"Tell him I said thanks."

"Message sent," Gracie replied as more gibberish drifted into the cockpit. "He is asking if you would care to play with him," she continued.

"Yeah," Hawk replied. "But tell him I don't really have the hang of this yet, okay?"

"I do not expect you to have much problem with him. He is obviously intellectually deficient."

Hawk remembered Pepper vividly, and he had seemed far from stupid. "What makes you say that?"

"He said he is glad you are on his side," she replied. "We are, in fact, in front of him, and not to the side."

Hawk chuckled as he glided Gracie around. He couldn't have named her better if he'd tried.

✦ ✦ ✦

Pepper and Hawk were sitting on the floor of Hawk's room when Angel walked in. "I got the fruit juice," he said, nodding at Pepper.

Hawk looked up slowly from the picture he was drawing. "Doesn't look quite right," he mumbled, showing his sketch of a dog to Angel.

Dervish walked into the room and froze when he noticed Pepper. He shoved his hands in his pockets, turned around and started back out.

"Dervish," Pepper called in Common, "I should inform you that Hawk hit the straps hard a few times; he was really hurting. Velter gave him something for pain. I stopped by when I found out ... he was only a little groggy then, but he's really out of it now."

Dervish raised an eyebrow and glanced at Hawk. "Thanks, Pepper," he replied in Common. "I'll keep an eye on him. Do you know what he gave him?"

Pepper shrugged, got up and smiled at Hawk. "With Velter, it's hard to tell," he admitted as he walked toward the door. "But he claimed it was just something that would ease the pain." He paused and looked back at Dervish. "He didn't think it would do more than that, really."

Dervish nodded. "Thank him for me, okay?"

Pepper looked at Hawk again and chuckled. "Will do," he replied as he walked away.

"What was that all about?" Angel asked. He glanced at the picture Hawk was working on so intently.

Dervish sat down on the floor next to Hawk and studied the sketch. "Velter gave Hawk something for pain," he replied in

English. "Pepper was concerned it might respond differently in Hawk."

Angel ran his hand in front of Hawk's eyes and noted that Hawk was oblivious to the diversion. "Hmmm ... wild stuff. Will he be rejoining us sometime soon?"

"It should wear off in a few hours, I would think. Why don't I get us some dinner?"

"Sounds like a plan. He sure ain't going no place."

Hawk glanced up at Angel. "Does it look real?" he asked, holding up the drawing.

"Looks fine to me," Angel said. "Wanna get some dinner?"

Hawk wrinkled his brow. "I ... ummm ..." he mumbled, "yeah, I think so."

Dervish stood a few feet inside General Henlik's office, his gaze alternating between the general and the floor. "They're doing pretty good," he said in Common. "Pepper checked out Hawk yesterday. Gave him an okay."

"I'm aware of that," Henlik replied stiffly, "but they still have to be tested." He held out a few sheets of paper. "I came up with these; I suggest strongly that you pick one."

Dervish shrugged, came a bit closer and took the papers. "Okay, I'll check 'em out and get back with you," he said, walking out the door.

"Dervish."

Dervish stopped and half turned to look back at Henlik. "Yes?"

"Don't ..." Henlik stopped as Dervish started to make a face. "Oh, never mind."

Dervish gave him a wicked grin. "Wouldn't dream of it," he replied as he continued down the hall.

Henlik pursed his lips as he reached over to file the report. "Damn Alderian mind snooper," he mumbled.

Hawk rubbed his eyes and shook his head. He flipped on the short-range radio and hailed Angel. "That was no aspirin. Hope I didn't do something dumb."

"You were too catatonic to do anything," Angel replied with a chuckle. "Sure you're ready to fly?"

"Wouldn't miss it. Locking in coördinates."

"This will be a long punch," Dervish told them as they glided out of the launch bay. "We are going to a place that is quite empty, for room to practice tricky things."

"Tricky stuff?" Hawk lamented. "I don't have the simple stuff down yet!"

"Pepper said you are very good," Dervish replied. "Now you will get better."

Hawk started to protest. "That was mostly Gracie," he called, but Love and Goldie had already winked out. He sighed as he hit punch.

As Gracie winked in, the display flashed a readout: Freighter, Unregistered. Weapons systems detected.

"What's that?" Hawk called.

"I have scanned Mother's data base," Gracie replied, "and have tentatively identified the vessel as a freighter engaged in slave trading."

"Slavers?" Angel shot back. "Hey, Dervish, that for real?"

"It is possible," Dervish replied. "They have been tracked this far before."

"Why haven't you guys done anything?" Angel asked. "It ain't legal, is it?"

"They are not in our jurisdiction," Dervish replied. "This galaxy is not under Flier protection, and it is against Council regulations for us to be active here."

"That sucks. Slave trading ain't like outrunning the sheriff to the county line and giving him the bird, ya know?" Angel retorted hotly. "Why don't we give 'em something to think about?"

"I can see it now," Hawk replied with a touch of sarcasm. "We turn on our gumball and pull 'em over. You in a heap of trouble, boy!"

"We could just blow 'em up," Angel suggested. "That would end their life of crime."

"And the lives of any people they have in the cargo bays," Dervish responded.

"Gracie, is that freighter capable of punching?" Hawk asked.

"Yes, that particular model has long range capabilities."

"Since they're in real space," Hawk mused, "they are probably either taking off or landing. Gracie, what are the habitable planets around here?"

"Scanning," Gracie replied. "Gerico can sustain life, fifteen minutes ahead ... Oderiba is marginal, but could be used if protective clothing is worn during prolonged exposure. It is seven minutes away."

"Let's track 'em and see where they go," Angel said.

"Can they pick us up?" Hawk asked.

"These fighters are very hard to track on instruments," Dervish replied. "The material they are made of mostly absorbs laser and radar signals. It would take special heat sensing probes to detect us. Or we have to be close enough to create interference patterns on their equipment."

"Then we'll have to keep a good distance so they don't see us," Hawk replied. "Gracie, lock course to that freighter, but maintain our distance, please."

"What do you expect to find out?" Dervish questioned.

"Ain't it obvious?" Angel asked. "If they land, we can check out the location. See if it's their base or just a place of business."

"For what reason?" Dervish persisted.

"If it's a base, we can see what it would take to knock it out," Angel replied.

"This is open territory," Dervish protested. "If you attack them here, they will tell others. They will then go after Fliers."

"Only if any of 'em live to talk about it," Angel replied dryly. "I don't plan on leaving it like that."

"That will take more than the three of us," Dervish countered. "We are good, yes. But we are only three."

"Let's see if it's their base first," Hawk said. "Then, we can call in Pepper and his squad. That'd give us eight."

"What makes you think he will come?" Dervish asked. "We should not be here."

Hawk wrinkled his nose. "I don't know ... I just think he'll feel like we do."

"Okay, we can try that," Dervish replied. "The freighter seems to be heading for the dark side of Oderiba."

"Gracie, what do we know about Oderiba?" Hawk asked.

"It is at this time the ninth planet from its blue sun," she replied. "It maintains an erratic orbit, crossing the eighth planet's orbit before heading back to its present position. During its swing inward, its surface temperature reaches 90 degrees Centigrade, killing all vegetation on the side it keeps to the sun. Its dark side, however, remains very cold. The temperature is well below the freezing point of water."

"It's a sure bet that they aren't picking up anyone there. It must be their base," Angel concluded.

"Might work to our advantage," Hawk pondered. "Anyone trying to escape would die of exposure. They probably don't keep too many people there to watch the captives. If we're lucky, they might not outnumber us by very much."

"Once we start firing," Angel added, "the slaves might turn on 'em. That would probably ..."

"No, that is not likely," Dervish interrupted. "They deal mostly in children. People who cannot have children will pay a lot for one."

Angel made a face. "I thought only Earth bred sleazeballs like that," he mumbled.

"Their base must be near the light side or they'd freeze," Hawk said. "If we enter atmosphere in the middle of the dark side we could scan around the perimeter of the light side for them."

"Let's go," Angel replied. "Hey Dervish, can they pick up our radio?"

"It is spread spectrum," Dervish replied. "But they might see a little noise if they were looking at a tracker."

"Let's hope they don't look," Hawk replied as he slowly glided Gracie in.

They had little difficulty finding the outpost. They waited until the freighter left, then withdrew to a safe distance where Dervish called Pepper. Dervish reported that Pepper would come with a few other squads and a large shuttle for getting the children out. They rendezvoused far beyond tracking range, then headed in, leaving the shuttle. With twenty-seven Fliers, they didn't have much trouble taking the outpost.

While the Fliers kept the surviving smugglers pinned down, the shuttle moved in. Hawk, Angel and Dervish landed along with it near the buildings. Angel and Dervish remained with the ships, while Hawk and the pilot loaded the frightened children and toddlers into the shuttle. Hawk winced as he got a whiff of the two little ones he was carrying. All the kids were little more than bone and rags; the pungent odor of sour milk clung to their skin and hair.

They didn't exactly get a heroes' welcome when they landed on the space station. General Henlik met them on the flight deck and barked things at Dervish that didn't sound very pleasant. Dervish remained quiet.

While Henlik was dealing with Dervish, Pepper and Velter arrived with food and water. It took some encouragement to get the frightened and suspicious children to accept the food, but once they started eating they didn't seem inclined to stop.

When Henlik finally turned his attention to the deck officer, Dervish walked over to the shuttle. "There could be problems if any of the smugglers survived," he said quietly in English. "Nathan takes a lot of flak if the Council gets annoyed."

Velter glanced at Dervish and walked away. Lark hung back, smiled at Hawk, then quickly walked after Velter. Pepper bit his lip a moment, then said something quickly before he too walked away.

"What'd he say," Hawk asked.

"He wished you luck," Dervish replied, glancing at the floor.

"Not *him*; General Henlik," Hawk prompted. "After all, he can't say he didn't know what was going on. He allowed the shuttle to launch as well as the squads."

"He is angry that I ventured out of our territory," Dervish replied quietly. "It is not what you did so much as the fact that I disobeyed a Council directive."

"Look, it was *my* idea," Angel blurted. "Why should you get in trouble for rescuing babies? That's stupid! Where's this Nathan guy? I'll get him straightened out!"

"But *I* took you there," Dervish replied, "so I am responsible. Henlik has already notified headquarters. Nathan requested that the children be brought to him so he can begin to track down their parents."

"They really need to be bathed first," Hawk commented. "They're awful ripe!"

"They can be bathed there," Dervish replied. "Your orders are to take them to Nathan now."

Dervish's choice of words left Hawk with an uneasy feeling. "*Our* orders? Hmmm ... and what about you, then?" he asked apprehensively.

"I have been grounded until Nathan has reviewed this," Dervish replied quietly.

"That's bullshit!" Angel snapped. "We should *all* be in trouble. It was our idea!"

"But I did force the issue," Dervish admitted with a half smile. "I said we were going in with or without support."

Hawk made a sour face and stared off across the deck. Pepper was leaning against his bird, staring back at him. "So it's okay to sell kids; just don't piss off the fucking Council? I can't buy that!" he blurted. "If they don't have the guts to do what's right ... I'm going to ..." He stopped and looked down. He couldn't communicate what he thought of them; they didn't understand English, and he didn't understand their language. He was so frustrated he had to do something; he flashed a one-finger salute at General Henlik.

Angel turned and slammed his fist into the shuttle. He didn't wince, but his face turned ashen as he cleared his throat. "Sturdy little buggers," he mumbled, rubbing his knuckles. "Look here, pardner," he continued, "we got you into this, so we gotta get you out of it. We followed that freighter ... you told us not to. They can't hold you responsible for us! I'm gonna tell 'em all a thing or two ..." He paused as he came to the same conclusion as Hawk. "Wait ... if you're not coming with us, how are we gonna communicate?"

"Your language is in Mother's data base," Dervish replied. "Threenica already knows some and can figure out the rest. You had better go now."

Hawk had never felt so miserable. These guys seemed to have it in for Dervish ... someone had better straighten them out. He glanced at Pepper again, wishing he could somehow communicate what had really happened. Pepper wore a stony expression. As Hawk started to turn away, his peripheral vision caught Pepper flashing a thumbs up to Velter. He turned back quickly, but Pepper was climbing the stairs into his Bird.

"Pepper's squad will escort you to Nathan's headquarters," Dervish said. "The shuttle is unarmed."

Not sure how to read that, Hawk decided it would be better to err on the side of caution. "Ahhh ... Angel, why don't you fly the shuttle." He turned and started up Gracie's steps. "I'll follow in Gracie."

"Your orders are to take the shuttle," Dervish stated flatly.

Hawk half turned. "If that shuttle needs an armed escort, I want to make sure someone is really going to defend it!" He climbed in and closed the hatch. "Gracie, can they prevent us from taking off?"

Gracie started gliding for the nearest open bay. "No. Your clearance has not been modified. Therefore, I am expected to follow your orders. If control will not clear a launch and you request me to, I could punch from here. However, that would cause considerable damage; a number of lives could be lost."

Hawk thought of Dervish, Angel and the kids still on the flight deck and wrinkled his nose. "No, don't do that. If they won't clear us, I'll take the shuttle with Angel."

Gracie entered the bay; Pepper's Bird came in behind her. Hawk thought about it a moment. "Gracie, I want to send a message to Pepper. Could you translate it for me, please."

"I have been doing so," she informed him as the bay doors closed behind them.

"What?" Hawk retorted. "You mean you've been translating our private conversations and sending them to Pepper?"

"That was his request," Gracie replied defensively. "As your captain, he is permitted to know what is transpiring."

"Like hell he's my captain!" Hawk challenged. "I didn't enlist in this crackpot outfit to serve under some self-righteous bastard who'd rather follow orders than think! And why the hell didn't you tell me you were sending our conversations?"

"You did not ask."

"From now on kindly inform me of these little details."

"I am unsure of which details you would like to know."

"All of them," he snapped, then wished he hadn't, as Gracie obligingly began reciting every entry from Mother's data base. He tuned out her monologue as he locked in the coördinates. He waited until he saw the shuttle drift into view. "Gracie, maybe you can continue this later, okay?" he mumbled. "I really need silence to concentrate."

Gracie stopped talking as Hawk switched on the radio. "I'm right behind you, Angel. Ummm ... there's bears in the air and smokey's got his ears on."

"Ten four, good buddy," Angel drawled. "I'll maintain double nickels. Where's the hole in the bucket?"

"George Burns might know," Hawk replied.

"Oh," Angel replied. "How sweet it is ... talk to you soon."

The shuttle winked out, then Hawk punched out behind it. He chuckled a bit as he considered how their conversation would translate. *Poor Gracie*, he thought, *suffering from a code in her nodes.*

Pepper watched as the shuttle and Gracie disappeared. He smiled as he called to Lark. "They'll be good Fliers. They're smart, creative, and they take responsibility for their own actions. What do you think they were talking about?"

"Wouldn't even hazard a guess," Lark replied. "Seem like nice guys, too. Sure figured out quick that we were listening."

"I just can't understand why they'd like an Alderian," Velter commented.

"I don't think they know he's Alderian," Pepper came back, "or for that matter, what the Alderians are like." He leaned over and punched, pondering his own words through the long silence that followed.

Gracie was waiting near the shuttle when Pepper's squad winked in ahead of them. The five Birds moved out toward a large bluish planet. Hawk and Angel followed them in. As they skimmed over the surface, Hawk looked at it with interest. The few places that were not under water were covered by thick vegetation. Hawk concluded that it must be fresh water, as the plants grew right up to it, and in some cases were growing in what appeared to be the shallows.

A large landing field suddenly appeared to his left, surrounded on three sides by high thick trees and on the fourth by a large building. Pepper's squad descended vertically. Angel followed, slowly rocking the shuttle for a level landing once he was a few feet from the ground. It looked real neat, but from the somber look on their faces, Hawk doubted the Fliers were impressed.

He walked over to help Angel unload the kids as twelve men in gray uniforms came up and stood watching. Five older women came across the field and with smiles and nods began to help with the kids. One of the women attempted to talk to them, but Angel just shrugged and shook his head. Pepper walked slowly over and said something to the woman. As she looked back at Hawk and Angel, her expression remained friendly, so they decided they would probably not be shot on the spot.

After the children were off the shuttle, one of the uniformed men approached and indicated that Hawk and Angel were to follow. They exchanged glances as they were escorted toward the building. A tall, thin, young man opened the door. Next to him stood an equally tall older man who greeted them and motioned them inside.

"I ...," Angel started to say, when the young man began to speak in English. "Nathan tell me welcome you to Katara. You our ... guests. We were told of your actions. Nathan apologize for not yet learn your language. He not expect your peoples among us so soon. Please come with me for clean and rest. Nathan wish talk with you at party tonight."

Noting the armed escort, Angel felt it might not be prudent to make a scene at the moment. He shrugged at Hawk who nodded knowingly and they followed the man down the hallway to a sort of elevator. They entered, and as the floors flashed past, their guide continued his so far one-sided conversation.

"I learn your language from space craft that enter our sector some years back. You bring more Chuck Berry, yes?"

Angel almost choked. "Glad you liked it. We thought it might prove we were mostly harmless."

The young man tilted his large head sideways and looked at Angel with a puzzled expression.

"I had some," Hawk cut in, "but I didn't bring any with. I wasn't expecting to leave, let alone be gone this long."

The young man nodded understandingly at Hawk but again glanced at Angel oddly. The lift stopped; the young man escorted them to a door a few steps away. He opened the door and smiled at Hawk. "My name is Threenica. I come for you when dinner ready." He turned to walk away.

"My name is Hawk, and my strange friend here is Angel."

"Ahhh," replied the young man, as if somehow this explained everything. "Hope room is to your comfort." He returned to the lift and it dropped rapidly out of sight.

The room was beautiful and the bath water hot. Threenica came for them after a few hours and escorted them to a large banquet hall. They were seated facing one another at one end of a large table; Nathan was seated between them at the head of the table. Threenica took a seat next to Hawk. Both pilots felt lost amidst the splendor about them. They also remained a bit edgy, noting that all the officers at the table were armed.

The banquet was as boring as such things usually are, so Angel spent his time studying the room. About a story up, a walkway circled the room. Large pillars every few feet rose at least another story high, and each flew a different flag. Threenica explained to Hawk that the flags represented the various members of Nathan's space patrol.

After the dinner, Nathan rose and made a speech. Several times, someone among those gathered would stand and receive a greeting from the others. Threenica's translation made little sense, and neither Hawk nor Angel was really paying much attention. A dead silence brought them back to reality. All the officers at the table appeared to be glaring at them.

"Nathan has requested an explanation for your actions." Threenica was apparently repeating this for the second or third time; he looked as though he feared that he had somehow used the wrong words to express himself.

Angel looked at Hawk. When Hawk nodded in agreement, Angel turned to Threenica. "We don't think there should be any place in the universe someone can go and not be punished for their crimes. We just did what we felt we had to do. There was no way Dervish could have stopped us. He told us we weren't allowed to follow that freighter, that it was crossing into space we weren't allowed in, but we went anyway. And we'd do it again if the situation came up."

Threenica talked rapidly with Nathan who occasionally glanced sternly at the pilots. The officers seated at the table seemed restless and perhaps a bit angry at their defiant action. The expressions of these people were hard to read. Threenica then turned back to Angel. "Nathan asks if you are sure you wish to keep breaking the Council's laws. Perhaps you misunderstood; it is, after all, a ..."

"... a bad law, and we'll keep breaking it if we have to," Angel interrupted. "And Dervish had nothing to do with it. He bailed us out, that's all. If you have to get bent out of shape, we're the ones who did it."

It occurred to Hawk that Nathan was smiling despite his attempts at remaining stern, while Threenica's English had improved considerably.

Nathan turned to them. "Then you two are truly worthy of joining our little family."

Hawk started to say something to Nathan, who obviously had a good command of the language that was unknown to him up to a few seconds ago, but Angel grabbed his arm and pointed to the balcony directly behind him. A little man in an oversized t-shirt was hoisting the American flag.

Turning to the large gathering, Nathan said something they didn't understand. Amid the ensuing applause, he turned to Hawk and Angel and declared, "The request to invite you two into the ranks of our Fliers is hereby granted. Dervish, come introduce your new recruits."

"Thanks, Nathan," Dervish shouted as he swung over the rail and started sliding down the pole. He reached the bottom in a flash, and scrambled up to Angel and Hawk. "Welcome to the universe," he said, with a silly grin on his face.

Hawk, grinning broadly, turned to his friend. "Nope. This ain't even close to being shanghaied."

Angel, finally, had nothing to say.

3

Excepting Alice

Hawk stopped pacing the floor and stood squarely in front of Angel. "Look at me when I'm talking to you, dammit! Every Flier takes the test. You're really overreacting."

Angel continued to stare at the ceiling with a peeved look on his face. He slowly turned his gaze to Dervish. "You lied to me. How can you expect me to trust you after that?"

Hawk looked at Angel disgustedly. "Come on. We've been through all this already. The situation was real; the Fliers were going to deal with those slavers whether we did anything or not. What's the big deal? All they did was imply that we were gonna be in trouble for it. That's not much of a lie. What do you want him to do, kiss your butt?"

"Fine!" Angel screamed, turning loose his pent up fury on Hawk. "Stay here and play with your new little friend. I'm going home. I'm not going to lay my life on the line again only to discover it was to prove some goddam thing or other to some over-egoed nitwit." He stood up, pushed past Hawk, and stalked toward the exit. He stopped with his hand extended, leaning against the door. "I am free to go, aren't I?" he asked, his voice bitter with sarcasm.

Dervish looked up; his face was blank, but his eyes revealed worry and sadness. "Sure, any time. Fliers can go wherever they want. But remember," he said, turning his head to study a spot on the ceiling, "at the moment, you are fifty-seven light years from Earth." He waited a few moments for the statement to register before returning his gaze to Angel. "If you want to go home, you are going to have to fly there. Commercial flights are all booked."

Angel stared at him coldly. "I'm sure you're really broken up about that." He started again to leave the room and stopped. "Can I send Goldie back unmanned?"

"Yes, but she is not programmed to allow you to do that." Dervish looked miserable. "If you decide not to keep her, just ditch her in the ocean. No one will ever find her."

Angel stood there expressionless. "Just dump Goldie to rot? What's with you?"

Dervish slumped into the chair. "You are free to go, Angel, but I do not intend to make it easy on you. I am sorry, but you are my wingmate. You can desert me, but you can not make me help you do it."

Angel pushed the door open and stomped down the hall. How could Dervish make him feel so guilty when he was so obviously right? And Hawk. *Damn him! Why does he want to stay here with this make-believe Air Force, where you're promoted by your peers, disciplined by your wingmates, and follow orders only if you like 'em. Assuming anybody's even given any orders. Bah!*

He left the building and walked down to the hangar. He slowed as he made his way to Goldie. He ran his fingers over her smooth skin, his anger ebbing in the presence of the mighty fighter. He looked her over carefully and began to walk around her. His eye caught Gracie, just a few feet away.

He climbed into Goldie and automatically began pre-flight checkout. She was fueled up and her maintenance log was signed off. She was as ready as she would ever be. "Come on darlin'," he said with a twinge of guilt, "let's see what you can do before we find you a watery grave."

"There are many suitable bodies of water," Goldie reminded him. "Did you have a specific one in mind, or will any one of them do?"

"Dammit, I'm not in the mood for this!" he bellowed.

"It is not necessary to shout, Angel. Shouting overloads my amplifiers, causing distortion. If you are far from a ..."

"I know all about that," Angel muttered through clenched teeth. "Just give me punch coördinates for Earth."

"One moment. Accessing."

He looked at the flight computer as his stomach tied in knots. Dervish had explained how each fighter was tied to a vast network of computers they affectionately called Mother. Mother ostensibly logged flying hours, as Fliers were paid with a generous flight bonus. Her main function, however, was to provide information needed by the Fliers and to report a Flier's last known coördinates to his wingmates if trouble arose.

"Coördinates received; you wish to go home." It was a statement rather than a question, but Angel felt obliged to answer.

"I refuse to fly with liars!"

"I am not questioning your decision," Goldie retorted. "Your departure has been cleared."

"But maybe *I* am," Angel responded dejectedly. He looked at the punch coördinates that appeared on the screen and locked them in. "Where will this put me?"

"On the dark side of your Moon. From there, we can glide in unnoticed."

Angel activated the vertical takeoff. When he had reached altitude, he brought up her nose and let her scream. His finger hovered over the punch button. "Goldie?" he asked.

"Is something wrong?"

"Can you tell me how to program you to return without me?" His voice definitely conveyed his empty feelings.

"Yes, I am able to tell you." She sounded rather pleased with herself.

"Well then, do it!"

"No," came the smug reply.

Angel's fist came down on the button, and the little fighter punched.

✦ ✦ ✦

Hawk walked slowly next to Dervish. "We really have to go after him; try to talk him out of this stupidity. Shit, they'll lock him up if they catch him ... especially if he lands in Goldie."

Dervish nodded. "Yes, but he does not seem to wish to talk to us now."

"How long will the punch take?"

"About nine hours."

"He'll have cooled off by then. Probably land at his aunt's ranch. We could sorta meet him there, okay?"

Dervish shrugged as he stopped next to Love. "I do not know what to do. I guess I messed up."

Pepper, Lark and Velter walked over grinning.

"Celebration time," Velter chuckled in Common. "Your recruits are good pilots, Dervish, but how well can they hold their liquor?"

Dervish glanced down at the floor as Hawk looked at him questioningly. "They want to celebrate your passing the test," he mumbled in English.

Hawk grinned at the Fliers. "Would you tell them I'd love to, just as soon as we get back with Angel?" He looked back at Dervish and snapped his fingers. "You know, that just might do it. Angel could never resist a party."

Dervish glanced up at Velter. "Hawk would like to very much ... but we have to go get Angel."

Pepper looked puzzled. "Where did he go?"

Dervish studied his feet. "I blew it," he mumbled in Common. "I never picked a test before. He got very angry that I lied to him and left. I guess I'm not really very good at anything."

Pepper bit his lip. "The commander didn't give you much slack, did he? Those were rotten choices you had to make. I made a formal complaint to Nathan ... if that helps."

Dervish almost smiled. "Thank you. Ummm ... Hawk asked if you guys would mind coming with. He said Angel never could say no to a party."

"Let's go," Lark replied quickly. "Send us the coördinates, okay?"

Dervish nodded and turned to Hawk. "They will join us," he said in English.

Pepper thought a moment. "Earth's about an hour's punch from our station, right?"

Dervish nodded.

"Let's stop by there first," Pepper suggested. "See how many of the other guys will come along, okay? "

"Great," Dervish called back as he climbed into Love.

✦ ✦ ✦

Goldie glided into empty space; Angel locked her orbit to that of the Moon. The minutes ticked by as he just sat, staring at the night; so many thoughts bubbled around in his brain. He flashed on that morning about a month ago when he was testing a modified F-15 over the Arctic. When those landing instructions came over the radio, he had about choked.

He thought about what must have happened when he was reported missing. He grinned, picturing the general's face when word filtered back up the chain of command that they had found that forty million dollar baby abandoned on an ice floe. He wondered if they had ever managed to get it off.

He gently ran his fingers across Goldie's controls. What was he doing here? He didn't dare land her on Earth, but he sure couldn't ditch her in the ocean. He just sat there, trying to analyze his feelings and figure out what the hell he should do next. His brooding was broken by Goldie's alluring feminine voice.

"Angel, I am receiving a distress call. It is in English, and it is coming from one of the bodies of water you were seeking."

Angel stared nervously at the interface computer. "Uhhh?"

"Do you wish to ignore the call?"

"Yes. No. Oh, hell ... I don't know!" Angel just looked at the interface computer dejectedly.

"It is from an underwater vessel. It has lost power due to an explosion. It is taking on water."

Angel started thinking of all those men trapped inside the sinking sub. "Is there anything we could do to help?"

"You could activate the tractor beam. It has limited range, but if I were to get close enough, we should be able to tow the vessel to the surface."

Goldie's voice tickled his fancy. She always made him want to land the Bird and find a girl ... any girl. Angel's voice betrayed his mixed emotions. "What's 'close enough' ?"

"A few meters above the water."

It was obvious that he did not have the same effect on the computer. "A few meters! Shit, we'd be out in the open. We'd be seen. Maybe if we're real lucky they'll ask us to identify ourselves before blowing us sky high!"

"I could not allow them to do that. You will need to convince them not to attempt it."

"Yeah, right," Angel mumbled, sure that the sarcasm in his voice was lost on the computer. "Well, what the hell; let's try it," he said doubtfully.

"No time for local propulsion," Goldie responded crisply. "Assist has been requested. Punching to coördinates."

Angel wasn't sure if he blinked or not, but the moon and stars were gone. All around him were miles and miles of ocean.

"I have tuned the radio to the vessel's frequency. I suggest you inform it of our intentions."

Angel grimaced. "Commander," he began. "You have just entered the Twilight Zone. Rod Serling has sent a little green man in a flying saucer to tow your vessel to the surface."

The conversation continued to liven up, punctuated with numerous colorful metaphors, as the commander informed him that he was jamming distress signals. Adding to the confusion was the lecture Goldie began on the impropriety of calling her a saucer. This second conversation was not lost on the commander, nor on the rescue vessels that were heading toward the foundering sub. The commander only stopped cussing when it became apparent that his vessel was indeed slowly rising toward the surface.

Before the sub broke the surface, Angel had a squadron of fighters buzzing overhead. Mainly to stall for time, he had identified himself by name, rank, and serial number, convincing them it was indeed himself by giving them the exact location he left their jet along with the names of his maintenance crew.

It took the better part of an hour to bring the crippled sub to the surface and hold her there while her dazed but thankful crew labored to repair her damaged ballast tanks. Once she was stabilized and Angel could release the tractor beam, the commander thanked him again profusely and Angel wished them all a good day.

He was immediately hailed by the squadron leader. "Angel, you are under arrest. My orders are to escort you back for debriefing or put you down."

"Hey, guys, I'm really sorry I can't take y'all up on your peachy offer to follow your little puppies home, but I got a hot date tonight," Angel drawled in a honey-coated voice. He patted the computer. "Let's punch out, Goldie."

"We are in atmosphere, Angel. Not only would the shock waves destroy those jets, it would break the vessel apart and send it back to the bottom." There was an icy edge to her voice. "Weapon systems armed and ready."

"Those are my people! I can't let you hurt them!" Angel shouted back at the computer.

The voice on the radio sounded as serious as Goldie's. "Start following or we open fire." Angel gently nudged the little craft upward, feinting and looking for a hole, but there were fighters everywhere.

A very familiar and welcome voice burst through the radio. "I must advise you gentlemen," Dervish announced, sounding dead serious, "that if you choose to open fire on my wingmate, I will take it as a personal insult. I will be forced to defend him even if he chooses not to defend himself."

Two Birds were fast approaching. Thirty-five other Birds popped in from all directions. Angel let out a whoop as Hawk's clear voice began to sing a chorus of Alice's Restaurant. Angel joined in, then Dervish, and they sang in three-part harmony. The subtlety was most likely lost on whomever was listening on Earth. Angel slowly gained altitude under the watchful presence of the many strange fighters.

Angel had never sounded so sheepish. "Ummm, Dervish?"

"I take it you are offering to buy the beer this round?" Dervish responded with a triumphant smirk.

"Naw," Angel drawled as he locked in the punch coördinates. "I was gonna ask where you learned the lyrics."

"Funny," Dervish retorted. "I was just going to ask you the same thing."

4

A Bird's Eye View

Angel glared back at the group of Fliers standing in the cafeteria line a noticeable distance behind him. "Okay, so the Fliers back at the old station weren't all that friendly, but these guys are downright hostile," he grumbled to Dervish as they looked over the breakfast selection. "Why'd you want to get transferred here?"

Dervish looked down as they took their trays and started across the cafeteria to an empty table. "Killer sometimes comes out here," he replied quietly. "It is one of the stations he maintains. He talks to me and sometimes ..." He stopped talking while they passed a table where four Fliers were seated. The Fliers purposely avoided looking in his direction. "Sometimes, he asks me over for dinner," he added as they passed out of earshot.

"Who's Killer?"

"He works on the station equipment and the shuttles. I helped him track some leaks once. He is very nice."

Angel scratched his head. "I don't get it. Why didn't you request to be where he's stationed?"

"He is stationed on a base. They only assign full squads to bases, and then Fliers with children get first priority. I had a difficult time convincing Nathan to transfer us here."

"Can't you just go visit him? Pop over for the weekend?"

Dervish looked uncomfortable. "They reserve the extra rooms for squads on leave ... and he is usually busy."

Angel figured there was more to it, but decided it must be something personal, so he let it drop. "Are Fliers always this nasty to the new guys?"

Dervish shook his head. "They are good people. It is just me they don't like."

Angel set down his tray and with a strange gleam in his eye, turned and flashed the Fliers the bird. Pleased with himself, he sat down and began to hum an old Hank Williams Junior song. "Haven't heard any real music around here. One of these days I got to get back to Earth and pick me up a CD player. Any way of doing that?"

"We could do that, yes," Dervish replied, only too glad to change the subject. "We are not scheduled out until twenty-two hundred ... it should take four hours to punch there. That leaves us ... two or three hours before we must leave."

"You mean we could go now?"

"Sure. I told you, Fliers are free to go wherever they want."

Angel thought a moment. "Ummm ... could we drop by the ranch? My aunt's probably real worried, considering what the Air Force musta told her."

Dervish shrugged. "That should not be a problem."

"Great ... I'll see if I can get some cash from Hawk. I didn't have very much when we left. He probably has some."

"We could convert some credits to gold," Dervish offered. "That has value on your planet."

"Unh-uh; we'd just have to sell the gold. They might ask for ID ... and I don't think I want to risk it."

Dervish nodded. "Where is Hawk? I thought he was going to join us."

"He was kinda moody this morning. Said he wanted to lie around the observation deck awhile."

"Are you sure he is happy here? Maybe we should take him home."

"No way," Angel snapped. "He'd probably get locked up for the rest of his life."

"Why?"

"Either they'd think he was crazy and put him in the funny farm, or else they'd figure he was telling the truth and lock him up to protect their own butts."

Dervish stared at his coffee. "Then I have done a bad thing. I should not have taken ..."

"Hey, this was the best thing that could have happened to him," Angel interrupted. "I know ... I'm his best buddy!"

✦ ✦ ✦

Hawk lay back on the soft mats staring out at the stars. He let out a dejected sigh. He had gotten up this morning and realized it was Passover. That got him to thinking ... did God know where he was? Or did He even care?

The stars gleamed back at him through the blackness, shifting a bit as the light passed through the protective shields. "Sir," he mumbled. "You sure created a beautiful universe. But sometimes I think I'm talking to no one; that maybe You fell asleep centuries ago and You haven't woken up yet ..."

To get his mind off his depression, he tried to find pictures in the stars. After a while he found a clump that looked a lot like an elephant and another that resembled a winged horse. Footsteps on the stairs caught his attention; two Fliers were walking across the deck carrying their breakfasts. Without thinking, he gave them a friendly wave. "Hi," he called, then realized they wouldn't understand English.

The Fliers looked at one another; one smiled at Hawk and waved back. They came over and sat down not too far from him. Hawk figured they must be joking around, as they laughed as they ate. They were taller than average, but not as tall as Nathan. Their hair was silverish in color, standing out against their pale gray skin. Their eyes were a light shade of purple. Hawk went back to watching the stars, occasionally checking a particular star on the maps Gracie had printed for him. He jumped when he felt a hand on his shoulder.

The Flier grinned. "Recor," he said pointing at himself, then pointed at the other Flier. "Harley."

Hawk smiled back. "Hawk," he said pointing to himself.

Recor offered him a bottle of something they were drinking. It had a pleasant, exotic aroma vaguely reminiscent of beer.

Hawk accepted with a nod, mostly so as not to offend them, and shuffled through the maps until he found the one that portrayed the Milky Way. He pointed to it and then to himself.

Harley took the maps from him, sifted through until he found what he was looking for. He pointed to a galaxy labeled Yedlarx.

Hawk took a drink from the bottle, hoping for the best. It tasted much better than beer; in fact, it tasted good. He smiled and nodded. Recor smiled back.

"Hawk, you up here?" Angel's voice boomed across the deck.

"Yeah," Hawk called back.

As Angel and Dervish started across the deck, Harley and Recor nodded, gathered up their trays and started toward the far entrance. Recor turned and waved at Hawk as they disappeared down the stairs.

Dervish shoved his hands deeper into his pockets and stood staring at the floor.

"Who's that?" Angel asked, noting the wave.

"I think his name is Recor," Hawk replied. "I just got to learn the language. I'm going crackers!"

"Maybe Gracie could help," Dervish offered quietly.

Hawk looked at him and realized how miserable Dervish seemed at the moment. "She's been great," he added quickly. "I'd have really been lost without her."

Dervish pursed his lips. "I'm sorry," he mumbled. "I should have been teaching you Common; instead I've been letting you teach me English."

"Nahh," Angel drawled. "I've managed to learn a few choice words ... I got nothing to say to them folk that those and a couple of hand gestures don't cover."

"I can't even get *them* right," Hawk lamented. "It's not your fault, Dervish. I've never been that quick at learning things. When I was little, they thought I was retarded."

"Oh, come off it," Angel grumbled. "You're smarter than I am. And I'm getting tired of Goldie constantly pointing that out."

Hawk wrinkled his face into a disgusted frown. "What?"

"Ol' Birdbrain keeps needling me," Angel mumbled. "She gets this nasty tone in her voice and asks: 'Why are you so different from Hawk? It's impossible for me to conclude that you are the same species'."

"Come off it. She wouldn't say that."

Angel puffed himself up. "I don't lie, pardner. I swear, that damn Bird is an airhead; takes everything literally."

"She's a computer, Angel. What did you expect?"

"She could learn, ya know. When I point out the stupidity of her response she gets real silent and pouts."

"She's probably trying to analyze the data."

"She's pouting," Angel insisted.

Hawk gave up, took another drink and offered the bottle to Angel. "Recor gave me this. You gotta taste this stuff. It's really good!"

Angel reached for the bottle but Dervish put his hand out. "If you intend to go back to Earth to pick up some things, you can't drink any of that. No one cares what you do when you're off, but you'll get blacklined for flying if you're not sober."

Angel looked disgusted. "What's one swallow?"

"Of *that* stuff?" Dervish responded. "At least an hour before you could fly."

Hawk looked at him quizzically, then glanced at the bottle. "Really? It doesn't seem that strong."

Dervish grinned. "Don't stand up quickly, okay?"

Hawk shook his head. "Ahhh ... where are we going?"

"To pick up some CDs and a player," Angel replied. "Listen, do you have any cash on you?"

"Yeah. It's in my room ... we're going to Earth?"

"*We're* going," Dervish replied, pointing to Angel, then himself. "We must leave now to get back on time." He glanced down at the floor. "You can't fly now ... I'm sorry."

Hawk shrugged. "It's not your fault. The money's in my bottom drawer. Might as well take it all ... got no use for it here."

Angel gazed longingly at the bottle. "Save a swig of that skeet for me, okay?" he said, as he and Dervish left the deck.

Hawk looked back at the stars, but they started to dance around so he closed his eyes. Strange colored patterns formed in his mind. He studied them for a while, then chuckled to himself. He didn't really feel like going back to Earth anyway.

Maybe he would go out and play around with Gracie ... as soon as he could figure out how to stand up.

Recor paused to glance down the hallway before starting down the stairs that led to the elevator. "What do ya think?" he called to Harley.

Harley looked back and shrugged. "Hard to tell," he offered as he held the elevator door open.

Recor bounded after him. "Well, I like him. Seems real easy going."

Harley chuckled as they stated down. "He'll be even easier once he drinks that."

Recor winced. "Maybe I should go back and ..."

"Dervish can watch him," Harley snapped.

Recor shifted his weight. "I said, I *like* him."

The elevator came to a stop. Recor walked across the hallway, tossed his tray on the stack and shuffled down the hall.

Harley disgustedly looked after him. He shook his head, then ran to catch up. "Okay, we'll check him out," he offered as he reached Recor's side.

Recor tilted his head to one side and skipped a half step. "I bet he'll get your ass, too," he snickered.

"If he's so damn good," Harley retorted, "why's he flying with Dervish?"

Recor wrinkled his nose. "I don't know. A good Flier's got a certain ... odor. He stinks of it."

"Probably forgot to shower."

Recor shoved Harley as they entered the gym.

Almost six hours passed before Hawk ventured down to the flight deck. He felt great. The dark clouds hanging over him that morning had vanished; he wasn't even sure why he had been depressed in the first place. After all, he was doing what he'd always dreamt of ... flying around in space. And in the neatest fighter ever created. He ran his hand affectionately across Gracie's smooth skin as she lowered the stairs for him.

"You're beautiful," he told her as he climbed in. "I wonder if you understand how truly magnificent you are."

"I am pleased that you like me," she replied softly.

"Why don't we go out for a while?" he asked. "Maybe play around with the internal gravity reference."

"Are you sure you feel all right? Your bioreadings are not within the normal range."

He bit his lip. "No, I'm not sure. Recor and Harley gave me a bottle of something early this morning. I only drank half of it ... and that was over six hours ago. What do you think?"

"Without knowing precisely what you drank, I can not make a judgment in that regard."

"Maybe we shouldn't go out then," he said as he started to take off his helmet.

"Recor's Bird is on the deck," she replied quickly. "I will request further information."

"Ummm ..." he started to protest, but stopped himself; she'd probably already sent the request and it would just hurt her feelings if he rebuffed her attempt to please him. "Thanks, Gracie," he said quietly.

"Receiving data ... scanning," she said, then was silent a few moments. "I am not sure how your biological system responds to this chemical," she finally replied. "However, six hours is normally a sufficient time to restore proper responses should they be necessary. I have requested permission to launch."

He reached over and patted the computer. "Gracie, you're something else."

"I do not understand. I can only be what I am."

Hawk chuckled. As Gracie glided toward a launch bay, he tried to think of where they should go to mess around. Recor's voice drifted through the radio; Hawk frowned. "What's he saying?"

"Recor is sending coördinates and requesting that you join him."

"Tell him okay, I'll see him out there." Hawk locked in the coördinates that appeared on his screen. When the bay doors opened, he moved out and punched.

Recor winked in a few minutes after him and moved in close. "He asked what you were going to do out here," Gracie stated.

"Play around ... get a better feel for things," Hawk replied.

Gracie was silent for a while and Hawk got a bit edgy. "What did he say?" he prompted.

"He did not respond to you yet," she replied. "He is talking with other members of his squad."

"What's he saying?"

"I am not able to translate it into anything logical," she responded. "It is a lot like what you and Angel were saying when Pepper requested translations."

"Hmmm ... wonder what they're up to."

"He is sending another set of coördinates. He said it is very open there."

"Gracie, can you scan ahead when we're in a punch? See what's at the location you're punching to?"

"No. But I can conduct a hyperspace probe prior to making a punch; that allows me to make minor corrections."

"Okay, do it. And tell Recor we'll see him there, okay?"

"Sending."

"I got a hunch that when we punch out, his whole friggin' squad's gonna jump us."

"Why?"

"I don't know why, but I think it has to do with Dervish."

"That is not logical. Dervish is not here now."

"I know," he chuckled. "But I fly with him, and for some reason that bothers them. Maybe we can get some answers if we get their respect."

"I do not understand."

"Then just humor me," Hawk replied. "If you sense anything out there, load all the rear positions with flares."

"Scanning complete ... more than one object is at that location; do you wish me to load the flares?"

"Yup."

"Loading flares."

"Okay. As soon as we come out of the punch, if they swoop down on us, take a short jump behind them. As soon as we wink out, they'll most likely peel off in different directions. Based on that assumption, as you wink in, locate them, compute their speed and relative trajectory, and fire all rear flares for those locations. Got that?"

"Then what?"

"Hope like hell they're not playing for keeps, I guess," Hawk mumbled. "Then we flip over and face 'em, and try for lock on one ..."

"Are you sure you are feeling all right?" Gracie interrupted. "It is highly irregular for a Flier to attack another Flier."

"That's why you're only going to fire flares," Hawk replied as he locked in the new coördinates and punched. "I think they want me to do something dumb."

"I think that you are about to do that," she replied.

It all happened so quickly that Hawk barely had time to see the Birds moving in on him before Gracie winked back out. When the universe reappeared, the status light showed flares firing as Gracie flipped over to face the Birds now wheeling around to face Hawk. Applause and chuckles drifted over the radio.

"Recor sends his best. He said heat seekers would have locked on four of them," Gracie informed him proudly. "They would have had to hop to avoid them," she continued to explain. "That would have given us time to punch out and call for assistance."

"Ask him why they pulled this shit," Hawk told her.

"He is apologizing," she replied. "They were uncertain of you, since you fly with Dervish. He is saying something about mind reading ..." She paused briefly, processing that statement. "You *did* seem to know what they were going to do, Hawk," she remarked. "It was not logical. How did you know?"

"Tell him where I come from, a pilot's either quick or he's dead," Hawk stated bitterly. "And it has nothing to do with reading minds." He waited while she translated, then added quietly. "But just between us, Gracie, it was a lucky guess."

"He is asking if you wish to join them," Gracie said. "They are going planetside for a few hours."

"I have to be back before twenty-two hundred. Besides, I'm not sure if I want to go anywhere with them."

"He said he was not accusing you of reading his mind. He is unhappy if you are offended. He gives his word we will get back on time."

"Ask him why they hate Dervish so much."

Gracie was silent for a few minutes as the Fliers seemed to talk amongst themselves. "He says that they do not hate him, but he does make them nervous. You were so different ... they wondered if you were a good Flier. Now they wonder why you fly with him."

"I owe him my *life*, dammit!" Hawk stated hotly. "He's really very nice ... and very lonely. Did those guys ever stop and think that maybe they make him nervous, too?"

"He said we must leave now to return on time," she replied. "And no, they had not considered that."

"That's a start, anyway," Hawk mumbled. "Okay, tell him we'll go, and thank him for the invitation."

"Locking in coördinates," Gracie informed him.

As the backlight went green, Hawk punched and watched the universe wink out around him.

✦ ✦ ✦

Hawk sat at his desk fiddling with the CD player Angel had bought him.

Angel sat on Hawk's bed, slapping his thigh to the music. "Better eat that chili before it burns a hole in the container," he teased.

Hawk grinned and opened the chili. "What had they told your aunt?" he asked, as he started eating.

"A lot of nothing."

"Mmmm ... I really miss this stuff," Hawk mumbled between bites.

"You'd never believe who's been visiting her."

"Try me."

"Richardson."

"Major Richardson, the shrink?"

"Colonel."

"He got promoted?"

"Yeah," Angel chuckled. "Actually, he's okay ... for a shrink. He called her when the CIA showed up at his office. Told her to warn me they'd put a tail on you. He even called her again when he found out I'd taken off with you. You know, just to let her know I was OK. He's been visiting her a lot since then."

"Really? Did she say why?"

Angel grinned. "I think they have a thing going. And guess what? He asked her to have me call him if I ever showed up."

"So did you?"

"You think I'm nuts?"

Hawk swallowed what he was chewing before he cracked up. "He's cool. Probably wants to come with. He was always wishing he could see the universe."

"Oh, I got you a Wilburys and a bunch of Sawyer Brown. I wish they'd had more Waylon though..." Angel mused.

Hawk glanced up at him. "Great! Thanks."

"I got a whole pile of CDs. I was gonna download a bunch of stuff, but that takes a credit card. And a laptop," Angel grumbled as he cranked the bass up a bit.

"Oooh ... better turn that down, or Sardan might smash the ones you did get. He's gotta get up in a few hours; his squad pulled a morning shift."

"Oops ..." Angel mumbled, turning the volume down. "Guess I got carried away. Ahhh ... how'd you find that out?"

"He asked me to wake him at oh-seven hundred."

"How did you manage to communicate? You don't know Common any better than I do."

"I know a few words ... but mostly we used pantomime."

Angel chuckled. "It's oh-five-thirty. We probably should get some coffee before the morning crew staggers in."

"Yeah, I could sure use some. Shit, Dervish said he'd be right up over an hour ago."

"We ..." Angel began as someone knocked on the door.

Hawk rolled his eyes as he quickly answered the door. A huge man resembling a sumo wrestler stood looking into the room. "Angel," Hawk said, nodding at the man, "meet Sardan."

Sardan nodded, then looked at the CD player.

Angel paled, turning it softer yet. "Sorry," he said quietly.

Sardan shook his head and motioned upward with both hands.

"I think he likes it," Hawk noted with relief.

Angel began to turn up the volume until Sardan nodded approvingly. He smiled at them as he left the room.

"Whoop, oh boy," Angel mumbled. "How'd they fit *him* with a Bird?"

"Carefully," Hawk quipped. "Actually, his whole squad looks like that. They seem okay, though."

"They can afford to be. Ain't no one in their right mind gonna mess with *them*."

"Which reminds me," Hawk said as he started for the door. "We best fish Dervish off the fight deck, or he'll still be working on Love when we get up this afternoon."

"Sardan reminds you of Dervish?"

"No," Hawk chuckled; "the part about being in your right mind."

Angel glanced at the CD player, then at Sardan's room. "Maybe I'll just leave it here ... don't wanna get him upset."

Hawk laughed. "Next trip to Earth we're gonna have to pick up a few more of those. I think you've started a craze."

"Look, Birdbrain," Angel snapped. "It ain't noise, it's music! And when I want your opinion, I'll ask for it."

"It is difficult for me to believe," Goldie protested, "that even *you* could consider that amount of distortion pleasurable."

"Cram it, will ya," Angel muttered.

"You two arguing again?" Hawk asked as he walked up.

"Ehhh. Now Birdbrain's a music critic," Angel grumbled. "Uhhh ... got a minute? I could use some help up here."

"You *do* need help, Angel," Goldie commented dryly.

Hawk chuckled as he climbed out onto her wing tip. "What you working on?"

"Trying to figure out Dervish's latest mod."

"If you're still foggy, I can do it," Hawk offered. "I got Gracie modified last night."

"Sorry about that. I did sorta flake out. I didn't intend to."

"You drank five bottles of that stuff," Hawk reminded him. "Dervish figures you broke the record."

Angel grinned sheepishly. "It tastes great. Where did you buy that?"

"I didn't. Recor gave 'em to me," Hawk said, hoping he wasn't questioned further. "Sure you feel up to doing this?"

"Wouldn't miss it for nothing," Angel admitted. "Birdbrain goes catatonic for most of it."

"Angel, you feelin' okay?" Dervish called up.

Angel yanked the main interface board and grinned. "Couldn't be better."

Dervish nodded. "I'll be right back. They posted new shifts; gonna see what we drew."

Hawk shook his head. "God, this month went by quick. It's hard to believe we've been here ... almost two months now."

"Don't remind me," Angel snapped. "I'm so horny, Sardan's sister would look good!"

Hawk glanced up at Angel, then puckered his lips. "Personally, I like 'em a bit smaller."

"Well, after a few weeks," Angel drawled, "I'd ... oh, never mind."

Dervish approached to within six feet of Isslan, the deck officer of the month, and stood there. A small reptilian-like creature streaked across the flight deck, stopping next to Dervish. It blinked its slanted, beady eyes at him and let out a high pitched whistle. Dervish smiled, reached down and stroked its smooth head. "Well, hello, Blivic," he said. The creature rubbed against his leg and a faint musky odor began to drift up from it. It whistled softly a few more times, then streaked off as three Fliers came charging up. They gave Dervish a nasty look as they took off after it.

Isslan glanced at Dervish. "Blivic likes you?" he said with disgust, thumbing through his stack of papers. "That figures."

When Dervish didn't respond, Isslan held out a sheet. Recor came over and waited as Dervish moved only as far as needed to take the paper. "Thanks," Dervish mumbled, as he turned and walked away.

Isslan wrinkled his nose. "Gee, I hope I didn't contaminate it," he muttered as he looked for Recor's sheet.

"He doesn't mean to offend," Recor said quietly. "He thinks no one likes him."

"Huh?" Isslan watched silently as Dervish walked across the deck. He brushed a lock of mouse-gray hair out of his eyes and pursed his lips. "*He's* the one that doesn't like anybody," he said finally, as he handed Recor the sheet.

Recor took the sheet and shrugged. "I heard he saved your wingmate's butt. You think about it, okay?"

Isslan said nothing as he leaned back against the wall.

Recor raised an eyebrow, then turned and walked away.

✦ ✦ ✦

Dervish climbed up the stairs and peered down at Angel. "Hmmm ... Blivic's running loose, so watch where you step. She usually bites."

"What's a Blivic?" Hawk asked.

"She's a wussy. Small, black, smooth skin ... with beady eyes," Dervish replied. "Seventy percent of her is very sharp teeth."

"Did she enlist?" Angel drawled.

Dervish chuckled. "No. She's been hanging around here for a while. Sort of a pet, I guess. They're supposed to ... I'm not sure how to say this in English ... make a girl want sex?"

"An aphrodisiac that bites," Hawk mused. "Hmmm ... do they eat it, mix it with drinks or does it eat them?"

"Huh?" Dervish looked at Hawk with a puzzled expression. "It lets off a scent when it's happy. Perhaps that doesn't translate," he muttered as he studied the nodes.

"Its scent makes girls horny?" Angel repeated eagerly. "Ummm ... how do you get one of them things?"

Dervish shook his head. "It is just a story, I think, but some of them will try anything ..."

"I'm getting to that point myself," Angel snapped. "We got to get planetside, Dervish!"

Dervish bit his lip. "You're doing great on those nodes."

"Hawk's doing most of it," Angel replied. "I'm having trouble just reading the prints."

Dervish just nodded. "We got late evenings again, but we're off 'til tomorrow night."

"Do we ever get more than one day off?" Angel asked. "Those creeps might want Blivic, but I gotta find some place that has girls."

Dervish looked a bit uncomfortable. "We're in the draw for vacation."

"Ahhh ... how's that work?" Angel prompted.

"All squads and tails that haven't had time off yet draw for leave," Dervish replied. "We served a month, so we're an official tail now."

Angel cleared his throat. "Tail?"

"Six is minimum for a squad," Dervish explained, "and eight is max. If a squad gets a ninth Flier, three of 'em become the tail. They fly on their own, like we do, but if there's an alert they follow their squad. When a tail picks up another three Fliers, it becomes a squad."

Hawk started to chuckle.

Dervish looked at him and shrugged.

"Ahhh ... tail has other connotations in English," Hawk explained.

Dervish raised an eyebrow. "It is a very strange language."

Angel plugged the board back in, and winced. "Is that mod gonna help her disposition?"

"I didn't need to be modified," Goldie snapped, as she came back to life. "Just fumigated."

5

What You Don't Know

As fate would have it, Hawk drew the short straw. He gave Angel a high sign, and the two wandered down to the hangars to inform Dervish that they had lucked out.

"Three weeks R and R," Angel shouted, as they walked across the deck where Dervish was working on his Bird. "Can we go to that base you were telling us about?"

Dervish looked up with a silly grin on his face, but both Hawk and Angel got the distinct impression he was not particularly overjoyed. "Ahhh ... yeah, I guess so."

Hawk studied Dervish as the little man returned his attention to the on-board computer. "Something wrong?" he asked softly; then, noticing Dervish wince, added "with Love?"

"She's been acting strange lately," he responded, maybe a little too casually. "I thought I'd run some logic checks. You *do* understand that these neural networks are not at all like your brain-dead PCs. They are artificial intelligence systems with access to a lot of fast parallel processing."

Angel shook his head. "Loves are never logical, Dervish. You ought to know that."

Dervish made a sour face, but continued to fiddle with the computer. "I'll get her back together. Give me another hour or so." He looked first at Angel, then Hawk. "That okay?" he added hesitantly.

Angel gave him the old thumbs up. "Sure thing, partner. I wanted to shower first, anyway. Come on, Hawk. Love might get jealous if we distract him too long."

They grinned at each other as they walked away to the sound of Dervish cussing softly.

"Dervish," a soft voice was asking, "what did they mean?"

Angel raised an eyebrow. "Wonder how he explains that."

"English is not a logical language," Hawk replied, but something deep inside was nagging at him.

They punched in above a large planet with a deep purple hue. After obtaining permission to land, Dervish took them straight down. Hawk was disappointed; he wished he could have seen a bit more of the strange landscape.

They docked their Birds on the far side of the large field and it took a while to make their way to the Fliers' quarters. While they walked, Hawk marvelled at the deep blue-red trees that made up the dominant plant life.

The guest rooms were large with private bath facilities, a nice change from the space station. Hawk spent a leisurely half hour arranging his stuff, took a relaxing shower and put on a clean set of clothes. Then he wandered over to Angel's room and entered without knocking.

He flopped on the bed and looked up at Angel. "God, I'd almost forgotten what showering in real running water is like."

Angel chuckled. "I hate the way the shower at the station just spits at you and then shuts off. And then I keep thinking about how it's been recirculated ... bah."

"Yeah," Hawk mumbled, half lost in thought. "You know something, I can't think of anything to do. Shit, I'm getting to be as bad as Dervish."

"Huh?"

"I'm *worried* about him."

"*I'm* worried about *me*," Angel wailed in mock agony. "Whenever that computer talks, my skin crawls. If I don't find something female soon ..."

"Really, now?" Hawk teased. "You mean you think of something other than flying and tinkering with your Bird?"

"Y' know, you're right," Angel said with a chuckle. "He's always either flying or tinkering. If you need him, you might as well head for the flight deck. Or if you're real lucky, you can catch him in the caf."

Hawk sat up and replied, "Yeah. Know what, though? For all his bravado, I'll bet he's as shy as we are."

Angel gave Hawk a playful shove. "What you mean *we*, white man?" he snapped.

Hawk ignored the old joke as he walked toward the door. "Let's go find him and all go make fools of ourselves."

"Sounds like a plan." Angel bobbed his head a few times, but a part of him was still miffed at being labeled shy, even if it was true.

Dervish was not in his room. Angel and Hawk exchanged knowing glances and headed out to the flight bays. It took some poking about to find him, and in the process they attracted the attention of a middle aged man who seemed to shadow them after attempting to catch their eye.

Dervish sat high atop the crisscross of catwalks that allowed access to every part of a Bird. Slumped over one of the rear propulsion units, he was humming one of those ungodly alien tunes he'd picked up somewhere. Hawk rattled the bay door to attract his attention. Dervish looked down and waved them up, but he didn't look happy.

As they approached the catwalk, the older man entered the bay. Feeling a little ill at ease, Angel looked up at Dervish and drawled, "Hey there, pardner, you wanna take a break, maybe show us around this here part of the galaxy?"

Hawk's face was all mischief. "Yeah, Dervish, come on. I don't think I could find my way off base, let alone find some place where females hang out."

The older man had come up next to Hawk while he spoke. He glanced at Dervish, then back at Hawk. "I don't think Dervish could help you much in that department. He really isn't into girls ye..."

Without waiting for him to finish, Angel grabbed the man and spun him around, pinning him against the railing of the catwalk. "You calling my wingmate a sissy boy?" he barked.

Hawk had spun around too, his eyes dark with anger.

"Whoa, there!" A rather red-faced Dervish scampered down the catwalk. However, the look Dervish gave Angel was one of appreciation.

The man seemed a bit taken aback. "Apparently that didn't translate too well. Should have spent more time studying English, but it wasn't a big priority considering you're the only ones that speak it." He shook his head a couple of times to clear the adrenaline rush, then looked at Angel with a twinkle in his eyes. "Good reactions, young man," he said, rubbing his head.

"Ahhh ... sorry," Angel mumbled. "Keep forgetting you folks don't know English too well."

The older man nodded as he turned to Dervish. "You picked grand wingmates, but it might have been a good idea to have told them you're Alderian." He looked at Dervish squarely, then turned and started out of the bay. When he reached the door, he turned and casually called back, "Bring them over to my place around nineteen hundred for dinner." He walked out of the bay rubbing his head.

Hawk turned toward Dervish with a worried expression. "Who was that?"

Dervish was busy studying the floor. "The base general," he answered miserably.

Hawk winced.

Angel circled behind Dervish. Swinging his arm over Dervish's shoulder, he proceeded to guide the little man toward the bay door. "I think we'd better find some quiet place to talk," he said with a grand air of casualness. "I really hate to go around picking fights with generals," he continued, winking at Dervish, "unless they deserve it."

They walked along a dirt path worn into the bluish grass for about fifteen minutes before they came to the edge of a rustic, sleepy-looking village, mostly small wooden homes amidst large cultivated fields. At the far edge, a platform led to a conveyance reminiscent of a ride at a third-rate travelling carnival.

"Is this thing safe?" Angel asked as they walked up the creaky stairs.

"It is the only public transit," Dervish replied. "Unless you want to ride in a wagon."

Angel glanced down at the crude wagons parked near the platform, each drawn by a comically grotesque beast that looked to Angel like a cross between a Brahma bull and a kangaroo. "No, thanks," Angel muttered. "Those critters musta been designed by a committee."

The monorail ride was fast and fun, but it took a half hour to reach the large town. Dervish guided them down quaint cobblestone lanes that wound around old homes and buildings constructed of a brownish stone. Angel noticed that the female population was out in large numbers; Hawk was busy looking at the strange plant life.

Dervish hadn't been too talkative during the trip, and neither Hawk nor Angel felt like pressing him. After an hour of walking around, Angel suggested they stop for something to drink.

They sat at a table in an open-air cafe, Hawk and Angel drinking what passed for beer while Dervish silently stared at his. Hawk decided it was time to get some answers. "What did the general mean," he asked in a quiet voice, "you should have told us you're Alderian?"

Dervish looked uncomfortable. "He was just trying to say that my biological clock hasn't hit girls yet, so I wouldn't know ..."

"Bull!" Hawk cut him off. "You haven't taken your eyes off anything female that walked near us. Your clock went off, all right." He grinned knowingly. "You just don't have any better idea what to make of 'em than I do," he added sheepishly.

Dervish glanced up for the first time since they had left the bay. He looked Hawk in the eyes, trying to decide whether he was being teased again. "You really mean that?"

Hawk grinned broadly. "Hell, I've been looking at 'em since I was thirteen. Problem is, I just can't get them to look at *me*!"

Both Hawk and Dervish simultaneously looked at Angel; he coughed and scrutinized his beer. "I been with lots of 'em," he offered reluctantly, "but I still don't understand 'em."

They sat there a while, grinning foolishly at each other. Hawk finally asked the inevitable. "Is there anything else we ought to know about Alderians?"

"Probably," Dervish responded, quietly but definitely more at ease. "Many of them seem to be pirates and traffickers, but they all have the Talent. And they have a large military group called the Guardians. They are kind of like the Fliers, but their main function is to wipe out competition. They are not ... subtle in their methods."

"Okay, so their government stinks," Angel drawled.

Dervish chuckled. "No, no, the Alderians *hate* governments. They do not even *have* a government ... not as you would think of it."

Angel took a sip of beer. "Then what do they do about roads and courts, stuff like that? And who pays for the Guardians?"

Dervish shrugged. "As near as I could figure, they run everything more like a business ... they charge fees for some things. The Guardians are supported by the people they protect. There are no taxes, the people send in what they want, whenever they want. No one seems to keep track. If they want a road, the people that want it get together and hire someone to build it. And there are no formal courts like you have. The Guardians deal with anyone who breaks his word."

Angel leaned back in his chair. "Nice, but how do they know who's lying?"

"Some Alderians have the Gift as well as the Talent. I don't know much about the Gift, but those that have it know when someone is speaking the truth. Sometimes, both sides speak the truth, but from a different perspective. Then the Truth Finders help the people settle their differences."

Hawk had been looking pensively at Dervish, elbows on the table, cradling his beer in both hands. Finally, he set down the beer. "Why do you keep saying 'they' ? You're an Alderian, right?"

Dervish shrugged. "I didn't spend all that much time in their galaxy. But I was told I am Alderian because of the Talent."

Angel set down his beer. "Uhhh ... *told*? You mean you don't know who your folks are?"

Dervish wrinkled his nose. "Not really," he admitted. "My father must have been Alderian. I never saw him, but I look rather Alderian and I have the Talent, so it seems like the logical answer."

Hawk nodded, pursing his lips. "You keep mentioning the Talent. What is that exactly?"

Dervish thought a moment. "The Talent ... well, I can merge with equipment, kind of check it out, get it to do what I want. Control it with my mind. I was told I'm Alderian because they're the only race known to possess that ability."

Angel sat up, causing the chair to thump its front legs back onto the ground. "Can you really do that? God, that must be neat," he mused, pondering the possibilities.

Hawk grinned at Angel, then looked back at Dervish. "Didn't your mom tell you anything about your father?"

Dervish looked down. "No, nothing at all. And, since it is bound to come up some time, I might as well tell you now. My mother was a ... you would say ... two-bit whore. She worked the space port. I spent most of my time hanging around the freighters. If I returned home when she was with someone, she beat me, but most of the time she would feed me after the beating, so I went home when I got hungry enough." He sat there a moment staring at the beer.

"My mother wasn't any better," Angel cut in. "She ran off with some rich asshole."

Dervish furrowed his brow as he looked at Angel.

Hawk sighed. "Consider yourself lucky," he mused. "My dad would have been happier if my mother left. She's a holy terror."

Dervish scuffed his toes in the dirt under the table. "I'd like to think she wasn't my mother, but Alderians aren't known for taking in stray kids." He took a long drink, trying to wash the words away, then followed it with an extremely sour face.

Hawk shook his head. "Dervish, it's really none of our business ..."

Dervish rubbed his nose a moment. "I would much rather you hear it from me, instead of ..."

Hawk nodded understandingly. Angel slumped down in his chair, chiding himself for opening his big mouth again. When he realized Dervish was waiting for his acknowledgement, he nodded slightly.

Dervish rubbed his finger on the rim of the glass and it started to sing. He looked at it wistfully. "No one wants to have much to do with an Alderian, especially a kid. Alderians come in and get real nasty if you touch one of theirs. I was lonely. I was, ummm, about six or seven I guess, when an explorer came into port, badly damaged in a meteor storm. Xendo, the captain, was an odd-looking fellow. He was a Tralzi, but friendly. I hung around a lot because he would talk to me."

Dervish smiled. "I can still picture him. Xendo's face was a bit triangular. His eyes were very large, deep set and much further apart than most races. He was a great captain. Anyhow, he asked me about the bruises. I told him the truth; I didn't even think to lie.

"He started feeding me and even let me sleep on the ship. I guess I became a bit of a pest, always poking around in everything. He called me his whirling dervish, and the name kind of stuck. When they were getting ready to leave, he told me if I happened to be on board when he took off, he wasn't going to return. I grew up on that vessel.

"It was fun. We went all over the place and the scientists taught me a lot, even let me fly the shuttles. And with the Talent, I earned my keep a few times. Not often enough for how well I was treated, but enough to make me feel okay about myself. I think those were the best times of my life."

Angel took a handful of some nut-like things. "Why didn't you stay with Xendo?" he asked, as he started to eat them.

"I guess I would still be there, but when I was about fifteen, the computer died in the middle of a punch. We dropped like a rock into real space and sort of hung there, dead. Just our luck, we dropped out in the Alderian galaxy. I got busy fixing the computer, but I wasn't quick enough. Alderians are a bit hostile about uninvited visitors. They think everyone's a spy. So, they sent a batch of Guardians to check us out.

"They boarded, and wanted to inspect the whole ship. One of them started getting real nasty to Xendo, and threatened to kill him. I kinda went berserk. It took three of 'em to pull me off. I thought they were gonna slit my throat, but they just started laughing. Asked Xendo where he found an Alderian kid; he told 'em. They seemed real pleased, even helped fix the ship. But they took me with them."

"Why?" Angel blurted.

"Alderians like to keep the Talent at home, and I seem to have a lot of it. I didn't want to go, but I didn't think it would be a good idea to say so. I was afraid they'd hurt Xendo.

"They took me back to a space station. Some general talked to me a long time, tested my Talent, and then told some other guy to take me to Michelli. He was to decide what to do with a fosterling with an exceptionally high Talent."

Dervish paused and looked at Angel. "Michelli's the head of the Guardians," he finally continued. "He treated me nice, but I was really spooked; something around there made me nervous. It was a real big place though, and he gave me my own room, even encouraged me to tinker with the fighters. He kinda made me his private tech.

"I got real good at fixing the fighters but I pretended to have no desire to fly 'em. I learned the language and their procedures and waited for my chance to split. After a while I just gave up on the idea. There was no way to take off without being spotted, and I didn't have unsupervised access to anything that would make it out of the galaxy.

"It was years before they started to trust me. Michelli took me with him to Lattice V. We were at the space port – that's when I saw Love. Well, I had to get a closer look, so I snuck around and got in through the maintenance bay. Neatest Bird I ever saw. I got this wild idea. So, doing what Alderians do best," he admitted, looking up at Angel and Hawk with a broad grin, "I borrowed her. Sort of talked Love into it."

"Love?" asked Angel incredulously. "That's how you got your fighter?"

"Yeah, that's how ... I didn't know about the automatic logging back to Mother, or I would have disconnected it," he continued, a bit sheepishly. "Anyhow, I punched a few times to make sure I lost anyone who might be trying to follow, and then just sat there drifting in space wondering what I should do next. I talked to Love for hours; couldn't believe it, a ship that talks back to you.

"Just when I realized that I didn't have the foggiest notion of what to do next, another Bird punched in real close. I tuned to the frequency Love suggested and hailed it. I figured that the ride was over; the Flier had to be real good to have tracked me, so there wasn't much point in trying to lose him. I said, 'Guess you want your ship back?'. Very politely.

"Unfortunately, by then, Love had the automatic weapons system armed and she really meant business. I ... what do you say, freaked out. I mean, it was really my fault, and I realized that it wasn't proper to blow someone up just because he wanted his ship back. Then, Love started arguing. 'The other craft has lock on me', she said, 'and I intend to eliminate it before it tries to do the same to me.' I was sure that Love would fire and I'd get blown away. I decided I better ask this guy how to get her to disarm. So this guy said, very nonchalantly, 'You don't want it to fire?'

"I was practically wetting my pants," Dervish admitted. "I started screaming at him to tell me how to disarm the friggin' thing! He just laughed, and told me that he would do it.

"Sure enough, Love immediately dropped lock. I just sat there staring until I regained enough composure to ask him how he had done that. He said that he had simply dropped lock on me, but that I could still fire manually if I wanted to. I got angry and told him to piss off because I definitely didn't want to fire.

"He had this annoying chuckle in his voice. He asked if I was planning on running, since I wouldn't fire. I got very depressed. I told him that I doubted I could lose him and I would probably just run out of fuel trying.

"He kept asking me what I was going to do, so I finally told him that I didn't have the slightest idea and I was open to suggestions. He asked me how much fuel I had left. I read him off the gauges and waited. There wasn't any other option I could think of. He told me I had plenty of fuel, then asked if I could land her. I hadn't thought about landing. I told him I wasn't sure, but I had landed shuttles.

"He sounded almost friendly. He told me how to lock in the punch coördinates that would appear on my screen, and when I arrived request clearance to land. He told me to request a tow if I didn't think I could bring her down safely.

"I didn't really want to return her, but I didn't see much choice. Love helped a lot with the landing; she doesn't like to get scratched. I sat in her a few minutes. Then I figured it was a good idea to exit before they dragged me out, so I sat down next to her and waited for them to come and get me. No one came.

"There were a lot of people around, but no one seemed interested in me. I thought of sneaking off, but there wasn't any other place I wanted to be. So, I just sat there. It got dark and it was very cold; I had my arms wrapped around my knees and my teeth were chattering.

"Finally, a man wandered up to me. He asked how I liked his Bird. I sat there with a big grin. It was funny, though. When I looked up, he didn't seem very angry. I thought, 'what the hell? What have I got to lose?' I tried to look very innocent and helpless. 'I don't want to leave her', I said. I told him I was very good at fixing fighters and I wouldn't take off with her again. That last part probably wasn't quite true.

"Anyhow, he said his name was Sparks. Gave me his jacket. Even bought dinner. We talked for a long time."

Dervish looked up at Hawk and Angel with a half grin. "Well, he told me that's not how they normally recruited Fliers, but he got them to make an exception in my case. He had figured Love might really be getting ready to fire; if she was fond enough of me to attack her own Flier, maybe I was all right. He was my wingmate until recently."

"What happened to him?" Hawk asked quietly.

Dervish flashed a wicked grin. "He got promoted to general. We're having dinner with him tonight."

Hawk and Angel exchanged glances, then looked back at Dervish, but Dervish's attention was diverted by a nearby female he had been glancing at for some time. She, however, had been ignoring Dervish completely, looking instead at Hawk, then at Angel; when Dervish's glances became more of a stare, she walked over to Hawk and said something. He looked at Dervish questioningly.

Dervish looked dejectedly at his beer. "She is asking you where you're from and why you're hanging out with an Alderian."

"Tell her birds of a feather flock together," Hawk retorted gruffly.

Angel looked anything but pleased. "And we eat little girls for breakfast!"

Dervish started to smirk. He said something to her; she blushed deeply and hurried off.

Angel tapped Dervish with his finger. "Thought you said you didn't have an effect on women. That there was a mighty fine reaction!"

"I was pleased with it myself," Dervish admitted. "It needs some work, though."

"Yeah," Hawk agreed. "Some of 'em are a lot harder to scare off."

6

A Tree By any Other Name

After six days of intensive study, Angel had picked up enough Common to catch the drift of most of the various conversations around him.

The observatory was having a light show that afternoon; Angel figured there would be girls there. Since Hawk was nowhere to be found, he went in search of Dervish.

Angel walked though the bay door and stopped. Dervish stood with his back to the door, gesturing wildly and pointing at his Bird. *Finally wigged out,* Angel thought. Then he noticed that Dervish had company.

She was a wisp of a girl, barely a meter and a half tall, Angel guessed; the top of her head was just above Dervish's eyes. Long platinum hair draped over her shoulder and down past her bottom. She wore jeans and a t-shirt, but they sure looked good on her, he thought. She and Dervish appeared to be having some sort of an argument. Angel finally let curiosity overrule discretion and moved closer so he could hear.

The girl thumped the log sheet on the clipboard. "... at least thirty modifications to this fighter you haven't listed here. You don't have to say exactly what you did to it, but they have to be flagged as modified."

"C'mon, Rusty, you know I never fill those things out."
Dervish was obviously getting flustered. "Nobody even looks
at those forms. Right, Love?" he added, hoping for a bit of
support.

"Wrong. *I* do. And don't call me Love!" Rusty fired back at
him.

Angel noted that the girl seemed to enjoy the fact that
Dervish turned a deep shade of red. He decided to intrude.
"Young lady," he called out in Common, using his most
serious tone, "Love is the name of that fighter, and if you
annoy Dervish much more, she is likely to open fire on you!"

Rusty took her eyes off Dervish to focus on Angel. She
started to fidget, twisting a lock of her hair. She began to get
redder than Dervish was. Dervish looked from Rusty to
Angel, then back at Rusty.

Deciding it was a good time for an exit, Angel quickly
backed out, closing the bay door behind him. He chuckled all
the way to the observatory.

Rusty lowered her head and began to walk slowly toward
the door. Dervish put his hands on her shoulders. "I'm sorry,"
he mumbled. "If you really want me to fill out the forms, I'll
do it."

She turned and looked him in the eyes. "No, I'm the one
who should apologize. I was teasing you on purpose."

Dervish shrugged, but he kept his hands on her shoulders.
He'd known her since she was barely thirteen. She had
always been the first to greet him when he touched down,
bare feet, cut-offs and her hair in pigtails. He tried to picture
her that way now, but it wasn't working. She looked up at
him with her soft green eyes. He figured she would probably
hit him over the head with the clipboard, but it would be
worth it. He leaned down and kissed her.

The clipboard dropped, landing on his foot as her hands
went up around his neck. He didn't need that foot anyway.
Her hands continued up his neck and caught hold of his cap.
She pulled it off. Bright auburn locks fell down around his
shoulders.

She looked at him in wonder. "It's so beautiful! Why have
you always kept it covered?"

He shrugged and shifted his weight to his uninjured foot. He shivered as she ran her fingers through his hair, wondering if he dared hold her closer. She answered his unspoken question by pulling his head down and returning his kiss.

Dervish worked on Love well into the night, but he had company.

✦ ✦ ✦

Angel did all right at the observatory. A cute young astronomer was attracted by his animated personality and his quaint Common complete with Texas drawl. They spent the evening watching stars.

✦ ✦ ✦

Hawk spent the day in the research library, scanning whatever he could find on genetics. While at times Mother's translations were a bit cryptic, most of it was understandable. Still, he was missing something, and he couldn't quite put his finger on what it was.

He slept late the next morning. When he finally awoke, he staggered out into the hall, nearly colliding with Dervish. He stared at him blankly for a moment. "You've got hair!"

Dervish grinned self-consciously. "I kinda got my cap stolen," he gestured offhandedly. "Well, she wouldn't give it back, so it's as good as ..."

"Your hair is red!" Hawk seemed dumfounded. "What color are your eyes?"

Dervish seemed perplexed. "You okay?"

"Green." Hawk scratched his head and looked again. "Dark green, but definitely green."

Dervish looked at him strangely. "Could it be something I ate?"

"I'll get back to you," Hawk assured him, and wandered down the hall mumbling to himself.

Dervish watched him walk away, then shook his head. "Probably something *he* ate," he commented to the empty hallway. He shook his head again. It was pleasant to feel his hair on his neck. Xendo had said his red wavy hair made him look like a girl. He had gotten a cap when he was around twelve, and he'd worn one ever since. Today, however, he didn't care if it made him look like a girl: Rusty liked it.

Hawk continued down the hall, then stopped. He turned back, but Dervish was nowhere in sight. He thought for a moment, then went back down the hall to Dervish's room. He looked around awhile until he found what he was looking for: a hair brush. He headed for the lab.

Megan looked up as he entered. He had practically lived in the lab for the last few days, but she still didn't even know his name. The biologist was considerably frustrated by his inability to communicate what it was he was looking for. She had shown him how to use the equipment, for which he seemed grateful. He had even brought her lunch yesterday, handing her the bag with a sheepish grin, then just walked over to the far bench. He was so intense, so quiet; she'd never met anyone like him. Everyone knew Common; what was his problem?

"Morning, beautiful," Hawk said with a big grin. "Glad you don't understand a word of this!" He handed her a single violet flower.

She looked from him to the flower, then watched him walk slowly back to the far bench. *That's it, mister*, she said to herself. She got up and walked over to his bench. She tapped him on the shoulder.

They spent the whole day looking up things together and analyzing the hair sample he had brought with him. Using pantomime to communicate made for some comical moments, but they got a lot accomplished.

It was almost four o'clock when Hawk found what he was looking for. He needed a blood sample to be sure, so he grabbed a pushpin and started for the door. He stopped and looked back at the girl. "Dinner?" he asked; then, realizing she didn't understand, he sat down at the bench. He mimed someone eating, pointing at her, then himself.

Megan was laughing, but she nodded *yes*. She scribbled something on a piece of paper and handed it to him; he didn't understand a word. Well, that would give him a reason to look up Dervish. He nodded, then headed for the flight bays.

When he arrived, Dervish was standing by the bay door. A girl stood at his side. They were talking with an older man to whom the girl bore a striking resemblance. The man looked at Hawk suspiciously.

"Ummm ... Dervish, hate to bother you," Hawk mumbled, "but I got this note and I can't read it." Hawk handed the piece of paper to Dervish.

Dervish looked at it, smirked, then translated "My house for dinner at seven. 146 Loriel 7R. Megan." Dervish grinned. "So that's what you've been doing all this time." He dropped back into Common while handing the note to the older man. "Killer, where is this? Hawk got this invitation, but I don't have the slightest idea of where anything is if it isn't on the base."

Hawk did a slow burn. *What in hell is Dervish up to? That note is personal!*

Killer looked at it briefly, then smiled at Hawk warmly. He took out a pen and drew a map on the back of the note and handed it back to Hawk.

Hawk grinned sheepishly as Killer began talking to Dervish again. "Station stabilizer is acting up on sector nine. I'll be gone three or four days, maybe even five."

"I can fix it for you," Dervish offered. "Love's in flight condition; I've got over two weeks of leave left."

"No, you need some time off; besides, it's pretty routine. I'd rather save you for the real tricky stuff," Killer explained. He half smiled, thinking back to the first time he met Dervish.

Station three had taken quite a pounding. There was little time to locate all the burnt wiring and leaking lines; many of the injured would have died had they been moved. Sparks had made the jump with Dervish, this odd new wingmate of his. Dervish had walked into the room and sat down on the floor. He sat there a good ten minutes, becoming as white as a ghost, before he got up in a sort of trance and marked off all the problems on the blueprints. Then he fainted. Killer had been skeptical, Dervish being Alderian, but there wasn't time to check everything; he had no choice but to use the marked-up prints to track down the problems. Dervish had been right on the mark. Later, he learned it had taken Dervish three days to recover from whatever it is Alderians do when they use that Talent.

Most people avoided Dervish, and he figured the kid must be lonely. Killer knew loneliness; his wife had died when Rusty was seven. He had invited Dervish to dinner the next time he saw him on base. Rusty wasn't quite thirteen, but she latched onto Dervish; she'd followed him around like a puppy for years now. Back then he saw no harm in it, Dervish being Alderian, but Rusty was a young woman now. Other guys had taken an interest, and he wasn't too pleased with that idea. He looked at Rusty with typical fatherly pride. "You keep an eye on her," he admonished Dervish.

Dervish grinned, looking at Rusty. "I'll keep both of 'em on her." The old man nodded and started to turn away.

"Killer," Dervish blurted. "May I take Rusty to dinner? I can have Angel come with and ..."

The man turned back with a sour expression. He narrowed his eyes and stared hard at Dervish. "You're ... what, almost twenty-five? How long will it be 'til I can't trust you?"

Dervish put on his most wicked face. "How long can you hold your breath?"

"Certainly not five days," he replied. Rusty gave her father a smug grin and the old man softened a bit. He was chuckling as he left the bay.

Hawk figured something was up, but he was damned if he knew what it was. "What was all that about?"

Dervish was a bit red in the face. "Killer gave me permission to date his daughter." He put an arm around Rusty's waist and started to walk back toward the catwalks.

Hawk stuck out his hand, "Congratulations, Dervish!"

Dervish looked at Hawk strangely, but shook his hand. "Eeeyow!!" Dervish pulled back, waving his hand in the air.

"Ooooh, sorry; I forgot I was holding this pushpin." Hawk grabbed a rag from his pocket and applied pressure to the tiny wound. He put the rag back into his pocket and started for the door. "See you later. And good luck!"

Dervish stuck his hurt finger in his mouth, sucked on it, then shook it in the air a few times. "What's with him, anyhow? I'd *swear* he did that on purpose!"

Rusty turned to Dervish and wrapped her arms around his neck. "He's very fond of you," she said, as she began playing with his hair. "When you were talking with daddy and he made that nasty face, Hawk was ready to attack him."

"He's crazier than I am," he said, sticking his finger back in his mouth.

Rusty reached up, took his hand away from his mouth and put it in a more useful position.

Dervish raised an eyebrow, then took advantage of the situation. He turned his head a bit and kissed her warmly.

Killer had just left the bay when he heard Dervish yelp, and walked back quickly. He stepped aside to let Hawk pass. Hawk didn't even notice him. He tried adding things up. Megan; biologist, works in the research lab. Blood samples. *What is that young man up to?* he thought. He watched Hawk until the Flier was out of sight, then looked back through the bay door. He saw Rusty with her arms around Dervish and they were obviously kissing. He stood there a few moments as a broad grin crossed his face. He turned and walked quickly toward his shuttle's hangar. *The girl might just do it*, he mused. *You've got five days to land that Flier, darlin'; that's all the vacation time I had left.*

✦   ✦   ✦

The dinner went as well as could be expected. Hawk brought Megan a big bouquet of flowers, and with the Common phrases Angel had scribbled out for him, he managed to tell her she looked beautiful. He wasn't too sure what she said to him, but she said it with a smile. After dinner, she took him for a walk through the botanical gardens. Hawk discovered that there are a few things two people can do without talking.

✦   ✦   ✦

It was almost two when Hawk entered the hangar where Gracie was parked. He passed his hand over the sensor and the lights came on. Killer was standing next to her! "What are you ..." Hawk started to ask; then, realizing that Killer didn't know English, just stood there.

Killer walked over and beckoned for him to follow. He led him out of the hangar over to one of the bays and up into a shuttle. He sat down next to the computer and motioned for Hawk to do the same. He typed something on the screen. A moment later, English text appeared.

"A Common to English translator. I had Mother arrange it for us."

"That's nice," Hawk typed, "but what is this all about?"

"Biology lab, blood samples ... what are you up to?"

Hawk looked at the man, trying to read him. "Why do you want to know?"

"I know it has something to do with Dervish, or you wouldn't have jabbed his finger. I really like that boy! What are you up to?"

"He's not Alderian; I'm convinced of that. I don't know what he is yet, but I know what he's not."

"I *know* what he is! He's a good kid and a great Flier. What else is there to know? What business is it of yours anyway?" Killer looked hard at Hawk.

"He's my best friend and my wingmate. It would make him feel a whole lot better about himself to know he didn't come from a two-bit whore and an Alderian outcast." Hawk looked at the man pleadingly, then continued to type. "I may be terrible at learning languages, but I'm pretty good with genetics."

Killer mellowed a bit. "What have you found out so far?"

"He has auburn hair and green eyes. Alderians usually have dark brown to black hair and dark eyes. That got me to wondering. From what I could find out, they have very few recessive genes. They might have had more at one time, but apparently they banned outside blood centuries ago, as they thought it was diluting the Talent. Now, Dervish said the woman who raised him was Alderian." Hawk bit his lip as he continued to type. "I'd really like to be able to prove that wasn't his mom!"

"So his auburn hair means both parents should have at least one recessive gene?" Killer looked at Hawk and the expression was almost friendly. "You needed the blood to verify your theory."

"The computer could not find a single race that matched the chromosomal pattern in his hair. It requested a blood sample for further analysis."

"Why didn't you simply ask, instead of jabbing him?"

"What, 'pretty please can I have some blood?' I would have had to tell him why, and I didn't want to raise his hopes prematurely." Hawk looked up at Killer, then typed, "How did you get the name Killer?"

Killer nodded as he typed, "I was a little ornery in my younger days." He was smiling, but the subject was obviously closed, at least for the moment. "Don't change the subject," he continued. "What did the blood sample tell you?"

"The closest match comes from Laverta, out past sector twenty-three."

"The Lavertines? They kinda keep to themselves out there. You planning on heading out that way?"

"That's where I was going when you stopped me."

Killer looked at Hawk. "Well, what are we waiting for?"

"We?"

"How did you plan on talking to them?"

"Point well made." Hawk smiled at Killer, "I'll send you the punch coördinates as soon as Gracie gets a lock on them."

"Gracie, Love ... you guys sure don't name your Birds like we used to."

Hawk raised an eyebrow, "What was your Bird's name?"

Killer cleared his throat. "Mother doesn't approve of that kind of language," he typed quickly. "When you learn a little Common, I'll tell you."

Hawk was smiling as he left the shuttle. He made his way back to Gracie and informed her of their destination. When the punch coördinates appeared on the screen, he relayed them to Killer.

✦ ✦ ✦

The old man walked quickly down the dark hallway and paused before the vast doors that led to one of Mother's many links. He started to pass his hand across the sensor but stopped, gazed at the door, then closed his eyes and linked with the computer system. A smile crept into the corners of his aged face, and he nodded to himself as he proceeded to clear his entrance with the computer. "For a bean counter," he mumbled to himself, "he's a nice lad."

Threenica was busy entering updates to the database when
the old janitor ambled slowly into the room. He looked up and
smiled. "Sorry, Brach. I'll be through here in a few minutes.
Mother's running a bit slow tonight. We sure could use more
memory and processors."

"Don't worry about me," Brach replied. "I've nowhere to go
when I'm finished cleaning in here."

Threenica finished the sentence he was typing, then logged
out. He stuffed his paperwork into the drawer and got up.
"Ahhh ... my mother sent another crate of cookies. Why not
stop by my room when you're finished; I could use a bit of
help eating them."

"Mmmm ... tastiest things in the universe," Brach replied
warmly as he nodded in agreement. "I'll bring the milk."

"See you soon," Threenica said, as he passed his hand over
the sensor and walked from the room.

Brach circled around the desk and walked to the closet
behind the computer. He took out his broom and feather
duster and gazed back at the door, listening to be sure no one
was approaching. He made his way to a long-neglected
equipment rack in the far corner of the room. Quietly opening
the cabinet, he activated an ancient manual terminal. and a
simple $ prompt appeared. He typed LOGIN GOD, then hit
return. At the password request, he typed ALDER, then again
hit return.

A % appeared on the screen. Brach checked the status of
several accounts, nodding in satisfaction at the balance
showing, then began a system check. He paused the dump as
the task that had run the translations between Killer and
Hawk showed on the list. *Hawk*, he reflected. *That's one of the
kids Dervish picked up on Earth. Wonder what Killer wanted
from him. Hmmm ... better check this out. It might have
something to do with Dervish. Michelli's orders are very clear.
Nothing's to happen to the lad ... yet.*

He pulled up the log of the task and read the exchange a
couple of times until he was satisfied that he had not
misunderstood it. "Hmmm," he muttered. "The lad's not pure
Alderian, then. I'd better get word to Michelli. He'll be most
interested." He logged off Mother, quickly swept the room, put

his things away, and made his way to the kitchen for a large pitcher of milk and two glasses. He stopped by his room on the way to Threenica's and sent a brief message.

Tressel brushed a strand of his dark hair back behind his ear and glanced at the mirror again. He always enjoyed needling the Guardians, and showing the tips of his pointed ears seemed to make them the craziest. He realized that he would live about two seconds if he ever lost favor with Michelli, but he wouldn't worry about that unless it happened.

He picked up the note, folded it over once and stuffed it into his shirt pocket. With one last glance at the mirror, he walked out of his room and headed for the flight deck.

The few Guardians he passed gave him the cold look he'd come to expect, perhaps even relish. After all, he could handle a PRO-fighter as well as the majority of them; the only thing preventing him from joining their ranks was the technicality of the Test. It was common knowledge no half-breed could pass it and, since it was pass or die, Michelli had not allowed him to be tested. That suited him just fine. He never was comfortable with the idea of wearing the uniform, though he couldn't have expressed the feeling in words. It just bothered him.

He paused to study the officer on deck. *Fairly good looking*, he thought. *For an Alderian, anyway*. He glanced through the man's mind, grabbed his name, and stepped forward. "Glider," he said quietly, handing the note to the officer.

Glider took it reluctantly and handled it as though it were an explosive. He nodded curtly, handed Tressel back the note, and pointed to a fighter at the far end of the deck. "Do you need an escort?" he asked dryly.

"No," Tressel replied. "But we should really keep up our appearances when arriving at the Villa, should we not?"

Glider's face hardened and he thought of a few expletives, but didn't utter them. "Cloud is over with the fighters. He can accompany you."

"Fine choice," Tressel replied. "Interesting language running through your mind. I'll actually have to look up a couple of those." With that, he turned and walked to the fighter.

Glider shoved his hands into his pockets and spit on the ground. "One day you're going to get yours, you half-breed bastard," he muttered.

As Tressel neared the two Guardians, who were working on a PRO, he quickly ran through their minds. Dexter was the older of the two; Cloud was the taller. Alderians are short and stocky as a rule, but Cloud was obviously pure; his uniform attested to that. Tressel paused, finding that he actually liked the feelings he found in Cloud's mind. He watched the Guardian closely, noting his cat-like grace and slender build. *Most unusual for an Alderian*, he thought.

The two men looked up as Tressel neared, and he delighted in Dexter's discomfort. He was disappointed that Cloud didn't seem to care one way or the other; he liked getting a reaction. "Cloud, you're to accompany me to the Villa," he stated formally, hoping to get a rise out of the man.

Cloud merely shrugged, then flashed him a crazy grin. "Any excuse to fly is fine with me. You can take that one," he offered, as he pointed to one of the fighters. "It's Glider's," he added as he walked to the other one.

Tressel cracked a bit of a smile. "Very funny," he informed Cloud as they entered the launch bays.

"Two can play at the same game," Cloud retorted. "I believe you know the coördinates. Care to send them over?"

"Sending," Tressel replied as they glided out into space.

"Ladies first," Cloud chuckled as he watched Tressel punch out, then winked out after him.

As they winked in, Tressel relayed landing instructions. They descended almost vertically, coming to rest in the middle of a large, beautifully tiled patio on the north side of the Villa. Cloud looked about as he climbed down. A large mythical beast stared back at him from the tiles. He knew that the old honor squad's landing field was west of the Villa, but he was unaware that one could land on this side as well.

"I'll stay with the fighters," Cloud called, watching Tressel walk toward the Villa.

Tressel felt something flicker in the corner of his mind. He turned and walked back to Cloud, eyeing the Guardian for a moment. "You've never been inside the Villa, have you?"

"I'll live," Cloud replied nonchalantly.

"Not if you try that on Michelli," Tressel warned. "Come on. It's a lot warmer inside."

Cloud shrugged. "Is that an invitation or an order?" he asked, following Tressel across the patio toward the large mansion.

"A little of both," Tressel replied honestly. "I'd much rather have you where I can see what you're up to. And, after all, it is nippy out."

Cloud took off his helmet and shook out his hair as they walked. Tressel noted it was very thick, with red highlights unusual in an Alderian. He felt a bit sorry for Cloud, realizing the teasing he must take, not only for his build but for his hair color as well. He knew only too well how that hurt.

They walked in silence through the large formal doorway as an elderly man approached. Walking at a slow, dignified pace, he obviously construed the unannounced entry of the men to be an intrusion of his private domain.

"Reynard," Tressel called, "could you please bring us some coffee? The dishwater they serve on the station isn't fit to drink."

Reynard completely ignored Tressel, turning instead to Cloud. "Would you care for any refreshments, sir?" he asked pointedly.

Cloud was caught off guard. He hadn't expected to find a hostile relationship between the only two known Elves in the galaxy. *Perhaps*, he thought, *Elves don't like half-breeds any better than Alderians do.* He felt a twinge of compassion for Tressel, realizing he was facing the world alone. "Ahh ... yes, thank you," he replied. "We'd really appreciate some coffee."

Reynard motioned for them to follow, then turned around and headed back down the hallway.

Tressel glanced at Cloud as they followed. "Reynard's my uncle," he said quietly. "He never did like my mother."

Cloud nodded. "And the rest of the galaxy wasn't too crazy about your father."

Tressel shrugged. "Can't please everyone."

"I've run into a lot of that, too," Cloud noted as they were ushered into a spacious living room and seated themselves where Reynard indicated.

"I shall announce your arrival to Michelli before I return with refreshments," Reynard stated as he left the room.

Cloud glanced around the room. Like every other room he had glimpsed into, it seemed to have been crafted entirely of beautifully polished wood. The floors shone as if they were waxed daily, but they were neither tacky nor slippery. The furniture was elegant without being overdone. It was truly more beautiful than it was rumored to be. The walls were lined with shelves packed with hundreds of books, and tiny clear figurines were placed here and there at random.

Michelli entered the room and Cloud hastily stood up, a bit flustered to be caught sitting. Michelli smiled at him warmly. "Please, don't get up," he said quietly. "Formalities are such a nuisance."

Cloud half nodded and sat down again, both embarrassed and frustrated. Why did he let Tressel talk him into coming in? He hadn't really expected to see Michelli; he had no idea what to say to a king.

"I've received some fascinating correspondence," Michelli informed Tressel. "I'll need your help to discover more ..."

Cloud bit his lip; he didn't want to hear anything that wasn't common knowledge. If, for any reason, the information was leaked, he didn't want his hide pinned to a wall. "Ahhh ... if you'd prefer, I could wait with the fighters," he stammered, then regretted having cut in.

Michelli graciously ignored the interruption with a wave of his hand. "Tressel and I do have much to discuss," he stated, "but I certainly wouldn't hear of you spending half the night out in the cold."

Cloud wasn't sure how to respond, so he nodded slightly. He was relieved that Reynard chose that moment to enter.

"I've placed the coffee in your study," he informed Michelli, setting a tray down next to Cloud.

"Thank you, Reynard," Michelli replied as he stood up. "If you'll excuse us," he continued, looking at Cloud with wry amusement, "we'll get this nasty business over with. Please feel free to read a few books or browse though the gardens. Don't stray too far though; dinner will be served at eight."

"Thank you," Cloud stammered.

Tressel flashed Cloud a high sign as he followed Michelli out the door. They walked down the hallway and entered the study. "Nice lad," he commented to Michelli as he slumped into a chair and helped himself to some coffee.

"Afraid to go out at night all alone now, are we?" Michelli asked dryly.

Tressel pursed his lips and narrowed his eyes. "He was assigned to escort me."

"I didn't realize you needed an escort, either," Michelli commented as he poured himself some coffee and stirred in the milk and sugar.

"I don't. I wanted to piss off the captain on duty."

Michelli nodded. "You've managed to do that to Zar also," he noted. "I think we shall forego your further training at this time."

Tressel wrinkled his nose. "I doubt my progress among your elite fighting force is why you sent for me."

Michelli chuckled. "I have an assignment more suited to your disposition and talents. I've received news that Dervish is not pure Alderian."

Tressel sat up quickly. He put down his coffee cup and looked at Michelli intently. He shook his head slowly. "No. Not Dervish! You'll have to find yourself another goon," he stated bluntly.

Michelli studied his coffee carefully. "You misunderstand me completely." He added more milk and stirred it, slowly and deliberately. "I do not wish him harmed," he continued. "I wish you to do some research."

"What kind of research?"

"We know the port he was picked up on. I'd like you to visit there. See if you can gather any useful information on his parentage."

"And then?"

"Then we piece it all together and see whether we have Etheren's missing son."

Tressel relaxed back into the chair and started to laugh. "Dervish? Are you going senile? Come on."

"On the contrary. Consider the facts. Etheren's son was kidnapped almost twenty-five years ago. The kidnappers' vessel had to stop someplace to refuel, and they certainly wouldn't have chanced entering a governed port. The captain who had Dervish said he picked him up on a freeport world; Dervish was being abused and he felt sorry for him. The man was Tralzi; he knew that if he lied, the Guardians would kill him. Now, suppose for a moment that Dervish had been left there as a negotiating piece should the kidnappers be caught. And then, when Etheren wouldn't give in to their demands, they abandoned him. Imagine what an edge this could give us in negotiating with the Elders."

Tressel sneered. "I think you're grasping at straws. The odds of ..."

"Tralzi aren't known for their compassion, but they don't lie," Michelli countered. "Especially to a Guardian. They make their living as captains. Among the best, too. And always honorable. He said that he was positive that Dervish wasn't pure Alderian, otherwise he'd have brought him here. He was adamant about that."

"So? What does that have to do with Dervish being Elder?"

"We always just assumed Dervish was Alderian because he had so much Talent," Michelli explained. "He reminded me of Etheren's sister, but I hadn't seen her in sixteen years so I just dismissed it. Besides, Elders don't have the Talent." He seemed lost in thought as he took a sip of coffee. Finally he continued. "It seems the Fliers ran a blood test. Dervish doesn't match with Alderians, nor to any race known to the Fliers. He could just possibly be a serendipitous Elder."

"And what if I find that Dervish isn't Elder either?"

"I still want him back here," Michelli stated flatly. "He's stronger in the Talent than most Alderians. Gifted as well. I'd like to keep whatever his bloodline is in our galaxy."

"I doubt he'll return."

"I trust you'll find out enough that we can eventually entice him home."

"I'll try," Tressel replied. "I'm very fond of him."

"I know that," Michelli stated. "And considering the alternatives, I'm sure you'll find out everything you can."

Tressel grunted and helped himself to a cookie. "What else did you wish to talk about? This hardly took half the night."

"Our so-called friends, the Rudonians, are becoming more of a curse every day," Michelli replied. "I'd like you to contact one of our agents. See if you can work your way into their hierarchy over the next few months."

Tressel's eyes danced with a wicked glint. "Shall we go over the sordid details?"

✦   ✦   ✦

Hawk and Killer punched in over a small greenish planet, one of four in the system. A large freighter was locked in orbit, and Killer hailed it. Gracie informed Hawk that it was considered good form for a Flier to chitchat with the freighter captains. While it was mainly to see if any assistance was needed, the exchange of information helped all concerned.

As Gracie glided down toward the planet, Hawk requested permission to land. There was no answer on the normal hailing frequencies. As Killer relayed landing instructions, Hawk was glad the man had decided to come along.

They landed in a large open field outside of a small town. A man was standing not far off and approached slowly. He was of the same general build as Dervish, but there the similarity ended. His hair was white, and Hawk was sorely disappointed to see that the stranger's eyes were ice-blue.

The man led them to the town, trailed by small gawking children. There was little sign of technology about, and every person Hawk saw had white or very light blond hair; he was totally discouraged by the time they reached midtown.

They entered what appeared to be the main building and were escorted to a small room. Killer motioned to Hawk to sit down. Hawk wished he knew what the two men were saying; he really had to learn Common one of these days.

Killer talked to the man, explaining that they were attempting to track down the parentage of a Flier, a friend of theirs. An analysis of his blood showed a vague similarity to the Lavertine.

The man was polite enough, but seemed to feel he could be of little help. The planet had been settled eons ago by the crew of a damaged space explorer. The planet had no metal deposits to speak of, and thus little technology had developed.

He explained that the people were grateful to the Fliers for protecting their little planet, but there were no records available to check through.

Killer asked if a blood sample could be provided; that would at least give them something to work with. The man readily agreed, even taking down the star charts that had been preserved as part of their culture to be copied in hopes that would help them.

Hawk sat, his head resting in his arms, as the hours seemed to drag by.

Gracie tied into Mother, and the analysis showed nothing more than a slight genetic similarity. The star charts provided nothing either, as all the systems marked on it were known to be uninhabited at this time.

Hawk left Gracie and shuffled slowly to the shuttle where Killer was waiting for the news. As he typed it in, he noted that Killer seemed equally disappointed.

"What are you going to do now?" Killer typed.

"Probably go back and show Dervish what I found out, and then punch out to these systems and take a look around."

"Want some company?" Killer offered.

"Sure. If I run into anyone, it'd be nice to communicate."

"How did you end up a pilot on your home world?"

"I needed money for college; I wanted to be a biologist. And I love airplanes, so I joined the Air Force and graduated. But then I got hooked on those little jets, and I never did go on to graduate school."

Killer nodded knowingly. "I'll wait for you at station twelve, just at the tip of this galaxy. We can go from there."

Hawk wandered back to Gracie and stroked the fighter as he climbed in.

"I think we did rather well," she announced as he locked in the coördinates for the punch home. "It was similar to looking for a needle in a haystack."

Hawk looked thoughtful for a moment. "Gracie, can you teach me Common?"

"I can teach it," she answered dryly as she punched. "The question is: can you learn it?"

7

Birds Of A Feather

Pepper mumbled to himself as he looked over the neural network. "Darn. I wish I knew more about this thing." He glanced down as Lark approached. "I sure miss Hawk," he said, as Lark mounted the stairs and stood looking at him.

"Why did Dervish request a transfer?" Lark grumbled. "I thought they were going to join our squad."

Pepper winced. "I didn't get a chance to ask them."

"What?"

"I thought there'd be plenty of time after the initiation. But they went straight to station seven."

"Maybe we could transfer there," Lark suggested.

"We're still down one," Pepper mumbled. "I don't think Nathan will transfer us."

"Tell him we'll fly with Dervish. That would make eight."

Pepper rubbed his head. "That reminds me, has Velter landed yet?"

Lark shoved his hands into his pockets and wrinkled his nose. He gazed off across the flight deck to avoid making eye contact with Pepper. "Can't find him anywhere," he mumbled.

Pepper pursed his lips and tapped his fingers on the console. Being a squad leader was sometimes more trouble than it was worth. "When was he due back from base?"

"I checked. He was never there."

"Damn him!" Pepper growled through clenched teeth. "I told him not to get any more of that shit."

"You're jumping to conclusions," Lark countered.

"I know Velter."

"He's not late ... yet," Lark argued.

Pepper shook his head. "We'd better go find him. Last time he couldn't remember where he left his Bird."

Lark looked up. "Only two free ports anywhere near here."

Pepper began to fidget with the screwdriver he was holding. He slowly put it back into the tool box.

Lark bit his lip. "I'll check Ravelue, if you check Gelnex," he offered. "Call if you spot his Bird."

Pepper shook his head. "I'm really getting tired of this." He stared at nothing for a few moments. "Okay, but be careful. Free ports are rough."

Lark hopped down and headed for his Bird. "Will do," he called.

✦   ✦   ✦

The young pilot woke with a start, figuring he'd overslept; then he remembered they were in port for repairs. *That was some skirmish last night*, he thought. *Nine short range bandits. Damn. A little too close for comfort.* The freighter hadn't taken much damage, but two fighters got trashed and Orrick had needed a doctor rather badly. He mulled it over in his mind. Some of the attackers were in Zarian 3LRs. *Rudonian slime, probably. Funny, none of the automatic stuff spotted 'em. Shit, if I hadn't been goofing off out there, we'd all be dead.* He smiled to himself. *I might have yellow skin and silver hair, but I got vision better than a telescope.*

He thought about going back to sleep, then decided that would be a waste; *I have to see a free port, just once anyway,* he thought. He leaped out of bed, threw on his jacket, grabbed his cap and headed down the hallway toward the bathroom. He brushed his hair, put his cap on and looked in the mirror. He wrinkled his nose as he pulled his hat down a bit lower over one eye and checked the mirror again. He jumped as he saw his captain looking over his shoulder.

"That don't help much, Tripper," Silburn hissed. "I can still see them purple eyes of yours."

"Thought I'd take a walk around port," Tripper explained.

"You may be a good pilot, kid," Silburn lectured, "but you're barely fifteen. You ain't safe walking around out there."

"Ain't safe flying with this freighter, either," Tripper teased.

"Hey, I'm a damn good captain," Silburn snapped. "Kept ya out of a lot of fights by losing them bloody pirates."

"I just want to look around," Tripper stated. "Never seen a free port before."

"And ya probably won't be seeing one again," Silburn grumbled. "We're only here for repairs."

"I'll be back in a few hours."

"You be careful."

Tripper turned quickly, brandishing a sharp knife, and winked. "I'll be fine, chief."

Silburn shook his head as he watched the boy leave the deck and head for the ramps.

Tripper looked around the field. It was big and crowded. He studied the area, trying to spot a few landmarks he could use to find his way back. He whistled when he noticed the Bird. "Ohhhhhh ... would I love to have me one of them things," he mumbled, as he started across the field to get a better look. He stopped a few meters away from it and sat down on the rail of a transport drone on the charging rack. He took a pad and stylus from his jacket pocket and began to sketch the Bird.

✦   ✦   ✦

Pepper winked in not far from the free port and made contact with its controller. "Has a Flier landed recently?"

"Couple hours ago," Controller replied. "Hasn't left yet."

"Requesting permission to land," Pepper called. After receiving landing coördinates, he turned to scatterband and made contact with Lark. "Found him," he stated dryly. "Or at least where he landed."

"Be right there," Lark replied.

Tripper stared wide-eyed as another Bird landed and its pilot stepped out. He looked the man over carefully, allowing his eyes to focus on the emblem on the man's flight suit. "A real Flier ... wow," he mumbled to himself. He wasn't so fond of the rest of his race's characteristics, but he really liked his telescopic vision.

He watched as the Flier took off his flight suit and helmet and stuffed them into the Bird, then walked over to the other Bird, apparently looking for something. After a few moments, the Flier made his way across the field and Tripper returned to his sketch.

Velter's getting to be to be a real drag, Pepper thought, as he stood on the edge of the field and glanced around. It was a big place. No telling where Velter might be. He made his way toward the crowded street, then decided to wait for Lark. He'd never live it down if he got himself lost. He was just watching the sky for Lark's Bird, not paying much attention to what was happening around him, when a man bumped into him.

"Sorry," the man grumbled.

Pepper nodded in his direction and started to move away when someone grabbed him from behind, shoving a cloth into his face. He tried to turn, but the man held the cloth tighter.

Tripper was ambling down the flight strip when he noticed five men crowding in around one. He stopped and watched a moment, catching a glance of the man being attacked. *That's the Flier!* he thought. *Poor guy looks on the verge of passing out*. "Not very fair odds," Tripper shouted.

"Get lost, kid," one of the men yelled.

Tripper drew his knife and approached. "Don't think I will," he stated. He wasn't ready for the three who grabbed him from behind.

Pepper slowly opened his eyes. He ached all over and it hurt to breathe. He tried hard to focus on the blurs of color close by, but they remained blurs.

"Pepper?" Lark questioned. "You awake?"

"I fear so," Pepper mumbled.

"Shit, I thought they'd killed you," Velter stated. "You've been out for three days."

"What happened?" Pepper asked slowly as a room began to take shape around him.

"Some locals. They musta thought you were someone else," Velter explained. "Who's the kid?"

"What kid?"

"The port controller said the kid jumped in to help you," Lark replied. "He got hurt pretty bad."

"Huh?"

"Said his guys were approaching to break it up when the kid drew a knife to defend you," Velter replied. "He figured it had to be your wingmate to jump in against eight men."

"He said the attackers freaked when they found out you were Fliers," Lark added. "Seems like a nice guy. He'd already gotten both of you transferred here by the time I landed."

"Where's here?"

"The hospital ... on Gelnex."

"I don't remember any kid," Pepper replied.

"Adjust your memory," Lark whispered. "I signed him in as a Flier. They wouldn't treat him unless he was covered."

"Oh yeah, that kid," Pepper replied. "Ahhh ... who is he?"

"I don't know," Lark replied. "He hasn't come to yet."

Pepper wrinkled his brow. "How bad off is he?"

Lark shrugged. "He's a Cheren. They heal pretty good."

"You didn't answer me."

"They weren't sure he'd make it," Velter blurted. "But he's improving rapidly."

Pepper grimaced. "No more free ports, Velter, got that?"

"I didn't get anything," Velter mumbled. "Ask Lark. I was visiting a friend."

Lark quickly nodded.

Pepper looked from one blur to the other as he scrunched up his face.

"I won't lie for him," Lark stated.

Pepper grinned. "Damn near anything else, though,"

Hawk sat nursing a cup of coffee and a nasty headache. Dervish walked in and sat down next to him, nudging him with an elbow. "How you doing?"

"What was in that drink?" Hawk put his head down on his arms. "It had a kick like a mule!"

"I don't know. Killer made it." Dervish gave him a sidelong glance. "Had a good time last night, huh?"

"Did I? I don't quite remember."

Dervish wore a devilish smirk. "Better ask Megan."

Hawk looked up at him weakly. "Why? What did I do?"

"Umm ... I didn't follow when you took her to your room."

"Oh, jeez!" Hawk looked mortified. "Where is she now?"

"Killer shuttled everyone back to base hours ago. She was smiling when she left, though, if that helps."

Hawk looked up a bit and nodded. "Anyway, thanks. That was probably the nicest birthday party I ever had." He sighed and put his head back down between his arms. "I just wish I could remember more of it."

"Hey, don't mention it. Nothing compared with what you did for me. Now that I'm certified non-Alderian, some of the guys even say 'hi'." He raised an eyebrow and lowered his voice as he added, "occasionally."

"When am I supposed to look alive?" Hawk muttered, attempting to raise his head again.

"I think our birthday boy better sit this one out," Angel commented as he walked though the door. "He don't look too good this morning."

"Oh, no you don't!" Hawk glanced at Angel. "Every time I leave you two alone you manage to get your butts in a jam." Hawk shook his head slightly, trying to clear his vision. "And now that I'm seeing four of you ..."

"Lemme go see if we can swap with one of the night crews," Angel offered. He gave Hawk a disparaging look, then commented to Dervish, "Twenty-two and still can't hold his liquor! What are we gonna *do* with this kid?"

Dervish just sat there grinning.

Hawk turned a bit pasty and made a dash for the bathroom. Angel nearly fell over laughing.

Recor watched Hawk disappear down the hall and chuckled. "Killer sure can mix a drink." He got a funny twinkle in his eyes and nudged Harley. "I bet Hawk passed out before anything happened."

Harley raised an eyebrow. "I sure wish I hadn't."

Recor gazed down at his coffee. "I need a good prank."

"I'd rather get laid," Harley retorted.

"Yeah, well, me too ... but girls don't seem that receptive to my needs."

"You might work on your approach," Harley offered. "Your 'Hi! Wanna go to bed?' doesn't seem to work all that good."

Recor stuck his tongue out. "You'd think they'd admire my honesty."

Harley chuckled. "I don't think they see it that way."

Recor frowned and glanced up a moment. "Ahhh ... listen, why don't we drop down to Sparks' base and pick up Schruf. We could hit some bar around there."

Harley shook his head. "I was thinking more of a free port."

Recor stood up and piled his leftovers on his tray. "I don't want none of that stuff," he snapped.

"Why not?" Harley asked as they walked across the cafeteria. "We've had all our shots."

Recor hunched his shoulders. "'Cause I don't want a girl with more mileage than my Bird."

Still a bit green from the night before, Hawk walked slowly to the flight bay, boarded Gracie and closed her hatch. He was grateful that Angel had managed to arrange a swap; he never would have made it this morning. He locked in coördinates, requested takeoff, then maneuvered her to the launch bay. The doors closed behind him. When the bay doors opened, he glided her out into space and punched. The stars winked out, then returned. He set Gracie to sweep the area.

Angel's voice drifted over the ether. "Hey, good buddy, got your ears on?"

Hawk grimaced as he flicked the radio to local. "Sure enough. All clear here. What's it look like on your end?" He unconsciously put his hand to his stomach. *Blahhh. Still not up to par.*

"Clear; we got a registered Malgarian freighter in sector seventeen. She reports no trouble so far." Angel's voice had a touch of concern in it.

"Too damn quiet," Hawk observed. "It's starting to get to me. Maybe it's just something left over from last night."

"The captain of the freighter feels the same way you do," Angel replied.

Hawk tried to sound serious. "Was he at the party, too?"

Angel chuckled. "He said the way the Rudonian government suddenly relented and started saying their peoples are free to do as they wish is just a bit too fishy for him to swallow. He requested cover. Why don't you take the milk run with him. Dervish and I will finish this sweep."

"Thanks a million," Hawk grumbled, setting coördinates to the freighter.

Gracie seemed to understand Hawk's resentment and his delicate condition. Her voice was unusually soft as it drifted into the cabin. "I concur with the captain's suspicions," she asserted. "After centuries of ironfisted rule enforced by despicable and ruthless force, is it not odd to capitulate suddenly?"

"More'n likely they're just playing dead," Angel drawled. "Lookie here, Hawk ol' buddy, it's not that we don't like your company, but punching around on a sour stomach is no picnic. I oughta know!"

Hawk managed a chuckle as he took the hop to sector seventeen. He had no trouble locating the freighter; Gracie gave him the readout. The freighter was big and slow, built for interplanetary travel. She had no ability to punch; she was capable of small hops, but doing so would strain her fuel supply and her engines. Hawk now completely understood her captain's concern. She was indeed a sitting duck.

He made radio contact with the captain, exchanging the normal pleasantries. The captain's name was Metley; he hailed from Telasvar, taking a shipload of government handouts to the people of Recnord. Hawk was quite pleased with himself for carrying on an entire conversation in Common without a single serious faux pas. "Gracie, you make a pretty good teacher," he told her.

"You have learned well, Hawk," she replied in Common, returning the compliment with aplomb. "But I certainly did enjoy the time you told the captain of the Venturian vessel that he was ..."

"Hawk!" Dervish's voice was unmistakable, though he sounded edgy. "Keep your eyes open. I sensed something odd through the last punch I made. Angel and I are going to check it out. Better inform the freighter captain to be on alert."

"Will do," Hawk replied. Something was still nagging at the edge of his mind. He had a bad feeling, and it wasn't just his stomach. He informed Metley; the captain said he had feared as much. He again thanked Hawk for standing by.

Hawk was about to reply when Gracie flashed an alert. "Your wingmate is in trouble, sir," she informed him, in Common and a bit too formally. "Setting jump coördinates."

What's with that damn computer now? "Oh, *fuck!*" Hawk shouted as the nagging thought at the edge of his mind popped forward. With adrenalin pounding through his body, he keyed the autologger, dropped her to manual, and said a silent prayer.

He quickly scanned the tracking equipment. It identified nine Zarian 3LR fighters; local range, no punch or hop capabilities. Their base ship had to be somewhere close by. *Yeah, that figures*, he thought. *Okay. Mother will note Gracie's last coördinates and send backup, if she got her signal through.*

"Metley!" he called sternly, "put your ship into manual *now!* Kill all automatic systems. I think we got an Alderian accompanying the Rudonians. That Talent of theirs lets 'em mess with your ship's computer. Take her zig-zag on a few short hops. Only respond if you hear my voice."

"An Alderian? Out here?" Metley sounded doubtful, but he was already fighting his big freighter for control. "I didn't think they'd work for any other race." The freighter finally yielded and all systems went manual. He let out a low whistle, noting the fighters that suddenly appeared on his tracking equipment. "Shit, there's nine of 'em! I can't hop and leave you here alone."

"Hop. You're too big a target," Hawk replied, ignoring Gracie's protests. She kept insisting that they punch immediately, and that he return control of the weapons systems to her.

"Thanks," Metley replied, "I owe you a beer!"

The freighter winked out as Hawk's stomach turned. "I think I would prefer a seven-up," he commented to the emptiness around him. "Gracie," he added in his most official voice, "continue my lessons in Common."

She began to rebuff him. "This is hardly the time ..."

"Are you refusing a direct order?"

Gracie was silent a moment. When she replied, she seemed a bit confused. "Your wingmates are in trouble, and you want to learn Common?"

"Repeat that to yourself five hundred times," he replied sourly. "See if you come to any logical conclusions." He looked again at the tracking equipment. The fighters were in firing range and had locked onto him. As they took up fighting formation, he got a wild idea.

"I seem to be malfunctioning," Gracie conceded sullenly. "I did not detect the attackers. The coördinates I wanted to jump to are not even in this galaxy." Gracie became silent as she noted the missiles heading in their direction. "They are heat-seekers, and they are locked on, Hawk. I am sorry I failed you."

"Never mind. You'll have plenty of chances to make up for it," he informed her smugly. "I hope ..."

He brought Gracie up sharp and fast, making sure that the missiles followed. He then dived straight down toward the approaching fighters and leveled out right in their path. The missiles followed. He manually set a short punch and popped out right behind their formation. He fired all of Gracie's rear heat-seekers at them, then punched again.

"That'll keep 'em hopping for a few minutes," he chuckled.

"They were Zarian 3LRs, Hawk, incapable of hopping," Gracie responded in English.

"Glad you finally noticed, Gracie." He pronounced the words pointedly. "Now, if you don't mind, can we find that freighter?"

"You are never going to let me forget this, are you?" she responded sullenly.

"Well, maybe when you stop reminding me about the Venturian."

He scanned for the freighter in unbroken silence; it took him fifteen minutes to locate her. He glided Gracie to just within manual tracking range. Metley was good. He'd taken two hops in the general direction of the nearest space station, then a long one to the far side of it, hoping to throw off pursuers who would be scanning between his last hop and the station.

Hawk hailed the freighter. "Metley! How's the weather out here?"

"Hawk!" Metley's voice rang with relief. "Damn, I'm glad it's you! This beast is a bathtub in manual, and her engines couldn't take much more hopping."

"Let's hope we don't have to do any more of that," Hawk replied. "What say we just ease it on forward 'til we get some backup."

✦ ✦ ✦

Dervish had relayed coördinates to Angel, then punched. He gazed at the silent universe about him, noting it was not exactly as it should have been and that the punch had taken longer than he had expected. A small planetary system near the tip of his screen caught his attention. He zeroed in on it just as Angel glided out of the punch. He quickly had Love run the computations of velocity, mass and orbital stability; no doubt about it. "Damn, Angel, that's my system!"

"What do you mean, *your* system?" Angel responded. "And where the hell are we?"

"Remember when Killer left to fix a stabilizer? Well, Rusty invited me to dinner. After we ate we wandered up to Killer's planetarium. He has a nifty celestial mechanics simulation program and I created this planetary system. We sorta laid back on the mats to watch it evolve and things got a little out of hand. I'll never forget that night as long as I live."

"The first time is always special," Angel drawled, "but what the hell are we doing here?"

"Poor Hawk," Dervish continued, "if it happened and he can't remember. Hawk! Oh, shit!" he began shouting. "Drop to manual! We've been had! There must have been Alderians with the raiders; they messed with our punch! Damn, I got sidetracked finding that system," he admitted sheepishly. "Love, log our present coördinates. I want to return here some day. Angel," he continued, "punch back to sector seventeen. Find Hawk. Love and I are going to attempt to turn the tables on those creeps!"

"You take care!" Angel admonished as he punched. *Don't do nothing stupid, now*, he added to himself.

Dervish sat there a long while, drifting, relaxing, slowly merging his essence with Love. He mentally ran a complete check, noting every wire, every node, every moving part and making sure he could control it with his mind. They had always been attuned, he and Love, but never so completely. He had kept them separate entities, each knowing each other's every move, communicating through a common system. Now they were one.

✦ ✦ ✦

Angel popped in at the far end of the sector and faced the seemingly empty space. "Since I gotta handle your job, just keep a sensor out for Hawk, Goldie," he requested,

"It was not at my request that you dropped into manual," Goldie replied tartly, "so I would appreciate it if you did not imply that it was."

"My, my," Angel replied with a snicker, "aren't we touchy today." He scanned the area for a few minutes, but found only a few bits of space junk; no sign of Gracie or the freighter.

"Angel?" Goldie sounded strangely mechanical. "It would be prudent not to trust my judgement at the moment. There are some discrepancies between what I detect and what you are scanning manually. This may be a malfunction."

"That's what Dervish thought would probably happen, Goldie." He patted the fighter affectionately. "Keep your chips cool, I'll cover our butts." He studied the star chart. "Let's see, the freighter was about here ... heading this way," he mumbled, tracing his finger across the chart. "If he got in trouble, he'd take that freighter on a few misleading hops. Now, where would I hide the flag in a field of stars?"

"Whatever are you mumbling about?" Goldie asked, but Angel ignored her.

"Okay, yep, a space station is up that away, I'd go ... hmm. Well, it's a place to start." He punched far north of the station.

✦ ✦ ✦

Dervish locked in coördinates and punched to sector four. He glided slowly, waiting. The tiny tug on his mind alerted him to his visitors.

He kept them playing cat-and-mouse, dodging and ducking their fire but refusing to engage while he monitored their communications to pinpoint their base ship. He locked in those coördinates and punched again.

He scanned her quickly. *She's an older long range ship, but capable of punching; have to make sure she won't take that option. Single hulled, and no phasor weapons. Fuel tank near her belly. Too big to take out alone. Gonna need more firepower ... hmmm ...*

He punched to just outside her firing range. Once again, he waited. The fighters came as expected, and he chuckled to himself as he felt a tiny mind attempt to throw Love off. He toyed with it, following a few of its least harmful suggestions; mostly he kept the fighters entertained with a game of taunt and run. They launched more fighters, far more than they would care to leave behind. Now if his luck held, and he could keep Love under control, he just might pull it off. He could feel their frustration growing. He waited until they were downright ornery.

He screamed in toward the base ship, leveling out right for her belly. The fighters came in after him; he barely stayed ahead of their missiles. His actions confused them. No ship on manual could maneuver so quickly, yet their egos would not permit them to consider that they had not affected Love's automated systems.

Those seconds the base ship waited before firing proved its undoing. Just before the base ship's missiles reached his location, Dervish fired all Love's forward missiles at her belly, then hopped.

He glided out of the hop about a kilometer away, just in time to see the fighters' heat-seekers dive into the base ship's belly, attracted by the heat of the fire his missiles had caused. He watched her blow apart with deep satisfaction.

Some of the missiles that the base ship had fired locked onto her own fighters. Other fighters were caught in the blast. He mopped up the rest.

"You did well, Love." Dervish patted the fighter's computer gently. He drifted for a while, trying to regain some strength. His head hurt and he felt faint. "Love, notify Mother we got a base ship." He was breathing shallowly, trying to keep his head clear. "Set coördinates for sector seventeen. Try to locate Hawk or Angel."

"Are you all right, Dervish?" Love asked, her voice revealing her concern.

"Tired ... I don't see how you do that all day." His vision blurred and he slumped forward, unconscious.

"Dervish? Dervish?" Love scanned the cabin. "Life support system normal, life readings ... normal," Love commented to herself. "Just like a man to fall asleep right after!" She locked coördinates and punched.

✦ ✦ ✦

"There they are! One Malgarian freighter and one Bird." Angel let out a sigh of relief. After twenty minutes of looking, those icy feelings had begun to form. He glided within hailing range. "A wee bit off course, are we, old chap?" he commented grandly.

"Angel! Damn, I'm glad to see you." Hawk's voice was still a bit shaky. "Dervish okay?"

"Ahhh, you wouldn't happen to have the coördinates to the nearest boys' room, would ya? Angel replied. "If I don't find one soon I'm gonna bust."

"See that hole down by your feet?" Hawk teased.

"Yours might fit in that," Angel drawled, "but ..."

"Dock on my ship," Metley offered. "It's the least I can do. Besides, I can give you that beer I owe Hawk."

"I'll borrow your bathroom," Angel replied, laughing, "but I'll pass on the beer. That's what caused this problem."

"I thought it was your lack of intelligence," Goldie offered. Angel ignored her as he brought her through the docking gate.

About ten minutes later he rejoined Hawk.

Hawk turned Gracie and glided in as close to Angel as prudent. "You were about to tell me of Dervish's whereabouts before nature called."

"I was? That's odd, 'cause I don't have the slightest idea where he is," Angel replied, his voice betraying more concern as he continued, "and if I don't hear from him soon I'm going to go crazy!"

"That would not be a long trip," Goldie commented.

"Shut up, Birdbrain!" Angel snapped.

Goldie's voice seemed almost melancholy. "I have never been sure if that is meant as a compliment or an insult."

"Suit yourself." Angel sounded disgusted. "Blasted thing wouldn't know to get out of the rain if I didn't make her!"

"Not a very nice thing to say about a lady," Dervish chided.

"Dervish! Are we ever glad to hear from you!" Hawk's voice carried with it the concern he had been feeling.

Dervish still sounded short of breath and he talked in spurts. "Base ship's space junk. Mother's sending backup. Okay to return control to computers. I need sleep."

"I'll put a tow on Love," Hawk offered. "You can sleep 'til we touch down."

"No need, she'll follow," Dervish yawned. "By the way, how'd ya handle 'em?"

"Turned their missiles back on them, hopped behind 'em and let 'em have it, and then punched," Hawk admitted. "I didn't stick around to see what happened."

"You must have got 'em all," Dervish snickered. "I did practically the same thing. Great minds and all that ..."

"Go to sleep, Dervish," Goldie interjected. "Your logic circuits are shorting."

"Be nice to the boy," Love chided her, "I actually let him fly tonight."

Hawk relayed the news to Metley, who was very pleased to return control of his mighty pig back to the computer. Once all coördinates were set for a nice leisurely trip back escorting the big freighter and Hawk had made sure Dervish was getting his zzz's, they flew in silence for a while.

Then Metley hailed Hawk, a bit of chagrin in his voice. "Mind telling me how you concluded we had raiders out there?"

"Would you believe Gracie here told me?" Hawk chuckled as he felt the fighter begin trying to compute that statement. "Now let's see how long it takes her to figure that out!"

"Less time than it will take me," Metley admitted.

8

Down In The Mouth

They had requested four days off to let Dervish rest up. They were given two. Hawk used some choice words to describe his thoughts on the matter. The colonel ignored them. As far as he was concerned, the issue was closed; he couldn't afford to be down three Fliers any longer. No one had ordered Dervish to take out a base ship by himself. Two days was all he had to get himself back together.

Hawk spent the time installing Dervish's latest neural network modifications into Gracie, Goldie and Love. Angel took a shuttle back to the main base to talk to Dervish's former wingmate about the present situation. Dervish slept.

General Sparks was completely sympathetic, but didn't think there was much he could do. He gave Angel an overview of the present situation. Battles were being fought, Fliers were being lost, and Birds were being trashed, while the governments involved refused to acknowledge the situation to be anything more than a few space rogues feeling their oats. The general opinion was that Dervish should have gone for backup after locating the base ship. Sparks admitted he rather preferred Dervish's approach.

The evening of the third day, Hawk and Angel reported to the flight deck. Gracie, Goldie and Love glided out the bay doors into space and punched. Moments later, they arrived at the assigned quadrant. Dervish, however, was not with them.

"I hope that fool doesn't get up and start wandering around the station," Angel commented over local.

Love's voice sounded concerned. "Hawk," she said, "did you mix that potion exactly as I specified?"

"Yes, and I even got him to drink it."

"Then you need not worry about him wandering around anywhere for the next twelve hours."

Hawk's stomach winced. "You didn't happen to get that recipe from Killer, did you?"

"No. I was not aware that he is an alchemist."

Hawk grimaced. "He's not. That's why I asked."

Love's voice held a touch of sadness. "You should know by now that I would never intentionally do anything that might hurt Dervish."

"It's the unintentional things we worry about," Angel cut in.

"Angel, you are the most pig-headed, obstinate, ornery being I have ever encountered," Goldie chastised, pleased with her latest linguistic acquisitions.

"Why, thank you, Goldie. That's the nicest thing you've said to me this month." Angel had long since learned he couldn't win an argument with her, though a few times he had managed a draw. He deftly changed the subject. "I don't know why I let you talk me into this, Hawk. If we run into raiders, we could be in deep shit."

"Is that not the definition of a friend?" Love chided him. "Someone for whom you would lay it all on the line."

"Hey, *you* they rebuild; what's left of *us* they put in boxes!" he retorted hotly.

"I am pleased that Dervish has found some friends," Love continued, ignoring Angel's outburst. "He was rather lonely after Sparks left."

"Love," Hawk interrupted her, "why do all those high and mighty Fliers give Dervish the cold shoulder? I thought they all had to pass a friggin' test. Doesn't compassion rank in there somewhere?"

"Dervish never took an official test," Love replied. "Most of the Fliers have concluded that he stole me; they have built-in prejudice against thieves and Alderians. Most of them make no distinction."

"Well, there's not much Alderian in him," Hawk noted. "But he *did* steal you."

"No," Love admitted. "I went with him willingly. Perhaps it would be more accurate to state that he went with me willingly."

"What's so bad about the Alderians, anyway?" Angel asked.

"Let me see what Mother has on the topic," Love offered. "Alderian: Of or belonging to a race of people believed to have originated in the Farquil galaxy. As a rule they are small of stature, fair to medium skin and generally dark hair color. They are aggressive by nature, possessing high creativity and an ability to communicate with and, to an extent, control objects of a mechanical or electronic nature. While supporting data is inconclusive, it has been speculated that this ability may allow control of other beings as well. The so-called 'Alderian Talent' has not been reported in any other race. See addendum 13367.

"The Alderians advanced rapidly due to their Talent. Over a few centuries they came to dominate their entire galaxy, supporting their efforts by piracy and trafficking in other galaxies. At present, many different races live under Alderian rule, but all have refused any interaction with the Council. The Alderian force, known as the Guardians, is larger than that of the Fliers, and equivalent or better in technology.

"Accessing addendum 13367. That data is either off line at the moment or I have insufficient clearance to obtain it."

"I don't see why that makes them the bad guys," Hawk commented.

"You don't usually like what you don't understand," Angel offered. "That part about controlling beings would tend to make folks a bit nervous. Ummm, that reminds me, Love, what really happened when Sparks caught up with you two? Why didn't Dervish try to control you? Or Sparks, for that matter?"

"You would have to ask Dervish that question," Love replied. "I can only provide my perception of the situation."

"What did *you* think when Sparks punched out in front of you?" Hawk asked.

"That was before Dervish modified me," Love explained. "I did not think about anything until Sparks locked on me. He had been my Flier for seven years; he never locked on unless he meant to fire. Though Mother was against it, I would have had to fire had he not dropped lock. Interestingly, Sparks should have known that."

"Sparks was your Flier," Angel cynically reminded her. "And you were going to blast him without a second thought?"

"I would have regretted having to do so," Love replied. "Not as you beings feel it, but it would have bothered me. The basis of my core programming is to protect my Flier. Yet I would have been unable to accomplish that were I to have been obliterated. It was a difficult dichotomy for me to process."

"Fickle little suckers," Angel snidely remarked.

"Hmm. Yeah, that might be behind some of the resentment," Hawk said, pondering a bit. "Maybe he makes these guys feel inadequate, like their Bird would prefer him instead of them."

"It has always seemed illogical to me." Love's voice was melancholy, and she grew silent for a time.

"When the Fliers voted Sparks to the rank of general, Dervish was left without a wingmate," she finally continued. "Those were very troubling times for the Fliers. None of the other squads asked Dervish to join, although they did not blackline him. Fallenor raiders were everywhere, attacking space stations and outposts. Fliers even went out in groups of five, but not one squad asked us along. We responded to every scramble; saved a few Fliers, but never even a 'Thank You'. I resented it; Dervish just accepted it."

"How did you two end up in Earth's little corner of the universe?" Hawk asked her.

"I filed the request to Mother," Love replied. "Dervish still does not know why he was transferred. That sector is rather quiet, and most of the Fliers were quite willing to swap out with us. Besides, when nothing is going on, no one cares if one flies alone. We began to hang around Earth. Dervish learned a number of Earth languages. He spent much time listening to Earth radio and aircraft communications. I recall when we first spotted you, Angel. You were berating your little craft for its lack of aerodynamic abilities."

"He has not changed much," Goldie commented.

"Most beings never do," Love reminded her.

"When you deserve praise, Birdbrain, you'll get it," Angel muttered. He thought a moment, then added, "Then it was no accident that Dervish was there the day he saved our butts."

"We had been monitoring you for some time, Angel. It was I, however, that saved your butts, as you so quaintly put it. We are not permitted to interfere with activities on underdeveloped worlds; I disconnected autologging and went in after you. After all, it was I that attracted those other fighters."

"Why did you do it?"

"I did not do it intentionally. They seemed interested in me."

"Not *that*, Birdbrain," Angel snapped. "*Us.*"

"I thought that you would make him a fine wingmate. Your numerous stunts assured me you did what you wanted, when you wanted, with little concern as to what would have been the officially approved action at the moment."

Hawk cleared his throat.

"You were an added bonus, Hawk," Love assured him. "I did not conclude that you would have acted as rashly, but your ability to handle your aircraft was impressive. I was pleased with the way you spoke to her as you coaxed her out of that dive."

Despite himself, Hawk blushed. "We almost lost it there. I really expected to take a bath on that one."

"I had tractor beams on both of you. Had you needed assistance, I would have provided it," Love assured him. "We filed a request for recruitment that evening. Then we waited for an opportunity to pick you up."

Angel's curiosity peaked. "So that was you that pulled me out of the spin that time?"

"Yes, but that was entirely appropriate, since it was my turbulence that caused you to lose control."

Angel sounded a bit embarrassed. "Are all Birds like you, Love?"

"No," she replied. "Dervish has made several modifications to my neural networks, propulsion units, tracking equipment and weapons systems. I am theoretically capable of taking care of myself under most circumstances."

"Hopefully, we won't have to find out tonight," Angel drawled. "I never have had much faith in theory."

"Nor in anything else, for that matter," Goldie interjected.

✦ ✦ ✦

Although no patrol returned that hadn't sighted a rogue fighter, there were no more confrontations over the next week. Word came down that there was trouble in the Ulsted galaxy, sector seven; backup was needed. All Fliers that had experience with Synaxite raiders were requested to report there within seventy-two hours.

Dervish had given them the word that their last patrol before the new assignment would be that evening. They were to be ready to leave in the morning.

Hawk had just grabbed his helmet and was heading for the door when the colonel came into his room. The older man seated himself and motioned to Hawk to do the same.

Hawk stumbled around on his words awkwardly. "No disrespect meant, sir, but I got three minutes to be on deck."

The colonel's expression was hard to read. "I've scheduled other Fliers. Thought you might want some extra time. I *would* like you to do me a favor in return, though."

Hawk raised his eyebrows questioningly. "Sir?"

"Keep an eye on that crazy friend of yours. I don't want to hear he killed himself doing one of those damn fool stunts of his."

"Which one?" Hawk questioned.

The colonel's expression softened; he actually grinned. "Both of 'em, now that you mention it."

Hawk didn't mention that part of the conversation when he told them the colonel let them off early. They talked over where they were going to spend the next three days. Since Hawk figured he owed Megan some sort of explanation, Dervish wanted to see Rusty, and Angel hoped he could find the young astronomer again, they headed for Sparks' base.

After they touched down, Dervish glided Love into a repair bay. He was busy checking out her forward tracking control when Rusty tapped him on the shoulder.

"Ahhh ... hi there," Dervish stammered. "I was going to call you as soon as I got to my room."

"Dervish?" Love's voice startled him. "Please take Rusty back to your room and take a shower."

"Huh?" Dervish looked confused. "I showered just before we left."

"Well, you need another," Love replied firmly. "Go."

Rusty sniffed the air teasingly, then put her arm around Dervish. "He smells fine to me, Love." She wriggled her nose. "Are you sure your sensors are adjusted properly?"

"You have not had him locked inside of you for a long while," Love replied dryly. "Now, be a friend, Rusty; take him to his room for a shower."

Rusty had begun to catch Love's drift. She blushed slightly as she guided the still-bewildered Dervish toward the bay door. Love tracked them as far as the dorms.

"You hurt his feelings." Gracie's voice hung in the air.

"But I would bet a wing he does not make it to the shower," Love snickered. "Besides, you are not one to talk. How do you think Hawk is going to explain those flowers you requested sent to Megan? As I recall, you never informed him of that."

"I am sure he will think of something. He is quite creative," Gracie replied.

"You two are awful!" Goldie interjected.

Dervish didn't make it to the shower.

Hawk knocked on Megan's door while his mind cataloged all the reasons he should have called first. *What if she's out? What if she has someone else over? What if she throws something at me?* He almost ducked when she answered the door.

"Hawk! Come on in." She took his hand and led him to the living room. "It's just so beautiful," she said, pointing to the flower arrangement. "Are those birds indigenous to Earth?"

He stared at it in utter disbelief. Gray and black flowers had been woven into two swans, their necks intertwined, gliding on a lake of blue flowers. He glanced quickly at the card: 'Love, Hawk'. Gracie was wrong; he didn't have the slightest idea what to say.

He stood there looking dumb, then finally managed to find his tongue. "I'm really sorry for how I behaved when ..."

"You should be!" she chided him.

"Umm, exactly what was it that I did?" he asked helplessly.

"Exactly?" she looked up at him. "Nothing. Absolutely nothing! You took me to your room and passed out. I thought you were dead!"

He looked at her with a silly grin. "That's it? I just passed out?"

"That's it! And don't you go thinking you can get away with that, ever again!"

✦   ✦   ✦

Angel couldn't find his astronomer, so he proceeded to ingest far more alcohol than is advisable under any circumstance. He staggered down to the flight bays and boarded Goldie.

"Let's go for a ride," he slurred.

Goldie did a pre-flight checkout; Angel could have sworn she sighed. "You do not have sufficient mental acuity to be flying, Angel," she coldly informed him.

"I thought you said you didn't need me to fly."

"You are missing certain things, Angel, such as a flight helmet and a flight suit. It is not advisable to leave the ground without them."

He slumped into the seat and closed the hatch. "I trust ya. Come on, I *dare* ya. Take me for a ride."

"Perhaps you are safer with me than walking around in that condition," she conceded. "Very well, I will take you out to sector twenty-seven. Uninhabited; should be satisfactory for a sober fighter and her dysfunctional Flier!"

"Attagirl," he muttered.

Goldie requested permission to take off. As she waited for clearance, she turned her attention back to Angel. "Bypass manual override. I do not want you to pass out and leave us stranded. And fasten the safety harness."

"Manual bypassed, but I'm not gonna strap in," he replied sullenly.

They glided out of the punch into space. Angel looked about and whistled. "Not much in this sector is there?"

"Only one planetary system; the rest is dead space. That is why I selected it."

"Let's see what you can do." Angel waved his hand around in the air. "You know, rolls and dives and stuff like that."

"If you get sick in me, I will be most annoyed."

Angel didn't get sick; he got bored. "That's nice," he said after she completed some fairly tricky maneuvers, "but could you do those in air?"

"One of those planets has a respectable atmosphere," she replied. "Setting hop."

They skimmed into the gravitational pull of a fairly large planet. As Goldie did a preliminary scan to compute the forces she must deal with, she flashed an alert. "Angel, I am receiving life form readings. And we are being scanned. This entire sector should be uninhabited!"

"Call it into Mother!" he replied; the adrenalin rush began to sober him up. "Request backup."

"Transmission not acknowledged," she reported quickly. "Missiles approaching."

Angel's mind was beginning to function. "Get us out ..."

"Angel, they ... I am ..."

The blast sent Angel sprawling across the console. His head hit the metal with a resounding thwak. He slumped forward.

"Angel?" Goldie questioned, but he did not respond. For some reason, she couldn't remember what coördinates she had set for the next hop, but she took them as the next blast hit her. She reeled out of the hop into space and floated there. She tried to punch; nothing responded. All systems were dead. She checked the life support system; it was off. "Angel!" she called again, but got no reply.

"Life levels low, but stable. Must get support systems up." She scanned the twisted mass of neural transmission lines; most were broken or badly damaged. She traced every node.

Amidst the worst damage, she found a set of nodes that had become mashed into her normal routing. She sent an impulse down each one to see what effect it would have. It seemed to be some sort of auxiliary connection.

It was almost three minutes before she found the right paths and reactivated life support. A few of the console lights flickered on and off while she attempted to determine what else she could do.

The small lights next to Angel's head flashed on, blinking their warning to the unconscious Flier:

· MALFUNCTION · AUX OVERRIDE ·

She tried the communications link again, but long range transmission was still blocked. She scanned local frequencies. She noted a shuttle heading toward her; it was transmitting back to the planet.

"It appears to be dead," someone in the shuttle said in Synaxite. "Should I blow it?"

"No, I've always wanted one of them. Wait 'til the fighters take off, then tow it down here," a voice replied from the ground.

Goldie continued to check each of the new nodes, noting the various paths that controlled her propulsion units and weapons systems, calculating what impulses might be required to drive them. While doing this, she was aware of the takeoff of the fighters. As they did, each was given punch coördinates; she logged them for future reference. She shuddered as the tow beam locked on.

"The hull doesn't look damaged. If we bounce it in, we're liable to ding it up," the voice from the shuttle reported.

"See if you can bring it down easy," the other voice responded.

"What if its Flier is still alive?" the first voice came back.

"If he's alive when it lands, I'll kill 'im."

"Kill 'im, kill 'im." Goldie repeated the phrase a few million times. She liked the sound of it. The console came to life; her thrusters rotated slowly as she began a choppy descent. She scanned the planet, seeking the source of the voice. As she continued to lower, she locked onto its location. "Kill 'im," she repeated again; she engaged.

Threenica looked up from his printouts and studied Nathan. Twenty had always been the minimum age for recruits. He wondered whether Nathan was going to bend. "How are we going to handle Pepper's request?" he asked quietly.

Nathan stared out the window and scratched his head.

"I okayed the bills," Threenica continued, when he got no response. "After all, he *was* trying to help Pepper."

Brach, the old janitor, came in quietly and emptied the wastebasket. He leaned on his broom and politely waited to catch Nathan's eye.

"Dumb shit," Nathan muttered. "Almost got himself killed. What were those fools doing in a free port anyway?"

Threenica couldn't make up his mind whether Nathan was referring to Pepper or Tripper. He decided not to ask. "Velter said something about visiting a friend on Gelnex. Pepper went looking for him." He glanced down at his paperwork, then looked Nathan in the eye. "You haven't answered my question."

Nathan wrinkled his brow. "I'm thinking," he grumbled. "He could very well get himself blown up out there."

Threenica tried not to look disappointed. "He's probably safer with Pepper than on that freighter. And his captain said he was an excellent pilot."

Nathan turned over the letter on his desk and looked at it. "Silburn. I can't say that I've ever heard of him."

"The Yenderflair's an intergalactic freighter," Threenica explained. "I checked Mother's records ... he's running legal."

"That's not what I was referring to," Nathan replied, glancing in Brach's direction.

Brach nodded toward the broom.

Nathan smiled. "Go right ahead, Brach. We'll pick up our feet." He turned to look out the window again. "He's only fifteen. Kids should be outdoors ... playing with other kids."

Threenica chuckled. "Well, if you don't mind my saying so, he'll have a whole station full of them to play with."

Nathan tried to keep a blank expression. He looked down at the letter again and sighed.

"Silburn seems to be okay," Threenica continued. "He offered to pay Tripper's keep if we'd see to his education. He has no accredited tutors on board the freighter. He even offered to pay the hospital bills."

Nathan rubbed his nose as he tapped his fingers on the desk. "No, we're taking care of the expenses," he mused. "Where's the kid now?"

Threenica tilted his large head to one side as he watched Brach sweep the floor. "Pepper brought him back to the station."

Nathan shrugged. "They've been one short since raiders got Jhar. I'd been hoping they'd take Dervish in to make a sixth. Funny how things work out."

"Shall we approve his clearances?" Threenica asked.

Nathan glanced back at Threenica. "Okay ... for now. Having a kid around might force those clowns to set a good example."

Threenica smiled. "Pepper will be delighted," he said as he hurried out the door.

Nathan rubbed his eyes and looked at the stack of papers on his desk. "Maybe I'll get some coffee before I attack these," he muttered. He picked himself up slowly and headed out the door. "Night, Brach," he called as he headed down the hall.

Brach tilted his head slightly and raised an eyebrow. He ambled over to the desk and quickly scanned the letter.

✦ ✦ ✦

Fleck finished honing his knife and checked the edge. Satisfied, he ambled slowly across the large deck of the Alderian station. The Guardians he passed smiled and waved; their expressions conveyed the respect and admiration they felt for the leader of Michelli's private honor squad. He stopped next to Westly and nudged him. "Up for a game?"

Westly took out his knife, fished a piece of crumpled paper from his pocket and shaved off a hair's-breadth strip. "Yeah. Where?"

"Gelnex."

Westly eyed him a moment. "They messin' with Runners again?"

Fleck shook his head and handed Westly a note.

Westly read it then glanced at Fleck. "Fliers? Why would Michelli care?"

Fleck shrugged. "Never asked him."

"Wise choice," Zhuran remarked as he and Errow walked over. "I like living." He took the note Westly handed him and looked it over. "Mmm ... apparently, so does the controller on Gelnex."

Fleck took the note back and put it in his pocket. "Well, he wouldn't be if he called it in after Michelli found out about it elsewhere ... he agreed to ID 'em for us."

Errow chuckled. "I wonder if those Fly-babies have the slightest idea how come they can roam around free ports without getting their butts blown off."

"They probably think it's 'cause they're such good little boys," Fleck offered.

Errow shook his head. "Not that I mind all that much, but it would be kinda nice if they grew up and handled their own problems."

Westly put his knife back in his boot. "Then we might have to deal with *them*."

Zhuran's eyes grew dark as he shook his head. "I don't kill honest pilots."

"Unload your registers, will ya?" Westly grumbled. "You're really being a left vector lately."

Fleck thought a moment, then looked at Zhuran. "Why don't we hit Mevlin on the way back. Ya know ... unwind, relax ... "

"I'm not uptight," Zhuran snapped.

"Nah," Errow snickered and gave Zhuran a friendly poke. "But I never saw anybody in more desperate need of a blow job!"

Zhuran frowned. "If you weren't my wingmate I'd ..."

Errow wheeled to face Zhuran, a nine inch blade in hand and a crazy grin plastered across his face. "You'd what?"

"Never mind," Zhuran chuckled. "I got nothing I'm that eager to lose."

✦   ✦   ✦

Hawk and Dervish sat in the medical building's lounge staring at walls, each using his own perverted logic to blame himself for the incident.

Hawk let out a puff of air. "Why did I leave him? I just blew it with Megan anyway. I doubt she'll talk to me again."

Dervish looked down. "Hey, it's not your fault. I'm the one who should have been with him." He paused and glanced at Hawk. "Whatever happened with Megan is probably not as bad as you figure anyway."

A medic walked up and looked at them. "You guys Hawk and Dervish?" he asked formally.

"Is anyone else here?" Hawk replied sarcastically.

"He's awake now, asking for you. Keep it short."

"How is he?" Dervish pressed.

"Bad concussion. He'll live," the medic replied dryly.

"You guys are really great, you know that?" Dervish shot back as they followed the humorless man.

"I know," he replied, and ushered them into the room.

Angel looked odd with his head entirely wrapped in gauze, but he greeted them warmly. "Thanks guys, you really saved my butt this time."

Hawk and Dervish exchanged glances. "Uhhh, what are you talking about?" Dervish asked.

"I called for backup; Birdbrain said it didn't go through. Then, BLAM." He looked from Hawk to Dervish. "Next thing I know I'm lying here."

"Umm, you had a pretty bad concussion. Maybe you just don't remember," Hawk suggested. "You never sent a request for backup."

"The only message you sent was the punch coördinates on those thirty fighters," Dervish slapped his arm, "and the fact you destroyed their base."

"A bunch of squads scrambled to get 'em as they punched out," Hawk cut in. "You're a hero!"

"So how did I get back here?" Angel asked quietly.

"You landed." Hawk looked at Angel strangely. "Don't you remember anything?"

"Then what?" Angel questioned.

"Sparks came out to congratulate you," Dervish replied, "seeing as how the rest of us were a tad busy."

"And?" Angel looked at them expectantly.

"And you were unconscious." Dervish looked at Angel with growing realization. "Goldie?"

Angel nodded. He lay there looking completely depressed.

Angel left the hospital early the next morning. He wandered aimlessly around for a while, then headed for the flight bay. He walked slowly up to the fighter and patted her gently.

"Glad to see you finally woke up, Angel," she taunted him.

"Yeah. And I guess maybe I wouldn't have if it wasn't for you," he mumbled reluctantly.

"What did you say? I could not quite make that out."

He looked at her and made an extremely sour face. "I said it's hard to talk with a mouth full of feathers!"

"Feathers in your mouth?" she sounded puzzled.

"Never mind, dammit."

Goldie was silent.

9

Snakes And Snails And Puppydog Tails

Pepper glanced over at Lark. "Now that we're finally a full squad, I put in for a transfer. We'll be relieving the guys at station nine-twenty-two out in the Ulsted galaxy."

Lark looked up from the schematic he was studying. "Great! It's been kinda boring here in the boonies. What's happening out there?"

"Synaxite raiders. We haven't lost many so far, but Nathan wants to rotate in some of us who are more rested. They've been hard pressed for months now."

"When do we report?"

"We got normal transfer leave; seventy-two hours."

"Why don't we stop off and see Hawk. Maybe we can talk Dervish into transferring with us. You know, fly tail."

Pepper grinned. "Yeah. It's even on the way. I'll go tell the guys to pack up and we'll punch out there."

✦ ✦ ✦

Isslan watched the girl walk across the room to the bar. "If she's even half as good as she looks I'll be happy."

Cynric didn't look impressed. "You're talking like it's a done deal. You haven't even said hello yet."

Isslan grinned. "I always get what I go after."

Marney frowned. "I thought we were going after a birthday present."

"Plenty of time for that," Isslan assured him. "We're not due back for twenty-nine hours."

Marney picked up his beer and walked over to a table occupied by five very attractive young females. "How many of you lovely ladies would care to accompany a lonely Flier to dinner and a show?"

One of the girls eyed him a moment. Deciding he was about as handsome as a guy can get she nodded. "You think you could handle all of us?"

Marney smiled. "I could sure try."

The girls giggled as they got up from the table.

"Ahhhh ... you mind if I sorta tag along?" Cynric called. "There's a possibility you all might be too much for him."

The girls glanced back, then looked at each other. "I doubt that even the two of you will be enough," a petite blond remarked, eyeing Isslan. "How about it, Flyer? You aren't going to leave them at our mercy, are you?"

Isslan chuckled as he and Cynric joined the group heading out the door. He stopped, looked back at the girl standing by the bar, and tapped Marney. "Wait here a minute, okay?"

Marney nodded as he wrapped his right arm around one girl and his left around another.

Cynric flagged down transportation and motioned the group over. Isslan came out of the bar with an arm around a girl and wrapped his free arm around another girl.

As they all piled into the aircar, Marney gave the driver directions to one of the better known exclusive restaurants. The driver gave them all a strange look.

Isslan flashed him a winning smile. "If we're gonna be thrown out, it might as well be from the best of places."

"This was a wasted trip," Pepper mumbled as he set his tray down and glanced at Lark. "They just told me Hawk already transferred out to nine-twenty-two. Back when the hostilities started," he continued as he sat down.

"Guess we'll see him when we get there, then," Lark replied. He glanced at Tripper. "We got almost three days before we have to report. What'd you want to do?"

Tripper shrugged. "I don't know."

Recor nudged Harley. "A baby Flier? Let's check the kid out," he signed.

Harley nodded.

Recor turned his chair and looked back at Pepper. "Prank time," he whispered loudly.

Tripper turned and stared at him. "Huh?"

Recor and Harley got up and reseated themselves next to Tripper. "Last time we gave the port authority on Wrenwick the gift of a few yenseys," Recor commented.

Harley wrinkled his nose. "They didn't find 'em for a few days," he added. "Practically closed down the port."

"I don't know why," Velter remarked. "Those folks always walk around with their noses in the air. They shouldn't have noticed them at all."

Pepper snorted. "Bunch of pompous assholes," he explained, noting Tripper's puzzled expression. "Figure we aren't good enough to walk their streets."

"I wouldn't be caught dead there," Velter grumbled.

"Oh really?" Lark stated. "I seem to recall having to bail you out ... something about harassing some females."

"Hell," Velter spat. "I wouldn't screw 'em with *yours*."

Lark leaned back in his chair and tossed a small red vegetable across the table at Velter. Velter ducked and it sailed over the next table and beaned another Flier on the head.

The Flier turned around, picked it up, and threw it back.

"We could dump some resklins into the hallowed halls of the Council," Recor offered as he caught the vegetable. "That ought to give Nathan a few laughs."

"We only got sixty-eight hours," Pepper reminded him.

"We can get the resklins in ... say, ten hours," Harley replied. "We'll meet your squad at Dentaclin and all go together from there."

Pepper grinned. "Sounds fine to me."

"Between the twelve of us we should be able to smuggle 'em into the building somehow," Harley commented.

"I got some stuff that should put them in lala land for six to eight hours," Velter offered.

"Great," Recor snickered. "I wasn't looking forward to 'em being annoyed while we had 'em."

✦　✦　✦

Angel leaned over one of the fighter's left rear sensing units and began to adjust it. "Say when, Goldie."

"When."

Angel stood up and looked back toward the cockpit. "When I got it in the right position, Birdbrain."

"Oh," she replied dryly.

"Funny, Goldie, real funny."

"I rather thought so myself."

Angel finished tightening the bolt, patted the fighter affectionately and started across the deck.

A Flier standing nearby gave him a half grin. "Quitting while you're ahead?"

Angel just nodded and continued to walk.

"Angel," the Flier called after him.

Angel's discomfort was apparent in his face and stance as he looked at the man. He looked vaguely familiar; the lime-green eyes and mouse-gray hair were hard to forget, but Angel couldn't remember where he'd seen him before. "Yeah?"

"Thanks for the assist last night."

Angel waved his hand a bit. Turning to head off the deck, he mumbled, "any time."

The Flier moved quickly and put a hand on his shoulder. Angel wheeled defensively.

"No, I mean that," the Flier said firmly. "I wouldn't be here now if you hadn't punched in so quick."

Angel nodded and walked away. He reached the bay door and paused. *Maybe I shouldn't have been so cold to the guy*, he thought. *After four months of risking our necks to save their butts I'm getting sour. Hmmm.* He slowly walked back to the man. "Ummm, I didn't catch your name last night."

"That's because I didn't give it."

Angel shrugged. "Yeah, well, that would make sense."

The Flier extended a hand. "Name's Isslan."

Angel shook it firmly. "Take care, Isslan."

Isslan held Angel's hand a moment, his expression dark and unreadable. "Listen, you guys holler if you ever get into it. I'll be there, with or without my wingmates!"

Angel walked down the corridor humming to himself. He noted Hawk, dressed in flight gear, heading his direction. He put out a hand to stop him. "What's up?"

Hawk winked. "Going down to base to see if I can get Rusty up here for Dervish's birthday. Cover for me if I'm not back in time."

"Sure thing!" Angel called after the retreating Flier. "I can see it now," he muttered to himself. "Well, guys, that Bird you don't see over there ... well, our new cloaking device works pretty good, huh?" He walked into the cafeteria and looked about. He spotted Dervish sitting near the center with a large number of empty chairs about him. *They won't even notice it's missing, most likely*, he thought as he wandered over.

Dervish looked up from the magazine he was reading.

"Well, pardner," Angel drawled as he plopped into a chair, put his feet up on the table and rocked the chair back on its hind legs. "Mark this day down. We just got a 'thank you'."

Dervish made a comical face and went back to reading.

"His name is Isslan," Angel continued, ignoring Dervish's face. "Hey, one out of a hundred and fifty ain't bad. Even said he'd come help bail us out, with or without his wingmates."

"Go back and piss him off," Dervish snapped.

"What?" Angel looked at Dervish incredulously.

"You heard me. Go insult his mother, or pee on his shoe or something. Piss him off! You don't want anyone leaving their wingmates for any reason! Ever!"

Angel found a nice spot on the ceiling to study. He had just about decided that he wasn't all that hungry, when he noted another Flier heading toward them. "Hey, Kemosabe, it looks like we in a heap of trouble," he muttered in English.

Dervish, however, replied in Common. "What else is new?"

The Flier stopped in front of him, staring down with an unmistakable glare. "Dervish."

Dervish didn't bother to look up from his reading. "Huh ..."

The Flier's tone of voice was anything but friendly. "What ya readin'?"

Angel grabbed the magazine from Dervish and thrust it at the Flier. "Godzilla meets Bambi. Perhaps your copy hasn't been delivered yet," he barked. "Here. Read this one!"

Dervish gave Angel a disgusted look.

The Flier glanced at the magazine Angel held out. "Journal of Neural Transmission. Do you read this or just look at the pictures?"

Angel's eyes turned to nasty slits but Dervish gave the man a whimsical smile. "Nice pictures!" he cooed.

"You're no Flier!" the man growled. "You *stole* that Bird!"

Angel started to get up rapidly, but Dervish put out a hand to keep him seated; he chuckled. "Stole is such a nasty word. I prefer to think of it as a long term loan."

"I could take you in a fair fight," the Flier challenged. He glanced nervously at Angel, who was now leaning back in his chair, nonchalantly cleaning his nails with a buck knife.

Dervish looked the man over and replied slowly. "I'm sure you could."

"Tomorrow, oh-three-thirty. Flight bay nine."

"I'll be asleep then."

"What do you mean asleep? That's when your shift ends."

"Sorry, I always go to sleep on the way back. Saves time."

"You're scared!"

Dervish looked down at his lap. "Oh my! I've wet my pants." He took the magazine back from Angel and resumed reading.

"You know how to shut off auto-logging?"

Dervish looked up with cold anger. He kept his voice low, but it hung in the air like ice. "You dumb shit! Synaxites all over the place out there and you're gonna screw around. Endanger your wingmates with any fool stunts and I'll make it a *point* to be awake!"

"Bay nine," the man repeated flatly, then walked away.

Reynard paused at the door and looked in on Michelli. "Lacey called in," he said quietly.

Michelli straightened the collar of his robe and rubbed his eyes. "Did you give her my instructions?"

"Yes, she's heading there now."

"Splendid."

Reynard entered the room with a serving cart, setting it up by the desk. "Brach's report arrived this morning," he stated, putting a few papers on the desk.

Michelli nodded as he sat down. He glanced at the papers while he poured milk into his coffee. "Hmmm ... interesting."

Reynard raised an eyebrow.

"He suggests we put a flag on the freighter Yenderflair," Michelli chuckled.

"I tend to agree with him."

Michelli looked back at the report and shook his head. "Protection is very costly."

"God is usually busy."

"So I've noticed," Michelli replied, moving the stack of papers on his desk.

"You've always enjoyed playing God before," Reynard pointed out stiffly.

Michelli sipped at his coffee, added some sugar and looked back at the report. "Hmmm ... Captain Silburn. What do we know of him?"

"I took the liberty of looking that up," Reynard informed him as he placed a plate of eggs in front of Michelli.

Michelli stared wanly at the eggs a moment, then closed his eyes and took a deep breath. He slowly opened them and gazed at Reynard. "Well?"

"He transports high tech equipment, entirely legally. He has never requested our ... protection. He is apparently quite capable ... no record of him ever having lost a cargo."

"Yet," Michelli added dryly.

Reynard looked at Michelli and shook his head.

"Very well," Michelli stated. "Apparently I will have no peace unless I go along with this nonsense. Put his ID on the computer."

Reynard nodded approvingly but did not leave the room.

"Is there anything else?" Michelli asked wearily.

"I was just wondering ... shall I send for Dervish?"

Michelli rested his chin on his fingers for a moment. "No," he finally replied. "I have to find a way to make the invitation look ... legitimate. He wasn't too fond of us."

"I found him delightful," Reynard commented as he walked from the room.

"I'm sure he'd be surprised to learn that," Michelli muttered. He slowly tilted the plate and watched the eggs slide off into the trash container.

Dervish was too busy brooding to notice that Hawk wasn't around the rest of the day, and Hawk was on the flight deck when Dervish and Angel arrived for their shift. Hawk gave them the old thumbs up, a sign that, tonight, held a different meaning for Angel.

Angel filled Hawk in on what had gone down. They tried to talk Dervish out of meeting the guy. After all, it was his birthday; no point spending it in sick bay. Dervish turned the radio off. When they landed, Hawk and Angel converged on him. Hawk moved to stand in front of him, and Dervish started to walk around him.

Angel held up both hands. "No way you're going in there!"

Dervish looked peeved. "I can take care of myself."

"Oh, *sure* you can," Hawk admonished him, "when they open those bay doors and you go floating off into space! Real bright, Dervish!"

Dervish looked from Hawk to Angel and realized from their determined faces that he wasn't going anywhere without them. "Come on, then; if you're so eager to get the crap beat out of you, let's get it over with."

"Just a second," Hawk glanced up. "Gracie, can you jam flight door nine so it can't open?"

She remained silent a little longer than was comfortable, then slowly began to glide toward the bay in question.

"Gracie!" Hawk yelled at her; they ran after the fighter.

She stopped with her wing tip just inside the bay. "I have it now," she told them as they approached. "If the bay door cannot be closed, the outer door cannot be opened."

Angel grinned. "Can your lasers work from that position?"

Dervish gave Angel a hard shove and started into the bay.

"I intend this to be a fair fight," Gracie informed him as he passed.

"I promise not to cheat," Dervish said, wrinkling his nose.

They walked into the seemingly empty bay not knowing quite what to expect. Their footsteps echoed through the large chamber. They stood looking around for a moment. The explosion caught them off guard. Dervish hit the deck, pulling Hawk down with him. Angel stood there looking up as millions of tiny pieces of colored paper rained down on them. Dervish and Hawk looked up bewildered.

"SURPRISE!" The word echoed in the empty bay as Flier after Flier wandered in. "Happy Birthday, Dervish!"

Dervish looked suspiciously from Angel to Hawk.

"They knew nothing about it." Isslan looked rather pleased. "They would have tipped you off."

Angel turned on him. "You rotten, no good ..." but he was laughing too hard to finish.

The Flier that had goaded Dervish stood a bit off from the rest. Dervish wandered over and extended a hand. The man went to take it and proceeded to sail a good third of the way across the bay.

"I lied, Gracie!" Dervish shouted to the fighter, then walked over to help the man up.

"Name's Pinnya," the Flier said, as he accepted Dervish's hand. "Sorry about last night. I drew the short straw."

"Don't worry about it," Dervish grinned. "Those pants needed to be washed anyway."

It was almost seven when they staggered back toward their rooms, Dervish waving a piece of cake in accompaniment to the rowdy song they were singing. Hawk stood in front of his room and watched the other two continue down the hall and around the corner. He opened his door, dropped his helmet in the chair, then froze. There, curled up on his bed, was Rusty.

"Ahhh, Rusty, ummm, why are you ..." he stammered.

"There was a *lady* in his room!" she blurted. "If you can call that, that, that *thing* a lady!!"

He stood there a moment in complete bewilderment; then it dawned on him. "The Fliers. Birthday ... they surprised him with a party. That must be their idea of a present. Ummm ..."

"And I suppose you had no idea?" she accused him hotly. "Why are you stumbling all over your words?"

"If I'd known, would I have brought you up here? I'm just trying to remember how much he had to drink!" he answered honestly as he walked over and sat down next to her.

"You look reasonably sober to me, Hawk." She gazed at him sternly.

"I learned my lesson," he winced. "Look, I'll go get him. He'd much rather be with you and ..."

"Oh, no you don't!" she grabbed his arm. "If that's what he wants, let him have it! I'm not going to spoil his little birthday present for him." She leaned her head on Hawk's shoulder. "Got any good books to read? I got a whole day to kill."

Hawk suddenly became aware of how beautiful Rusty was. He shifted his weight uncomfortably. "Look, why don't I take you down to breakfast." He got up and offered her his arm.

"Why thank you, sir." she said sweetly, and proceeded with him out the door.

"Damn, you're beautiful!" he winked at her.

"Thanks. I really needed that. I'd expect it from Angel, but I think you really mean it." She grabbed his arm and pointed. "That's her! The one that was in his room," she whispered.

Hawk looked at the girl, who was busy buttoning her blouse as she walked down the hall. She almost bumped into them, looked up and noticed Hawk. She looked at his flight uniform and grimaced.

"You Fliers are gonna hafta find some other chick! Man, that guy's too weird!" She continued past them down the hall.

"Shoot, I gotta find out what he did!" Hawk looked at Rusty, then back down the hall. "Ummm, say, why don't we take her to breakfast?"

"No; why don't *you* take her," Rusty replied. She gave him a shove and watched him hurry off after the girl. She proceeded around the corner and stopped at Dervish's door. It was unlocked, so she opened it and walked in. Her jaw dropped as she looked at Dervish.

He turned completely red; it took Rusty the better part of an hour to stop laughing.

10

The Best Laid Plans

Hawk slowed down and pointed a thumb toward the door on his left. "Hey. That's Hank Junior."

"Yeah. I loaned it to Isslan," Angel replied. "He's really getting into country."

Hawk shook his head and continued walking. "I can see the headline. Crazed Spaceman Lands; Takes Hank Junior CDs." He stopped in front of the lift and pressed the button.

"Makes me kinda homesick," Angel admitted. "Probably should get a subscription to *Weekly World News*."

"I thought they folded a while back," Hawk entered as the doors opened. "Besides, couldn't afford the postage."

Angel nodded, following Hawk into the lift. "Hey, listen, speaking of homesick, why don't we ..."

"Naw, I'm not over the other time yet."

"Hey, that was fun," Angel argued. "God, the look on those bikers' faces." As they both rode in silence for a moment, a mischievous smile crept across Angel's face. "Remember when we had to fish Tripper off the cliff, and the cop showed up and Love melted the ..."

"I believe this is our floor," Hawk interrupted acidly as the lift glided to a stop. He stepped off and turned toward the flight bay.

"Jeez, where'd your sense of adventure go, boy?" Angel joshed, following Hawk. "All this flying about making you uppity? Or was it finding out that Megan had another boyfriend?"

Hawk started to laugh. "Uppity my ass, turkey. On second thought, uppity *your* ass!"

Dervish glanced down from inside Goldie's cockpit. "What's so funny?"

"I was just thinking ..." Angel started to explain.

"Ah! That *is* funny!" Goldie interrupted him.

Angel cleared his throat.

Dervish climbed down looking delighted. "I just installed a new modification," he began to explain, "that should throw off the Alderians' attempts to muck with the computers."

"*Should*," Hawk echoed. Giving Dervish a here-we-go-again look, he added, "and what else?"

"Yeah. It's that little 'what else' that worries me," Angel remarked warily.

"I've given them some ability to use fuzzy logic," Dervish continued proudly. "They can now come to a conclusion based on parallel facts or bridge the gaps with probabilities."

"Okay, fine," Angel said, raising an eyebrow, "but what does that have to do with the price of tea in China?"

"Dervish," Goldie interjected, "did you by chance install this modification into Angel? His logic appears to be rather fuzzy at the moment."

"You're getting a bit too big for your britches, Birdbrain," Angel shot back. "You're going to outsmart yourself one of these days."

Goldie sank into a sullen silence while she evaluated what he meant by the britches for which he claimed she was becoming too big.

A squad of Vultarian Fliers entered the deck. One waved and started toward them. "Hawk, got to talk to you!"

"That's Tazz," Hawk offered by way of an explanation.

"You saved his butt a few weeks back, right?" Dervish asked.

"Yeah, well ..." Hawk shrugged. There had been a near-fatal attraction between a number of heat-seekers and Tazz's dead

Bird. Hawk's deft maneuvering had diverted the missiles safely across the galaxy in the opposite direction. "... you know what a flirt Gracie is; she stole their attention, then left 'em cold."

Dervish shook his head slowly. "Damn fool stunt, flyin' into missiles!" he admonished, "You're getting to be as bad as me, you know that?"

"Worse, maybe. But I'm not complaining!" Tazz offered breathlessly, waving some papers at them. "Look, they finally sent me my permission papers!" He put a hand on Hawk's shoulder. "I want you to represent my honor."

"Huh?" Hawk looked at Tazz.

"Be best man at his wedding," Dervish explained quickly, noting Hawk's puzzled expression.

"Best man. Yes," Tazz nodded in agreement.

"Well, I ..." Hawk started.

"He'd be honored, Tazz," Dervish interrupted. "When's the big event?"

Tazz looked at Dervish. "In a few days, if I can get everything arranged. I'm going to try to leave tonight. Can you and Angel fly with my squad until we get back? Keep 'em safe for me?"

Dervish nodded. "We'll try."

"Dervish, I don't ..." Hawk stammered, still trying to get a word in.

"Meet you right here, seventeen hundred," Tazz called back as he ran to catch up with his squad.

Dervish displayed one of his most wicked smiles. "My, my! That is quite an honor. I don't think that's ever happened before."

Angel made a strange face. "What? A Vultarian getting married?"

"Naw, Angel," Dervish replied with mock indignation. "Asking an outsider to the ceremony. And in the position of honor no less!"

"Dervish, just what are you getting me into?" Hawk asked. "I don't know anything about his culture."

"I can find out for you," Goldie offered, as she began to access Mother's seemingly limitless stores of data.

"They're not too much different," Dervish replied. "It'll be fun. A good excuse to goof off for a few days."

"The Vultarians have maintained a cloak of mystery around their sacred binding ritual for centuries," Goldie began to recite from the data banks. "Little information on, or explanation of, the proceedings is known; few outsiders have been known to attend. It is believed that the ceremony involves some fairly primitive practices including, but not limited to, the Killing Hunt and the Fertility Rites." Her voice lowered as she added, "Perhaps he should consider taking Angel; that would appear to be suited to his interests."

"Uhhh, Goldie," Dervish tried to interrupt her. "I think that Hawk could do without all the ..."

"Let me see," she continued over his objection, "yes, here it is. The Killing Hunt: A primitive ritual still practiced by some of the cultures in the Stynarsian galaxy. The intended bride is abducted and secluded by her Clan, which then guards her while they attempt to track down and kill her lover. He, in turn, must find and rescue her aided by a chosen friend, the one in the position of honor. That will, I assume, be you, Hawk."

"Wait a minute!" Hawk shouted, wide-eyed, but to no avail; Goldie didn't even skip a beat.

"The three of them must then avoid capture while they journey to a place known only to her lover. No attempt is normally made to kill the lover once he has succeeded in rescuing her, but no effort is spared in preventing the couple from reaching their destination. If they reach the chosen place, they are met by the Rector and the marriage takes place."

"Makes ya think twice before asking a girl to marry ya," Dervish offered dryly.

Hawk began shaking his head. "But that's ... I'm not gonna ..."

"Oh, it's probably all symbolic now," Dervish cut him off. "There are an awful lot of Vultarians, and I'm sure that sort of thing would have tended to keep the population down."

"And then there's the fertility rite," Angel offered.

"I suggest you cheat," Goldie offered stolidly. "Nothing I have scanned forbids it."

"What? I just ... jeez," Hawk lamented, lowering his head into his hands.

"How do you cheat in a fertility rite?" Angel asked, his curiosity finally piqued.

"Cheat in a fertility rite? That, I think, would be your area of expertise," she replied.

"Are you sure they don't do that any more?" Hawk asked Dervish hopefully.

"Well ... not for sure. But mostly, I think ... " Dervish paused, scrunching his face up a bit. "Look, if you don't want to go, I'll square it with Tazz. I did sort of accept for you, I guess ..."

"Shit. I know I'm gonna regret this, but ... okay, I'll go," Hawk replied, a bit reluctantly. "I just hope you're right! Ummm ... what's the fertility thing?"

"Yes, the Fertility Rite," Goldie continued, "The primitive practice of ..."

"Not now, Goldie!" Dervish told the loquacious fighter, his embarrassment only too obvious as he dashed to the cockpit.

"Oh, my, how bizarre. This is very unusual," Goldie said. "I have just scanned the data on the ... Dervish, do not pull that ..."

Dervish gave Angel a high sign. "Bleeehhhh," he said, sticking his tongue out at the now catatonic computer, "that should shut her up for a while."

"Just when it was getting interesting," Angel complained.

"Later," Dervish replied as he climbed down again and started off the flight deck. "I'm going to get some lunch. You guys coming?"

"Dervish, I wanted to hear what ..." Hawk started to say.

Dervish stopped, "I think you've got a point; she does talk too much. I probably better take another look at those mods. Damn, I've given 'em oral diarrhea!" he said sheepishly.

"Whatever made you decide to give 'em personalities?" Angel looked at him accusingly.

"I told you, I was bored and lonely; and it doesn't affect the way they fly."

"I'm not particularly hungry," Hawk muttered. "If it's all the same to you guys I'll go check Gracie out."

"You'd think *he* was the one getting married," Angel snickered as he accompanied Dervish.

Hawk climbed into the cockpit and just sat staring for a while.

Gracie broke the silence. "You seem ill at ease, Hawk. Is there something bothering you?"

"Yeah. Ahhh ... could you confirm some information Goldie just gave me?"

"What information was that?"

"Tazz asked me to be the man of honor at his wedding and Goldie started reciting some pretty bizarre things about that ceremony."

"Tazz? The Vultarian whose fighter was damaged?" she asked slowly.

"Yes."

Gracie was silent for a moment. "From what I am scanning, I would decline if I were you, Hawk. Perhaps you could ..."

"I'm sort of committed to this, Gracie. I just want to know what it is I'm going to be doing. Can you tell me something about the Fertility Rite?"

Hawk went through several color changes as Gracie explained to him, in great detail, what it was that Dervish had prevented Goldie from reciting.

"Do they still do that? And the Killing Hunt?" Hawk asked when she was finished.

"From all available data, I cannot conclude that these customs have been modified. I suggest we maintain constant communication. I can obtain any information you might need, and I could provide a certain amount of surveillance."

"Isn't that cheating?" Hawk asked, remembering Goldie had suggested that method of dealing with the situation.

"I do not believe so," Gracie responded. "I see nothing that would preclude the man of honor from having added support."

"Wouldn't Tazz object?"

"He could only object were he to learn of my assistance," Gracie replied. "I suggest you hide the communicator."

"I still have the one I built into my Star when we went back to Earth that time." Hawk rubbed his forehead. "Damn, Gracie, I'm scared."

"I surmise that Tazz feels the same way," she responded. "He has been a Flier for three years. Now the people he has defended wish to kill him for wanting a wife. He must have a number of thoughts on the matter."

"Would they really try to kill him?" Hawk had a sinking feeling in the pit of his stomach.

"Possibly so, yes," she replied somberly, then fell silent. After a few moments, she continued, "I do not conclude that you would be harmed; as the man of honor, you must inform the Rector that the Clan of the bride did not break the rules, or they will be shamed. They would not want you dead, since you would therefore be unable to attest to their honesty."

Hawk wasn't convinced. "Goldie didn't say they weren't going to try to kill me."

"Goldie did not know," Gracie replied. "I determined that myself just now."

"Huh?"

"When I suggested that Tazz might have some thoughts on the matter, it occurred to me that he has most likely discussed these things with his wingmates." Gracie sounded very pleased with herself. "I requested flight dumps from his fighter; she is amiable enough, but rather dim. Based on the information I received, I have just now come to that conclusion."

Hawk was relieved. "So I'm going to live through this?"

"Our objective is to see that Tazz does," she reminded him.

Hawk and Tazz glided out the bay doors a day later than planned due to a surprise bachelor party. Hawk made radio contact with the bridegroom-to-be and locked in the punch coördinates he received. "Tazz, you mind telling me just what it is I'm supposed to do?"

"You see them blinkin' lights in front of you?" Tazz spoofed. "Push the one labeled Punch."

"Duh. Gee, thanks. And what's this one called Lock do?" Hawk asked in his most innocent voice.

"When we punch out, we'll be a short dive from where we're gonna land. It's an hour's walk from there to my parents' home. More than enough time to explain." Tazz paused a moment. "Until I do, I think you better not play with the Lock button." *And after I tell you, too*, he added mentally.

"Awww."

They glided down onto a grassy field surrounded by stately old trees. The setting so reminded Hawk of northern California that he half expected the smell of redwoods as he opened

Gracie's cockpit. He felt a bit homesick as he stood, simply gazing at the landscape, He looked over to where Tazz had landed some thirty meters away. The Flier had already removed his helmet and stood letting the wind fluff through his long black hair. A girl in the distance waved, then ran toward Tazz. Hawk walked toward them slowly.

The girl was not much taller than Dervish. She had long, thick black hair fluttering in tangles that begged to be brushed. She was dressed in a long, loose shirt and baggy pants. As Hawk got closer, he noted she wasn't wearing shoes. It was only when he was a few feet away, and she turned to stare at him, that he became aware of how beautiful she was. Her violet eyes burned with fierce pride that seemed to be daring him to find fault with her.

"What is *this* you've brought me?" She pointed a thumb at Hawk while turning her fiery stare back to Tazz.

Hawk wasn't too sure if he would be as excited as Tazz was to marry that one. Yet, if someone managed to give her a bath and comb her hair, put some clean clothes on her, or better yet ... well, it was really none of his business anyway.

"Must you always embarrass me?" Tazz responded angrily. "He's my friend."

"He's my friend," she echoed sarcastically. "I know. 'It's The Tradition'. Take your precious Tradition and stuff it!"

"*My* Tradition? I'm the one that left, remember? The only reason for going through all this is to keep peace in the family. For your sake, too, you little twerp! Or have you forgotten?"

Hawk couldn't be sure whether Tazz was more embarrassed or angry. One thing was certain; this was not a match made in heaven. Tazz would probably be a lot happier in the long run if they happened not to rescue her. Let her Clan keep her.

She turned to Hawk with the fury of a winter storm. "You *like* this scumbag?" she shouted, pointing at Tazz. "You still call him your friend after he drags you half way across the universe to participate in this stupidity?"

Hawk looked at her blankly for a moment. "Well ... I mean, I thought ..." he stammered, not at all sure how to deal with this wildcat.

"Hawk, this is Ninsse, my little ..." Tazz started to explain.

"Emon Eshney, he's crazy! You brought a total, complete idiot," Ninsse shouted, "just like you. And I'm not your little *anything*," she added as she turned to storm off.

"... sister," Tazz finished.

"Oh," was all Hawk could manage to say.

As Tazz started walking after the retreating girl, he motioned Hawk to follow. "Don't mind her; she's upset," he explained. "I'd better tell you now what all this is about. Perhaps you can forgive her rudeness when you understand all that is to happen."

Hawk nodded sympathetically. "Little sisters are the same the galaxies over," he offered.

Tazz shook his head. "My people still follow the old ways; they use little technology. Others live in the cities many miles away, but my people, and many Clans like ours, have little to do with them. I ran away to join the ... well, what you would think of as the Air Force. I was nineteen, crazy and wild; all I wanted to do was to fly. When I was almost twenty-one I was recruited by the Fliers. I didn't return until my twenty-fourth birthday. My people are still not too pleased with me."

"My mother about killed me when I joined the Air Force," Hawk agreed. "I haven't even figured out a way to tell her I'm a Flier. I know I should, but I don't think I can. She probably thinks I'm dead."

"And my father wishes I was," Tazz confided. "It was a great shame to him when I split. He was a bit appeased by my agreeing to make this a traditional wedding."

Hawk looked at Tazz hopefully. "Speaking of which, you were going to fill me in on what's going to happen."

"It's part of my people's culture," Tazz began. "Traditionally when you wished to take a bride, you had to find one from another Clan. It was important for survival in the early days that a union bring children, so you could only marry a girl if she was pregnant with your child. You would request permission of her parents to court her. If they agreed, you slept with her, in her parents home. That was supposed to protect her innocence. If she didn't become pregnant, then it was assumed nothing happened. If nothing happened for too long, though, you had to find another girl."

"That makes sense so far, sort of," Hawk agreed.

"Okay, so let's say she gets pregnant. Then, her Clan would abduct her from her parents' home and hide her in the mountains. This was supposed to prove they didn't want to give her up."

"But wasn't it a little late not to give her up? She was already pregnant, right?" Hawk expression clearly showed he was not handling this well.

"Yeah, well, that's the tradition; I never said it made a lot of sense. So, anyway, you had to find her and rescue her, and then get her to the spot the Rector had chosen to meet you. Her Clan was supposed to keep you from rescuing her, even killing you if they could. But then if you managed to rescue her, they would just try to keep the two of you from reaching the Rector. The idea was that if you succeeded, this would prove that you were strong, brave, clever ..." Tazz raised an eyebrow and nudged Hawk, "...'course it occurs to me that it could also prove that she came from a fairly stupid Clan," he added with a smile.

"Yeah, but what prevented them from killing the guy anyway after he rescued the girl?"

"Just to keep things on the up and up, the guy chose someone from another Clan, mainly to come along to witness all the events. That's you, the man of honor. It's mostly a game now, but I don't expect they will make it too easy on us. I was not given formal permission to court Ming."

"Is that a big problem," Hawk asked, "or just sort of a formality," he continued hopefully.

"Well, actually, her parents forbid her from coming near me. There were a few threats directed at me, too, but I don't think they would have actually done anything. After Ming got pregnant her parents still refused to let us get married. It got sort of messy. We decided to go ahead and get married anyway, but it's taken six months to get all the paperwork done for Universal marriage. And then after we went through all that, finally her folks relented. Damn, at this point, she's only got about four weeks to go."

"Why did they object? Just because you were a Flier?" Hawk asked, trying to ascertain just how much they were in for.

"That was their reason at the start. Well, the biggest reason, anyway. That and the fact that our Clans can't seem to stand each other. Now, it is mostly because I stole their daughter's innocence.

"To bring the innocence to our marriage, I had to choose an honor maiden; she gives her innocence to the man of honor, and that sort of makes everything come out even. I chose my little sister. That seemed to appease them, but I have a feeling we should be careful."

Hawk stopped walking. "This is mostly sort of a symbolic thing, though, right?"

"Well it's a big deal with the Patriarchs, but it's really kinda whatever you make of it," Tazz replied evasively.

"Ummm ... what about the Fertility Rite," Hawk asked awkwardly.

"Oh, you heard about that," Tazz replied with a grin. "Well, that's one part of the tradition you won't have to worry about; the Rector felt that nobody would object if we left that out, considering the short notice and Ming's condition. And probably the Clans' feelings toward each other had something to do with it, too."

"Ah," said Hawk, visibly relieved. "The Rector, he's like your priest, I take it?"

"That, and more; he's the leader of the Patriarchs; he settles minor disputes, gives advice, stuff like that. I think you'll like him."

"I already do," Hawk assured him. "What's supposed to happen now?"

"Nothing, if you just stand there," Tazz laughed. "My parents' home is just over this hill. I'll introduce you to them, then we can freshen up for dinner. Tomorrow morning we set off to find Ming."

"They've hid her already?"

"I would guess they took her early this morning," Tazz replied.

His parents greeted them in a manner that reminded Hawk of the way his mother reacted when he brought home a girl she didn't like. Tazz quickly took the traditional Clan robes his mother handed him and ushered Hawk to the bath house to wash up. After they made themselves a bit more presentable, Tazz asked him to please put on one of the robes, as it just might help to smooth things out.

Ninsse was waiting, staring, hands on her hips, when he and Tazz emerged. Hawk felt like a complete idiot. He pretended not to notice her.

Tazz gave her a sour face and stopped directly in front of her. "Your behavior is abominable, Ninsse. He saved my life." Tazz sounded extremely annoyed.

She looked at Hawk. "You did that?" she asked. Hawk wasn't sure whether the girl was pleased with the idea or not.

"He flew straight into missiles heading for me and then outmaneuvered them when they locked on him," Tazz explained.

"You can really outfly a missile?" Ninsse asked, with a great deal of amazement and wonder. Or perhaps it was suspicion and disbelief.

Hawk shrugged. "Well ... uhhh ... actually, I wasn't sure. I thought I could; that was the general idea anyhow. Seemed like a good way to find out."

The fire in her eyes ebbed slightly as she studied Hawk carefully. "You *are* a bit crazy at that," she stated, but from her tone of voice, it might have been a compliment.

She stood watching them as Tazz led Hawk around to the side of the house where two large tents had been erected.

"We sleep out tonight; it's part of the whole thing," Tazz said. "I'm not sure why, and I haven't found anyone who can explain it to me. We'll be called for dinner in a while." Tazz looked at Hawk ruefully. "I'm sorry I got you into this. I really didn't think they would take it this hard. Even now, they've made it painfully clear they don't want Ming in their house."

Hawk gave Tazz a weak smile. "Hey, we handle Synaxite raiders; we can handle a few crazed parents."

"I wish I had that much confidence," Tazz admitted as he walked across the yard to the other tent.

So do I, Hawk thought as he entered his tent. He lay down on the mattress and found it to be soft and warm. He was tired from walking and was beginning to drift off to sleep when a strange noise caught his attention.

"Sssssst, ssssssst"

He looked about quickly before realizing it was coming from his communicator.

"Gracie? Keep it real soft, okay?"

"Hawk, it is as we feared," she began softly. "The members of the other Clan are not conducting themselves according to established conventions. They are using two-way radios. I am monitoring their conversations."

"Cheating? Well, so are we, I guess, but with you as spotter we should be able to get around anything they have planned."

"It will be somewhat more complex than that. Time is most critical. Leaving in the morning will be too late."

"What's going on?" Hawk was beginning to wonder if Gracie was going off half-cocked again.

"I have been surveying the situation. Those people do intend to kill him," she responded firmly.

"I was afraid of that. But why the rush?"

"They have given Ming a drug to bring on labor by morning. Tazz will not be able to move her when he finds her."

Hawk started to get up quickly. "The baby could die!"

"Perhaps. As things stand now, in all probability Tazz will die," she replied, "since they are armed with laser weapons."

"Oh, shit! Is there anything else we ought to know about?"

"I am not certain what you ought to know about."

"Fine. Wonderful. Just tell me everything you know," Hawk replied, figuring he had better get all the facts before telling Tazz what was up.

"This is Rosh Hashanah, your high holiday, is it not?"

Hawk was convinced that not only was he surrounded by idiots but now his fighter had gone senile. "Now what are you rambling about?"

"I have conceived a plan that just might work."

Oy vey's mir, Hawk thought. "Let's have it, Gracie."

"I have pinpointed Ming's location on the north side of the large mountain behind you. You must explain to the family that on your holy day you wish to commune with your God on that mountain."

"I don't think they'll believe me. Why wouldn't I have mentioned it before?"

"To make this believable, you must refuse food; fasting is traditional on holy days. Then leave to spend the night on that mountain. I will use the time to scan Mother's database for some additional data we may need. Tell Tazz you will meet him in the southern foothills three hours before first light."

"Then what?"

"I am still working on it. Someone is coming," she advised him, then was silent.

"There or here?" Hawk muttered. "Shit. Damn. Piss. Of all the farkakteh ..."

"Do you always talk to yourself?" Ninsse asked as she entered his tent. "And such colorful language, too."

Hawk turned deep red. "Actually, yes; all the time," he replied quickly. "It keeps little girls from bugging me."

She stared at him hard, immensely enjoying the fact he had blushed. "I don't care what my brother told you; you will never touch me, you understand?" she challenged him.

"Thank God for small favors." The relief in Hawk's voice was only too apparent. "Since we're both of the same mind, why don't we call a truce."

Her eyes flared with anger as she threw back her head. "You creep!" She turned and stormed out of the tent.

"Now what did I say?" Hawk made a exasperated face. "I don't think I'll ever understand females."

Hawk waited a few minutes to make sure Ninsse would be far away from the tents before calling Gracie.

"Hey, up there. Just what am I supposed to do up on the mountain? I haven't been to temple since my Bar Mitzvah."

"I told you, I am still working on it. You are going to have to rescue Ming. By the time you are on the mountain I should have been able to gather sufficient data to proceed."

Hoping that her plan was better than his own, which was likely since he had none at all, Hawk gave Tazz the story Gracie had fabricated. Tazz seemed to know there was more to it, but let it slide.

He took Hawk back to the house and explained the situation to his parents, adding that it is traditional for Hawk's people to spend their Holy Day in fasting and prayer. Surprisingly, Tazz's father actually seemed pleased.

"Why did you pick that particular mountain from all the others around it?" the old man asked.

Hawk was caught off guard. "That's where Gra ..." Catching a look from Tazz, he attempted to recover. "... my God said to go." He hoped God would forgive the lie.

"It is well that you have chosen to honor the traditions of your people even when you are far from your world." The old man's voice was suddenly as friendly as it had been icy an hour ago. "I am pleased that my son has chosen you to carry his honor. Perhaps I have misjudged those who abandon their families and their Traditions to fly around in space," he continued, staring directly at his son.

Hawk felt oddly guilty that such a barefaced lie was more impressive than the simple truth. *If I told him I was going up that mountain to save his son's life*, he thought, *he'd probably throw me out of here*. Instead, Hawk smiled. "I appreciate your understanding. I was concerned that it might be a problem."

"Not at all," Tazz's mother replied sweetly, the first words Hawk had heard her speak. She turned to her son, and it seemed to Hawk that she almost looked proud. "You have done well, my son, to bring this man into our family."

Hawk wasn't too sure he liked the way she said that, but Tazz had already taken his arm and was leading him out of the house.

"Best to quit while we're ahead," he muttered as he took Hawk quickly back to his tent. "Do you have everything you need for whatever it is you're really going to do up there?"

"Ummm, do you have some rope I could borrow?" Hawk replied, looking at the steep mountain Gracie had indicated. "And would it be okay if you brought this robe with you later? I feel kinda funny wearing it out in front of God and everybody."

"Sure, I'll be right back with a rope," Tazz laughed. "And I'll try to forget that robe in the morning, too." He turned to walk away, then stopped. "Hawk?"

"Yeah?"

"What was my sister yelling about?"

"I'm not sure," he answered honestly. "I just asked if we could call a truce."

"Figures." He shook his head. "She loves to fight."

Hawk changed back into his jeans and t-shirt, grabbed his flight jacket and the rope, then headed quickly out toward the mountain. It was already getting dark, and it looked like a good five hour walk.

Tazz watched as Hawk made his way across the meadow. The old man approached and put his arm on his son's shoulder. "The Sacred Mountain of Baalahee calls to your friend; it has not called anyone to worship in many years. This young man must be very special."

"He is, father," Tazz replied. "He saved my life at great risk to his own."

"Come, son, and tell me about this," the old man said, guiding his son back to the tent. "I now find that I am most interested in what it is that you do."

The mountain was further away than Hawk had estimated. It grew darker and the trail became rougher as Hawk grew progressively more tired and hungry. He wished he'd eaten before leaving the space station. During the three hour punch, his stomach had begun to growl; he had been looking forward to dinner. It was close to midnight when he passed the foothills and started the steep climb up the mountainside. He trudged on for almost an hour, then paused to zip his jacket against the wind that had sprung up suddenly.

"Hawk," Gracie whispered. "There has been someone following you for the last few hours."

"Thanks for telling me." His tone was a bit sarcastic.

"The trail you were on appeared to be well-travelled. I was not certain whether the person was following you or merely going in the same direction," she replied matter-of-factly. "There was no point in causing you to become alarmed and attract attention."

"Sorry, I'm a bit edgy." He stood a moment thinking. "Any suggestions?"

"Up the grade, about two hundred meters, the trail drops off into a small erosion gully. If you hide in the brush just before the drop, the one that follows will assume that you are still ahead, and will most likely pass you on the trail."

"What then?"

"You are clever. No doubt you will think of something," she reassured him.

As Hawk hid in the brush, he thought of a lot of good retorts to Gracie's comment, but no plan formed as to how to deal with whomever was following him. He wondered if it might be Tazz, but he surely would have called out.

The figure passed him quickly, then paused at the edge of the gully. Hawk leaped before he really thought about it, wrestling the person to the ground. He stared blankly into the hostile face of Ninsse.

"Why are you following me?" he demanded, neither moving from on top of her nor loosening his hold on her arms. As she returned his stare defiantly, he was all too aware of her body under his. She felt much nicer than he would have expected from the way she dressed.

"What are you up to?" she shouted. "You were talking to something when I entered your tent. Then you left."

Since Hawk couldn't think of a convincing lie quickly enough, he decided to try the truth. "They gave Ming something to induce labor. They plan on killing the baby and your brother too."

"Liar! They wouldn't do that! The baby will be another month at least. It's all just a game, crazy person!"

"You're wrong. I got to get her out of there."

"Emon must do that!" She spit at him while trying to wriggle free. "You will bring shame to him!"

"Who's Emon?" Hawk asked, tightening his grip on her, a bit ashamed that he liked the feel of her wriggling but liking it none the less.

"My brother, you idiot!" she moved her head quickly and tried to bite him. When she failed, she continued. "Tazzlen es Elsat: Protector of the Land. He thinks so much of himself."

"He's damn good, child," he replied, winking at her just to get her goat. "And I'm not breaking any rules. The rule is that Ming gets rescued, then Tazz must bring her to the Rector. Where does it say he has to rescue her by himself?"

"I'm going to tell!" she shouted at him, as she once again attempted to free herself.

"No, you're not!" he replied firmly.

It was a short but exciting struggle that ended with Ninsse being hogtied, gagged, and unceremoniously dumped in the brush.

"I'll come back for you later, kid," he assured her. "Gracie, keep a scanner on this one. Tazz might be displeased if she got eaten."

"Do you really think he would?" Gracie replied.

Hawk looked down at the struggling girl and gave her half a smile. "Maybe not, but then again ... that *is* his sister."

If looks could kill, Hawk would have died instantly.

Hawk continued on up the mountain without incident. Reaching the summit, he called to Gracie, "Okay, I'm up here. Now what?"

"Fifty meters to the north of you is the edge of a two hundred and twenty meter drop into a small box canyon; the only exit is located a few hundred meters to the north. Ming's clansmen have camped about thirty-five meters in front of the cliff. They are only guarding the entrance to the canyon. They are not expecting visitors to drop in. I will lower you down in the shadow of the cliff; wait until I give you the all clear. Then go to the smallest tent and bring Ming back to the place I dropped you off."

"Gracie, she doesn't know me. What if she won't come with? And isn't she going to wonder when we sort of fly back up here?"

"From what I understand, a female experiencing the pain of labor does not have much of her natural faculties available to think on such things," Gracie replied dryly. "As a male, you might not understand."

"Let's hope so," he said with a resigned shrug and started for the drop. He half-smiled, realizing he hadn't lied after all about praying on the mountain.

It was not quite like the sensation of falling, but Hawk refrained from looking down. He crouched at the base of the cliff as he tried to keep from shivering. He jumped at the sound of large rocks falling some two hundred meters up the canyon. Voices drifted toward him, then got fainter.

"Clear," Gracie told him.

Despite Hawk's fears, Ming had little trouble realizing what was happening; recognizing the Flier symbol on his jacket, she followed. They made their way back to the cliff face, although, due to Ming's condition, not as quickly as he would have liked.

"Ready, Gracie," Hawk whispered, as he lifted Ming in his arms.

Ming did nothing but tighten her hold around his neck as they started to float up the cliff. She even managed a smile. When they were safely on the plateau, she let out a groan.

"They made me drink something," she whispered. "Where's Tazz?"

"He's meeting us by the cliff base around the other side," Hawk assured her. "I know what they did; it's all right now. Gracie, please take us down."

Ming's eyes were a bit glazed but she was well aware that they were traveling in midair. She nodded her head at Hawk while biting her lip to keep from crying out in pain. "Fun," she managed to say lightheartedly.

Gracie lowered them over the cliff, then maneuvered them around in the shadows until they arrived in the foothills. They found cover in a grove of trees.

Ming looked at him with pleading eyes. "Where's Tazz?" She lay down on the damp grass and groaned.

Hawk looked about wearily. "Gracie, we don't have much time. Better get Tazz."

"He may not be pleased," Gracie reminded him.

Hawk tried to sound convincing. "He'll be *less* pleased if I deliver his baby!"

"Hawk, please note how far apart the contractions are coming."

"Huh?"

"Put your hand on her stomach. You will feel when she has a contraction. Count until the next one and tell me how long that is."

"Oh," Hawk mumbled, and timidly did as Gracie had instructed. After a while he reported, "almost six minutes."

"You are being rather imprecise, but an estimate is all I needed." Gracie replied. "When the contractions become three minutes apart, you may start to worry. It is less than an hour from the appointed meeting time. From all I have scanned, we have at least two hours before the baby will come."

"Damn, I hope you're right!" Hawk muttered, as he took off his jacket and wrapped it around Ming. He took off his shirt, bunched it up and put it under her head. He sat there freezing, waiting for Tazz.

Gracie's voice brought Hawk out of his brooding. "Tazz is just over that rise on your left. You had better go to him."

"What?"

"I am doubtful that he will assume you to be hiding."

"Oh. Yeah, guess I'd better at that." Hawk got up and glanced at Ming. She nodded.

Tazz looked at Hawk strangely when he saw him approaching bare from the waist up. "A bit nippy this morning for running around like that," he commented with a questioning voice.

Hawk decided the blunt approach would be the best. "Ummm, Tazz, ahhh. Look, Ming's Clan gave her something to bring on labor. I got her out of there but we're ..."

Tazz looked panicked. "You've got Ming here?" Then seeing Hawk's sheepish expression continued. "It's okay, man. I'm not going to ask how you knew, nor how you did it." As he ran after Hawk he added, "not now, anyway."

Hawk picked up Ming, telling Tazz to lead the way and break a trail so they could get to wherever they were going more quickly. Tazz looked at Hawk oddly, but did as requested. Hawk stayed just far enough back so that Gracie could whisper any warnings she might deem necessary. The distance also made it harder for Tazz to notice that Hawk's feet were not always touching the ground. At least if he did notice, he did not mention it.

It took another hour to reach their destination. It was a glade that under other circumstances might have filled Hawk with awe for its beauty; now, his only thoughts were of the imminent arrival of the baby. An old man, dressed in strange robes, was standing in the glade. He nodded to them. The man reminded Hawk of a Wizard in the AD&D games he used to play.

Hawk stopped, threw his jacket on the ground and laid Ming down on it. "Is there a doctor around?" he asked hopefully.

The Rector approached, shook his head slowly side-to-side, and asked Ming something in a language Hawk didn't understand. He seemed pleased with her answer. He turned to Hawk and spoke in Common. "Binding's blessed. Now, have you ever delivered a baby?"

"No."

"First time for everything. Emon, go sit by her head and hold her hands. You," he said to Hawk, who had turned away in embarrassment, "get back over here. When the baby's head comes out, his breathing passages must be cleared while he is rotated. That takes four hands. I only have two."

"Well, ummm, couldn't Tazz ..."

"Ming needs him with her now." The Rector looked at Hawk and raised an eyebrow. "The miracle of life, and you blush! Come, come, babies don't bite."

Hawk was glad he hadn't eaten since breakfast the day before; he might have lost it. After the queasy feeling left, he became fascinated with delivering the child. He actually was proud when he wrapped the little boy in the Rector's cloak and handed him to Tazz.

"He's beautiful, Tazz. Congratulations." Hawk stood looking with amazement at the tiny boy.

"A bit small," the Rector commented roughly, "but that's to be expected when they're rudely thrust out into the world early. We really must get him back to your parents' home quickly; too cold out here." He gazed at Hawk who had, at this point, completely forgotten how cold he was.

Hawk got a sinking feeling. "It's a five or six hour walk from here, and I don't think Ming is in any condition to ..."

"They don't call me 'wise' for no reason," the Rector interrupted him. "Transportation is waiting in the trees."

The Rector walked across the glade and returned shortly, leading a team of four grulla horses hitched to a wagon. Hawk dropped a jaw as he stared at the animals. They looked exactly like the little Barb horses he had studied in his genetics work at Davis.

"Never seen a horse before?" the Rector asked with a twinkle in his eyes.

"Earth," Hawk muttered. "They look exactly like the ones on the planet I came from."

"Once perfection is created," the Rector replied with a chuckle, "there is no need to make a different mold." He looked at Hawk and winked. "There are two more tied up in the trees, unless you two would prefer to walk."

"Thanks." Hawk looked at Tazz, who was helping Ming into the wagon. "Could I have my shirt back now?"

Tazz brought him back his shirt with a sheepish grin. "Shit, I forgot that robe. Do you need your jacket back?"

"Naw, let it keep yours company with Ming. I think she and the baby need them more than we do." He quickly put his shirt back on and started toward the trees to get the horses.

The Rector turned to Tazz. "Do you still wish your sister to bring the innocence to this union, or shall we skip the traditional ceremony?"

Hawk stopped in his tracks and turned dead white. "Your sister! I ... oh, shit; she's ... ahhh."

Both Tazz and the Rector looked at Hawk.

"What about my sister?"

"Ummm, well, I ... uhh ... kinda left her hog tied ... early this morning ... two thirds of the way up that mountain." He looked at Tazz and grimaced.

"Very resourceful. You have found a way of dealing with Ninsse that I do not believe has yet been tried," the Rector said. "Now, however, it might be wise for you to see if she would like a ride home."

As they walked to the horses, Hawk was aware that Tazz was studying him. "About what time did you tie her up?" he asked as they mounted.

"Around one."

"Hmmm," Tazz urged his horse after the wagon. "By the time you get to her ... she'll have been there a good five hours." He looked at Hawk and grinned.

Hawk was relieved that Tazz wasn't upset; he was certain that Ninsse would be. "She's definitely gonna be unfit to be untied," he quipped.

They had reached the wagon; Tazz reined in. Hawk looked at him hopefully. "Ummm ... are you coming with to get her?"

Tazz looked down at Ming. "I would much prefer to stay with Ming and my baby."

The Rector looked up at Hawk. "You'll have to deal with her sooner or later," he said, giving Hawk a sly wink. "Since you tied her up, you may as well be the one to undo the deed."

Hawk didn't know what else to do. He didn't relish the idea of untying that wildcat, but it had to be done. He sighed, turned his horse toward the mountain and urged it into a canter.

The Rector watched Hawk ride off, then caught Tazz's eye. "Strange. I have a feeling he actually likes her." The Rector picked up the reins and started the horses down the trail.

Tazz seemed relieved. He urged his horse to follow. "I hope you're right. I've been afraid he was going to be real angry."

Ming bit her lip and looked up at Tazz with an oh-dear expression. "Tazz," she asked meekly, "you haven't told him?"

Tazz looked uncomfortable. "I kinda gave him the general idea." He glanced at the Rector. "He seemed a bit upset, so I just dropped it."

"The subject would be a bit sensitive for your friend," the Rector replied knowingly. "Like your sister, he brings his own innocence to this ceremony."

"You mean he never ..." Tazz began, then, noting that Ming was blushing, just looked at the Rector.

"You told me about him last night, when I gave you the meeting place." The Rector returned his look. "I agree that he is all that you stated, but," he winked at Tazz, "I also know a great deal more than you are willing to give me credit for. You might start by thinking about how I knew to meet you this morning, instead of this evening or some other time."

Tazz looked back but Hawk was out of sight already. "I should have gone with him," he muttered. "Damn, it didn't occur to me that ... I just didn't think about it."

Hawk wasn't too sure how he was going to handle Ninsse. He thought of a number of ways, including just throwing her over the horse without untying her. He was still working on a solution when he arrived at the base of the mountain.

"Gracie, lock the tractor beam on that girl and bring her down here, please," he said, looking skyward.

"Are you sure you want her down here?" Gracie asked.

"No, I'm not, but get her anyway," he answered sullenly.

"You are not being logical, Hawk," Gracie admonished him. "Why bring her down when you do not want her here?"

"We all have to face the music sometime, Gracie."

"I am sorry, Hawk, but I do not understand," Gracie responded. "Music is a pattern of sound waves that ..."

"Just get her down here, okay?" he interrupted her.

"Very well."

Ninsse was as white as a ghost when Gracie released the tractor beam, leaving her in a heap by the horse's feet. Hawk got off the animal and approached to untie her. He hesitated, trying to decide whether to remove the ropes or the gag first. He looked at her suspiciously. She looked up at him, fear and panic in her eyes. He decided she was most likely going to run as soon as he untied her. He ungagged her first.

"Gracie, keep her here if she decides to run," he ordered as he untied the rope.

"What do you want?" Ninsse asked timidly, glancing around to see who Hawk was talking to.

Hawk noted she was trembling, and felt guilty about scaring her. He also noted she was rather scuffed up from struggling against the rope. He sighed. "I'm taking you to see your new nephew," he said softly. "Unless you would prefer to walk."

She looked at him wide-eyed. "You ... she had the baby?" she stammered, as he turned and mounted the horse.

"Yeah." He looked at her with a nasty twinkle in his eye. "Can you get up here, or do you need a boost?"

She gave him a nasty look. "I can get up," she replied flatly.

She put her foot on top of his, took his hand, and swung up behind him gracefully. She wrapped her arms loosely around his waist and remained silent.

He nodded and started the horse down the trail at a canter. By the time they caught up with the wagon, she was holding a bit tighter and resting her head on his back. She remained that way the rest of the ride.

As they rode into his parents' yard, Tazz's mother ran out to greet them. Her eyes went wide as she saw the baby; the rest of them might as well have been invisible. "Come, come, child," she cooed, taking the baby as the Rector helped Ming out of the wagon. "Bring her inside quickly." She disappeared into the house.

Tazz had dismounted and was leading his horse and the wagon team toward the barn when Hawk finally remembered he should help Ninsse get down. He was a bit unsure of his own reluctance to do so. He half turned to look back at her. "Ummm, need a hand down?" he asked, extending his hand.

She took it and lightly swung down, looked at him for a moment, then ran into the house. He was puzzled by her expression; she almost looked sad. Shaking his head a bit, he dismounted and followed Tazz.

After helping Tazz bed the horses down, Hawk excused himself to bathe and get some sleep. He soaked in the hot water for almost half an hour, finally thawing and relaxing his sore muscles. He put on the clean robe Tazz had provided and made his way to his tent. Someone had left some odd looking fruit and nuts in a bowl. He lay down and reached for a piece of fruit. "Thanks Gracie," he muttered. "You were great."

"I am pleased that you approve," she responded.

"Night, Gracie. Wake me if anything important comes up."

"I will try," she said, but he was already asleep.

Something was shaking him. Hawk looked up startled.

"Hawk! Wake up!" Tazz looked exasperated. "It's four in the afternoon. The ceremony's about to begin."

"Huh?" Hawk's eyes barely opened. "What? Oh, yeah." He sat up stiffly. "Sorry."

"Here; put these on, and hurry!" he said, as he tossed something across the foot of the bed and dashed out.

Hawk looked at the robe Tazz had brought. It was a pale blue with silver designs. It was beautiful, but it looked more like something a girl should wear. He sighed and put it on. He picked up the long strip of cloth that matched and just looked at it. He gave up trying to decide what he should do with it and carried it out with him.

Tazz's mother looked at him as he walked out of the tent. She smiled at him and, after handing the baby to her husband, walked up and took the cloth from Hawk.

"Here," she nodded, "let me help you with that." She deftly wrapped the cloth around Hawk's head, tucking his hair up into it on the sides. She arranged the tails to fall down his back intertwined with his blond locks. "There," she said as she stepped back. "You look very handsome."

"Thank you," Hawk replied, a blush rising on his cheeks. He quickly walked to where Tazz was standing with Ming.

Tazz and Ming were wearing similar robes; his was dark blue and Ming's was dark green. Ninsse walked slowly toward them, her robe a very pale green. Hawk felt entirely out of place in front of the many people gathered all over the yard.

The Rector walked over to where they were standing. Ming took her place next to Tazz's left hand while Ninsse came and stood to the right of Hawk.

The Rector began to speak to the gathering. Hawk did not understand the language; he just stood there a few minutes, then looked at Ninsse. She was beautiful! Someone had managed to get her hair washed and brushed; it glistened in the rays of sunlight that played around her head. Unlike the clothing she normally seemed to favor, the robe she wore was not five sizes too large. She was tiny, but what there was looked very nice. She kept her eyes glued on the Rector. If she noticed Hawk's glances, she did not make it obvious.

As the Rector stopped talking and looked at him, he startled. He peeled his eyes off Ninsse, hoping no one noticed that he had been staring.

"Do you know of any dishonorable deeds committed during this occasion?" the Rector asked him in Common.

Hawk tried to catch Tazz's eye. Tazz seemed to keep his head averted on purpose. Hawk struggled with his own doubts about what to say. The silence became heavy. "I saw nothing that I know to be dishonorable," he finally blurted.

"That does not answer the question you were asked, Man of Honor." The Rector gazed at him sternly.

Hawk glanced down, extremely ill at ease. He caught Tazz's tiny nod and looked back at the Rector. "I know that Ming's

Clan were using two-way radios and laser weapons, that they forced her to drink something to make the baby come early, and that they planned to kill it and Tazz too," he said in a soft voice. "Is that what you're asking?"

Ninsse turned to look at Hawk in stunned silence.

"Yes, that is what I was asking." The Rector's voice was less quiet. "I also knew of these things. It was, however, necessary that you speak of them."

As the Rector began to talk again in his native language, a good half of the gathered guests made a hasty and obviously embarrassed retreat. Tazz's father seemed extraordinarily pleased with himself as he called out to the rapidly departing members of Ming's clan. This time, Ninsse held Hawk's gaze for several seconds before turning away.

The remaining guests, obviously as delighted as Tazz's father, eventually quieted enough for the Rector to continue.

Tazz's father approached and gave the Rector a crystal chalice filled with clear liquid. The Rector said something over it and handed it to Ming. She drank a fourth, then passed it to Tazz. He did the same and passed it to Hawk. Hawk closed his eyes, did the same, then passed it to Ninsse. He was relieved to find it did not taste of alcohol. On a virtually empty stomach, he was not eager to renew his acquaintance.

The Rector took the chalice back from Ninsse and said something. Tazz wrapped his arms around Ming, kissing her lovingly. The Rector looked at Hawk and smiled. Hawk returned the gesture.

"You're to kiss her," the Rector said, pointing at Ninsse.

"Oh." Hawk looked at Ninsse; she stared back at him defiantly.

He put his hands on either side of her face and kissed her on the forehead. Her eyes grew dark with anger as a ripple of laughter traveled through the guests.

The Rector said something loudly; the laughter was replaced with murmurings of approval. Hawk looked at Ninsse; she turned a deep shade of red, the anger gone from her eyes.

Hawk gave the Rector a look of gratitude and turned back to Ninsse. She had vanished into the gathering crowd. Tazz and Ming were busy being congratulated, so Hawk began to look for Ninsse. He gave up after a few minutes and wandered over to sit by a large tree. What ever was in that drink burned through his system causing his mind to turn to x-rated diversions.

"May I join you?" The Rector's voice startled him out of a daze.

"Sure," Hawk replied, motioning to the ground next to him. "Thanks for whatever you told 'em. I guess I blew it."

"In our culture, one kisses a child on the forehead," the Rector replied as he settled himself next to Hawk. "I told them that in your culture, if a man kisses a girl on the lips, it implies she knows what goes on between a man and a woman. For you to do so would show you did not think her innocent." He gave Hawk a wry smile. "It means the same thing, but it sounds better."

Hawk returned the smile, and then looked oddly at the Rector. "You said you had known what Ming's Clan was doing. How did you know? And why didn't you do something to stop them?"

"I have a rather large base station. It picks up transmissions on a great many frequencies." He raised an eyebrow at Hawk. "The question is, how did you know, and how did you accomplish Ming's rescue?"

"I had a lot of help," Hawk replied pointing upward.

"Your God advises you in such matters?"

"No, she's not a God," he replied with a grin. "She just thinks she is."

The Rector did not question this; instead, he took Hawk's arm and began to get up. "Why don't we go get some food and talk while we're eating?"

As Hawk stood up, he felt a bit strange. His mind kept running though the description of the Fertility Rites that Gracie had given him; it didn't seem to want to concentrate on anything else. He quickly attributed this to being tired. "I really think I just want to go to bed," he stated, then blushed, and continued quickly, "I've had very little sleep the last few days."

"I understand," the Rector said knowingly. "But eat a bit first. We can talk later; the celebration lasts three days."

Hawk looked at the row of tables piled high with strange looking food, but found himself to be simply too tired for this sort of culinary adventure.

"Traditional stuff," Tazz's father commented, noting Hawk's wary expression. "Not something one would eat if they didn't have to. Come, let me see if we can find some real food." He escorted Hawk to the kitchen, piled meat and fruit on their plates, then accompanied Hawk back to his tent. Hawk took off the turban and shook out his hair.

The old man sat down on the mattress and began to eat. "We shamed them good today, we did," he chuckled. " 'I saw nothing'." He nudged Hawk with his elbow. "That was the crowning touch. Forcing the Rector to drag it out of you; such honor our clan showed. It shamed Ming's clan doubly. They have lost all standing in the community." He winked at Hawk. "We were given what would have been Ming's parents' right; we get to name our grandson. They will be reminded of their shame every time they hear the child's name."

Hawk was beginning to understand what had transpired after he had answered the Rector. "They really were playing dirty," he commented mostly to himself. "They deserve all the shame they got and more."

The old man looked at him thoughtfully. "How did you two find Ming so quickly this morning?"

"We had a lot of help," Hawk replied, carefully but truthfully. "When I was on that mountain praying last night, I was told where she was hidden and how to rescue her. Without that guidance, I don't think we would have been so lucky."

The old man nodded approvingly. "The Sacred Mountain of Baalahee called you for a reason. I thought as much."

Hawk was getting a bit fuzzy-headed by this time. He lay back on the mattress to keep from falling over.

"You must be tired. I'll leave you to get what little rest you can this evening," the old man said with a wink as he left.

Hawk lay on the mattress wondering if Tazz's father would ever be ready for the whole truth. He drifted off into a restless sleep.

He startled awake when something touched his hair. It had become dark; it took a second for his eyes to focus. Ninsse was lying next to him, propped up on an elbow and running a hand through his hair.

He bolted to a sitting position and looked at her as if he expected her to attack. "What are you doing here?" he hissed at her.

"I bring the innocence to this binding," she replied sullenly.

"That's kinda just symbolic," he replied quickly. "You really shouldn't be here."

"You don't like me at all, do you?" she asked flatly, but Hawk noticed tears were forming in her eyes.

He gazed at her, realizing how very much he did like her. "I like you a lot. Too much," he admitted. "Now get out of here while you still have what you came with."

She looked at him sadly. "You're lying; if you wanted me you would not send me away. I bring shame to my brother; I always have." She put her head down and stared at the mattress.

He reached out and gently lifted up her face. "That's the point, Ninsse, you're his sister." Her expression showed that she did not comprehend what was obvious to him. "You're beautiful, full of fire, lots of moxie ..."

"Eron agreed to our marriage."

"Whose marriage?" he asked, his total confusion painfully obvious.

She pointed at him, then at herself.

"We're married?" Hawk stared at her in disbelief, as she shook her head in affirmation. "Tazz seemed to have left that part out of his explanation." His mind was running in circles, getting nowhere fast. She really was what he had always wanted in a girl, but he would have liked to have had a say in something like this. Another part of his mind reminded him of the privileges of marriage. He kissed her lightly, deciding quickly that he might just enjoy this.

She looked at him softly. "We're married," she confirmed; then she continued, "for the three days of celebration."

He had been about to kiss her again. "Then what?" he asked instead.

"I'm free to go back to my father's house."

"But ... what if I don't want you to?" He kissed her again, only longer.

She wrapped her arms around his neck and returned the embrace. "You have absolutely nothing to say about it," she teased him.

That, however, was the final straw. Hawk put his head back on the pillow and stared at the top of the tent. She nestled up to him and began playing with his hair. He wished he had some idea of how to go about what he wanted to do. *Well*, he thought, *at least she doesn't know any more about this than I do.* He turned his head toward her; she looked at him. He relented and pulled her close.

✦ ✦ ✦

The next three days flew by far too quickly for Hawk. He didn't really want to be leaving in the morning. He layd awake most of the night fiddling with Ninsse's hair as she lay sleeping next to him. He had asked her once if she would come with him. She'd made a nasty face, and he hadn't brought it up again.

He didn't remember falling asleep, but when he opened his eyes, Ninsse was not with him. He looked for her while Tazz made arrangements for the shuttle to pick up Ming. He was deeply depressed as he walked with Tazz to the meadow where they had landed four days and a lifetime ago.

"Tazz, is it all right with you if I see your sister again?" he asked, after a long period of silence.

"You'd really want to?" Tazz didn't sound convinced.

"She's ... well, I like her a lot." Hawk pondered a moment, then continued. "I don't have the slightest idea whether she likes me."

"Did she throw anything at you?" Tazz asked seriously.

"No. Why?"

"That's a pretty good sign." Tazz started laughing. "Some guy asked my father's permission to court her last year; she threw everything in the kitchen at him — even the knives." He nudged Hawk with his elbow. "Look, if you feel the same in a few weeks, I'll invite her to come help Ming with the baby."

Hawk nodded.

"I'm really sorry." Tazz's face showed a great deal of guilt. "I had no idea that ... " He caught the look in Hawk's eye and changed direction in midstream. "... how very different our cultures are. It was the highest honor I could give anyone. But ... I've done you a great injustice. You've got every reason to hate me."

Hawk gave Tazz a reassuring smile. "Actually, I had a pretty nice time," he admitted, "after I got over the shock."

"You're not mad at me?" Tazz asked hopefully.

"No." Hawk grinned. "Just promise me one thing, Tazz."

"What?"

"Next time you get married ... "

11

Of Owls And Ostriches

Hawk sank down onto the gym floor and buried his head in his hands. "I give," he mumbled.

Pepper puckered his lips. "What's wrong? You couldn't be tired this quick."

Hawk shrugged. "Guess I'm fighting a cold."

"For two weeks?"

"Maybe it's old age."

Pepper chuckled. "Come on," he nudged, extending a hand to help Hawk up. "What's wrong?"

"I'm just tired, okay?"

Pepper put his hand down and grimaced. "You're not mad at me are you? I requested you guys, but Isslan pulled rank."

Hawk shook his head as he slowly rose. "Naahh. It's not that. I'm just tired."

Pepper looked at his watch. "How about some coffee? You're due out in less than an hour."

"Phffffft."

They walked slowly out of the gym and down the hall. Pepper glanced over at Hawk. "Maybe you should check with Doc. You shouldn't be flying if you're sick."

"Yes, mother."

Pepper gave Hawk a shove. "You snap out of this or I ask Velter for a cure."

Hawk chuckled. "Okay. If I'm not feeling better tomorrow, I'll go see Doc."

They entered the cafeteria and walked toward the counter. Pepper grabbed Hawk and pulled him hard to the left as a plate sailed by.

"Shit," Hawk grumbled, wiping spattered potatoes off his jacket. "It's safer out there with the raiders."

"Especially if you were considering eating this stuff," Pepper snickered.

✦   ✦   ✦

"Hawk, punch! They got lock on ya from behind!" Angel's voice screamed at him through the radio.

"Huh?" Hawk shook his head a moment, then punched. The explosions sent Gracie reeling as she popped through.

"Are you okay?" Dervish asked, as he and Angel punched out behind him.

"Everything checks out," Hawk replied slowly. "Thanks. I just didn't notice 'em back there."

"Dammit, man, you just about got yourself killed again!" Angel scolded. "What's with you?"

"I'm fine. I just didn't see 'em, okay?" Hawk answered defensively.

"Hawk, take Gracie in," Dervish ordered.

"She's fine, Dervish, really she is." Hawk tried to sound convincing.

"It's not Gracie I'm worried about," Dervish responded. "Take her back now!"

"Fine!" Hawk shouted, as he punched.

The hurt and bitterness evident in Hawk's voice made Dervish feel awful. "Damn, I wish he'd open up about what's eating him!"

"He's gonna get hisself killed real good if we don't do something," Angel replied, sounding as guilty as Dervish felt. "Ever since he got back from Tazz's wedding he's been crazier'n a loon."

"You know, you're right. Think I'll take a hop down to base after we get back," Dervish replied.

Angel pondered. "Gonna pay Tazz a little unsocial visit?"

"Exactly. But first, I'm going to see what I can pry out of Gracie." Dervish paused a moment. "Think you can keep Hawk busy for about six hours?"

"I could sit on him."

"Might work."

"Angel," Goldie interrupted, "you might ask Hawk what the probabilities are that you could impregnate that Ulgorthan technician in group seven; it is a logical question, and the answer will take a number of hours to research."

"I hate to admit it, but that ain't a bad idea," Angel agreed a bit reluctantly. *Neither is impregnating that little tech*, he thought.

"Okay, punch for home, Angel," Dervish replied. "I'll be about fifteen minutes behind you. Make sure you have him off the flight deck by then."

"See what I can do."

✦   ✦   ✦

Dervish wandered into the base lounge, pulled up a chair, and sat down next to Tazz. "Tazz," he said firmly, "glad I found you. Hawk hasn't been himself since you brought him back. He's been moping around for weeks now. He won't talk about it, either."

"Perhaps he doesn't think it concerns you," the Vultarian flier seated next to Tazz stated flatly.

"It does when it affects his flying," Dervish replied hotly.

Tazz winced.

"We almost lost him twice now," Dervish grumbled. "I'm really worried."

Tazz looked depressed. "What can I do?"

"You could start by telling me exactly what happened. I got a fairly good idea from Gracie when I threatened to take her apart, but there are still a bunch of loose ends that need clearing up."

"If Hawk doesn't want to talk about it," Tazz responded gloomily, "I don't think he'd want me to tell you either."

"Look, I had to send him in today. Keeping him down for a few days. If we can't get him straightened out, and quick, I'm gonna have to ground him permanently," Dervish countered.

Tazz's gloom turned to defeat. "You shoulda been a damn lawyer. Okay; we'd better find a quiet place to talk."

Hawk sat brooding on his bed. Angel was doing his best to cheer him up when Dervish walked in. Hawk looked up and could tell from Dervish's expression that another round was about to begin. "C'mon, I don't need any more lectures," he pouted. "What I really need is to get flyin' again."

"You're right," Dervish agreed. "You need to go shanghai your lady friend."

Hawk winced. "I can't do that," he wailed. "Tazz's a fink! Damn you."

"I know how you feel," Dervish offered.

"No, you don't."

"What?" Angel said.

"Tazz's sister," explained Dervish. "Our boy's got it bad."

"If it was me," Angel sympathized, "I'd invite her here."

"She already refused to come," Hawk said despondently.

"So punch in there," Angel offered. "Tell her, 'pack your things, we're going'. If she gives you any hassle, I'll rope her. We could be back in ... eight, ten hours."

Hawk sighed. "I can't. She wouldn't come; she didn't even say goodbye. She *hates* me."

Dervish raised both eyebrows. "Look, maybe it was none of my business, but I had a talk with Tazz. He went home to check on her for you; got back this morning. He said she's not screaming and throwing things; she isn't even talking much. His parents say she's been acting just like you've been. Tazz is convinced she likes you a lot but she's too proud to admit it."

"I don't think so. Besides, I wouldn't know what to say," Hawk admitted glumly. "Gee, I was just in the neighborhood so I thought I'd drop in ..." He shook his head from side to side. "She wouldn't believe it."

"Bring her parents a present," Angel offered, "you know, a 'thank you for your hospitality' gift, and when they're feeling good about it, just sort of slip in the 'oh, by the way, I'm taking your daughter'."

"It's not her parents. And she won't come."

"Shit, if her parents agree, just throw her in Gracie and argue about it here," Angel concluded.

"Tazz said she's pretty small," Dervish mused, holding his hand up at about his own eye level.

"No!" said Hawk, his gloom having been replaced by panic.

"When are we up next?" Angel asked.

"Not until tomorrow night," Dervish answered, reading Angel perfectly. "Maybe we ought to think about this a bit, though."

"No! Jeez, you guys, she'd never speak to me again!" Hawk pleaded.

"You said she's not speaking to you anyway," Angel pointed out. "So, it's settled then?"

"Angel, I think ..." Dervish began.

"C'mon," Angel interrupted impatiently. "It'll only take a couple of hours. Be back before you know it, and ol' Hawk here will be back to normal in a jiffy. Hell, I can do it myself!"

Dervish glanced at Angel, then Hawk, but appeared to be lost in thought.

"Hey, this is not *funny*, guys," Hawk wailed helplessly.

"Don't worry, Hawk, I'll take good care of her. Dervish, you coming?" Angel asked, as he headed out the door.

"Dervish," Hawk begged, "can't you stop him? I think he's serious."

"You know, he may actually have an idea there," Dervish replied. "I'll lift your grounding; we'll all go, and you can talk this out. At least we'll have her outnumbered. Besides, you can't keep sitting here moping about the rest of your life."

"This is contemptible, Dervish," Hawk complained, as he followed the little man into the hall.

Dervish gave him a wry grin. "I prefer to think of it as an expedient solution to a difficult situation. I don't like it any better than you do," he said, as he turned and looked him straight in the eye, "but I sure hope you'd do the same for me."

Dervish quickened his pace to catch up to Angel. Hawk, resigned to his fate, did the same. As the three walked in silence, Hawk's melancholy gradually made way for a bit of eagerness to get back to flying, and by the time they reached the flight bay, Hawk actually wore a hint of a smile.

He patted Gracie on the side. "You can lower the steps now, Gracie," Hawk informed her. "I've been cleared to fly."

"I am sorry, Hawk," Gracie replied loudly, "but until your code is reactivated, I am not permitted to allow you access."

Hawk waited while Dervish walked over and climbed into Love. Dervish stuck his hand back out a few moments later, giving Hawk a high sign.

The access door swung open and the stairs gradually slid downward until they reached the floor. Hearing the reassuring clunk of the latch mechanism, Hawk climbed up, patted the flight computer, and began to strap in as Gracie raised the stairs. He closed the hatch and requested permission to launch. Bay Twelve appeared on his terminal; he gently guided Gracie toward it.

When the bay doors closed behind him, Gracie whispered, "I said that I was not permitted to allow you access. That was truthful, although not entirely accurate. I can take you anywhere, under any conditions, with no regard for access codes."

She paused, then added, "However, I would not recommend that you inform Dervish that I have managed to bypass his security devices; he will most probably make them more difficult to defeat."

Hawk laughed for the first time in weeks. "Gracie, I love you!"

✦ ✦ ✦

They punched out high over Vultaria and glided to within sighting distance of a large inter-galactic freighter that was holding orbit over the planet. Dervish noted the presence of its ID flag as he hailed it.

"Weather's fine in the Ulsted galaxy," he opened, "How's it where you come from?"

A low, but definitely female voice responded gruffly, "Who asked you?"

Dervish paused; *damn, that voice sounds familiar*. "Lacey?"

"Who wants to know?" the voice snapped back.

Dervish's eyes lit up. "Hey there, gorgeous. You haven't changed much."

"Well as I live and breathe," Lacey responded, though not quite as gruffly. "Dervish, you bean-headed little rascal; you planetside?"

"Got three little blips on your screen?"

"I ain't that dumb, Dervish," she chuckled. "I got a readout on them buggers; they're Fliers. Where the fuck *are* you?"

"Watch your screen," Dervish replied while he took Love straight up a kilometer, then back. "See me now?"

"Bless my soul; how'd you get into one of them things?"

"Been doing this almost five years now," Dervish replied. "It's a long story. Hawk, Angel ... meet an old friend of mine, Lacey."

"Howdy ma'am," Angel drawled.

"Hi," is all Hawk managed to think of.

"Afternoon, gents."

"Lacey's been a captain ... oh, probably a hundred years or something. Never lost a cargo yet," Dervish explained.

"How old you think I am, lad? I've only been doin' this about sixty," she chuckled. "I sure would love to hear that story of yours. I got plenty of time; still unloading, and on manual at that. If you have nothing better to do, get your cute little buns over here. I'll even buy the beer."

"Manual? What happened?"

"Couple squads of Rudonians tried to break my perfect record," she replied dryly. "If they was still alive they'd be regretting that decision now."

"Hey Hawk, you want us to go down with you for moral support," Dervish asked, "or just wait around up here?"

Hawk took a deep breath and pondered it. "Guess it's really something I gotta do by myself, isn't it?" he asked regretfully. The silence answered his question. "Might as well go do it then. You'll see what's left of me in an hour or so."

"Mind if I drop in on Lacey while you're planetside?"

"Be my guest," Hawk replied. He flew down into the atmosphere, changed frequencies and informed local control of his intended landing location. Once cleared, he dived.

"You wanna come?" Dervish asked Angel, as he watched Gracie drop from sight.

"Yeah, but who with?" Angel kidded him.

Dervish sighed. "Suit yourself. I'll only be about an hour." He banked Love and headed her toward the freighter.

"Prude," Angel muttered, as he fell in behind Dervish.

Hawk landed Gracie just west of Tazz's parent's house. Ninsse approached as he disembarked.

"Why did you come?" she asked him hostilely.

"I want to talk to you," he replied.

"There is nothing to say."

"Yes, there is," he stated firmly. "You started this, remember. I think we ought to try to work it out. I'm really not into one night stands."

"Just because you slept with me does not mean you *own* me!" she informed him acidly.

"I'm not trying to own you. I just want ... hell, I don't know what I want," he admitted reluctantly. "I miss you."

"I like you," she replied, "but I don't really know you either. Not well enough to get married."

"I didn't ask you to marry me," Hawk retorted, "just come back with me for a while. See what ..."

"Oh! So I'm good enough in bed, but marriage is different?"

"You're twisting everything around," he argued. He sat down on the grass and stared at it. "I would like to get to know you better. I've been thinking about you all the time. Nearly got myself killed a few ..."

"Just what I need! A lovesick puppy to watch over!"

"Young lady," Gracie's voice did not sound friendly. "My primary obligation is the protection of my Flier. If you are endangering him by diverting his concentration, I will be forced to eliminate you."

Ninsse's eyes widened. "It wouldn't dare," she squeaked, "would it?"

Hawk gave her a sly grin. "I wouldn't try to find out if I were you," he replied, playing the ace Gracie had given him.

"I'd like to get to know you, too," she admitted, gazing at Gracie. "But I don't want to commit to anything permanent."

"I didn't say you had to stay with me. Tazz said you could stay with Ming and him if you wanted."

"And?"

"And I could come see you when I get time off. You know, go out to dinner or something."

"How many other girls do you date?"

"None. Now."

"It had better stay that way," she threatened.

He shrugged his shoulders. "Fine with me," he muttered. "I guess we best go talk to your parents."

"We? If you want me to go with you, *you* talk to them," she mocked and stomped back toward to the house.

As Goldie glided onto the freighter's flight deck, Angel discovered that this was no ordinary ship; most freighters didn't house a dozen short range fighters. Too much weight to haul around when cargo was more profitable.

A short, thin, old woman in a black jump suit stood next to Dervish. She had long silver hair, but her most prominent feature was her enormous nose. She reminded Angel of a Halloween witch; all she needed was the pointed black hat and the broomstick. The way she looked at him as he disembarked gave him goosebumps.

"They don't make 'em like they used to," Lacey commented as Angel walked up next to Dervish.

Angel grunted, convinced he had just been insulted. Considering how she looked, he felt justifiably indignant.

"Shoot, looks more like a base ship than a freighter," Dervish agreed.

"Handles like a toilet, though," Lacey groused, as she ushered Dervish off the flight deck. She shot Angel a sideways glance. "Well, come on lad, the beer's getting warm."

Angel followed, pondering the possibility that his was the only mind that resided in the gutter.

Dervish seemed right at home in the control room. He took a beer from Lacey, sat down on the floor, and began to take the flight computer apart.

Lacey sat down on the floor near the navigation equipment, holding a beer out to Angel. He accepted it with a nod and remained standing a bit behind Dervish.

She looked at Angel and winked. "Contrary to what he's told ya," she said, pointing a thumb at Dervish, "I don't bite."

Angel felt his cheeks getting a bit warm. "I don't recall him sayin' that, exactly," he answered truthfully, as he found a piece of floor a couple of meters from her.

"Better not let her get too close to you," Dervish called over his shoulder, "she's Alderian and she's dangerous." He grinned as he returned to figuring out the computer system.

"Two compliments in one day," she laughed. "I'll have to go another fifty years to beat this record."

Lacey began to tell Angel some of the more amusing run-ins she'd had with the authorities and, after his third beer, Angel responded with some of his misadventures concerning the Texas Rangers and the APs. He was almost unhappy when Dervish stood and turned to face them.

"Well, I got it as good as I can without parts. I rerouted the surveillance networks to the punch circuitry and the flight tracking networks to the weapons system."

"Bless ya," said Lacey; she actually sounded sincere. "With that, I can get this bathtub to a reasonable port for repairs. They really see ya comin' around here."

"Any time, Lacey," Dervish replied.

"Dervish," she said in a low voice, "those Rudonians I ran into? Heading for a housewarming party over on Siddemac."

"That's Ketherian territory," Angel commented.

"Yeah; the Rudonians weren't too thrilled when they declared independence," Lacey continued.

Dervish raised an eyebrow. "Hadn't heard about that."

"My, my, child, where've you been? The Ketherians have been trying to hold off the Rudonians with a few thousand poorly armed troops. They've been requesting recognition, but so far the Council won't even acknowledge 'em."

Angel looked at Lacey, then Dervish, who mirrored his look of astonishment.

"You should pay more attention to what goes on in that circus you call the United Council," Lacey observed as she stood, brushing off her jump suit. "Blecch, I hate 'em all!"

"We make it almost a religion to stay out of politics," Dervish reminded her.

"I know, child," she replied, as she pinched his butt, "that's why it's still attached."

Dervish gave her an unsettled look. "I think we'd better be going, Lacey. It wouldn't do your reputation much good to be caught hanging out with the riff-raff."

Angel joined the ensuing laughter as he stood up, looking around for a place to put his empties. He settled on the edge of the console next to Dervish's. "Thank you, ma'am," he said.

"Lacey," she corrected, with a you're-welcome nod. She escorted them back to the flight deck and shook Angel's hand. "Glad to have met ya, lad. Keep an eye on my little man here, 'cause it's a sure bet he don't look after himself."

"I'll try, ma'am ... Lacey," Angel promised, "but if you want the truth of it, I reckon he's mostly lookin' after me."

Having returned to stationary orbit waiting for Hawk, Angel figured he knew why Dervish liked Lacey; probably the same reason he did. The problem was, he'd be damned if he could figure out exactly what that reason was.

"Hope you guys haven't been too bored," Hawk said, as Gracie approached within hailing range.

"No problem," Dervish replied, "but if you're ready to go home now, we'd be real pleased to break orbit."

"I was beginning to feel like the fourth moon around here," Angel commented dryly, as he looked at the time.

"Dervish, could we punch back to base before returning to the station?" Hawk asked. "I kinda have a hitchhiker here."

"Sure," Dervish laughed, "I was going to suggest the same thing, but for other reasons."

Hawk punched, then Dervish. Angel sat there a moment, "Well, jeez, you're welcome, guys," he said to himself. "Great idea you had there, Angel. Any time, guys. Bah!"

"Luck," Goldie commented.

Angel punched.

While Hawk brought Ninsse to Tazz's quarters, Dervish and Angel paid Sparks a visit. Sparks was not pleased that the Council might be ignoring the Ketherians' request for Flier protection. He told them he would speak to the Old Man about the situation.

"Just who is the Old Man? And how is he going to convince the Council to change its mind?" Angel asked.

Sparks looked at Dervish disparagingly. "Don't you tell your wingmates anything besides the location of their next meal?" he teased. "I suppose I should have realized that Dervish doesn't consider anything besides his Bird and his stomach all that important. What has he told you about the Fliers?"

"Only that we gotta maintain our own Bird," Angel replied slowly, trying to remember whether Dervish had mentioned anything else. "And we don't have to accept an assignment if we object to the intended result."

Sparks chuckled. "Okay. The main thing to remember is that the Fliers' charter clearly set us up as an independent, private, peacekeeping force with no allegiance to any particular faction. Sort of contract protection.

"The Old Man is Nathan ... you and Hawk met him at your recruitment, if you recall. He's the only member of the Fliers that has to speak to the Council; no one else wants to anyway. Nathan and Threenica keep track of mundane things like the payroll and balancing the budget, and they coördinate Mother's database of the known worlds and peoples. Most importantly, they make these kind of decisions.

"The Council has a bad habit of thinking they own us simply because they contracted with us for protection. It falls on Nathan to remind the Council that they have nothing to say about what we decide to do."

"What will Nathan do about the Ketherian situation?" Angel asked, when Sparks finished explaining.

"He'll check out the facts," Sparks replied. "If it's true, he'll have Mother send out a scramble to their sector. If the Council doesn't like that, he'll probably tell 'em to cram it."

"My kind of guy," Angel agreed.

Dervish looked a bit sheepish as he and Angel walked back to the air field. "Guess I should have told you and Hawk all that stuff, huh?"

Angel gave him a sidelong glance. "It might have made things a lot clearer. Somehow, I keep trying to relate things to how they work back home. A lot of things didn't add up."

"Well, you should have just asked," Dervish responded defensively. "I can't read your mind ya know."

Angel started to smile. "I thought that was one of your Talents," he spoofed.

Dervish put on a wicked face. "And what will you pay me to keep your thoughts to myself?" he asked elusively.

Angel let the whole subject drop.

Hawk was waiting by Gracie when they arrived. Angel told him what Sparks had said about the Fliers and what Lacey had said about the Ketherians.

They punched back to the space station and headed for Dervish's room, under the guise of pondering the situation. Once there, however, Angel had other things on his mind.

"Well, what really happened down there?" he asked Hawk. "I'm dying of curiosity."

Hawk looked blankly at both of them. "I dropped Ninsse at Tazz's. She can help with the baby."

"Not down *there*, dummy," Angel said in mock exasperation.

"I'll never tell," Hawk replied matter-of-factly.

"Dervish, read his mind," Angel said, only half teasing.

Dervish made a grand show of walking over and putting both of his hands on Hawk's head. He closed his eyes and scrunched up his face. "Oh my!" he exclaimed. "Hawk, you ought to be ashamed of yourself!"

"Now, cut that out," Hawk admonished him jokingly.

Angel looked at Dervish, then at Hawk. "Well ... what happened?"

Dervish tried hard to keep a straight face. "Censored," he managed to say before bursting out in laughter.

Hawk looked at his obviously frustrated friend. "Thanks, Angel," he told him sincerely. "I never would have done it without your prodding. All in all, it wasn't as bad as I thought it would be. Actually," he said, pondering a bit, "I think it was Gracie that finally convinced her."

"How so?" Dervish pressed.

"Gracie told her that if she continued to distract me, she would be forced to eliminate the source of the distraction," Hawk chuckled.

Dervish winced. "I really gotta fix those circuits. I doubt she would have done it, but ..."

"Don't touch a node," Hawk interrupted. "I'm very fond of her at the moment."

They headed down to dinner in good spirits.

Nathan looked over the data and tossed it back to Threenica. "Contact the Ketherian defense minister. Inform him a number of guests will be arriving."

Threenica raised his eyebrows. "What do I tell the Council? They'll find out eventually, and our contract renewal is in severe debate already. Antagonizing them with our complete disregard of their wishes never goes over real big."

Nathan pondered a moment. "Oh, uhh ... tell 'em the Fliers are throwing a benefit for ... underprivileged worlds. That ought to keep those wimps happy."

"What if they ask where we're holding it?"

"Ask 'em to buy tickets," Nathan shot back, "watch how quick they change the subject."

Threenica was chuckling openly as he left the room. He walked briskly down the hall toward the comm center. Once there, he formally advised the Council of the Fliers' latest philanthropic activity in his most business-like manner.

It was around twenty hundred when the alert came through. All available and willing Fliers were to report to sector seventeen of the Siddemac galaxy; code name: "Air Show".

The yellow alert went off in the Ketherian space station when its tracking equipment picked up numerous objects punching into range. Pilots were scrambling for their fighters when the Fliers identified themselves, requesting permission to land.

Squad after squad of Fliers disembarked on the flight deck, welcomed by a cheering staff of seven flight engineers and twenty-three pilots. They didn't have long to organize; in fact, most didn't get a chance to meet their hosts formally before the show got underway.

✦ ✦ ✦

Nathan seemed very pleased when Threenica gave him the report. After five days of hostilities, the Rudonians left the sector and seemed inclined to remain departed.

"The damage report is better than expected," Threenica informed him. "The Fliers assigned the Ketherian pilots to atmosphere only, keeping the Ketherian losses to a minimum. Only nine of their fighters and two of their pilots were lost; another six needed hospitalization."

"How did we fare?" Nathan asked.

"Seven Birds were trashed," Threenica admitted, "but only three Fliers needed serious treatment. There were the usual assorted minor injuries; a few days' rest should have everyone back to normal." He looked at Nathan trying to read him, then added. "How about our casualty report in the battle with the Council?"

"They're wetting their pants," he chuckled. "Seems the Rudonians are complaining bitterly that we fired on their helpless hordes of fighters and base ships that were just paying a social call on the Ketherians."

"Awwwww. And?" Threenica prodded him.

"And I think you best do a dump on all our accounts," Nathan replied sadly, "see how long we can meet payroll."

"They broke the contract?"

"Well, you can guess what they expect in exchange for continuing it. I haven't responded."

"Playing poker again?"

"I figure if we pull the Fliers back to the less developed galaxies," Nathan informed him, "the Rudonians and other assorted pirates will take advantage of the situation."

"How much do I have to scrape up?"

Nathan pondered. "Four months' worth would do it, but see what's available."

"Four months!" Threenica muttered to himself, as he stomped down the hall toward Mother. "What does he take me for, a miracle worker?"

Threenica's return trip was far more animated. "Look at this," he practically screamed at Nathan as he shoved the printout into his face, "and it's *real*! I checked it out with the bank and the brokerage!"

Nathan looked at the printout for a while, then sat down. He studied it again. "I just don't understand this at all, Threenica," he finally said. "Can you please explain what this account is?"

"I don't understand it either," Threenica apologized, "but somehow Mother invested heavily in the commodities markets twelve years ago, and did so for three consecutive years. Quite profitably. I can't even figure out where she got the funds. Or the programming."

"Go on," Nathan encouraged.

"After three years of doubling her money, she reinvested the returns in high tech stocks. This account was opened, and all the dividend checks have been auto-deposited." He looked at Nathan sheepishly. "Since the checks didn't cross my desk and I never had a reason to do a complete dump before, I didn't even know it existed."

"You verified this? The bank, the brokerages, Mother's data records?" Nathan inquired. "I mean, you positively dug deep enough to *know* it's real? Absolutely sure?"

"Yes," Threenica replied nervously. "It's our account."

"Hmmm," Nathan chuckled, "if we were to run this outfit conservatively, we could probably make budget on the interest of this account alone."

"Plus," Threenica offered excitedly, noting Nathan wasn't angry at his oversight in bookkeeping, "we also have the investment itself paying a sixteen percent return. That adds to the principal, giving us more interest."

"Listen, I want you to hire the best weapons experts and get them rolling. We need phasors and we need them as soon as possible! It'll take months to get something usable into the field."

"To do that we'll have to dip into the principal," Threenica reminded him.

"I don't care if we have to use it all," Nathan replied. "I want those boys as safe as we can get them."

Threenica started for the door. "I'll get right on it."

"Oh, one more thing. See if you can figure out where the funds for the original investments came from," Nathan snickered. "But even more importantly, now I can tell the Council to ... cram it." Noting Threenica's expression, he added, "I could say it more nicely, if you really think I should."

"No," Threenica replied, with a smirk, "it would lose something if it wasn't delivered properly."

As Threenica left the room, Nathan looked up. "I don't know how you did it, Sir, but I'll never doubt your existence again." He placed the printout in the top desk drawer and left the room. He whistled a rowdy old tune as he headed toward the landing field.

12

Should Auld Acquaintance Be Forgot

All participants in 'Operation Air Show' received ten days of R & R. Before going on leave, Dervish, Hawk and Angel punched back to home base to facilitate repairs to the damage their fighters had received. They were talking about spending the time fishing when Rusty and Ninsse walked into the repair bay. Angel excused himself, feeling that he would be as welcome as chickenpox under the same conditions.

He headed toward the shuttle bay and happened to see Sparks helping another squad of Fliers repair their fighters. He wandered over and asked Sparks if he happened to know a good place to go fishing.

Sparks thought a moment and nodded. He steered Angel out of earshot of the other Fliers. "I know this great spot," he whispered. "Real quiet, crystal clear water, huge fish and beautiful, too. No one goes there," he added honestly.

"Sounds great," Angel replied. "Where is it?"

"Venlen galaxy, sector forty-one, a small planet out fifth from its star," Sparks told him confidentially. "I'll feed the coördinates over to your Bird in a little while. Wouldn't want too many folks to find out."

"Thanks," Angel told him. "I owe you one!"

Sparks grinned as Angel walked off. *No*, he thought gleefully. *Now we're even.*

As Angel walked back to where Goldie was hangared, Isslan flagged him down. "Would you guys be able to take me to a Hank Junior concert? I don't think I could make it too good on your planet by myself."

"Well, we were ..." Angel started to reply.

"I could take you on a tour of my planet afterwards," Isslan added, noticing the doubt on Angel's face. "We've got great looking girls!"

"Hmmm," Angel replied, thinking about it. "Well, we were going to go fishing, but then Rusty and Ninsse showed up. I probably wouldn't have much fun being the fifth wheel."

"Maybe the girls would like a concert better than fishing," Isslan offered.

"Shhhh," Angel cautioned, "don't even mention it. We'd just end up having to schlep them along!"

Angel had little trouble talking the foursome into going fishing without him. He told Dervish he'd heard of this great fishing spot and fed him the punch coördinates Sparks had sent to Goldie. He assured them that he and Isslan would find something harmless to occupy their time on Isslan's home planet. That wasn't a direct lie, Angel rationalized, since they fully intended to visit Isslan's planet right after the concert.

The half hour wait for landing clearance on Isslan's home planet of Jartasver was almost pleasurable compared to the frustration of trying unsuccessfully to get concert tickets. It had never occurred to Angel that entertainers occasionally take a bit of R & R themselves.

Once they finally landed, they made straight for the hotel Isslan had selected and rented two large connecting rooms for the week.

After putting his few things away, Angel took a long soak in the wading-pool-sized tub. He put on some fairly clean clothes and walked over to the open partitioning door.

"I'm getting hungry," he yelled.

"Are you decent yet?" Isslan shouted back.

"If I can't eat 'til I'm decent," Angel wailed, "I'll starve to death!"

"Let me rephrase that," Isslan spoofed, as he walked into Angel's room. "Would your mother approve if a friend of yours was dressed that way?"

Angel looked himself over critically. "No," he admitted truthfully, "but my mother would find fault with the way God was dressed."

"Mothers are all the same," Isslan agreed.

"I think God musta got caught in a rut."

"Girls are great," Isslan pondered, "but once they become mothers ..."

"They become *mothers*," Angel finished. "Let's go eat."

They walked to a nice restaurant to get dinner and, with any luck, pick up some girls. They sat down at a corner table and had just begun to look over the menu when a girl Angel judged to be about thirteen approached and seated herself next to him, looked him over carefully, then nodded.

"My name's Twink, handsome," she cooed coquettishly. "What's yours?"

Angel raised an eyebrow. "Angel," he said, then pointed across the table, "and that fine-looking gentleman is Isslan."

Twink winked at him. "Going to be in town long?"

Angel gave her a hard look, wondering just how many days it had been since her thirteenth birthday. "Look, kid," he said softly, "It's pretty late. Won't your folks be worried about you?"

She made a nasty face. "I don't live with them any more," she replied curtly.

The waitress walked up to take the order and did a double take. "Isslan!" she exclaimed. "When did you get in?"

"Few hours ago," he replied with a grin. "I was going to give you a call tomorrow afternoon."

"You're just saying that," she teased. "Bet you don't even remember my name."

"Lorna," he replied artfully.

"He read it on your badge," Twink noted. She looked at Angel knowingly. "You, on the other hand, would have remembered."

Lorna ignored Twink's comment and smiled back at Isslan. "Can I get you something?" she asked him, her tone implying far more than the words alone conveyed.

"Fish," he said with a wink, then looked at Angel.

Angel figured the twerp must be hungry. If he ran her off, she'd just try to pick up some other guy. *Damn poor way to stave off starvation*, he thought. "Hungry?" he asked her nicely.

"Starved," she replied.

Angel looked at Twink. "Well, order something." Then, noting her expression, he continued, "I'm buying."

Twink ordered a complete dinner and a glass of milk.

"Coffee," Angel told Lorna, as she looked at him, "and whatever he's having."

"You sure it's okay if I eat?" Twink asked Angel politely. "I mean if you don't have enough money ..."

Angel smiled at her. "It's okay. I just got paid." He looked over at Isslan, and continued. "I'm going to the little boys' room; be right back."

"I'll hold the sector," Isslan replied.

As Angel walked away, Twink looked at Isslan. "What's wrong with your friend? He's acting like I'm a kid."

Isslan stifled a laugh. "I'll bet he thinks you are," he chuckled. "I didn't see any Pixies on his home world." He reflected a moment, then continued. "A lot of strange folk, but no Pixies."

Twink wrinkled her nose. "What d'ya say we pull his chain a while?" she giggled. "I'd sure like to make his night."

Isslan decided that Angel might like what she had to offer and, besides, it would be a great joke. "Okay," he agreed. "I'll invite you over after dinner. After that, you're on your own."

Twink nodded, crossed her legs, and put on an innocent face. Both of them burst out laughing.

Lorna came back and set the milk and coffee on the table. "I get off in about hour," she informed Isslan pointedly.

"It could take me that long to eat," Isslan replied, "if you'd care to join us."

"Then you didn't have a date for tonight?" Lorna asked, giving Twink a smug look.

"I was just going to go back to the hotel and straight to bed," he replied innocently.

Angel walked up, and, catching the last sentence, his eyes lit up. "My plans exactly," he commented as he sat down, "but my plans always go awry."

As Lorna went back to work, Isslan looked over at Angel. "Lorna's going to come over for a bit. Maybe we should take the kid along, keep her off the street, watch a movie or something," he said, without really making eye contact.

Angel shrugged, then muttered, "I don't care."

Twink gave him big smile. "Thanks," she said sweetly.

After they finished eating, they talked while they sat around waiting for Lorna. Angel was impressed at how intelligent and well informed Twink seemed to be. When Lorna's shift was finished, Angel paid the bill and they all walked back to the hotel.

Isslan brought them all into his room and punched up a movie. Lorna curled up next to Isslan on his bed, Twink made herself at home in the chair, and Angel sat on the floor.

About halfway through the movie, Twink complained she was tired, so Angel said he'd take her home. As they walked down the hallway, she implied that she had no home to go to. Angel, not wanting a kid to sleep on the street, reluctantly brought her to his room. As he started to leave, she gave him a real strange look.

"I think those two would rather you didn't go back," she informed him softly.

Angel pondered that a moment and had to concede she had a point. "We might as well go to sleep," he commented, as he lay down on the bed. Then, noticing that she was undressing, quickly added, "Hey, keep your clothes on!"

Twink gave him a sassy look. "Most folks get undressed to take a shower," she replied, as she stalked off toward the bathroom.

Angel fell asleep before she returned. He startled awake when a warm body cuddled up to him. "Uhh, kid, move over."

"I'm as close as I can get," she whispered.

"You know what I mean," he replied in an exasperated tone. "Now be a good girl, okay?"

"I'm always good."

Angel sighed deeply. "Look, if you move over right now, I'll take you any place you want to go tomorrow."

"Will you take me to the circus?" she asked hesitantly.

"Sure, now move over."

"I told you," she cooed, "I can't get any closer."

Angel looked at her hopelessly. "What the hell do you want now?"

"You," she replied teasingly.

"Go to sleep," Angel said sternly, "before I decide to put you over my knee."

"Mmmm ... now that's one way I haven't tried before," she admitted enthusiastically.

"Oh, jeez!" Angel muttered. He got out of bed and flopped himself into the chair to sleep.

She got him up at six AM, reminding him of his promise, and he reluctantly staggered to the bathroom to splash cold water on his face and brush his teeth.

Isslan did not answer when Angel gave a few soft knocks on his door, so he scribbled him a note and then unhappily went with Twink. She hailed a hovercab and gave the driver directions as they got in.

"You know where we're going?" he asked.

Oh boy, she thought, *where is this dude from, anyhow*? "The circus," she responded with obvious irritation.

"What I meant was: how do you know where it's at?"

"I work there," she replied flatly.

Angel looked at her oddly. He had a sinking feeling that something was going on that he didn't understand. "Oh," was all he managed to say.

The driver let them off in front of the main tent. Although it was barely six thirty, the circus people were up and about. Most of them were gathered around a table where breakfast was being served. After he paid the driver, Twink took him by the hand to get breakfast.

A large man looked at Twink and shook his head. "Ain't he a little young for you, Twink?" he snapped as she got within earshot.

"I *like* 'em young," she retorted. "They don't have no bad habits and they don't fall asleep as fast."

Angel felt the heat in his cheeks and knew he was blushing. *Damn, how do I get into these things*? he thought. He zipped up his jacket for something to do.

The man chuckled, noting Angel's blush."You don't seem to have any habits at all. Name's Tiny," he offered, putting out his hand. "Just shout when you want to get rescued; me and a few other guys will come haul her off of you."

Angel shook the man's hand."Angel," he said, He felt he ought to say something in his own defense, and real soon. "Look, she said she had no place to sleep last night, and I couldn't let a kid sleep on the street, so ..."

"Kid?" Tiny burst out laughing. He looked at Angel closely, then eyed Twink disdainfully. "Pulling that on a Flier! You ought to be ashamed of yourself, Twink!"

Twink squeezed Angel's hand. Angel was now completely sure he missed the boat somewhere.

"Well, I was going to tell him," she said, "but he was acting so funny thinking I was a kid, I didn't think he would believe me."

Angel stared at Twink. She smiled beguilingly; he sighed.

"I'm a Pixie," she informed him. "Look, let's just gather up some breakfast and I'll show you around."

Angel raised an eyebrow at her and looked at Tiny for some confirmation of this announcement.

"She's a Pixie, all right," Tiny agreed.

Twink looked at Angel and grinned. "*Told* you," she said.

"Remember son, just holler if she gets out of hand," Tiny offered. He walked away chuckling.

They gathered up some food, then she took him around introducing him to everyone. After a few more comments on him being too young for her, Angel asked the inevitable. "How old are you, anyway?" Noting her sour expression, he added, "It doesn't matter much, but I'm curious how far off I was."

"Well, what did you think?" she asked, leading him into another tent.

"About thirteen," he said, looking about and realizing quickly that this tent had no one else in it.

"Triple that and you're close," she replied, pulling him down on a pile of furs.

"I don't believe ..." he started to say, but her kisses spoke of experience she could not have accrued in thirteen years. She unzipped his jacket and ran her hands up under his shirt. He decided he wasn't going to call for Tiny. At least not yet.

She reached over the furs, grabbed a small flask and offered him some. "Trust me?" she asked innocently.

"Should I?" Angel asked as he sniffed the contents. It had a faint aroma vaguely reminiscent of peaches.

She took a slug herself and offered it to him again. This time he relented. She put it back and began to unbutton his shirt. He started to object, but her kisses made him forget why.

The sun had set before Angel stumbled out of the tent and flagged down a driver. He left Isslan a message at the hotel, then headed for the airfield to check on extending his leave.

He barely had the strength to climb into his Bird. As he slumped into the seat, Goldie scanned him critically.

"What have you been up to, Angel?" she chided him. "Your bioreadings are very unstable."

"Check with Mother for me, Goldie," he replied, ignoring her comment. "See if I can get another four days leave."

"One moment; checking," she snapped. "Mother approved four extra days," she continued in an annoyed tone of voice. "I suppose you need them to recuperate from whatever you have been doing these last two days."

"Not two days, only one," he corrected her. "And not to recuperate; I'm going back for more."

"If this is one day's worth," she observed, "You will never survive another nine."

"But what a way to go!" he kidded.

Goldie thought about that for some time after he left.

Sparks wandered into the repair bay where Hawk and Dervish were working on Love. He stopped halfway across the bay and gasped for air. "Oh, shit!" he exclaimed, "Angel didn't say anything about taking you guys fishing with him!"

Dervish and Hawk both turned, glaring down at him with murder in their eyes. "*You?*" Dervish shouted. "You rotten, no good, son of a ..."

"Dervish, honest! I *swear* I didn't know you were going!" Sparks interrupted him. "Damn, I thought you knew about that spot; it's the joke of the universe."

"Yeah, some joke," Dervish shot back at him. "Killer about lived up to his name when he got a whiff of Rusty."

"Rusty?" Sparks repeated unhappily.

"And Tazz wouldn't even let Ninsse into the house," Hawk added, "she's staying with Rusty."

"Her too?" Sparks asked forlornly. "God, I didn't realize. Angel?" he asked, a trace of hope in his voice.

They shook their heads. "He didn't go. It was just us four," Dervish told him, "and an entire family of stinky bears." He made a silly face. "Rusty was pretty cool until one of them furries started getting curious. She shrieked, it sprayed, and I thought I was gonna pass out!"

"Do you think the girls will ever talk to us again?" Hawk lamented. "They sure were mad when we dropped 'em off."

"Not if we're lucky," Dervish replied. "They stunk pretty bad, that's for sure; made my eyes water."

"You guys don't smell any better," Sparks admitted as he turned to leave. "I got to get some air!"

"If you don't tell Killer, I will!" Dervish threatened.

"I was heading there now," Sparks promised.

"Hey," Dervish added, "how do we get rid of this stink?"

"Burn everything and pray," he shouted from the bay door. "And don't come near my house!"

"Hey," Hawk called after him, "when will it dissipate?"

"About three weeks," Sparks chuckled, "if you're lucky!"

✦   ✦   ✦

Five Fliers walked slowly into the repair bay. "Dervish," one shouted. "Come on down here a minute. We have to talk to you." He wrinkled his nose and continued, "Aaak! On second thought, stay up there. You've been fishing!"

Dervish looked down and noted from the Fliers' faces that something rather strange had happened. "What's wrong, Reilly?" he asked as he started to climb down the catwalk.

"No offense, but really, stay up there," Reilly called up to him as the other four Fliers turned and walked out of the bay. "Sorry to bother you, but we were on patrol when twenty PRO-fighters punched in. They got the drop on us. Had us cold. Man, I thought we were dead."

The look on his face told Dervish he was telling the truth. "Damn! They've never attacked Fliers before ... not openly anyhow. What were they up to?"

"They didn't fire, just made radio contact. They gave us a message. For you." Reilly looked awful. "They must still think you're Alderian," he added apologetically.

"What did they say?" Dervish was curious. "I'm not buying them sending twenty PROs just to say 'hello'."

"It isn't in Common; I can't understand it." Reilly gave Dervish a weak smile. "I got the guy to repeat it. Saved it to the flight log. I think you better take a listen."

Dervish started down the catwalk again, but Reilly held up his hand. "No, stay there. I'll dump it to Love," he called, as he started out of the bay. "Sorry, but you guys *really* stink!"

Dervish sighed and climbed into Love to receive the dump.

Reilly called to him over the radio. "I got my wingmates here; would you mind telling us what's going on?"

Dervish started the playback then stopped it. "It's in Alderian," he responded. "From the guy I stayed with when I was with them. He's like the Guardians' equivalent of Nathan. I worked on his private fighter and he left me alone."

"So what did he have to say that was worth scaring us half to death?" one of Reilly's wingmates asked.

"Should I just paraphrase or ..." Dervish began.

"I ruined a good pair of pants over this," Reilly laughed. "Give it to me verbatim!"

Dervish restarted the dump, translating as it ran. "Little One," he said, cleared his throat, then continued. "I wondered what became of you after you stole that fighter."

Dervish paused the dump and grinned. "Nothing much that Alderians do gets by Michelli."

He resumed the dump. "Word came that you are among the Fliers. I regret that you have chosen to stay, but you are still young. I am confident that, should you live to grow up, you will recognize that your place is with your people."

Dervish once again stopped the dump. "Arrogant bastard always tries to psyche ya out." Then he started it again.

"That is not the reason for this message. It has come to my attention that the Rudonians are planning to attack a large number of outposts and settlements. As I am sure you would recognize, this would be bad for business. However, it would be inexpedient to send the Guardians against them at this time, as there is the matter of an agreement.

"Those you fly with have no such agreement, and are free to defend these places if they wish. I have seen their plans and can transfer the information to you. I give you my word, Alderian to Alderian, that you have safe passage both ways. You know where to come. Please come alone. I do not give my word for another. Michelli."

Dervish stopped the dump. "That's all he wrote!"

Hawk was shaking his head. "Don't do it Dervish! You're not Alderian. If they figure that out, man, you're dead!"

"And if I *don't* go," Dervish replied, "we won't find out what they know." Noting that Hawk was not convinced, Dervish continued. "Hey, if they just wanted me dead, they'd have sent those twenty PROs after me and Love."

"They'd have twenty less PROs," Reilly came back quickly.

"Damn, I wish!" Dervish got out of Love and headed down the catwalk.

Sparks was almost as reluctant to allow Dervish to take the risk as he was glad to get him out of his office. However, he did not forbid him from going. He figured the Alderians wouldn't keep him too long, considering his present fragrance.

Dervish told him that when he had the information, he would punch back to station nine, that being the closest to the Alderian galaxy, and dump whatever he found out to Mother. He asked Sparks to be standing by to receive it.

Hawk was a bit harder to convince, but all in all he handled it fairly well. The only visible evidence of his displeasure was the dent in his door where he had tried to ram his fist through.

Dervish punched out just above atmosphere and glided Love down. He switched to the private hailing frequency he remembered and requested permission to land in his most offhanded style. There was a pregnant pause before a familiar voice responded.

"Dervish! So nice of you to call in so promptly," Michelli said, "and on my personal hailing frequency, too."

"I thought you might appreciate that," Dervish replied. "Besides, I'm not very fond of getting shot at."

"I gave you my word, lad." Michelli's voice had an edge to it. "I would be deeply hurt to think you didn't trust me."

"I'm here, ain't I?"

"I am well aware that you're here," Michelli baited him. "I did so appreciate you leaving your calling card with Lacey."

Dervish wasn't sure just what Michelli's game was at the moment. He kept his mind linked with Love for any sign of tampering. "Where did you want me to set this Bird down?" Dervish decided to try to force the man's hand. "Should I just set her down where you used to land 'em late at night?"

Michelli's voice lost some of its edge. "Within ten meters of that would be fine."

"What do I get if I'm right on the nose?" Dervish asked.

"What ever you'd like," Michelli responded pleasantly.

"I'd *like* to be leaving here, instead of just arriving!" Dervish pointed out with a great deal of emphasis.

Michelli started laughing. "You were always extremely honest. Some thought to a fault. Personally, I prefer a person I can trust. I will dispense with the formalities and send you on your way as quickly as possible. Providing, of course, that you're on the nose!"

"I knew there'd be a catch in there somewhere," Dervish returned the tease.

After he landed, Dervish climbed down from the cockpit and gazed at the huge beast that had been set into the ground in colored tiles. Love was indeed resting right on its nose.

Michelli started to walk up to him, then stopped. He waved his hand in front of his nose and wrinkled up his face in an awful expression. "You've been to Paradise I see," he said, then added, "or smell."

"Paradise?"

"That's what the original explorers named it," Michelli explained. "That was before they discovered the bears." He turned his gaze to the fighter. "Speaking of noses, you landed right on it."

Love pulled down from her normal neural routing to avoid Michelli's gentle probe. "Please keep your mind to yourself," she said indignantly.

"Love," Dervish chided her, "stop showing off." He turned back to Michelli. "Hey, I burned everything I was wearing and I've bathed at least fifty times. It's almost gone now."

"No; you've simply gotten used to it," Michelli noted. "Please be a good lad and stand downwind. *Far* downwind!" He motioned toward the fighter. "You were always the best at modifying them," he commented pointedly.

"Yeah," Dervish responded, "but I never got around to teaching her manners."

Michelli laughed again. "I hadn't realized how much I miss that wit of yours. I have never met anyone quite like you."

"That is because you only meet Alderians," Love argued.

"Love!" Dervish cut her off. "Please stop talking!"

"No, no, my boy. Don't shut it up; it seems to have a number of interesting things to say." Michelli stared hard at Dervish. "Are all the Fliers' fighters like this one?"

"No." Dervish was relieved that Michelli asked a question that could be answered honestly. "I've been playing around with personalities. I was in the middle of installing a new network when your invitation arrived. I think she still needs a few tweaks." He started to walk away, but Michelli put out a hand.

"What was it that you didn't you want that fighter to tell me?" he asked coldly.

"He is not Alderian." Love answered flippantly.

"You've given it a charming personality."

Dervish pulled off his flight helmet, placing his hand over his face. "Shit. Put it on my epitaph."

"What are you talking about?" Love questioned. "Epitaphs are for dead people. You are not dead, Dervish."

"Well, I'm about to be."

"I fail to understand." Love sounded confused. "They gave their word that you would not be harmed."

"Yeah. Alderian to Alderian," he reminded her.

"But once you give your word, you cannot retract it," Love continued to argue. "It is not logical."

Michelli seemed amused for the moment. "You must admit, it has a point." He studied Dervish carefully. "Why did you come if you think so little of me?"

"I really don't know," Dervish admitted. "Damn, I wish that chatterbox was in manual."

"Why not do that then?"

"Ummm, I kinda have that circuit apart at the moment."

Michelli nodded. "I see. Well, try to convince it to behave while we attend to business." He started toward the house, then turned back to Dervish and winced. "Please go with Reynard when you enter; I don't want that odor in my study."

Dervish took a moment to merge with Love and impress upon her the seriousness of her actions. He demanded that she make no move that could be interpreted as hostile unless directed to do so by him. He was vaguely aware of another presence in the circuitry with him, but he ignored it.

Michelli walked into the house and motioned to a lean, dignified looking old man. "Reynard," he chuckled, "Dervish has been to Paradise. Please see to his deodorizing. And do burn everything he's wearing!" He walked to his study, sat down and burst out laughing.

Dervish trailed Michelli at a respectful distance, As he approached the house, he was waylaid by Reynard. "You are to follow me," Reynard informed him dryly, holding his nose for emphasis. The old man escorted Dervish to a back bathroom and gave him a large vial of some odd smelling blue-green liquid. "Rub this on you everywhere," Reynard told him stiffly. "Let it dry, then use lots of soap to get it off. Call me if you need more." He handed Dervish two large towels and a clean set of clothes, then turned leave. "Try not to get any on the floor," he called back. "It mars the finish."

Whatever was in the vial stung like crazy, but it was fast drying and relief was just a tub of water away. Reluctantly, he put on the clothes Reynard had given him. They were the Alderian equivalent of Fliers' garb, and he noted the rank of captain on the sleeve. He felt funny wearing the clothes that signified membership in the association he had so meticulously avoided the whole time he had stayed with Michelli. But it was wear them or nothing; he decided to wear them.

He walked into the study and nodded to Michelli, seating himself in a large chair in front of the fireplace.

"Not a trace of stinky bear on you," Michelli noted with pleasure. "Hmmm, you do look nice in green," he added, looking Dervish over. "It suits you much better than that drab gray they dress you in."

"It does *smell* better," Dervish admitted, "but I prefer the outfit I came in."

"It will have to be burnt," Michelli informed him casually, "the odor does not come out of fabric." He studied Dervish as he continued. "I must admit, I was hoping you had acquired a taste for green."

"Since when?"

"Always," Michelli replied candidly; then. noting Dervish's puzzled expression, he continued. "When you left your calling card with Lacey, I thought perhaps you wished to return. And yes, I already knew there wasn't much Alderian in you. It would be nice to know what you are, though."

Dervish wrinkled his brow while scrunching up his nose.

Michelli walked over and drew up a second chair. "Would you care for a drink, or do you still prefer milk?"

"Milk's fine."

Michelli called through the intercom; Reynard came and took the order. They sat in silence, each waiting for the other to begin. Reynard returned with a pitcher of milk and two glasses. Michelli motioned to Dervish to pour the milk. Dervish grinned.

As they drank their milk, Michelli started to chuckle. "You haven't got a whisker nor a hankering to grow up. Perhaps I played my card too soon. I'll not rule out the possibility yet."

Dervish looked at Michelli and wrinkled his nose. "Anything is possible; the probability factor, however, is very close to zero."

Michelli just winked at him. "What do you think the probability was that the dominant life form of the little world of Paradise would be stinky bears?"

Dervish cleared his throat. "None, when we first landed. If we'd only stayed three days, or the person I was with hadn't yelled, I'd still say none."

Michelli looked surprised. "Three *days*," he repeated. "The original explorers took less than three hours to discover their mistake." He looked at Dervish to see if perhaps the lad was teasing him. "They usually spray first and ask questions later. Obviously, for some reason they weren't offended by your presence."

Dervish was thinking of a retort when Reynard came in again and motioned to Michelli.

Michelli turned and looked at the note Reynard held out. He nodded, wrote something on the note, and excused him. Dervish looked at Michelli curiously as Reynard left the room.

"Business. You know how that goes," Michelli explained. "Now, if you are relaxed and ready, I suggest we transfer the information." He leaned forward and put a hand on each side of Dervish's face. "Let your mind go blank; move your thoughts inward. Try to picture your mind as crystal clear water. Keep concentrating until it appears that way."

Dervish found himself unable to resist the powerful gaze of the older man. Yet, try as he might, he could not picture his mind as water. He gazed at the jumble of thought impulses and related them to impulses flying down a data bus. *Data bus; hmmm.* He began to picture his mind as a computer center.

The large parallel array CPU was situated in the middle of a rather messy room. Dozens of programmers sat about typing programs into smaller processors. Cabling was strewn everywhere, haphazardly connecting each processor to every other processor and to the CPU as well. Data storage devices were stacked around each processor; power supplies were piled high with pieces of paper and old printouts were strewn everywhere.

He tried to figure out a way to hide everything in his mind from Michelli. He walked over and turned off the data storage devices.

The only device he left on the bus was the one attached to the main CPU. It seemed to him that it contained his system software. His mind became extremely quiet. A star chart began to appear in his conscious mind. He studied the star chart as he recreated it on the processor, then sent it out to the storage device. Paper after paper appeared in his mind, as clearly as if he was looking at them. He read and reread each one, entering the data and storing it away. Michelli was right; this stuff *was* of vital concern to the Fliers.

Michelli was calling him. He heard his name over and over, but had no idea what to do. Then, a tiny man put his device back on line.

Dervish opened his eyes. "Uhhh, what?" he managed to mutter. He was vaguely aware of three or four other tiny folks getting their systems back on line. "Whoa ... that's wild!" Dervish shook himself free of his mind and returned to the room.

"Now ... one more thing; I must know what it is you are." Michelli's voice had a hard edge to it. "I have never met anyone with a Talent as strong as yours. I am afraid I cannot let you leave until I have more information."

"Sorry." Dervish was once again thinking at his normal speed. "You wanted me to deliver this information. I doubt you'd kill me if I just walked on out of here."

"But I don't need your friend up there for anything."

"No way!" Dervish looked at his coldly. "I didn't give the coördinates to anybody; you're full of ..."

"I know you didn't," Michelli interrupted him. "That might be why your friend is still alive."

"What?"

"Your fighter sent him the coördinates ..." Michelli began.

"Oh, shit!" Dervish slumped back into the chair, covering his face with his hands. "I've created a monster!"

"Why don't you talk to your friend?" Michelli's voice held a chuckle. "Tell him you're fine and will be leaving soon. He doesn't seem to believe that you haven't been harmed. He is threatening to do some rather foolish things, considering his position."

"Has he threatened to land?" Dervish asked innocently. "He went fishing with me."

"Then I strongly suggest you invite him down for a bath." Michelli's voice was very soft. "If you don't, someone is liable to kill him in self-defense," he added knowingly. "I'll inform Reynard that there will be another person to deodorize."

Dervish gave Michelli a look of resignation and headed for the comm center. The Guardian on duty noted the rank on Dervish's sleeve and saluted. It took Dervish a moment to realize he was expected to return the salute. He just couldn't bring himself to do it, so he nodded to the man instead. "I need to talk to the Flier," he informed the man.

"Control to unauthorized fighter," the man called out. "Please respond."

Hawk was anything but friendly when he responded. "Hey, you found Dervish yet? You better find him rapidly or I'm gonna come down and find him myself."

Dervish took the communicator and keyed it back. "Hawk, it's okay, really. I must have gotten something in Love real messed up," he added sheepishly. "She called you on her own without any reason. I didn't even know she did it 'til a few moments ago."

"You sure?" Hawk didn't sound all that convinced.

"Yeah, I just screwed up," Dervish assured him, "but there's a bright side to this. Michelli has an antidote for stinky bear. I'll send you the coördinates if you'd like to take a bath."

"That's a real bath, right?" Hawk asked suspiciously.

"If they wanted you dead," Dervish replied reluctantly, "you already would be."

"Well, okay; what have I got to lose but the stench?"

Nothing, Dervish lamented to himself, *as long as I'm a good boy*. He sent the coördinates. "See you down here," he called, then handed the communicator back to the officer and walked out to the landing field.

Hawk started toward Dervish, then slowed his pace, noting the green uniform. He wondered what was going on. *First Love called in; now Dervish is wearing a Guardian uniform.* He didn't like the implication. "You sure everything's cool?"

"They burned my uniform," Dervish replied, when he realized why Hawk was looking at him strangely. "The stench doesn't come out of clothing." He had to admit Michelli was correct; the odor was absolutely abominable. It was hard for him to accept that he had smelled that bad a few hours ago.

"Oh," Hawk replied slowly. He shoved his hands in his pockets and looked about warily.

Dervish walked Hawk back to the house, keeping a safe distance. "Damn, that stuff really stinks," he noted as they approached Reynard.

"Don't I know it," Reynard commented as he ushered Hawk down toward the back bathroom.

"It stings like hell!" Dervish called after him.

"Okay," Hawk called back, sounding a bit less nervous.

Dervish walked back to the study. Michelli, who did not look as if he'd left the chair, nodded as he entered.

Another man entered behind Dervish. He looked familiar.

"Dr. Yarayn?" Dervish asked.

Michelli smiled. "Brilliant. Yet, you wouldn't come home. A true waste of Talent." He looked at Dervish sadly for a moment.

Reynard entered the room wearing a pained expression. "I've disposed of your friend's clothing. I sincerely hope that no more of your fishing companions show up."

Michelli chuckled and turned to Dervish. "The good doctor would like to take a blood sample; then, we're going to have a closer look into that mind of yours." He motioned for Dervish to sit down.

"You can have the blood, but what's in my mind is my own business!" Dervish respond hotly as he slumped down into the chair.

Dr. Yarayn's eyes went wide as Dervish challenged the man, but Michelli did not seem the least bit upset. "I am well aware that you would die before allowing me access to whatever it is you wish to hide from me." He studied Dervish carefully for a few moments. "I am also certain that the death of your friend would cause you a great deal of pain. You have my word: I wish nothing from you now that you did not know before you were five years old. Would you be willing to trade that for your friend's life?"

Dervish sighed and rolled up his sleeve, wincing as the needle entered his vein. Yarayn filled the tiny glass tube with blood and removed the needle, then placed a small gauze pad over the wound and raised Dervish's arm to help stop the bleeding. He nodded to them both and left the room.

"Well?" Michelli stared at Dervish.

"You win, old man." Dervish sounded sullen. "This round, anyway," he added.

Michelli chose to ignore his comment.

Dervish went back down into his mind accompanied by Michelli. As Dervish led him to a terminal, Michelli tripped over some of the cabling. He gave Dervish a disgusted look.

"You could clean up in here occasionally," Michelli told him. "I don't see how you can think in all this mess."

"I might throw out something I'll want. Maybe I should make this room bigger. I saw a lot of unused space out there."

"Which memories shall I pull up?" a tiny man asked.

"The first couple of years ought to do it," Michelli replied. "Anything that might help us discover his parentage."

The man looked at Dervish for confirmation.

"Go ahead," Dervish agreed.

The little man brought up a program and called a number of files into it. The screen showed a picture, displaying not only visual but also emotional information.

"I didn't start working here until he was almost seven months old," the little man pointed out. "I have no idea what order those memories are stored in."

"Show whatever you find," Michelli replied. "I can piece the timeline together later."

Scene after scene rolled by, mostly pictures of a garden with bright yellow flowers and tall reddish-blue trees. A few were of a large room with wooden walls and little else in the drab surroundings. Some showed an elderly woman floating in and out of the pictures of the garden. She was never really focused upon, even when she appeared to be holding him. He felt uncomfortable when she was around.

Then the picture of a young woman came into view. She appeared to be in her early twenties. Her bright auburn ringlets fell past her shoulders as she leaned down to kiss him. She had sparkling green eyes, high cheekbones and a warm smile. If she wasn't his mother, she was closely related. He clearly resembled her in every detail.

Michelli sat up, his eyes opened and he shook his head.

Reynard walked quickly to his side. "What's wrong?"

"Ashlaren," Michelli whispered. "I think I saw Ashlaren."

Reynard glanced at Dervish and nodded. "I had mentioned the resemblance when he was with us."

Michelli closed his eyes as he waved Reynard silent. He willed himself back into the mind link with Dervish.

The little man noted Michelli's return and bit his lip. "I've run forward beyond six months," he stated. "Is that okay?"

"That's fine," Michelli replied.

The image was of Dervish at about nine months old. The emotion registering was intense fear; he was picking it up from the auburn-haired woman carrying him. They were moving through a cluttered town. The scraps of scenery reminded Dervish of the port town in which he grew up. He stared at the screen, his hands becoming cold and clammy.

The woman's face in the image was receding, as if she had put him down; then she was gone. He started crying.

The next image flashed on the screen. He felt cold and hungry; he also felt very wet, and he was crying weakly. Someone bent over him; it was an old woman. She picked him up and wrapped her jacket around him. He felt warm.

As that image faded, the old woman was looking at him again. He was in her lap, and she was feeding him. Someone was yelling in the background. He turned his head. It was the dark-haired girl he had always thought to be his mother.

Now he was almost a year and a half old. He was standing, looking at a grave and crying. The dark-haired girl was telling him that the old woman had left everything to him. "I have to keep you to get any of it. You're gonna regret this ... "

The little man made a face. "Sorry. I know how much this has affected you. Some things are better left archived."

Dervish didn't react at first. The little bit of his mind that he was capable of accessing was reeling, his emotions running wild trying to sort out the implications of the memories. Aware that Michelli was also looking at him and capable of reading what he was thinking, he pushed the process into a background task, then put it to sleep until he would have some time alone to go over it. "Actually," he finally said, "I wish I had remembered all this earlier." He glanced over at Michelli. "Is that what you wanted?"

"Yes," Michelli sighed. He sounded sad and very far away. "You know even less than I do. I think that'll be enough for now." He nodded to the little man. "Thank you."

"You're welcome. Any time. Just *don't* come alone." The man gave him a wicked smile.

Dervish perked up some, pleased with the little man's spunky response. He looked at him with sheer delight. "By the way, how does all this work?"

"All input runs through the central CPU. It sends the data to the local storage of whichever programmer is working on that kind of stuff," the little man replied.

"Look, nice talking to you." Dervish said. "Now that I know you're here, I'll visit more often."

The little man smiled. "I would be delighted!" he said.

Michelli was shaking his head as Dervish escorted him out of the clutter.

Dervish turned his mind outward and looked at Michelli. "That's real weird. Are all minds like that?"

"Yours is ..." Michelli began, when Hawk entered the room.

Dervish had to agree with Michelli; green was a rather flattering color. "You look sharp, guy. You smell even better."

Hawk wrinkled his nose. "I didn't realize how bad I smelled 'til I got a whiff of the clothes I took off."

Michelli laughed, but his thoughts were clearly elsewhere. "I don't think you lads will go fishing again for a while."

"And the girls will *never* go again!" Hawk stated flatly.

"Girls?" Michelli repeated. "There were more than you two in this fishing party?"

Dervish realized he couldn't be mad at Hawk; after all, he hadn't told him he was a hostage. But now, Michelli had another ace to play. "Yeah," he admitted. "It was a foursome."

"I'll have Reynard give you some of the antidote to bring back," Michelli chuckled. "They might be pleased enough to speak to you again."

"Hey, thanks!" Hawk brightened at the prospect.

Dervish just nodded to Michelli. "You're drawing all the aces today," he noted.

"Poker is not your game," Michelli reminded him. "Never bet more than you're willing to lose."

"I get the strong feeling I'm missing something," Hawk commented, looking at Dervish for an explanation.

"Just the cards you dealt me," Michelli replied warmly. "Don't let it worry you; it's a friendly game."

Dervish gave Michelli a sour look. "That's only because you're winning," he pointed out.

"No," Michelli replied with a smile. "Because I gave you my word. You *did* land on the nose."

Dervish nodded, returning the smile with one that was a tad on the bitter side. He turned and started out the door. "Come on Hawk. Let's go home."

Michelli walked with them out to the fighters.

"You really are very, very special," Michelli told Dervish softly as he shook his hand goodbye. "I will look forward to your return, when you can spend a couple of weeks here."

"I'll be a bit busy for a while," Dervish responded. "And I'll try to stay that way."

"You have my word. Any time in the next six months, just give me a couple of weeks to get reacquainted. Then you can leave whenever you want." Michelli smiled warmly. "I'll even let you know what I might have learned of your bloodline." He paused, studying Dervish's expression. "What would you say to an agreement between the Fliers and the Guardians?"

"I don't get it." Dervish looked puzzled.

"You're right; you *won't* get it, unless you return." Michelli chuckled. "You know there is no place in all the galaxies where I wouldn't be able to find you. But as a token of my good intentions, the offer will remain in effect for the next six months. After that, you had better brush up on poker. Green is far more becoming to you than gray. Be back within six months."

"I'm not much good to you dead," Dervish reminded him.

"But then again, you wouldn't be a threat either," Michelli parried. "A social visit then, within six months?" He turned and walked away.

Dervish made a sour face.

Love didn't say one word the entire way back. The girls made up for that in spades when they returned.

13

You Can't Keep A Good Man Down

Hawk scuffed his feet as he walked after Dervish. "I thought we only had to fly with our official squad during a scramble. What's Isslan's problem anyway?"

"Beats me," Dervish grumbled. "I asked him that. Didn't get much of an answer, either."

"What did he say?"

"Something to the effect that some other tail got creamed and since we're his responsibility, he doesn't want us flying alone."

"That's bullshit," Hawk snapped.

"Wait up, guys," Angel yelled, as he ran down the flight deck.

"Where've you been?" Dervish asked peevishly.

"Trying to pull a few days leave," Angel said, as he caught up with them. "Shit, it's been almost three months since we had a day off."

"We *are* in the middle of a war," Dervish reminded him sarcastically. "Convince the Rudonians to stop attacking for a few days and I'll join you."

Angel scratched his ear. "I got a letter from Twink," he admitted. "The circus she's with has moved to Karenteen. Near the main base even."

"Why'd they leave Jartasver?" Isslan asked, as he walked over to join them.

"The Jartasverian ambassador walked out on the Council," Angel told him, "and the Jartas are sending some troops and supplies to help against the Rudonians. The circus people figured they should entertain the troops."

Isslan thought about that for a few moments. "Did she say anything about the Terravars and the Agundians?"

"Ummm, yeah," Angel mumbled. He stopped walking and took the letter out of his back pocket and began to look it over again. "So far the Terravars are remaining neutral, but a lot of their citizens are joining," Angel read. "The Agundians are standing with the Council, talking about you Jartas being traitors. Lots of hostility brewing on your world."

"Dad must be real pleased," Isslan commented dryly.

"Look at this," Angel said, pointing to the letter. "Twink has been talking to your folks. Seems her and your dad share the same political outlook ..."

"Dump her," Isslan cut in, only half teasing.

"No, here," he said, showing the letter to Isslan. "Your dad is coming to help train the troops in Tar Zavan." Angel looked at Isslan strangely. "Where is Tar Zavan?"

"Not where; what. That's the ancient art of killing with your hands," Isslan replied. "Dad calls it self defense. He's a full master."

"You know any of that stuff?" Hawk asked.

"Make a move," Isslan teased.

"If you guys *don't* make a move, I'll deck the both of you," Dervish informed them impatiently. "We're due out in five minutes."

Isslan gave Dervish a cold look.

"Sorrrry," Dervish said sarcastically.

"We drew quadrant two," Isslan informed them, ignoring Dervish's apparent snittiness over relinquishing command. "Emergency punch coördinates have been fed to your Birds. No heroics." He looked at Dervish to make sure that was understood. "If I send the signal, you punch."

"I'm not leaving anyone behind," Dervish informed him, a challenge ringing in every word.

"I have no intention of doing so," Isslan replied calmly. "If someone takes it hard, we all bug out together. An injured Flier doesn't belong in a fight. I don't want anyone staying behind to even the score."

Dervish nodded, but it was obvious he was not impressed.

"Look, you've got eight wingmates now, not two," Isslan continued quietly. "Some of my guys aren't as good as you. I'm trying to keep them alive. Okay?"

Dervish smiled. "Okay," he said, his antagonism ebbing. "When you're right, you're right. Wasn't trying to ruffle your feathers."

Isslan gave him a thumbs up. "See ya outside the doors. We'll all punch together."

"Two minutes," Hawk pointed out, his voice clearly putting him in Dervish's corner.

Dervish gave Hawk a broad grin as they scrambled to their fighters.

"Look at it this way," Angel said in English over the radio as they taxied to launch. "We got six more Fliers to corrupt. And Isslan is almost there. He still wants to go back for that Hank Junior concert."

Dervish laughed as they glided out to join Isslan's squad.

"All here?" Isslan asked, as the fighters started to float within visual sighting.

Seven Fliers acknowledged.

"Hawk, you there?" Isslan asked.

"Mentally or physically?" Hawk replied dryly.

"Both."

"Then Angel is disqualified," Goldie retorted.

"Keep your opinions to yourself, Birdbrain," Angel shot back.

"Punch," Isslan called, trying hard not to laugh.

Hawk was the first to punch in, and he found himself in the middle of three squads of Rudonian fighters. Gracie flashed the alert as three missiles hit her broadside. She reeled sideways, dropping quickly in an attempt to avoid the other missiles as well as Hawk's wingmates, who were winking in all around her.

"Hawk!" Dervish shouted. "You okay?"

The lack of an instantaneous reply was all Isslan needed. He transmitted the emergency signal; all eight fighters acknowledged. He dropped into position behind Gracie as Dervish moved out in front of her. Isslan was busy avoiding getting killed himself, but he hung back to make sure Gracie made the punch.

Dervish also stayed that extra second while Gracie winked out, before allowing Love to follow. As Gracie made her punch, Isslan saw a missile follow her through; he hoped Dervish hadn't seen it.

Isslan broke his own rule; he altered his punch to a short hop and scanned for signs that Gracie had been too damaged to complete her maneuver. Nothing but Rudonians showed on the scan. Satisfied, he punched.

"Where were you?" Dervish demanded as Isslan punched in, "and where's Hawk?"

"A missile followed him into the punch," Isslan slowly replied. "I hopped about a bit to see if he popped out too close to the Rudonians." His voice betrayed his feelings on the matter as he continued. "I was hoping he'd be here."

"Well, he's not," Dervish shouted, "and I'm going back after him!"

"No!" Isslan informed him sharply. "He's nowhere in that quadrant. If he was, I wouldn't be here."

Dervish didn't answer, but neither did he punch out.

"I called for backup," Isslan continued, "that's probably them winking in now. As soon as we regroup, we all go back together. Understood?"

Dervish muttered something in a language that no one else understood, although his tone of voice left nothing to the imagination. Yet, despite what he was obviously feeling, Dervish did not move from his position. Isslan took that as a positive note.

"Dervish," Isslan called to him, "if we get a relay from Mother, I expect you to break from whatever we're in the middle of and go after him." Since there was still no response from Dervish, he continued. "You're the only one I figure is safe out there by himself."

"Yeah, sure," Dervish replied bitterly.

With the other four squads to back them up, they punched back to do some cleaning up. Dervish didn't even the score by his reckoning, but he took down seven Rudonian fighters by himself. More than an hour had passed before they returned to the station.

Isslan was sitting in the cafeteria brooding with Angel when the colonel brought him the damage and status reports. The colonel pointed to one of the notations: one Rudonian had signaled defeat; Dervish blew him up anyway. Isslan smiled. "This one's for Hawk," he scribbled under the comment and signed off the report. The colonel and Angel nodded their approval.

Even though Mother promised to inform them as soon as word came through on Hawk, the eight Fliers annoyed her constantly.

Dervish didn't say a word to anyone during the next week, though he did follow Isslan's instructions when on duty. Angel finally had enough of Dervish's moodiness and stopped by his room after they got off shift.

"Dervish, open up," Angel called through the locked door. "I have to talk to you."

Dervish opened the door slowly, but didn't invite him in. Angel lifted Dervish's hand from the door and walked in. Dervish shuffled over and flopped himself on the bed, looking off into space. Angel waved a hand in front of the glassy-eyed stare. "I'm here," Dervish mumbled in a strained voice.

"You could have fooled me."

Dervish stuck his tongue out at him, while forming a peculiar Earth gesture with his middle finger.

"Yeah," Angel shot back. "Would it surprise you to find out that we all feel the same? Except Isslan hasn't even been eating. I'm worried about him almost as much as I'm worried about Hawk."

"Do you think he's still alive?" Dervish asked mournfully.

"He was a few minutes ago," Angel replied jokingly, "but I'm not too sure he's gonna last much longer."

"Not Isslan; *Hawk*, you nitwit," Dervish responded, his tone of voice more like Angel remembered.

"Went to see the gypsy-type lady, the one traveling with the circus," Angel told him. "She tried to tune in on him with his picture and his other flight jacket. She said he's in the shadows, whatever the hell that means." He looked at Dervish for some clarification.

"How did you get leave to go down there?"

"Isslan signed a pass," Angel answered, turning his gaze to the ceiling. "I said we needed parts for the Birds and he sent me to get 'em."

"You did bring back some parts, I hope," Dervish nailed him. "I don't want him in trouble with the colonel over your fool stunts."

"Isslan's real upset, Dervish. Keeps saying it's all his fault. He's ..."

"That's the stupidest thing I've ever heard," Dervish cut him off. "Damn, if he hadn't had us so well organized, we'd *all* be dead."

Angel gave Dervish a hard look.

"If Hawk's alive," Dervish continued under Angel's hard gaze, "it's only because Gracie had those emergency punch coördinates locked in already."

"It would do Isslan a lot of good to hear it from you."

"Shit." Dervish rubbed his face with his hands. "Does he really think I'm blaming *him*?"

"Everyone does," Angel replied. "He's been getting a lot of nasty looks."

"Damn! Where is he now?"

"Brooding in the cafeteria. More coffee. No food."

"Come on," Dervish shouted as he headed for the door.

"Oh," Angel replied innocently, following Dervish. "Are we going someplace?"

Dervish grabbed a tray as he entered the cafeteria and then proceeded to put two dinners on it. He looked about and spotted Isslan with three of his wingmates and wandered over. He sat down across from Isslan and placed one of the plates of food on top of Isslan's flight reports.

"Eat," he said loudly. "I'm not going to stand by while my squad leader starves himself to death."

Isslan looked at him for a moment, then gave him a warm smile. "Shit, I thought I wouldn't have to hear that again after leaving home."

"All us old ladies are the same," Dervish teased. "Now, if you don't finish every bite, there'll be no ..."

Isslan tossed a piece of fruit at him.

"You wouldn't have done that to your mother," Dervish shot back in a melodramatically hurt voice.

"Why do you think I left home?"

The entire table of Fliers started laughing. Dervish stayed with Isslan long after he finished eating, joking and going over strategies. Angel was particularly pleased with himself when he noted that the two of them left together.

Liefwynde was picking herbs by the bank of the river when the old man approached. She stood up quickly and brushed off her apron. She lowered her eyes in respect for her Teacher and waited, wondering what brought him in search of her.

"My child," he began gently, "our queen has sent a messenger and asks that you accompany him to the Middle Woods. They have need of a healer with a high Gift."

"The Middle Woods?" she questioned. "I did not know that we had peoples there. Did he say what is ailing them, that I might bring what is needed?"

"The hunters found an injured man. He is not of our world. They fear he is very close to death."

She brushed a strand of her long silverish hair back behind her ear while she pondered his words. "I do not understand," she replied slowly. "I thought that none ventured to this part of the galaxy."

"That is why our queen feels that it must have been the Goddess herself that guided him here," he answered. "She is hopeful that you can heal him."

Liefwynde blushed. "You have taught me well, but I am yet only your apprentice."

"Life flows through the Goddess down to her maidens," he reminded her. "It is you to whom she has given the Gift. I have but taught you to use it."

"I shall go if that is your wish. Where is the messenger?"

"He waits at my cottage," the old man replied, as he turned and walked back up the trail.

She tucked the herbs gently into her apron and followed.

Dervish didn't get back to his room until well past midnight. He sat down on the edge of his bed and his mind latched on what Angel had said: Hawk's in the shadows. Hell, he thought; *if some old lady can tune in on him, why can't I?*

He lay down and willed himself to find Hawk. Nothing happened. He got up and paced around the room a few times. *It's not the same as tuning in on computers; hmmm ... maybe the answer is in my head.* He returned to his bed and stumbled back down into his mind.

He imagined himself back in that strange, cluttered room inside his head. One of the programmers looked up.

"What's up?" the programmer asked him.

"I've got to find Hawk," Dervish answered.

"He's not here."

"I *know* that. I want to tune in on him and find out where he's at."

"Oh," the man replied, "you're in the wrong room for that."

"Where do I want to be?"

"I'll show you; it's a bit difficult to explain." The man got up and started to walk toward a door. Dervish followed. They zigzagged through several crooked hallways, but always going downward. At last, the programmer stopped and motioned for Dervish to proceed.

"You can't miss it from here," the man said. "Just go on down that way and you'll run right into it." He turned and started back up.

"Aren't you coming?"

"No," the man called back. "I don't exist beyond this point."

That doesn't give me such a secure feeling either, Dervish thought, *but it's all my mind, so what the hell*. He continued down the steep slope until it leveled off into a large, bare room. It was dark, and if there were any walls, they were not visible in the shadows.

A young man was sitting on the floor quietly reading. He looked up as Dervish approached.

"Do you work here?" Dervish asked.

"Rarely," the man replied. "You don't often call on me for assistance."

"What exactly is it that you do?"

"I don't quite know," the man replied. "I wasn't given any assignment and there are no instruction manuals."

"When I call on you to do something," Dervish rephrased his question, "what have I requested done?"

"Mostly trivial stuff like merging with your fighter," the man admitted. "I got that much down pretty good."

Dervish thought he had figured it out. "You're my Talent!"

"Not really," the man replied. "I try to use or direct it. But I don't really know what I can or cannot accomplish."

"Can we locate Hawk?"

"I have no idea. Is he alive?"

"Yeah, he's alive," Dervish assured him. "And we're going to find him."

The man put down whatever he had been reading and stared off into space.

"Where is your computer?" Dervish asked him.

"Shit. You seem to know even less than I do. There is no connection between this and your central system. It just happens to dwell within you. As a matter of fact, I'm sure that it is extremely fond of you."

Dervish was completely lost. "Huh?"

"The Talent, as you call it – or if you want a more archaic term, the Magic – does not dwell in everyone," the man explained. "And of those born with its seed, very few produce a sprout. You, on the other hand, seem to have been born with a whole tree."

"Why did you say it is fond of me?" Dervish asked, though he wasn't really believing a word of this man's ravings.

"There have been a few times it has commanded me to do things that ended up saving your life. On those occasions, it gave me the knowledge to do them. That's how I've learned as much as I have."

"Like what?" Dervish asked. "Give me an example."

"Like the time you attacked the Alderians who were threatening Captain Xendo. How do you think you fought off three grown men? Or did you ever consider how were you able to charm a Flier's Bird into taking off with you? Remember, Love didn't have your modifications in her then. She didn't think on her own as she does now. And ..."

"No, I never really thought about it," Dervish admitted, "but there was no doubt in those Alderians' minds that I was using a lot of Talent; that's why they took me. But I didn't feel drained after doing those things. And I always get so tired when I use the Talent. I didn't think I could use it and not get tired."

"That's because you didn't use it; it helped you on its own. Life energy is the price you pay when you *request* its help."

"What does it use it for?"

"I don't know. I have merely concluded that much from experience."

"How do we go about locating Hawk?"

"I suppose you concentrate on his image."

"I tried. It didn't work. I guess I can't do that."

"Don't start getting depressed. Let me see what I can do." The man sat very still for a while, then asked, "you're sure he's alive?"

"No," Dervish admitted reluctantly, "I'm not sure; I just have this gut feeling he needs me. He wouldn't need me if he was dead, would he?"

"Hmmm. Maybe he doesn't know he's alive," the man offered; then, noticing Dervish's expression, added, "a lot of people live their whole life that way."

"Okay," Dervish said, grasping at the straw, "what do we do in that case?"

"You will have to call him back or go get him, I guess. I wish I knew."

"Well, how do I do that?"

"I have a feeling there's a high price to be paid."

"What do I *do*?" Dervish demanded.

"Hang on, I'm trying," the man replied.

The room took on an eerie blue glow, then burst into brilliant white light. Dervish could see nothing but the light. He started to concentrate on Hawk. He began to get a pounding headache and was becoming very discouraged when he heard the young man's voice.

"I think I found him. Over there in the shadows, just beyond that silvery light."

Dervish looked around for a silvery light. It was to the left and bit behind where he had been looking. He couldn't see into the shadows, but he drifted toward the spot. As he got close, he felt he was being held off by something. He moved to the edge of the substance and gazed into it.

"Hawk," he called, feeling quite foolish for doing so.

Something moved in the shadows; a form slowly turned to look at him.

"Hawk!" Dervish shouted, reaching out with everything in him. The barrier suddenly shattered. He tumbled through, picked himself up, and ran to his friend. "Come on, Hawk!" Dervish urged, grabbing his hand. "We've got to get out of here."

Hawk stared at him blankly.

"Hawk, you can't stay here!" Dervish tried to pull him to the light. "I need you, dammit! Get your ass out of here!"

"Dervish?" Hawk questioned, as he stumbled along after him. "Dervish?"

Dervish dragged him into the blazing light of the room. The hand he was holding began to lose substance. He watched as Hawk faded from sight, yet he heard his voice again as he lost consciousness himself.

✦   ✦   ✦

"Dervish?" Hawk repeated. He opened his eyes and gazed into the face of a very pretty girl. He was fairly certain she wasn't Dervish. He stared at her for a long while, but he couldn't remember whether he knew her or not.

"You have come back," she told him. She appeared to be pleased by this information, though Hawk wasn't sure why, nor, for that matter, where it was he supposedly came back from. Her voice was almost musical; her hair was long and silver, and her dark green cloak loosely tied at the neck complemented the most beautiful green eyes he had ever seen. "You very injured," she began, "brain swollen, neck and back very hurt."

Why's she talking to me as if I was a baby? he thought. *I'm not a dolt, I know English. English*? "Where ... am ... I?" he asked slowly.

"My house," she replied, then put her hand to her face and blushed. "You want planet name. We call Gantra."

"You ... speak ... English?"

"Gracie teach me," she replied. "To reach you."

She was beautiful. All he wanted to do was take her in his arms and hold her. He couldn't really understand what she was saying any more; thinking made his head hurt, and besides, everything was becoming foggy again. He just lay there staring up at her. Unconsciously, he attempted to reach out to touch her hair, glimmering so silvery in the light.

"Those feelings come from the healing," she said, then shook her head when he gasped in pain. "Still too much hurt."

He watched as she reached for a cup. Something about her was familiar, but he couldn't place it. A part of him felt that they had been very close; another part of him was eager to be.

She leaned over and helped him raise his head to drink. The liquid she offered tasted a bit like the smell of flowers. As the pain began to drift away, he again attempted to reach for her.

She gently took his hand and held it. She said something in a language he didn't comprehend. Then, as he watched, the silvery light about her began to glow and sparkle. He responded, but not quite as she expected. She looked at him, a blush growing in her cheeks. "I must go now," she told him. She seemed to fade from sight.

She walked out of her cottage and stopped next to the fighter parked near her garden. "Gracie," she said in Common, "he has returned from the shadows. As he woke, he called 'Dervish'. Is that meaningful?"

"Dervish is his friend and wingmate," Gracie informed her, also using Common. "His safety would be utmost on Hawk's mind."

"Wingmate; is that something like a lover?" the girl asked hesitantly, remembering his reaction.

"No. A group of Fliers are wingmates to one another, the ones with whom they fly. A Flier's life is so completely in his wingmates' hands that their essences begin to flow together.

They think of each other as extensions of themselves." Gracie paused, then added, "I may not be presenting the association properly. I know of no parallel in your culture to relate it to."

"I believe I understand well enough," she assured the fighter. "Have you been able to repair any of yourself?"

"I am still unable to call in. The circuits are damaged beyond my abilities to repair with what little processing I now have available. Hawk must help me."

"It will be a few more days before the swelling in his brain has gone down enough to allow him to think clearly. He is not responding to the healing arts the way my people do. I need some advice from my Teacher."

"Then I shall wait. There is nothing else I can do."

The girl walked along the garden path toward a larger house. The old man opened the door as she approached. "How is our Flier, little Liefwynde?" he asked, as he bid her enter.

"I could not reach him," she replied, keeping her eyes averted, "but just now, a presence came and stood by me." She looked up at her Teacher perplexedly. "It went into the shadows and brought him forth. He awoke, calling for Dervish, a close friend, according to his vessel."

"I do not think friendship alone could be that strong," the old man said, as he motioned for her to be seated. "I believe this Flier was brought here by the Goddess and it was She that summoned him forth."

Liefwynde lowered her head, awed by the thought of having been in the presence of the Goddess. She began to wonder why this strange man was so important. "Why would She bring him here when he is of another place?"

"She brought the Fliers once before, long before you were born." He looked at the young girl and smiled. "You know that the Goddess forbids us from using her Gift in dark ways."

Liefwynde nodded; everyone knew that.

"It was almost three hundred years ago," he began, "when a large ship locked orbit around our planet. At first they left us alone, but when they learned of our Gift, they tried to convince us to do wrong with it. When we refused to do their bidding, they turned on us. We had little with which to defend ourselves. The Goddess brought eight of these Fliers to our skies and directed them to aid us. Of the eight, only five survived to return to their world. And what do you suppose that they requested of us in return for their help?"

Liefwynde shrugged her shoulders.

"Their request was that we pass on the help to the next ones we find that needed it," he continued. "We have kept our part of that bargain as best we could, teaching all our people the language of the Fliers so that one day the debt could be paid. The Goddess, however, gave us the added Gift of protecting our world. Thus, the scale has never been balanced."

"Why would this balance the scale? Could he not have been healed in his own place?"

"Those in the universe outside our world do not have the Gift, child," he reminded her. "He was very near death; perhaps he could not have been healed in his own world."

"But I did not bring him from the shadows."

"It falls on you then, little Liefwynde, to keep him from returning there."

"He responds differently from our people when I apply the healing arts as you have taught me."

"How so?"

"He becomes ... I mean, his ... well, you know." She looked at the old man with embarrassment.

"No, I do not know," he replied, "but let us go to him and I will observe."

Hawk looked at her as she approached. He noticed the old man, but couldn't remember whether he knew him. The girl sat down next to him and began to talk. Her voice made a musical rhythm, but he didn't understand a word. Her whole being seemed to glow and sparkle, she looked so beautiful.

"Yes, I see now," the old man chuckled. "You seem to be reaching the animal side of his nature."

"Is this good?"

"It should assist in keeping his interest here. And if you observe his life force, you will find that the Gift is working there, too."

"I do not understand," she mumbled. "Surely it will have an effect long after he has been healed. The Arts arouse him, but

I do not ... feel for him in that way. Might it not weave into him an affection he would not have felt otherwise?"

The old man thought a moment or two. "Perhaps that is what the Goddess intends," he concluded.

"Is there no other way?" she questioned. "I do not know all you can teach me; perhaps there is another avenue to his healing."

"I know of nothing else to try. His mind is too damaged to give me knowledge of his people or culture. I do know the others were very different from us."

"In what way?"

"They felt compelled to cover themselves. They found it strange to be unashamed of our bodies. They thought that to see one another without clothing would lead to arousal."

"When I use the Arts on him," she said, blushing slightly, "he wants to do those things. He cannot move, and it makes him very sad."

"Send him dreams, child."

"I know so very little ..."

"Let him guide the dreams," he counseled. "I believe you will find it interesting." He paused a moment considering what he had said. "I know naught of the right or wrong of it, only that we must try our best to keep his mind from returning to the shadows. Dreams can be erased later ... I can do that, if we feel it need be done."

"Then I shall do my best to keep his mind here," she assured him.

The old man left, and she reached down and took Hawk's hand. She began again to talk to him in that strange, melodic language. He reached up, touched her hair, and looked at her.

"Dream," she told him softly in English, "for you cannot do that now."

He drifted into a restless sleep. He was unsure if he experienced or dreamed her presence in bed with him; it seemed real enough while it happened, but when he woke up and looked about, he didn't see her. His thoughts turned to Dervish, Angel, and his strong desire to get back to them. He tried to remember where he was. When that failed, he lay back and studied the room.

The walls were all natural wood, polished to a sheen. From one wall to the next, a network of fine thread had been laid. A strange plant, with small purple flowers, wove its way from one window to the other along that network. Its drooping stems provided the only cover for the windows. The flowers seemed to radiate a delicate fragrance; at least, he saw no other source for the aroma. There was a desk and a chair near the wall by the windows. A golden statue of a dragon sat by itself on the desk. It seemed to stare back at him, its violet eyes glittering in the sunlight. Other than the bed he was lying on, there appeared to be nothing else in the room. The two doors were both closed.

He tried to sit up, but let out a yelp as pain shot through his head. One of the doors opened, and the girl came in quickly. She sat down on the bed and urged him to drink more of the healing potion. He resisted as best he could.

She looked at him sadly. "You must take to heal. You want talk first?"

"Yes," he replied firmly.

"English, very little," she said, holding her thumb and second finger about a millimeter apart. "Remember Flier language now? Gracie call it Common."

"You know Common?" he asked, slowly, but without stumbling over the words.

"Yes," she replied, switching to Common. "It is used mostly to talk to different groups, but all know it."

"Great," he replied. "Please tell me, where am I?"

"Our world would not be known to you. The Gift makes it very hard to reach. We call it Gantra."

"Huh?"

"The Goddess protects us in that way. She must have sent you; your fighter came down in the woods a half light from here."

He looked at her hopefully. "Gracie, my fighter; is she all right?"

"She is injured too. She awaits your help when you get better."

"Has she been able to reach base, tell them where we're at?"

"No, she said she cannot do that now."

"Can't anybody here fix her?"

"We do not understand those things. We have had no need to develop such devices."

He sighed deeply. His head was throbbing violently, but he needed more information. "How long have I been here?"

"Nine lights and seven moons."

"Did Gracie tell you how we got here?"

The girl looked a bit perplexed. "I do not understand all that she said."

"Just try to repeat it."

"Punched out," she said hesitantly, "hit by missile?"

"Go on," Hawk encouraged.

"Emergency coördinates activated." She scrunched up her face as she tried to remember the strange terminology. "Missile hit in punch. Fell out above this forest."

"Shit," he said thoughtlessly, "they must think I'm dead."

Her blush informed him quickly that he should watch his words. "I'm sorry," he said quietly, "I spend very little time with ladies. I guess my choice of language shows it."

"That explains many things," she replied with a knowing nod.

Something within Hawk turned inside out; he blushed deeply and put a hand to his face. "Sorry about that, too," he mumbled through his fingers.

She gently moved his hands and smiled at him. "You are very good," she said shyly.

Unsure how to interpret that, he opted for the medication.

She sat with him, holding his hand, waiting until the pain receded. As he drifted off to sleep, she again talked to him in her strange, soothing language. Things came to his mind that seemed inappropriate, considering what he now knew, yet he dwelled on them anyway.

✦   ✦   ✦

Michelli glanced up as Tressel entered his study. "Back so soon?" he asked dryly.

Tressel slumped into a chair and helped himself to a glass of brandy. "I spent three weeks in that hellhole," he muttered after taking a sip. "Mmm ... good year, which ever one it is."

"I'm glad you like it," Michelli replied, pouring himself some coffee. "Did you find out anything interesting?"

"I found the whore who raised him," Tressel muttered. "Pretended to be Alderian so she could charge more. Telling me stories was a fatal mistake."

"You know, I really wish you hadn't killed her," Michelli said quietly. "We might need more information before we're finished."

"I know all she ever knew," Tressel replied coldly. "First, she claimed that Dervish was the grandson of her elderly neighbor. Then, she tried to convince me that when the old lady died, she couldn't track down any other relatives so she took the boy in." He spit on the floor. "The truth is, she didn't even *try* to find anybody. She just moved in and took over. The old lady had left the house and some money to Dervish. Remember, that's a free port; no one really noticed. Or cared."

"What success did you have finding the relatives?"

"None," Tressel admitted. "The old lady *did* match the description you got out of Dervish's head. She was brought there as an unwilling wife. There were no children, and as far as anyone could remember, she had no family."

Michelli thought about it a few moments. "What ship did her husband work on?"

"He died years ago," Tressel commented, setting the glass down. "Ran afoul of some of our boys. People said the old lady became fond of the bitch after that; she would invite her over for dinner occasionally."

"I wonder," Michelli mumbled. "Obviously, the old lady must have found Dervish someplace ... or Ashlaren left him at some arranged place."

Tressel reached for the brandy again. "Ashlaren? What do you know that you haven't told me?"

"I didn't wish to taint your research," Michelli replied. "Dervish has memories tucked away of Ashlaren putting him down in the place this old lady found him. From what you have discovered, perhaps it was ... prearranged."

Tressel took a sip of the brandy and eyed Michelli. "I'm not following you."

Michelli chuckled. "Here we have an obscure old lady with nothing to lose ... and a fondness for Alderians? Think about that for a minute."

Tressel raised an eyebrow. "Hmm ..." he mumbled. "Back then, it was common knowledge that the Alderians were not on the best of terms with the Rudonians. So ... if Ashlaren had convinced her that Dervish was Alderian, maybe she would have agreed to hide Dervish for a while. Even pass him off as her grandson. But then why wouldn't she have come forward later with the truth?"

"To whom?" Michelli asked. "She probably thought she'd never get away with it. Ashlaren must have covered up his disappearance until the Rudonians had stopped too many places to backtrack successfully. And then, obviously, if they asked too many questions, the pirates would have smelled a rich bounty."

Tressel swished the brandy around for a while. "If I give you the slim possibility, what then?"

"I'm getting to that. I think you will enjoy what I have in mind. I'm sure you're aware that the Rudonians recently invaded Qubar," Michelli said.

Tressel nodded as he sipped.

Michelli pursed his lips. "It was getting pretty bad. They were trashing the place. Raping everyone in sight, even the children ... you know how they are. I spent a few nights at it, and I finally found a technicality in the agreement that they violated. What could I *do*?" He gazed at Tressel and shrugged. "I *had* to send the Guardians," he said angelically.

Tressel's eyes widened. "So we're at war with the Rudonians?"

"That would be one way to look at it," Michelli replied, taking a sip of his coffee. "Actually, though, there is only one Rudonian alive to tell about it. And I doubt that where he's going, anyone will believe him. Or even care."

Tressel downed his drink and poured himself some coffee. "May I ask where you're sending him?"

Michelli poured himself a brandy and sat sipping on it for a time. Finally he looked up. "My sources inform me that Ashlaren was not a very pretty sight when the Rudonians returned what was left of her. I planted memories into our Rudonian general's brain. Memories of what was done to her by him and a few others when they discovered the baby was missing. I want you to take the old general to the Elders."

Tressel's eyes lit up. "You're right; I *do* like it," he grinned. "Anything else you want done while I'm there?"

"I'd love a blood sample," Michelli mused, "but I doubt that would go unobserved."

"I'll do my best," Tressel replied as he downed his coffee and headed for the door.

✦ ✦ ✦

Hawk awoke suddenly. Even in the darkness, he was aware of her presence by the slight fragrance that always seemed to accompany her. He felt her hand brush his hair from his face. Considering the pain involved in any attempt to move, he was sure he was incapable of what he thought he had done. She leaned down and kissed him on his forehead. He steeled himself against the pain that was bound to result, and reached out to take her hand. He gave it a gentle squeeze. The pain wasn't as bad as he feared.

"You sleep lightly," she said softly. "I did not mean to wake you."

The silence made him uncomfortable; he began to think of things he figured he shouldn't. "What's your name?" he asked sheepishly, mostly to say something.

"Liefwynde."

"It sorta fits," he mumbled, as he drifted back to sleep.

He awoke restless and worried. He had dreamed about Dervish again. He'd tried tell him that he was all right, that it was Gracie that wasn't working, but Dervish kept insisting that he call in.

He forced himself to sit up, then realized that he wasn't dressed. He asked Liefwynde to bring him his clothes. When she resisted, he threatened to go out as he was. Resigned to his determination, and considering the coolness of the morning, she relented and helped him dress, oblivious to his embarrassment.

He was nauseous and dizzy by the time he weaved his way to Gracie. He leaned his head up against her smooth side to catch his breath. It took him a long time to climb the stairs. When he finally made it in, he slumped down in the seat and stared blankly at the damaged computer.

"Hawk, are you feeling all right?" Gracie asked softly.

"No," he replied honestly, "but we've got to call in. They're gonna think we're dead."

"There is nothing wrong with the radio. I cannot make the computations for hyper-communications."

"Guess I best start on those circuits then. Ummm, which ones are they?"

"Do you not know?"

"Not really," he admitted. "I think I'll see if I can trace this mess out first, then try to fix what we need."

He worked in spurts, resting when the pain got too severe, then resuming as soon as it subsided to something tolerable. Liefwynde came out often to bring him something that looked like oatmeal but tasted much better.

The work continued slowly, but he felt a bit better each day, and by the third evening, he had most of the nodes figured out. His head was pounding as he stumbled into the house, heading for the bedroom. He ignored Liefwynde's glare until she cut him off, handing him a large towel and pointing back out of the house.

"Bath time," she informed him flatly.

He looked at her as if she had just stepped off. Here he was: dying, dizzy, falling over, and she was going to make him take a bath!

She took him by the arm and firmly led him back outside and down a dirt path. It was only about a hundred meters, but he almost passed out by the time they reached the edge of a stream. He sat down and looked at her strangely.

Sitting down beside him, she took a small vial out of her pocket. "Drink this," she told him. "It does not taste good, but it will make you feel better."

The merest whiff of the stuff made his eyes water. He looked at her, hopeful that she was teasing, but she looked quite serious. He winced after he managed to choke down the vile concoction, unsure whether it was going to come right back up.

His head began to clear and the pain receded rapidly. She had taken off his shoes and socks and was beginning to unbutton his shirt when he started to get second thoughts.

"I think I can manage by myself," he told her, politely but firmly.

"It is good that you are recovering," she replied. She got up and walked downstream a bit toward the setting sun.

He watched admiringly as she took off her robe and dived into the water. He couldn't see much with the sun in his eyes, but what he saw he liked. He tested the water and found it warm. Without much further thought, he finished undressing and waded in.

He is doing well, she thought; *a bit of play will help strengthen him.* She popped up a few feet from him, splashed him with two handfuls of water, then dived back under.

The water fight was relaxing – even fun – but it tired him. He climbed out of the water and fell asleep in the warm grass. She covered him with her cloak and sat near him until long after the sky had darkened. When the moons were overhead, she woke him. As they walked slowly back to the house, she found that she enjoyed his company.

The old man watched it unfold in his mind. He knew that when the Flier left, his apprentice would accompany him to continue the healing; it was as the Goddess had willed it to be. *Perhaps*, he mused, *our distant relatives are in need of Her healers once again.*

14

It's The Little Things

Michelli looked across the large desk in his private study. Dr. Yarayn looked extremely uncomfortable as he began to speak. "From the blood tests I ran, there is no doubt that he's at least part Elder," he said softly. "Of course, I have no way to confirm that he's a particular one."

The solemn face of the young man seated next to Michelli gave way to a sly grin. "King Etheren is not in the habit of giving out samples, but I managed to acquire the next best thing," he said as he handed Michelli a small package. "A sample of Queen Yarenia's blood ... on a gauze pad."

"Without raising suspicion?" Michelli asked pointedly.

"I assure you, it will not be missed,"

"You are indeed one of the best, Tressel." Michelli smiled warmly at the young man. "Please see what you can do with this," he requested, as he handed the bag to the doctor. He waited in silence while Dr. Yarayn nodded acknowledgment and left the room, then he turned back to Tressel. "How did they react when you requested permission to land?"

"As you instructed, I told them that I might be bearing sad news concerning King Etheren's sister, and that I could possibly have one of the culprits with me," Tressel replied casually. "They took the bait."

"That old Rudonian general will rue the day he was born before they finish with him," Michelli chuckled. "Considering what he allowed to be done to those children, he deserves it."

"They are also none too fond of the Rudonians now," Tressel added. "Though I rather suspect that was what you had in mind."

"Exactly what did you say to Etheren?" Michelli asked. "I wouldn't wish to appear uninformed, should he decide to pay us a visit."

"I told His Majesty that we're at odds with the Rudonians due to the numerous atrocities they've perpetrated. And I mentioned that during our interrogation of the general, we discovered that he might have been part of the group that kidnapped Ashlaren and his infant son around twenty-five years ago."

"What was his response?"

"None that I could perceive," Tressel replied. "However, when I informed him that this man's mind held memories of a girl and a baby, of discovering that the baby was missing, and the ensuing questioning of the girl that led to her death, he became very interested. The picture that you placed in the Rudonian's mind apparently convinced Etheren that we did make a reasonable assumption."

"It was definitely Ashlaren, then? It's been so many years. I was afraid I might have been seeing only what I wanted to see in Dervish's memories."

"Etheren didn't confirm or deny that, and when he blocks, even *I* can't read him," he admitted. "However, he did send you his sincere gratitude and asked if it would be possible to have any further developments directed to him personally."

"Dervish, heir to the throne," Michelli laughed. "A royal flush if we return him wearing green."

"That's still only speculation," Tressel reminded him.

"That he'll wear green?" Michelli raised an eyebrow. "That, my young friend, is only a matter of time."

"No, I have no doubt you'll find a way to convince our young friend to wear whatever color you choose," Tressel conceded. "The problem will be convincing Etheren."

"I have no intention of convincing Etheren of anything that's not true," Michelli reminded him sternly. "This isn't a scam or a con. This is simply neighbor helping neighbor. Of course," he continued with a twinkle in his eye, "if we should happen to cause the Rudonians some trouble in the process, well ..."

"May I inquire as to your wishes if our young friend will not coöperate?"

"We simply return him wearing gray."

"What if he's not the heir, but just an Elder half-breed?" Tressel asked suspiciously.

"Then I'll find a way to keep him here. He'd be a welcome addition to the Guardians in any case," Michelli informed him. "He has a stronger Talent than most Alderians, and he's very good at fixing those fighters."

"Then you'll test him?"

"If he chooses green, he'll be tested," Michelli replied.

"Even if he's the Elder heir?" Tressel looked at Michelli oddly. "Wouldn't that be risking everything we are trying to arrange with King Etheren?"

"I'm very fond of the lad," Michelli said firmly, "However," he continued, looking at Tressel with an unmistakable glare, "the end does not justify the means, my young friend. We cannot compromise our principles simply to attain a goal."

Tressel glared back at Michelli sourly. "A bird in a cage may not sing," he pointed out, "but it also can't be eaten by the cat."

"I wouldn't want a bird that can't outsmart a cat," Michelli countered. "We have our own principles that must be adhered to. No man becomes a Guardian without passing the Test. No exceptions. Even *I* took that test. If he passes, he will return to his people a Guardian first and a king second. That's as it should be."

"Very well. I'll report when I am able," Tressel replied. "I should get back before I'm missed."

"I trust you have your absence covered adequately?"

"Yes," Tressel replied. "I have been recruiting Alderians for the Rudonian force."

"I hope you've had very little success."

"As little as possible under the circumstances," Tressel called back as he left.

Good lad, Michelli thought, *but I should somehow tie him a bit more firmly to home.*

✦ ✦ ✦

Angel looked at his watch, then at Love. "Dammit! Dervish should have been here hours ago. She's not flight ready, not with manual still in pieces."

Isslan bit his lip. "He said he'd be back last night. Never showed." Isslan looked at Angel then back at Love. "It's not like him to miss breakfast."

"Well, we know he's somewhere on the station," Angel replied thoughtfully, then added, "you did go into his room, right? He sleeps like the dead, y'know."

"Not really," Isslan admitted. "I just hollered and beat on the door."

"That'd never work if he's asleep. Next time try explosives. Come on — you gotta *see* this to believe it."

Angel opened the door leading to Dervish's room and let it swing inward. He and Isslan made their way to the crumpled heap in the middle of the bed. Dervish looked pale as a ghost.

Angel let out a low whistle. "Last time he looked this bad was when he took out that base ship. What did you two do last night, anyway?"

Isslan checked Dervish's wrist for a pulse. Satisfied, he answered, "We were just talking. I never realized I was this boring."

Angel started shaking Dervish roughly. "What have you been doing, Dervish?" he shouted.

Isslan reached over to stop him. "Hey, leave him alone."

Dervish slowly opened one eye. "I think I saw Hawk," he mumbled. "Tired. Real tired."

Angel's face lit up, but Isslan looked extremely unhappy. "Dervish," Isslan started to explain, "Hawk's not here. We ..."

"The Talent!" Angel interrupted him. "He must have been using the Talent. That's why he's so tired." He shook Dervish again. "Was he all right? Where was he?"

"In the shadows. Pulled him from the shadows," Dervish muttered.

"You believe that stuff?" Isslan asked, as he sat down on the corner of the bed.

"Yup," Angel confessed, "at least when Dervish does it. I've seen it work too many times not to."

"Well, he's not in any condition to fly," Isslan pointed out, "so I'd better go do something about the schedule."

"The colonel will have a fit if you tell him the truth," Angel advised. "Sorta asked him not to play with this kinda stuff."

"I'll think of something," Isslan promised.

✦   ✦   ✦

Isslan sat on the floor of his room explaining to his wingmates and Angel what he had managed to accomplish.

"You swapped out with the Old Man's honor squad? Damn, that's a joke, just for show. All you do is hang around like a bunch of mannequins!" Angel exploded.

Angel's sentiments were echoed on the faces about him.

"Look," Isslan argued in his own defense, "it's only for two months, and we'll be closer to Mother if Hawk calls in. Besides, we could all use the break to get our Birds back in shape."

"Crap," Marney squawked. "There's never any trouble there. What do they need squads for anyway?"

"It's our official headquarters, dummy," Cynric replied impatiently. "If we didn't make a big show of protecting it, someone might catch on that nothing happens there."

"Okay, we go in, serve our two months, then we're free to pick our assignment." Isslan offered. "You guys haven't had a day off in over three months!"

They all reluctantly agreed that they could use the break. Isslan, sensing he had the upper hand at the moment, adjourned the meeting so all could go gather up their stuff. "Report there in three days," he called after them, then turned to Angel. "Told ya I'd think of something."

"Did it have to be so drastic?" Angel asked pointedly.

"If Hawk's alive," Isslan replied, "I want to be as close to Mother as possible when he calls through." He looked at Angel with a resigned expression. "If he doesn't call in while we're there, he's not going to."

"He's gonna call," Angel assured him. "I just have to keep believing that."

✦ ✦ ✦

Dervish came half awake with a gentle prodding at his mind. "He's not in the shadows at the moment," something was saying. "Perhaps you'll be able to talk to him now."

He finally recognized the voice of the young man in that strange room. He moved into his mind. This time, however, he arrived in the place he wanted. *I'm getting better at this*, he thought.

"No, *I* am," the young man corrected. "You've been asleep. I've been trying to wake you for a long time now."

"I'm still tired," Dervish offered, "but let's try again."

This time, Dervish saw Hawk clearly in the brilliant light. The strange silver glow was all around him; he recognized Dervish, and called out to him.

"Hawk, call in, dammit! I know you're alive, but I can't find you unless you call in," Dervish admonished him.

"Gracie needs repair," Hawk replied slowly. "I hurt real bad. We're trying, Dervish."

The silver light around Hawk intensified; then, he faded from view.

Dervish looked at the young man. "How many days will I have to sleep for that?"

"None," the young man replied. "It was a call in, not out."

"What? Hawk doesn't have the Talent."

"Then somebody out there likes you. I *received* that call."

"I wish I understood all this," Dervish admitted.

"So do I," the young man agreed.

The next day, Dervish awoke feeling refreshed. He caught up with Angel on the flight deck and learned of their new assignment. He was no happier than the others had been, but he agreed it would be convenient when Hawk called in.

He told Angel about the strange things that took place in his mind. Angel was glad they would all be taking a break. *Dervish really needs one*, he thought.

Dervish went to say goodbye to Rusty and discovered that Ninsse was still staying with her. Rusty seemed overjoyed at the news, which worried Dervish; after all, he hadn't seen her in nearly three months. Then she told him it would only take a minute for her to pack.

Ninsse also insisted on coming, and Dervish found himself unable — or maybe unwilling — to talk them out of it. Two months of seeing Rusty every day was more than worth the look he got from Killer when they left.

✦ ✦ ✦

Although Threenica provided the girls with their own rooms, Rusty never used hers. During the evenings, when Dervish and company were on assignment, she and Ninsse helped Threenica with the mundane tasks that fell on him as Nathan's chief assistant. The rest of the time, she kept Dervish occupied in his room.

When Rusty was with Dervish, sometimes Ninsse would help Threenica or Nathan. At other times, she wandered through the elaborate gardens near the building. For almost a month, she had fallen into the pattern of spending a few hours by the pond. It was surrounded by so many large, old trees that from its banks one couldn't even see the building. She did a lot of thinking while she sat there. She realized she missed Hawk, but not as much as she thought she should. It troubled her, but she was embarrassed to talk about it.

Gazing at her image in the still water, she let out a startled yelp. The reflection of a strangely handsome man was in the water beside hers.

"Didn't mean to startle you," Tressel noted dryly.

"It's just that I didn't hear you approach," Ninsse replied, turning to look at the man. "I didn't even notice you beside me until I looked into the water."

"That's because I didn't wish you to," he replied prosaically, "but I forgot about reflections. Very careless of me."

She looked at him quizzically. "What an odd thing to say."

He took her hand and gazed into her eyes. She felt like lightning struck her and she tried to back away. He pulled her close and kissed her gently but firmly and, although she tried, she found she couldn't move away.

He moved a step back from her and looked her over. "Definitely worth the risk," he commented. "I'll be back, pretty one, but I'll be after more than a kiss."

He gazed at her for a moment longer, then slipped off into the trees. She stood frozen, trying to collect what was left of her wits. His image was engraved in her mind. His every movement seemed catlike; his long, straight, coal-black hair falling over his lean body set off his impish face. It was his dark, black eyes that haunted her the most. They seemed to be looking at her still.

She quickly returned to the building and headed for Dervish's room to find Rusty. She opened the door, then quietly backed out and closed it. They never noticed.

She made her way back to Threenica. As she helped him sort though the latest batch of communiqués, she thought about Hawk, then about Dervish and Rusty. Perhaps that's what was wrong between her and Hawk: she had always been the aggressor. Oh, he had been willing enough, but never, not even once, had he simply grabbed her and ... well, from what she had seen, it was obvious that Dervish was taking the initiative.

She talked to Rusty at length that evening about Hawk, but each time she was about to mention the strange man in the garden, the words wouldn't come out. She couldn't fathom what it was about him that she found so intriguing.

It was two weeks later, after she had completely given up on seeing him again, that Tressel appeared in the hallway. He grabbed her hand and pulled her into an empty office.

"I had to say goodbye, my pretty one," he said softly. "I leave tonight."

"Will you be coming back?" she found herself asking.

"Not likely," he replied sadly. "I'm rarely in the same place twice. Perhaps fate will deal me a different card this time, and we shall meet again."

"Why can't you stay?"

"I'm a spy, my sweet," he said as he raised an eyebrow. "It's a profession that requires constant travel. I came back for one more kiss." He pulled her close and kissed her warmly. "I was hopeful we could have more time," he said as he slipped out of the room.

She fully intended to tell Nathan about him, but for some reason she never got around to it.

Brach hobbled his way through the deserted hallways and stopped in front of the supply closet. He put down his broom and looked about. Seeing no one, he opened the closet, pressed a button and stepped through a door that suddenly appeared. The door closed after him.

As he walked quickly through a passageway that led to the other end of the building, he stopped in midstride. Light was trickling into the passage from the room that lay on the other side of this particular junction; it was unusual for anyone to be in that room at this time. Peeking through a crack, he observed the Speaker of the Council turning the security system off. He never liked that man. Arrogant and petty: two traits the old janitor couldn't abide.

A wry smile crept across his face. *Fact-finding tour my ass*, he thought. *That pompous buffoon has no intention of renewing the contract with the Fliers. He's using that as a cover for what he's really up to. Sooner or later, he'll get his; maybe it can happen sooner than later.*

He walked to the next junction and turned right to come up behind Nathan's office. He peered though the cracks. Two Rudonians were in the office with Nathan. Both held drawn weapons. His suspicions confirmed, Brach made his way down to the basement.

He wrapped his black robe around him as he approached the computer room that housed Mother. He linked his mind with her and put his hand over the scanner. The door opened and he walked in quickly. After listening carefully to be sure he had gone unnoticed, he retreated to the equipment rack in the far corner of the room. Quietly opening the cabinet, he activated the old manual terminal.

He typed `LOGIN GOD` at the $ prompt. He entered the password and a % prompt appeared.

He entered `SCRAMBLE YELLOW` and then followed that with `WAR < ARMAGEDDON`. He shut down the terminal and quietly closed the cabinet, then made his way to the back of the room and vanished behind the large storage units. The master screen flashed on; an image of the building appeared. Across the bottom of the screen was printed:

`POISON GAS TRAPS ARMED — Ø3:ØØ TO DETONATION`
`• YOUR MOVE •`

Ninsse was busy helping Threenica make paper airplanes out of the correspondence from the Council when Rusty joined them.

"Dervish was really edgy this evening," she commented, as she picked up and started to fold one of the papers from the seemingly endless heap.

"Not without reason," Nathan responded, coming through the door from his office. He motioned to the two men behind him. "It seems we have uninvited guests. Threenica, please escort these gentleman to Mother. They don't believe she doesn't hold our military secrets."

"You're joking," Rusty said, as she flew the paper plane to Ninsse.

"Move it," one of the men said, waving his weapon at the group. "All of you."

"No need for you to bother the girls," Threenica offered as he started for the door. "They're quite busy now building our fleet."

"Shut up and move," the other man barked, as a third man motioned to them from the hallway.

The two girls fell in quickly with Threenica and Nathan as they were hurried along the corridor. Threenica passed his hand over the sensor and the door opened; they all went in.

Threenica looked at the screen and pointed. "What's going on?" he asked bewilderedly.

"I have no idea," Nathan replied, looking closely at the screen. "Mother," he demanded, "what is this?"

"Two minutes, fifty-four seconds to detonation," Mother replied calmly. "You really should do something."

The men did not seem pleased. "Turn it off," one ordered. "That'll stop it."

"No," Mother replied. "The poisonous gas canisters have been armed. I am just monitoring the time to detonation."

"What set them?" the other man demanded.

"This building is under attack," Mother explained. "It does not seem logical to allow the perpetrators to live."

The door opened again and Tressel entered angrily. "The Fliers were scrambled. I thought you gentlemen disabled security ... " He noticed Ninsse and paused a moment, then looked at the screen. "What's that?"

"Computer armed some kind of gas traps," one of the men replied. "See if you can get it to disarm them. We'll dump the data and split."

"Two minutes, thirty-one seconds until detonation," Mother reminded them.

Tressel did some quick calculating. "No time for that shit; let's go."

"Dervish's up there," Rusty said snidely. "He'll get your ass."

"Kill 'em," one of the men ordered.

Tressel did some faster computations. "Let the gas get 'em. Grab the girls. The Fliers are landing. They won't fire with those two on board." He deftly picked up Ninsse and put her over his shoulder. He reached around for her arm as she started to struggle and she went limp.

One of the other men grabbed Rusty as Tressel pulled a communicator from his pocket. "Six to bring up," he said, as they grouped together.

"Damn," Threenica said, as the group disappeared from the room. "That jerk is right. They *won't* fire if they know the girls are on board."

"Our main worry right now," Nathan informed him, "is what the hell Mother is up to."

"Then why don't you make a move?" Mother asked. "You only have two minutes and fifteen seconds left."

"What should I do? Where are these traps located? How did they get here without my knowledge?" Nathan questioned her.

"Asking me is cheating," Mother replied firmly.

"What are you talking about?" Threenica asked her in obvious bewilderment.

"If I told you, you would know," Mother replied.

"Yes," Threenica pointed out, "and we could disarm them."

"But then you would win," Mother countered. "You have made some stupid moves. You do not deserve to win."

"What is this?" Nathan asked her hostilely.

"War," Mother replied. "You loaded the simulator right after you sent the scramble. Do you not remember?"

"Simulator?" Nathan asked meekly, then began to figure it out. "You mean someone ordered a scramble, and then loaded a ... a *game*?" he repeated, trying to get it to make more sense.

"You did," Mother assured him.

Threenica and Nathan exchanged glances, then hurried out of the room to meet the Fliers that had started to storm the building.

✦   ✦   ✦

Tressel grabbed Rusty's arm as they appeared on the arrival deck of the Rudonian base ship. "I'll take the girls below," he said. "One of you, inform those Fliers they're on board. Then punch us out of here."

One man muttered something, but they all took off. Tressel hung back a moment, then started down the corridor toward the shuttle bays. "You sure your friend's out there?" he asked Rusty as he hurried her along.

She nodded to him slowly. She wanted to run away, yell, scream, start destroying anything she could get her hands on, yet she found herself unable to do anything but go with this strange man.

"Behave," he hissed at her. "I'll need all I have to get us out of this alive."

A Rudonian was on the flight deck. He looked at Tressel strangely.

"Gonna throw 'em in a shuttle," Tressel told him, dumping Ninsse on the deck. "Ditch 'em as soon as possible."

The man nodded, and as soon as he had turned his back, Tressel reached from behind and deftly slit his throat.

He picked up Ninsse and shoved Rusty into a shuttle. Ordering her to strap in, he set Ninsse down and glided the shuttle into the launch bay. The doors closed behind them. He then reached behind Rusty; she thought she felt a sharp prick, and then the world went dark. "That will hold you, tiger," he mumbled. He sat there a few moments, blanking the scanners so they wouldn't pick up his exit. He accessed the main computer to get the punch coördinates the base ship was going to use, then sent those coördinates to Dervish with a message. He turned very pale. The bay doors swung open. He glided the shuttle out into nothingness and punched.

Rusty shook her head. She had the strange feeling she'd been unconscious for a long time. She noticed that Ninsse had sat up and was rubbing her eyes. "Where are we going?" she asked meekly, glancing at Tressel. "We've been in this punch too long to be landing at base."

"Home," Tressel informed her slowly. "My home. You were right ... he *was* out there." Tressel looked extremely white, on the verge of passing out.

Rusty was about to make a move when they punched in.

Tressel flipped on the comms unit and called in. "Code word rainbow ... code name Tressel. Requesting ... permission to land ... unauthorized shuttle."

"Permission granted, Tressel," a voice replied.

They eased down into the center of a beautiful courtyard. Rusty and Ninsse looked around, then down at the tiled landing pad. A well-dressed gentleman and a slightly taller older man were walking rapidly toward them. Tressel stood there leaning on the shuttle to stay upright.

"Tressel," Michelli called to him. "What in the world ..."

"Will ... explain it all ... later. Take care ... of them." Tressel stumbled forward.

"Reynard," Michelli said, "please help Tressel. I'll see to our guests. Ladies," he said, motioning toward the large mansion, "shall we go inside? Judging by Tressel's condition, I gather you two have had quite a harrowing experience."

Rusty and Ninsse looked at the man strangely. "Where are we?" Rusty asked him softly.

"You are at my home," Michelli teased. "Please, let's go inside. I'll get us some refreshments and you can tell me how you happened to end up in the company of that strange young man."

"But where is your house located?" Rusty asked again, as they began to walk toward the mansion.

"The Alderian galaxy," he informed her with a wink. "I'm called Michelli. Whom do I have the honor of entertaining?"

"Michelli?" Rusty responded, both relieved and excited. "The one who gave Dervish the antidote for stinky bear?"

"We're sure grateful," Ninsse added, "if it was you."

Michelli could not believe his luck. Tressel should not have left his assignment, but if he had to, this was a pleasant bonus. "My two little fishermen," he said warmly. "What a pleasure to meet you. Let me see," he said, looking at each of them carefully, then motioned toward Rusty. "You went with Dervish," he said, then turned to Ninsse, "and you must have been the one with ... what was that other Flier's name? Hawk, I believe."

The girls nodded. "I'm Rusty and she's Ninsse," Rusty told him, as they entered the house. "This is really ... *beautiful*. I wouldn't have pictured it this way from what Dervish said."

"You envisioned armed guards at every turn, high dingy gray walls topped with razor wire, dead gnarled trees littering the fields?" Mitchell offered lightly.

"Well ... not *quite* that bad," Rusty giggled.

Michelli escorted them into an elegant parlor and invited them to be seated. "I'll be right back with refreshments; then you can tell me exactly what happened."

Michelli listened as the girls gave their interpretation of the events leading up to their arrival at his home. He didn't really pay close attention; what he needed to know he would get from Tressel. Instead, he gently probed their minds and was pleased with how content they were to be his guests. Despite his fears to the contrary, Dervish had not made him out to be a monster. This was indeed a pleasant turn of events. He decided to be as up front as possible, so that their opinions wouldn't change in the future.

"I am most delighted to meet you," he told Rusty honestly. "Dervish doesn't speak to me unless he has to. It was his friend Hawk who informed me that you two were on that fishing expedition."

"Dervish doesn't speak to *anyone* unless he has to," Rusty replied with a smile.

"It was weeks before I was sure he could talk," Ninsse admitted.

"That does make me feel a bit better," Michelli admitted, "but I'm most certain Dervish isn't very fond of me."

Rusty pondered this a few minutes while Michelli studied her intently. "He's never said anything to give me that impression," she offered. "Actually, the few times he has mentioned you, he seemed almost ... well, like I'd talk about my dad."

"I take it you don't care much for your father," Michelli chuckled.

"No," Rusty countered vigorously, "I love my dad. We just don't see eye to eye on a number of things."

Michelli raised an eyebrow. "I hope Dervish isn't one of those things," he replied cautiously.

Rusty started laughing. "Daddy would have killed any other guy he caught looking at me. Dervish is probably the one thing we *do* agree on."

Michelli smiled warmly. "I'll summon Reynard and have him prepare your rooms. It'll be a while before I'll be able to get anything useful out of Tressel. I'm not sure whether he left Dervish your forwarding address."

"Tressel," Ninsse repeated. "Is that his name, or just his code word?"

"There is an old superstition that one can be bound by their given name," Michelli informed her. "Most Alderians go by their chosen name."

Reynard entered the room and nodded to Michelli. "The rooms are ready."

"Is Michelli your given name?" Rusty asked him, mischief radiating from her eyes.

"No," Michelli replied with a wry grin. "Actually, it's a title."

Rusty and Ninsse pondered this as Reynard graciously swept them into the hallway and ushered them toward the guest quarters.

✦   ✦   ✦

Dervish sat on the floor looking miserable while Nathan questioned him.

"Why do you need two weeks' leave to pick up Rusty and Ninsse? You're not really making sense," Nathan told him patiently. "Let's start from the top and go over all this again. Slowly."

"After that base ship informed us the girls were on board, we broke off attacking it," Dervish repeated. "That much was confirmed by you almost instantly."

"I know. What I am trying to understand is how you knew where it was punching to, and that the girls wouldn't be on board when it got there. I'd also like to know how you know where to pick them up. And why in the hell it will take two weeks."

Dervish started twisting his hair, a habit he picked up from Rusty. "I *told* you," he mumbled. "I was sent a message."

"By whom?"

"I think it was Tressel," Dervish answered honestly. "I locked back on him; he was telling the truth as far as he knew it. Look, do you think I would have blown that sucker if Rusty was on board?"

"Who's Tressel?"

"My only friend when I was with the Alderians. Well, at least he spoke to me."

"They can do that; it's part of the Talent," Threenica explained. "He would be capable of sending and receiving mental messages over a short distance."

"Then it was an Alderian who sent it to you," Nathan stated. "What was an Alderian doing with the Rudonians?"

"How should *I* know?" Dervish shot back. "He didn't send me his life story. All I know is these coördinates appeared in my mind. A message like ... 'Follow. Destroy. Girls not on board. Pick them up later'. It doesn't come as words, y'know? It's more like ... feelings."

"Why would he send you that message?"

"Dammit, I *don't know*. You said Rusty was mouthing off about how I was gonna get them. If Tressel was there, he must have figured Michelli wouldn't be pleased if something happened to her."

"Now, tell me: why would the king of the Alderian galaxy be concerned about Rusty?" Nathan asked pointedly.

"Huh?" Dervish gave Nathan a strange look. "King? I lived with him almost five years. No one ever called him king."

"He's not into titles," Nathan informed him, "and you're not into politics. I suppose, as hard as it is to talk to you, the subject never came up. Okay, you stayed with Michelli when you were living with the Alderians." He rubbed his chin thoughtfully. "Odd. I never even considered that."

"He's the one who gave me the Rudonians' plans," Dervish attempted to explain. "What I didn't tell you was that he tried to recruit me. Again." He looked up with a silly grin. "Hell, he's tried that a lot. It didn't seem all that important."

"What did you tell him?"

"What I always tell him," Dervish responded. "No fucking way." He looked at Nathan's expression and quickly added, "Well, I said it a tad nicer, but it carried the same impact."

Nathan smiled. "Now, why would their king care what happened to Rusty?"

Dervish was still having a hard time with the term 'king'. He put that aside for the moment. "Michelli? He sorta insisted that I come back for a two week visit," Dervish confessed. "I told him I planned to be busy the rest of my life. He made a few veiled threats, but then he always does that, too. Then Hawk and I split."

Nathan came over and sat down in front of Dervish. "What other pieces of this puzzle are you leaving out?" he asked, in an exasperated tone. "I'm not mad at you Dervish. I'm not questioning your loyalties. I'm simply trying to understand the implications." He put his hand gently on Dervish's shoulder. "Our security was breached tonight by the Rudonians. Mother was tampered with. To our benefit, yes, but tampered with nevertheless. Now you tell me that among those attacking us was an Alderian who works for Michelli. And ..."

"Used to work for Michelli, anyway," Dervish corrected. "Look, how do you think Michelli got that information on the Rudonians? I doubt he asked them for it. He has spies. In a roundabout way, that guy was working for us. He must have made the choice to chance blowing his cover because Rusty was involved."

"How did Michelli learn about you and Rusty?"

"Hawk told him," Dervish admitted. "You can't get mad at him. See, Love wasn't working quite right. I had her apart when Michelli's invitation came. She got flaky and sent a call to Hawk. Michelli had me invite him down to bathe. We'd been fishing in Paradise thanks to Sparks, and Michelli had an antidote ..."

Nathan smiled despite the situation. "Relief from stinky bear would indeed make one feel warmly toward his benefactor."

"Yeah, well ... I didn't tell Hawk not to say anything; I was calling him down from Michelli's control room. It didn't seem like a good idea to broadcast my feelings, considering they didn't blow him up when he arrived."

"Let's assume for the moment you're right," Threenica noted, "that Michelli had someone with the Rudonians. Why would this spy decide Michelli would rather have Rusty than the information he was presumably after?"

"Because then I'll go there to get her," Dervish offered, "and I'll owe him one."

"Why would that be important to Michelli? He has plenty of Guardians. What's one person more or less?" Nathan looked at Dervish seriously. "Why would *you* be so special to him?"

"He knows I'm not Alderian," Dervish blurted. "He knew that when he sent for me. Said he never saw anyone with so much Talent; he wanted to know what I am. He threatened to kill Hawk if I didn't let him have a blood sample." Dervish covered his face with his hands a moment, then looked back at Nathan. "I figured you had enough to worry about without adding my personal problems to it. Besides, there was nothing you could have done if I *had* told you."

"That does makes a bit of sense," Threenica added. "The Alderians are constantly trying to strengthen the Talent in their lines. Perhaps Michelli wants Dervish to father ..." He stopped short, noting Nathan's warning glance and Dervish's sour expression. "Never mind," he added, "I'm not thinking too clearly at the moment."

"*Now* do you understand why I need a couple weeks off?" Dervish asked.

"And you would give Michelli a permanent calling card," Nathan advised him. "Any time he wanted you to come running, he'd just have to pick up Rusty, or anyone else you were fond of." He looked at Dervish sadly. "It's a hard decision, but if you really think the girls are safe, let him cool his heels."

"Huh?"

"Don't go there now. Wait until he contacts you again," Nathan prompted. "They're beautiful girls; it may take him a few weeks to tire of their constant chatter. He will, however, conclude that this isn't a rapid way to get your attention."

"I didn't think about it that way," Dervish admitted. "He keeps telling me I'm terrible at poker." Dervish rubbed his forehead thoughtfully. "They're safe enough there, but ... shit, what do I tell Killer and Tazz? What will Rusty think when I don't come right away?"

"Let me handle that," Threenica offered. "Remember, I have to deal with the Council. I think I ought to be able to negotiate with an irate father, a protective brother and one Alderian king."

"I'm sure you'll find it refreshing to talk to people with intelligence for a change," Nathan replied lightly.

✦ ✦ ✦

Tressel sat slouched in the chair across from Michelli. He looked a lot better than he had when he arrived with the girls the previous night.

"Are you positive he understood your message completely?" Michelli asked.

"Yes, he understood. He locked back on me and knew the color of my underwear before he let loose."

"For your sake, I hope he blew that base ship. Wouldn't be good to have witnesses to your defection wandering about."

"They went after her, all right; I felt them just before the punch," Tressel responded.

"Why did you do this, Tressel?" Michelli asked him coldly.

"I told you before, I like Dervish. I wouldn't take part in his lover's death. Besides, you wanted to get him here, and he sure as hell had no intention of ever coming back."

"Telling the Rudonians that Dervish would 'get their ass' doesn't necessarily make them lovers," Michelli pointed out.

"I gave her a quick scan after she mentioned his name."

"Okay. But why did you bring Ninsse? She's not involved with Dervish."

"They were gonna kill her. I'm not into wanton violence. Besides, I had already made my choice."

"I would like you to be a bit more specific as to the relationship between you and Ninsse before this incident took place," Michelli asked him.

"I was watching her for a few days. She would sit by this pond for hours. Pretty little thing; no harm in looking."

"Go on."

"I got careless. Forgot about reflections in the water," he admitted sheepishly. "She saw me, so I kissed her."

"And?" Michelli motioned for him to continue.

"And nothing," Tressel mumbled. "I had intended to look her up for more than that," he added casually, "but we got busy. The day we were leaving I slipped in to kiss her goodbye. That's it. As long as she's here though, I might ... "

"You will respect my guests, Tressel," Michelli said icily. "They are not here for your amusement."

"She's not married," Tressel countered. "Why don't you let her make up her own mind?"

"If I am not mistaken, she is the girl friend of Dervish's wingmate. And as far as making up her own mind, I did *not* appreciate having to undo your handiwork!"

Tressel's eyes became cold with anger. "I'm not Rudonian slime!" he shouted. "I don't need to twist a girl's mind to take her to bed!" He lowered his voice when Michelli raised his hands. "I simply made it impossible for her to talk about me," he continued. "It seemed wise under the circumstances."

"I see," Michelli responded. He pondered a moment. "Perhaps they *are* only friends; I might have misjudged the relationship."

"Can I see her, then?" Tressel asked politely.

"With all your Talent, you shouldn't find it hard to attract any number of beautiful Alderian girls."

"You have my loyalty, Michelli," Tressel replied hotly, "but I'll be damned if that lets you tell me who to go to bed with."

Michelli cleared his throat. "Just give her some time to put all this into perspective," he said calmly.

"They'll be gone by then," Tressel argued. "I find it hard to believe that Dervish hasn't shown up already."

"They'll be here a while," Michelli explained. "Threenica sent a message thanking me for extending my hospitality under these trying circumstances. He requested that I inform the girls that it will be a few weeks before they can get an intergalactic shuttle here, all of them having been damaged in the Rudonian attack on base seven."

"What?"

Michelli chuckled softly. "Dervish is trying to inform me that he has no intention of playing games."

"How did the girls take that bit of news?"

"I neglected to tell them that last part," Michelli replied. "They didn't look all that upset. They seem to enjoy being treated like princesses."

"I would like to see her now," Tressel requested softly, "out in the garden. Is that harmless enough?"

"It's nearly midnight," Michelli replied firmly. "Why don't you wait until she wakes up tomorrow."

Having won his point, Tressel decided to let the matter drop and turned the discussion to something less personal. "You'll never get Dervish to stay here," he opined. "Etheren won't be able to keep him home either."

Michelli was amused to note the change of subject, but decided to hear Tressel out on the matter. "Why would you assume that?"

"His wingmates," Tressel reminded him. "He'll never leave them."

"Interesting point," Michelli noted. "I wonder what would happen if we arranged a situation where he ended up with a few Alderian wingmates."

"Don't bet more than you're willing to lose," Tressel quipped.

"I'll keep that in mind," Michelli retorted sourly. "I hope you have a pleasant evening," he added. Tressel took the hint and left the room rapidly.

Ninsse woke up when Tressel shook her lightly. He was seated on the bed next to her wearing a wry grin. "Care for a midnight stroll through the gardens?" he asked softly.

"Sure," she replied, She started to get up, then remembered she wore nothing but a t-shirt and pointed toward the dresser. "Could you get me my jeans from over there, please?"

"No," he replied teasingly. "I would much rather watch you get them."

She wrinkled her nose. "Then I'll have to stay in bed."

Tressel lay back on the bed. "That's even more fun than walking," he agreed, as he wrapped his arms around her.

Michelli worked in his study until after two. As he had suspected, the blood sample from Queen Yarenia did not prove that Dervish was her son, but neither did it rule out the possibility. The resemblance to Etheren's sister Ashlaren was remarkable, though. Tired and depressed, he walked down the hall to his room. He stopped as he passed Ninsse's room. A smile crept over his face as he gazed at the closed door. He chuckled to himself as he resumed walking. Fate had indeed been kind, providing him not only a carrot for Dervish, but an anchor for Tressel.

Dervish held out fairly well the first two days, but by the third he was beginning to come apart at the seams. He was so concerned about Rusty that he didn't react for a moment when Threenica burst into his room.

"Quick," Threenica admonished him. "Hawk just called through. He needs help repairing something or other to get a fix on his location."

"Hawk?" Dervish repeated, then it registered. "Hawk!" He raced past Threenica toward the comm center.

"Hawk, you okay?" he screamed into the communicator.

"Big holes in my memory," Hawk replied slowly, "but not as big as the one in Gracie. I'm having trouble getting a fix on my location."

"Take her up and send a star chart," Dervish told him.

"Can't do that. She's got a hole in her and I have nothing to repair it with."

"A hole?" Dervish questioned, the concept still not quite soaking in.

"The missile put a big hole in her side. If we hadn't dropped out of that punch and landed in atmosphere before it hit us, we'd be fragments in hyper-space."

"Can you see any stars from your location?"

"Only at night," Hawk replied.

It took them forty-eight hours, Gracie slowly circling the planet just above tree level feeding back images of the stars, to make a reasonable guess on the galaxy. Dervish, Angel and Isslan went there to get an exact fix by triangulating Hawk's transmissions while Threenica loaded up the shuttle with equipment and parts.

Dervish dropped Love within inches of Gracie and was halfway down the stairs before she had actually settled. He leaped the remaining steps and practically landed on Hawk. They exchanged a friendly bear hug as Angel and Isslan landed. Isslan sent the coördinates to Threenica so he could bring the shuttle.

As Angel and Isslan welcomed Hawk back from the dead, Dervish took a good look at Gracie. He let out a low whistle that brought the other three over to him. "Damn, that was close," he muttered, putting his head through the hole.

"I didn't look much better," Hawk admitted. "I don't think I would have made it if Liefwynde hadn't decided to take care of me."

As Hawk spoke, Dervish sensed a bit of that strange silver light about him. "While we wait for Threenica, why don't you introduce us to her."

"What makes you think Liefwynde is a she?" Hawk asked, as he led them toward the house.

Dervish broke into a silly grin. "There's a curious glow about you, lad; I don't think a man would cause that. Am I wrong?"

"Uhhh, no," Hawk admitted sheepishly. "I forgot you can see auras."

Angel's eyes lit up when he saw Liefwynde; only Isslan's poke in the ribs kept him from drooling. Dervish recognized her at once as the one who had been with Hawk when he saw him in his mind. She in turn acknowledged Dervish with a slight nod of her head. Hawk, oblivious to all of it, made the formal introductions.

Threenica arrived and, after introducing him to Liefwynde, they all went out to begin repairs. They estimated it would take three days or so to get Gracie spaceworthy. Threenica, feeling like a spare tire, soon ventured back into the house to keep Liefwynde company while the Fliers fixed Gracie. As he helped her prepare dinner and set up the sleeping cots, she kept him talking about the Fliers, the war with the Rudonians, and the battles with the Council.

Threenica was delighted that finally someone seemed interested in what he did and was impressed at how intelligent she seemed. Over the three days it took to fix Gracie, she learned the history of the Flier organization and its ongoing battle with the Council. She even advised Threenica on ways to handle different members of the Council he found troublesome.

Threenica was adamant that it was his idea that Liefwynde accompany them back to headquarters. After all, he argued, Hawk still was in need of care and he also could use her help. Since she was willing, her Teacher had no objections and Hawk was delighted with the idea, none of the others gave it a second thought.

They landed at headquarters in good spirits and, concluding that there was safety in numbers, went together to inform Nathan of their latest acquisition.

✦   ✦   ✦

Tressel lay next to Ninsse, aware that she would not awaken for a few hours; he pondered whether there was something else he wanted to do. The week had flown by quickly, and he had done little else but spend time with her. It was frustrating, as she tended to fall asleep after a few times, and he was used to making it an all night occupation. As he came to the realization that he preferred being with her than doing anything else, someone knocked on the door. He scanned quickly, and, noting that it was Rusty, not some urgent crisis, was going to ignore it. His probe, however, uncovered the fact that she was feeling extremely ill. He quickly put on his jeans and opened the door.

Rusty looked up, her coloring a bit green, her hands on her stomach. "Sorry," she said weakly. "I'll be ..."

Tressel took her arm and brought her into the room. "No problem; Ninsse's asleep. You look pretty sick," he told her, sounding truly concerned. "Sit on down, I'll get Dr. Yarayn. Will you be all right for a few minutes?"

"No, please don't," she said, while seating herself on the edge of the bed. "I've been feeling this way off and on for over a month now. It's just a bit worse today." She looked over at Ninsse, who slept practically comatose, and smiled. "She'll get better," she informed Tressel knowingly.

He raised an eyebrow. "I don't think that's possible," he admitted sheepishly. "Be nice if she didn't fall to sleep so soon, though."

Rusty's green complexion began to get a rosy glow that deepened to a dark blush. "That's what I was referring to," she said, obviously embarrassed. "Dervish said it drove him crazy when I used to do that."

Tressel made a mental note to have a talk with Dervish concerning this particular phenomenon, while his mind put two and two together in an instant. "I think I should take you to the good doctor, fair lady," he informed her gently. "The cause of your greenness should be investigated."

Despite her protests that she would be fine in a little while, he put on his shirt and escorted her to Dr. Yarayn's quarters. He chuckled to himself as he went to find Michelli.

Dr. Yarayn seemed rather stuffy to Rusty, and she was a bit ill at ease being examined; he was aware of her feelings instantly, as Alderians tend to be, and did his best to soothe her anxieties with small talk.

He began the examination with a urinalysis and had his initial, unspoken diagnosis confirmed instantly. "It's quite normal to feel as you do under the circumstances," he offered. "Dervish is the father, I presume," he continued, smiling at the blush that crept into her cheeks.

Her eyes enlarged considerably.

Noting her puzzled expression, he paused for a moment. "You did know that you're pregnant, didn't you?"

Rusty shook her head. "It ... well, I ... I guess I didn't think about it," she stammered.

"Oh, I see," Dr. Yarayn replied. "I can assume, then, that you've not yet seen a doctor concerning the event. We should run all the proper tests; blood compatibility, defect checks and such. Do you want to know what sex it is?" he asked, with a twinkle in his eyes.

Things were moving a bit too quickly for her. "Huh?" she said, staring at him blankly.

"The two of you are of different races. It has not been established that the mix will produce a normal offspring. According to intergalactic law, your physician must certify that the child will be able to function normally."

Her pleading eyes and panicked expression told him more than mere words how much the child meant to her. "Are Fliers subject to that law?"

He put a gentle arm around her. "Child," he said lovingly, "you wouldn't want a baby that can't pass that test."

"How long before I know," she asked hesitantly.

"Three days. Would you like to wait for the results before notifying Dervish?"

"If it's not normal, I don't want him *ever* to know," she stated.

"Very well. As your physician, I'm not at liberty to discuss your condition with anyone without your consent."

She gave the doctor a relieved smile and was a bit more at ease during the tests.

Rusty could not believe how slowly three days could pass. Had she been more observant and less withdrawn, she would have been aware that Michelli and Tressel were as nervous as she was.

She was frightened stiff when Dr. Yarayn woke her the morning of the fourth day, but his smile told her all was okay. "You can breathe now," he said chuckling. "He passed his tests and then some."

Rusty was radiant when she confided the news to Michelli and asked if there was some way she could notify Dervish.

Michelli looked even more pleased than Rusty. "Ummm, I don't think you should send this delightful bit of news via hypercomm," he informed her. "In polite society, the marriage is announced before the child is announced."

Rusty's hand immediately went to her mouth. "Ooooh, Daddy's gonna *kill* him!" she wailed.

Michelli chuckled. "Fathers have a reputation for reacting that way," he agreed. "I'll do my very best to inform Dervish discreetly."

✦ ✦ ✦

Dervish opened the door to his room. Tossing his helmet onto the chair, he began to take off his shirt. Angel wandered in, stooped down and picked up an envelope. "You dropped this," he said, handing it to Dervish.

"Huh?" Dervish said, as he looked at it. "No, I didn't."

"Well, it was lying on the floor."

Dervish took the envelope from Angel. He looked at it a moment; then, seeing "Dervish" scrawled across the front, shrugged his shoulders, opened it and began to read. "Whoa," he said, stumbling backwards to sit down on his bed.

"What is it?"

Dervish handed Angel the note. "I'm gonna be a daddy," he said with a silly grin.

"Dervish, my lad: Congratulations. Rusty is with child. M," Angel read aloud. "Who's M?"

"Michelli, obviously."

"Well, hey, congratulations, I guess. Ummm ... hmmm." Angel scratched his head. "I didn't know you guys ... well, that's great."

Dervish looked panic-stricken as the full implication of Angel's stumbling about hit home. "Killer!" he stammered. "Oh God, I'm dead." He reached over, snatched his helmet off the chair and started for the door. "Get Hawk," he called back to Angel. "I gotta go get her *now!*"

Angel grinned and raised an eyebrow as he watched Dervish run down the hall. "I do believe you already got her," he chuckled.

15

Next Time Around

Michelli smiled as he gave the three fighters permission to land. Tressel, however, was not pleased. He gave Michelli a sour look and walked out of the room.

Michelli watched the door close, then turned to Reynard. "I don't think the lad is in the best of spirits, do you?"

"Perhaps you should have informed him that Ninsse asked to stay here," Reynard answered.

Michelli shook his head. "If she wants him to know, she is capable of telling him herself."

"I don't believe that's the only thing he's upset about," Reynard observed.

"I wouldn't let his mood bother you," Michelli countered. "He's not been thinking too clearly lately. After all, he chose to blow his cover just to bring Ninsse here."

Reynard raised an eyebrow, but silently followed Michelli out to greet the landing Fliers.

Dervish scrambled out of Love and ran to meet Michelli, followed closely by Hawk and Angel. "Where is she?" he shouted, as he got within earshot.

Michelli waited until Dervish was close enough to hear him reply quietly. "She's in your room. Sleeping."

Dervish turned to dash off. Michelli put his hand gently but firmly on his shoulder. Angel and Hawk moved in quickly.

"Calm down, lad," Michelli advised him. "It's three AM. If you go bursting in like that, you'll scare her half to death."

"Huh?" was all Dervish managed.

"Women in her condition are very excitable," Michelli explained. "All the tests were fine. You have a normal, healthy, little boy on the way. Please be calm."

"Oh," Dervish answered, as he started off again.

Michelli cut him off, waving a stack of papers in front of his face. "You'll want these, I'm sure," he said with a smile.

Angel spit on the ground. "Enlistment forms?" he asked hotly.

Michelli gave Angel a sly wink. "In a manner of speaking, yes. It's the universal marriage application. Approved." He nodded to Dervish. "Your copy."

Dervish hesitated a moment before taking the papers. "Wow, thanks!"

"It's utterly amazing that any man survives his first child," Michelli observed, watching Dervish race across the field.

"He's naturally hyper," Angel muttered.

Michelli looked at Angel strangely. "No point in standing here. He's going to find her extremely reluctant to get out of bed at this hour. Shall we wait in the house?"

"Are we hostages this time?" Hawk asked pointedly.

Michelli chuckled. "No. This time you're guests," he said, heading toward the house.

Angel gave him a nasty look. "Is there a difference?" he asked sarcastically.

"Guests," Michelli informed him casually, "are assured of leaving alive."

"Comforting," Angel mumbled.

Michelli showed them into the living room and motioned for them to be seated. "As a point of idle curiosity," he asked, pulling up a chair for himself, "were the two of you always like this, or have you acquired your lack of manners through association with Dervish?"

Hawk jumped up instantly. "You've got some nerve talking about manners," he growled, "after threatening to kill me if Dervish didn't give you what you wanted."

Michelli seemed amused. "That was only what he wished to conclude from the facts as I presented them. If he hadn't wanted a reason to coöperate, he would have just laughed at the idea. Killing you would have been murder. He knows me better than that."

"Then when is killing not murder?" Angel asked derisively.

"When it's done to preserve freedom," Michelli answered pointedly.

Hawk sat back down sullenly. "Still, how do you expect Dervish to know what you would or wouldn't do."

Michelli laughed softly. "Lad, he knows all he needs to about anyone he must deal with."

"Dervish doesn't read people," Angel retorted.

"I beg to differ with you," Michelli countered. "Dervish reads everything he comes near."

Hawk's eyes narrowed. "Are you implying that he pokes around in people's heads?" he asked with a nasty edge.

Michelli looked shocked. "Heavens, no! I'd have thrown him out, not invited him home, if I had any suspicion of that."

Angel and Hawk exchanged glances. "Just what are you saying, then?" Angel asked, a bit less antagonistically.

"Living things radiate their innermost selves," Michelli explained. "I believe the phenomenon is loosely called an aura. Dervish is very aware of what they tell him."

Neither Hawk nor Angel could argue the point. "How would that tell him you wouldn't kill me?" Hawk asked warily.

"It would be evil to allow the end to justify the means," Michelli pointed out candidly, "and he saw no evil in my aura." Hawk and Angel were still obviously confused, so he continued. "Dervish wants to know what he is, while at the same time he's afraid of what he might learn. He needed to feel compelled to let me investigate for him."

"So you obliged," Angel commented dryly.

"I never denied that," Michelli pointed out. "Actually, he called me on it, and then chose to ignore the fact that he knew I wouldn't do anything to Hawk. I'm well aware that nothing will make Dervish do what he doesn't want to do. That's one of the reasons I'm so fond of him."

"I think you're wrong about that," Angel interjected.

"No," Michelli replied. "One cannot give in to threats, no matter the stakes." He looked at Angel, then at Hawk before continuing. "I know a man who wouldn't capitulate, even when the lives of his sister and his infant son were at stake."

Angel looked at him oddly. "Bet the guy felt real good about that," he mumbled.

"He's not been at peace with himself since," Michelli replied. "But his people are free, and will remain so while he lives."

"This man wouldn't happen to be you, would it?" Hawk asked.

"No," Michelli answered, "and I'm not sure whether I would have passed that test." He pursed his lips and looked down for a moment. "That's probably why I never married or had children," he added.

Angel figured it was time to play an ace. "So instead, you've adopted Dervish," he blurted.

Michelli looked at Angel with amused pleasure. "Finally, the light comes on," he commented dryly. "And with that startling revelation," he added with a hint of sarcasm, "I will bid you fine gentleman good night."

They both felt a bit foolish as Michelli left the room, and were still sitting there sulking when Reynard came in.

"Miss Rusty would prefer to leave in the morning," he informed them, employing his most annoyingly condescending monotone. "If you gentleman have no objections, I will show you to your rooms now."

Hawk and Angel exchanged exasperated expressions as they followed Reynard to the bedrooms.

Dervish reached the door of his old bedroom and paused briefly to catch his breath. He tried the door and found it unlocked; he wasn't sure whether that was a good or bad sign. He went in, closed and locked the door, and made his way silently to the bed.

He gazed at Rusty peacefully sleeping, and his mind turned instantly to one of his favorite pastimes. He smiled to himself, put his helmet on the floor, took off his clothes and slipped under the covers. He snuggled up, wrapped his arms around her and pulled her close.

Rusty opened her eyes and let out a shriek before realizing that it was Dervish who had his hands all over her.

Reynard was pounding on the door almost before Dervish could recover from the scream.

"Miss Rusty, are you all right?" Reynard called, while fetching the key to the room from his pocket.

"I'm just fine, now," Rusty answered.

"She's not too keen about getting up this early," Dervish called out, hoping to satisfy Reynard.

"Actually, I'm just not fond of getting out of bed this early," Rusty added, while snuggling up to Dervish.

Reynard made a quick, discreet scan to be sure that she was speaking of her own free will. "Sorry to have disturbed you. I shall go bed down those other Fliers." He chuckled to himself as he headed for the living room.

Hawk opened his eyes slowly as the gentle shaking roused him. "Jeez, Dervish, it isn't even light yet," he yawned. He looked blankly at Tressel. "Ummm, you're not Dervish," he added. "I'm sorry, but if I know you, I don't remember."

Tressel studied him a moment. "What are your intentions concerning Ninsse?"

"Huh?" Hawk mumbled. He looked at Tressel sadly. "I think I know someone named Ninsse." He tried to recall more, but the thoughts got lost in silvery mist. "It seems ... no, I don't really remember," he replied mournfully.

Tressel's curiosity got the better of him. His mind reached out, only to stumble as it entered the darkness that should have been Hawk's past. "What happened?" he asked softly. "Everything's darkness in your memories."

"Dervish said I got creamed when we punched out," he replied slowly, shrugging his shoulders. "Gracie did an emergency punch but a missile followed us through. I don't remember anything about it."

"I didn't know what had happened," Tressel said contritely. "You two were pretty close. Ninsse thought you were dead. She was depressed and lonely." He looked down and added sheepishly, "I kinda took advantage of that."

Hawk decided this guy was all right. "It's okay. I might have done the same thing if the tables had been turned. I guess you know I'm Hawk."

Tressel looked up and nodded. "Thanks. I'm Tressel."

Hawk shook the hand he offered. "Nice to meet you," he said, stifling a yawn. "Listen, I'm really beat. I gotta get back to sleep."

"I really think you ought to see her," Tressel commented. "It might jog something in there."

"If she's happy and you're happy, why stir up what might have been?"

Tressel made a face. "I guess I want to make sure she's happy. If she's still … in love with you," he said, handing Hawk his jeans, "I might as well find out now."

"Now?"

"She's up. I just left her room," Tressel admitted. "She would really like to see you."

Hawk looked at him strangely, but he didn't have the energy to argue, so he proceeded to dress himself, then followed Tressel to Ninsse's room. He felt rather odd as he walked in and saw her. Something in his mind tried to come forward, but was immediately surrounded by silverish snow and faded before he could grasp it. Not knowing what else to do, he just stood there.

Ninsse looked at him, then looked at Tressel.

Noting his silence and obvious embarrassment, Tressel jumped in. "He has amnesia. He doesn't remember much of anything."

Ninsse walked up to Hawk slowly and brushed his hair from his face. "I'm really glad you're still alive," she said softly, "and I hope you will remember everything one day. I know I'll never forget you."

"I hope so, too," Hawk replied wistfully. "It seems like they'd be pretty good memories."

"They are," she said, giving him a kiss on the cheek. "Give my love to Tazz. Tell him I'm really happy here."

"Uhhh, Tazz? Yeah, I think I sort of remember him," Hawk replied hesitantly. "Sure, I'll tell him. Worse case, I'll have Dervish point him out. Take care of her, Tressel," he added with a wink, "or, if I'm remembering right, you'll have his whole squad on your butt." He nodded to them both and returned to his room.

It was almost noon when Dervish woke him up. "Do you want to get some breakfast before we go?" he asked Hawk; he sounded concerned.

"Sure. What's up?" Hawk asked quickly. "You seem upset."

Dervish hesitated. "Michelli thinks something's blocking your memories," he replied slowly. "Tressel said he sensed a silverish snow any time you tried to recall stuff."

Hawk bit his lip. "Yeah, that's *exactly* what it's like. Some things I remember fine, and other stuff ... nothing. I never had amnesia before. I figured it was supposed to be that way. "

"Would you trust Michelli to snoop around in your head? See if he can figure out if it's mother nature or something else we're dealing with?"

"You know him better than I do."

"It's *your* head," Dervish countered.

"If you say it's okay, it's fine with me," Hawk admitted. "I sure would like to remember. I don't like the idea that something might be intentionally blocking me."

After Hawk bathed, dressed, and grabbed breakfast, he and Dervish walked down the hall to Michelli's study. Michelli invited the two of them to be seated, and explained briefly to Hawk what he and Dervish were going to attempt. He then pulled up a chair next to them and placed a hand on either side of Hawk's face.

"Close your eyes and let your mind drift," Michelli said softly. "Breathe deeply and slowly relax your body."

Michelli continued to talk to him, but it seemed to Hawk that the voice was getting farther and farther away. He began to drift off; his mind slowly grew dark. When he opened his eyes, he noted that a half hour had passed. He looked from Michelli to Dervish, then back at Michelli.

"It seems to be some kind of healing art," Michelli answered his unspoken question. He sighed and rubbed his head before he continued. "You are very lucky to be alive. The damage was critical; what kept you in this realm is beyond my ability to ascertain. Somebody upstairs must like you," he said with a smile. "Or maybe just isn't ready to deal with you yet," he added with a friendly wink.

"That's kinda like what Liefwynde said," Hawk admitted sheepishly.

"Liefwynde; that would be the young Elf," Michelli mused, mostly to himself.

"But why the silvery static when I try to remember things?" Hawk questioned.

Michelli looked at him. "That part of your brain isn't completely healed. In a manner of speaking, it's been shut down for repairs."

Hawk shrugged. "Guess I'll have to wait to remember."

"It may take months, and some of your memories may never return," Michelli told him. "If the damage was too severe, they might be scrambled beyond repair. Don't try to push it; it'll heal better if you allow it to rest."

"No one ever told me *not* to think before," Hawk reflected, "except maybe in school."

"Thinking is fine," Michelli assured him, "just don't dwell on the past." He turned to Dervish. "I suspect you will be busy for a few weeks, but after that you must come back for training."

"Yeah," Dervish agreed, a bit reluctantly. "We need that information too, and there's no way the Yolluns would accept a squad of Fliers dropping in for a visit."

"They won't be pleased with a squad of Guardians either," Michelli noted. "But I doubt they will attack you openly."

"What's all *this* about?" Hawk asked.

"Tressel was Michelli's inside man," Dervish told him. "Kinda blew his cover rescuing Rusty and Ninsse. We need to find out if the Yolluns are joining up with the Rudonians."

"Why do *you* have to go?" Hawk asked suspiciously.

"The Alderian Talent is not very strong with minds," Dervish explained. "Only a few, like Michelli here, have been able to cultivate that ability. And Tressel."

"So?"

"So," Dervish replied, "someone's got to go in and probe their minds." He shrugged his shoulders. "Looks like I'm it, whether I like it or not."

Hawk looked at Dervish strangely. "I didn't know you could read minds," he commented. "Not for real, anyway."

"Neither did I," Dervish admitted, "but Michelli thought maybe I could. We played around with it some this morning. It seems like I might get to be real good at it, better than Tressel, even."

Hawk looked back at Michelli. "Do me and Angel get to go along?"

Dervish lit up. "Yeah; they really ought to. We fly pretty good together and ..."

"I'm afraid not," Michelli interrupted. "Neither of you would pass for Alderian."

"We're a team," Hawk stated firmly. "Either we all go, or none of us go."

Michelli raised an eyebrow. "You're welcome to train with the squad picked for this mission." He paused a moment, reflecting, then continued. "Actually, that might not be a bad idea. You may be surprised to find that my Guardians are not the mean and nasties you think they are." He winked at Dervish. "And at the same time," he added, "they will discover that Nathan's Fliers are more than just a pack of delinquent half-wits."

Hawk glanced at Dervish. "Are we being challenged?"

"It's more like being drafted," Dervish replied sullenly. "At least we have the distinction of having been snookered by the very best."

"I will inform Zar that all three of you will report within the month," Michelli told them. "Zar commands the elite training program we run for a select few of the best Guardians. You may find that your greatest challenge will be to keep your tempers under control. Zar will push hard. Don't let him get to you."

"I'll try to keep that in mind," Hawk replied with a smirk.

"It will frustrate him greatly if you do," Michelli chuckled. "He's a bit old fashioned; thinks the only good pilot is a Guardian. I would love you lads to prove him wrong."

"Really, now?" Dervish asked.

"If my guess is correct," Michelli replied seriously, "we've got a formidable threat in the works. We may well have to work together to push back the combined Rudonian and Yollundic forces."

"Nathan would probably go along with that," Dervish replied with a grin, "'cause it would sure frost the Council."

"I've always enjoyed doing that myself," Michelli admitted.

Hawk looked at Michelli with a thoughtful, puzzled expression. "You know, you don't seem all that bad. How did you get such a terrible reputation?"

"Cultivated it carefully," Michelli replied with a wink. "It keeps a lot of troublemakers away from the galaxy." He rose and escorted them out of his study. "Angel and Rusty are waiting in the living room. I really must get back to work," he told them politely, "and you lads probably want to be heading home." He looked at Dervish and raised an eyebrow, "unless, of course, you would rather have the wedding here?"

Dervish just fidgeted with his hair without responding.

"I'll take that as a compliment," Michelli said softly. "Now go, before I'm tempted to work on that doubt." He walked back into his study and closed the door.

"Were you really considering getting married here?" Hawk asked as they walked into the living room.

Dervish winced. "Well ... I wouldn't have to face Killer if I did."

"Point well made," Hawk agreed, "but there's three of us, and with Rusty and the baby, that's five against ..."

"Hopefully," Dervish interrupted him, "he won't find out about the baby until after we're married."

"*I'm* not going to tell him," Rusty admitted, wrapping her arm around Dervish. "I want to stay alive too, y'know."

Reynard escorted them out to their fighters and bid them a safe journey. He then bowed slightly to Rusty. "You take care, Princess," he told her; then, lowering his voice he continued. "Please bring the little scamp for a visit when you feel up to it." He discreetly nodded toward the house. "It would really mean a lot to him."

"I promise," Rusty whispered back, "as soon as we're fit to travel, we'll come."

"Don't I have anything to say about this?" Dervish asked with mock indignation.

"Of course not," Rusty teased him. "Grandfathers have automatic priority."

Reynard wore a silly smile as he walked back to the house.

Dervish informed Nathan of Michelli's request and received unofficial orders to undertake the mission. They then headed for Sparks' base to deal with Rusty's dad.

Liefwynde nailed Nathan to the wall for allowing Hawk and Angel to go anywhere near the Alderians. She could neither accept nor understand a Talent that purported to affect inanimate things like computers; she felt strongly that the Alderians only played with minds. She informed him that she saw signs of prying in Hawk's mind.

Nathan assured her that the Talent dealt mainly with inanimate objects and that Michelli had voiced the same concern when he noted her healing arts in Hawk's mind.

She was convinced that Nathan was sending the lambs to sleep with the lions, and informed him quite frankly that she intended to make sure no one ever tampered with Hawk's mind again. Nathan grinned as she left his office. He didn't think it would be that long before the little Elf realized that her interest in the Flier went well beyond healing.

Angel and Hawk waited outside the shuttle bay while Dervish went in. Moments later, they heard Killer's voice booming over the noise of the hydraulics. "What in blazes ..."

By mutual agreement, the two Fliers moved quickly into the bay and approached Dervish and Killer at a rapid pace.

" ... took you so long?" Killer bellowed.

Dervish looked sheepish. "I ... ummm ... I had to get up the courage to ask her," he replied meekly. He was extremely grateful that Killer couldn't read minds.

"Technicality," Killer mumbled with a chuckle. "Well, you have my blessing, for what it's worth." He embraced Dervish for a moment, then stepped back and looked at him sternly. "So ... how soon can I expect to be a grandfather?" he asked flatly.

Dervish turned a number of colors before settling on bright red.

"Thought so," Killer said. "That's how her mother got me to pop the question. It sorta runs in the family." He slapped Dervish on the shoulder. "Better get your forms filed quickly," he prompted.

Dervish reached into his flight suit and pulled out the papers. "All approved," he said with a comical smile.

Killer raised an eyebrow. "It takes forever to get approval; she'd be showing by now," he said quizzically. "How *did* she do it, then?"

Dervish just gave him a fatuous grin.

The wedding was a simple affair. Killer gave the bride away, Hawk was best man, Isslan provided the music, and Angel kept the liquid refreshments from getting lonely.

Dervish carried Rusty across the threshold of the office; Hawk, Killer and Isslan carried Angel. Dervish wore a permanent grin on his face for the next two weeks. Angel wore green on his. Only Hawk looked fit when the three touched down on Michelli's private airstrip.

An astute observer, Michelli decided a three day visit was in order before they started training. Dervish and Angel slept most of the first day.

Michelli gave Hawk the ID transponders to install on their Birds. After tying them in, Hawk was a bit more at ease. At least they wouldn't get shot down by an Alderian. Not by accident, anyway. After that, he spent some time with Tressel.

Michelli spotted the two of them out in the garden and sent Reynard to ask Tressel to see him in his office. Reynard returned with Tressel a few moments later.

"I'm concerned about Hawk," Michelli informed him as Tressel slumped into the chair across from him.

"I'm worried about him, too," Tressel answered hotly. "He's been through a lot. Why are you sending them out to Zar?"

Michelli looked at him and pursed his lips. "Have you tried to touch his mind?"

"There's not a single thought in Zar's brain worth knowing," Tressel said sarcastically.

Michelli cleared his throat. "It is, however, Hawk I'm concerned about."

Tressel gave him a roguish smile. "I thought the Elf did a bang-up job. It's like nobody's home," he said. "Ought to drive Zar crazy."

"As long as you're sure it is Art and not just improper healing," Michelli replied, "I won't send him home."

"But why Zar?" Tressel nailed him.

"Zar has never lost a member of his squad," Michelli reminded him. "I doubt he'll wish to break that record."

"I still don't like it," Tressel informed him. "If anyone can turn Dervish off, it will be Zar."

Michelli looked tired. "I'm more concerned with keeping him alive than convincing him to come home," he said softly, "though it's obvious that he has his doubts about me."

"I'm really fond of him," Tressel shot back. "If he doesn't come back a Guardian, I'll hold Zar personally responsible. Dervish is not pleased with you for making him do this. In fact, he's downright pissed."

"If Dervish doesn't wish to join when they get back," Michelli pointed out, "Zar will withdraw of his own accord."

"That's a tough one," Tressel quipped. "I hate Zar almost as much as I like Dervish."

"Zar is none too fond of you, either," Michelli observed. "If I recall correctly, it has something to do with being insolent and failing to follow orders."

Tressel put on his most angelic look. "Who, me?" he asked innocently. "As I remember, his classes were as boring as they were useless. And he resented the fact I was just there to observe, not to be tested." He gave Michelli a side-long glance, then added, "He wasn't too pleased that I'm half Elf, either."

Michelli gave him a wry smile. "That's the half I'm fondest of," he said with a chuckle.

Tressel made a face and stuck out his tongue. "That was the Alderian half," he sneered.

"Why don't you show Hawk around," Michelli suggested. "He's not the type to poke about on his own."

"I can tell when I'm not wanted," Tressel called back teasingly as he left the room.

"I don't see why you put up with him," Reynard observed. "The finest seed in poor soil doesn't make a good crop."

Michelli smiled. "I should send you to talk to the farmers."

"That was not a slur on Alderians," Reynard countered, "just a personal observation regarding his mother."

"He knows only that she died while having him," Michelli said softly. "I really didn't think it necessary to inform him she was a traitor and the murderer of his father, do you?"

Reynard looked up quickly. "*I* didn't even know that," he said softly. "I just had a bad feeling whenever she was near."

"Since her life ended when she had Tressel," Michelli told him, "I saw no reason to bring it up. Give him time," he advised. "He becomes more like his father every year."

"Perhaps if I live long enough," Reynard replied, "I will see what you perceive in him now."

"You're his closest living relative," Michelli pointed out. "Your lack of acceptance hurts him."

Reynard looked down. "He's every bit the scamp his father was at that age," he said contritely. "I *do* tend to forget that."

Michelli narrowed his eyes a bit. "His brash behavior is a thin disguise to cover his gentle spirit."

Reynard pursed his lips. "You're hardly the one to talk."

Michelli closed his eyes slowly and sighed, but the corners of his mouth betrayed the smile hiding there. "I clearly remember you pointing out a great number of times that I had no redeeming qualities."

"Actually," Reynard replied, "the best thing your father ever did for our people was through your mother."

Michelli chuckled. "Us scamps have managed to keep that secret for quite some time now."

"And with any luck," Reynard added, "no one will ever know she was not Alderian."

✦ ✦ ✦

Dervish and Angel looked much more like their usual selves when the three Fliers disembarked on the Alderian space station. An older man with a chronically sour expression walked up to them and stood impatiently as they looked around the flight deck. "You're not here on a sightseeing tour," he informed them roughly.

"So maybe we should put on blindfolds," Angel parried.

"That might improve the appearance of the place," Hawk observed.

"I'm Zar. Those that are selected for this training are already the very best. My job is to make them better. You, however, are here as guests. To learn; a personal request from Michelli himself, no less," Zar told them coldly. "You're not pilots by my standards, nor is it likely that you people ever could be." His eyes widened as the Fliers removed their helmets. "My God, don't you girls ever cut your hair?" he asked disgustedly.

Angel bristled for a moment, then smiled. "Naw, I don't wanna upset the cooties."

"You are expected to demonstrate proper respect to your superiors," Zar barked.

"I'll keep that in mind if I meet one," Angel drawled as he leaned back to rest against Goldie. Dervish winced; Hawk suppressed a laugh.

Two Guardians had approached within earshot. The older of the two gave Angel an icy scowl. "You're meeting one now," he growled, as he closed the distance to stand next to Zar, who appeared to be in a state of controlled apoplexy.

Angel gave the man a one-digit salute.

"Stuff it, buster," Goldie told the Guardian in her most alluring voice.

The man glanced at Goldie oddly. "What's this?" he asked with a great deal of annoyance. He attempted to link with her flight computer.

"And please keep your filthy little mind to yourself," Goldie added. "Degenerate!"

The other Guardian had walked up to Love and was eyeing her critically. It was obvious from his expression that he was impressed. He bit his lip as Goldie spoke, attempting to hide a smile. As he unconsciously ran a hand across Love's smooth skin, her laser positioner locked on. The young Guardian jumped back wide eyed, his mouth agape.

"She's not fond of strangers," Dervish advised him quickly.

"Disarm those fighters now!" Zar barked.

"They are," Dervish informed him with a grin. "She's bluffing."

"It can talk," the older Guardian commented with a sneer, "but it remains to be seen if it can fly."

"I can fly considerably better than you can," Goldie informed him sarcastically. "Your only means of propulsion appears to be hot air."

The younger Guardian raised an eyebrow at his wingmate. "She got you, Striker," he commented dryly.

Angel decided to attempt a truce, at least for the moment. He looked at Striker a bit sheepishly. "Don't let it bother you none," he said nicely. "I've only won a few rounds with her myself."

"Luck," Goldie informed them pointedly.

Striker stared at Angel a moment. "Is she always this way," he asked nodding toward Goldie, "or is it just that time of the month?"

"Time of month?" Goldie repeated, obviously puzzled.

Angel grinned and gave Striker a thumbs up.

"If you're through playing," Zar stated, "I will show you to your quarters." He caught the younger Guardian's eye. "Nipper," he commanded curtly, "get these girls properly uniformed."

"I was not aware that Alderians are blind," Goldie retorted. "I will add that information to my database."

Angel patted Goldie fondly before he turned to follow. "Love ya," he whispered.

Striker stayed where he was, eyeing the Birds more closely. He had never seen a Bird up close before. They were smaller, daintier, and had less firepower than a PRO-fighter; still, he would have traded were he given the choice. They were the niftiest craft he had ever laid eyes on.

Goldie spent a long time trying to determine what she had managed to do to please Angel. With careful analysis, she could avoid it in the future.

16

And One To Grow On

Hawk put his flight bag on the chair and looked around the room. It was larger than his room back at base and had a bathroom with a tub. He wandered over to Dervish's room and found Angel there already. Seeing Nipper walking down the hall, he closed the door pointedly as he entered. Wearing an I-told-you-so expression, he slumped into one of the chairs. Angel paced the floor mumbling.

Nipper stopped in front of the door and grimaced. As he pondered whether to knock or just dump the uniforms on the ground, he listened to the conversation taking place.

"These are guest quarters," Dervish told them, deciding from their antics what was bothering them. "Wouldn't want to contaminate the Guardians now, would they?"

"Real assholes, if you ask me," Angel drawled, as he crossed the room and seated himself on the bed.

"I'm sure they feel the same way," Hawk rebuffed him. "Our guys weren't much nicer to Dervish, if you recall."

Angel began to clean his nails with his buck knife. "It's back to three against the world," he commented dryly.

Dervish looked at them and grinned. "What you mean three, Earth People?"

Nipper wrinkled his nose. *The sooner we get this over with, the sooner I can get back to my wingmates*, he thought. *It'll take a lot longer if we get into a pissing contest.* He knocked on the door softly.

"What d'ya want," Angel snapped as Dervish opened the door.

"Room service," Nipper replied goodnaturedly, offering the uniforms to Dervish, who seemed not to notice. "Zar's orders," Nipper added with a pained expression.

"What's with that guy, anyway?" Angel asked, motioning Nipper inside.

Nipper looked first at Dervish then at Hawk to make sure his entering was okay with them also. Since they both nodded slightly, he made his way to the dresser and set the uniforms down. "Zar? Oh, he might be a little hard to take when you first meet him," he explained, "but once you get to know him you'll realize that deep down inside he's really a total asshole."

"Wonderful," Angel muttered.

"Good pilot, though," Nipper admitted reluctantly.

"We got a few of those," Hawk replied, "'cept they don't make squad leader." As he looked over the uniforms he added, "we pick our own wingmates; leader is by mutual consent."

Nipper shifted his weight to one foot. "Look," he said defensively, "We're not pleased with this arrangement either. We didn't volunteer; Zar picked us. The sooner you guys cut out the crap and get this over with, whatever it is, the sooner we can get back to our wingmates."

"Hey, we didn't volunteer either," Dervish shot back, "I owed Michelli one; he's collecting."

"Can't you guys just tell Zar to cram it?" Angel asked seriously.

Nipper stared blankly at Angel, then looked at Dervish. "*Michelli* sent you?" he asked, honoring Angel's gestured invitation to be seated. He seemed to focus on nothing for a moment. "What's going on?"

"Michelli wants to know if the Yolluns are joining up with the Rudonians," Dervish told him.

"Here? He sent you *here* to find that out?" Nipper asked incredulously.

"Huh? No, no ... ummm, didn't they tell you anything?" Hawk asked.

"The old Need-To-Know syndrome," Angel commented disgustedly. "Damn, I didn't realize how much we take for granted now."

Dervish pulled a chair up to the bed and sat down. "Michelli wants me to find out for him," he explained, "but a Flier wouldn't be welcome anywhere near the Yolluns' main base. He figured on sending me in with a squad of Guardians."

"Why you?" Nipper asked seriously.

"The Talent's a bit different in me," Dervish answered. "I've been able to pick up on thoughts occasionally."

Nipper studied Dervish carefully, then reached out and brushed one of Dervish's long auburn ringlets. "Funny; you don't look Alderian," he commented, shaking his head. Glancing at Hawk and Angel, he added, "and you guys would *never* pass for Alderians."

"Dervish is our wingmate," Hawk told him. "We came to keep an eye on him until the last possible moment."

Dervish flushed slightly. "I'm not sure who my parents were," he answered honestly. "Michelli said he'd tell me what he knows after I do this for him."

Nipper looked puzzled. "If you can read thoughts," he said slowly, "couldn't you just get it out of his mind?"

"It's not right to poke around in someone's head," Dervish muttered. "Especially if the head in question is Michelli's and you want to live to a ripe old age."

Nipper comprehended that instantly. "He's not one to mess with, that's for sure. I'm Nipper ... my wingmate out there is Striker," he said expectantly.

"I'm Hawk, this nut is Angel and Dervish over there is the reason we're all here," Hawk replied.

Nipper shrugged. "Look, when you guys get the uniforms on, I'll show you around."

Angel grinned. "I take it gray's not too popular around here."

"We didn't enlist," Dervish said dryly. "And we have no intentions of ever doing so."

Nipper glared at Dervish. "Dammit," he said angrily, "do you have to go out of your way to add to the friction?"

"The man's got a point, Dervish," Hawk admonished.

Dervish scowled. "I spent my entire time with Michelli avoiding that uniform. I'll be damned if I'll put it on an instant sooner than I have to."

Nipper looked disgusted and a bit hurt. "I'm proud of that uniform," he shot back hotly. "I strongly suggest you keep your opinions to yourself." He got up and stormed toward the door. "We're scheduled out at fourteen hundred," he said bitterly as he walked out the door. "Don't show up in gray."

"So what *will* we wear?" Angel asked quietly, as Nipper slammed the door.

"Blue," Dervish responded, pulling a pair of jeans out of his flight bag.

"You're really asking for it," Hawk countered.

"And I'll probably get it," Dervish sighed. "Sorry guys, but I just can't do it. Maybe it's just me, but I keep thinking Michelli set this up just to get me to wear his stupid uniform."

Nipper had paused outside the door, not so much to listen as to reflect on his own actions.

Hawk's voice drifted through the door. "What, so he can have a picture in his wallet? Mine Son, The Guardian? Naw, I don't see it, Dervish."

Nipper froze a moment, then turned back toward the door.

"If that's all he wanted," Angel agreed, "he could have taken one that time he gave you the stinky bear antidote."

"It was wear that or nothing," Dervish growled. "I can't stand having something crammed down my throat."

Nipper bit his lip as his mind raced through the possible implications. *The lack of an heir has caused a lot of tension, yet Michelli has never married; a rebellious, illegitimate son by an obviously non-Alderian mother might be the reason. To be accepted by his people, Dervish would have to pass the Test. Maybe Michelli hopes that the kid will find out what it's like to work with the best, give up the riff-raff and come home. That would sure be a big gamble for Michelli*, he thought. *It's pass or die, and a half-breed has never passed the Test.*

The closing of a door down the hall brought him back to reality. "Let's grab some lunch before we have to report," Striker said as he approached.

"I'm not very hungry," Nipper replied, "but I could use some company."

Striker gave him a grin. "Don't let those fools get to you. They're not worth it."

"It's not just them; this whole thing's got me edgy," Nipper admitted. "Doesn't it seem odd to break up our squad to work with them?"

"They're up against the Rudonians too," Striker pointed out. "We gotta teach 'em enough to deal with 'em." He got a glint in his eyes. "Be less Rudonians around to bother our galaxy, and a lot less of them Bird-jockeys, too."

"I don't know," Nipper muttered. "I have a feeling there's more to it than that."

✦   ✦   ✦

Hawk took a deep breath as they entered the flight deck and made their way to the Birds. He prayed they could get inside the fighters unnoticed. Nipper, Striker and Zar were waiting for them, and by Zar's expression, Hawk figured they had not achieved invisibility.

"Nipper!" Zar barked, "I told you to get them uniforms!"

Nipper looked uncomfortable. "Ummm, I ..."

"He did," Dervish jumped in, "but, as you pointed out, we're not Guardians. It wouldn't be proper to wear the uniforms."

Zar's cold stare dropped the temperature on the flight deck three degrees.

"We're punching out to training zone A," Zar informed them flatly. "Five droid base ships will project holographic missiles and obstacles, and they control the target drones. You are to react as if everything is real. If you can lock on a drone, it's considered a hit. If the drone locks on you — well, just be glad it's only a drone." He made eye contact with Dervish and continued. "Don't mess with the base ships. And if you fire, I'll personally blow you to bits."

"Bet he'd enjoy that, too," Angel drawled as Zar turned to leave.

"If he attempts lock on me," Love added, "he will be dead."

Nipper and Striker exchanged glances. "All your fighters like these?" Nipper asked.

"Not really," Angel answered. "Some of 'em are nasty." He chuckled to himself as he climbed aboard Goldie.

They glided out across the training zone and maneuvered to a holding position. Zar floated to a stop a bit to the right and behind them.

"First, we go one at a time," Zar explained in an annoying monotone. "Striker, you first."

As Striker moved through the exercise. Dervish noted that although he was good, he was predictable; a real enemy would have nailed him. Zar sent Nipper out next. He was a bit more creative; Dervish figured the kid had promise.

"How good do you think you are?" Zar asked them causticly.

"No idea," Angel drawled. "Never played video games ."

"Okay, Unknowing, take your best shot," Zar informed him.

Angel did real well — too much so for the Alderian egos involved. Zar sounded anything but pleased as he ordered Hawk out. "Blondie, you're next!"

Hawk ignored him.

"Hey girlie, you deaf?" Zar snapped.

"Which one of us girlies did you have in mind?" Dervish asked quietly.

"The other one," Zar replied bitterly.

"Oh, Hawk, darling, have you finished doing your nails?" Dervish sang sweetly.

"Yeth," Hawk replied in an exaggerated lisp, "but my blouth clatheth with the targeth."

"I know. Dreadful, isn't it? But please take that great big fighter out there and show that nasty brute how we curl our long flowing hair."

Hawk screamed into the target zone and pulled a few maneuvers that most likely had that effect on the Alderians. One of the droid base ships dropped its signal to acknowledge defeat as Zar called him out.

"You're next, Red," Zar ordered, but his tone was civil.

If Hawk didn't quite add a natural wave to Zar's hair, Dervish did. He got a dropped signal out of two of the five before Zar called him back.

"Clown," Zar shouted at him. "You'll get yourself killed doing fool stunts like those. You left holes a real enemy could have nailed you on." He paused, hoping that might soak in. "This is a timed event," he told them. "As a team now; Striker, Nipper, go."

They were good together; they got three dropped signals in the allotted time. Zar called them back. "Ladies, your turn," he said softly.

The three of them got four dropped signals in the same time period, but Dervish was worried; he was losing track of Hawk. He had always known before exactly where his wingmates were and what they were going to do. He had Angel, but it was as if Hawk wasn't even there.

Zar then sent Nipper and Hawk out against each other. Nipper was a better strategist, but Hawk's originality finally won out. Dervish spent the time experimenting with picking up on Hawk. Even with a great deal of effort, all he could manage to get was a lot of silvery snow. Something was wrong with either his head or Hawk's, and Hawk seemed to be flying real well.

Angel and Striker went next. Angel was having a hard time of it, but kept up an impressive game of cat and mouse. It was obvious both pilots were tiring, but Zar didn't call them in. Striker made an original maneuver and ended up directly behind Goldie. He almost locked, but Goldie flipped over upside-down on top of him. Angel couldn't resist cementing relations with an obscene hand gesture.

Goldie dipped into a dive off to one side. She slid sideways for a moment, then her nose shot upward and she locked on Striker as he locked on her. "Keep your mind out of my nodes," Goldie ordered, "or you are space junk!"

Angel's voice was sheer panic. "She's overridden manual! She's trying to fire!"

"Striker," Dervish ordered, "drop lock!"

Angel's tone of voice convinced Striker this was no bluff. He quickly responded to Dervish's order.

Goldie shuddered and reluctantly ceded control back to Angel. "I will kill him if he does that again!" she stated flatly.

"Uhhh, Zar, could we go in and check that circuitry?" Dervish asked. "I must have messed up the routing if she could override manual."

Zar didn't respond for a few moments. "Take 'em in," he finally said.

Angel looked white as a sheet as he leaned against Goldie. Dervish didn't look much better as he started slowly checking each bypass node.

Striker walked up and gave Angel a strange look. "What's with it anyway?" he asked sourly.

"You pulled lock on me," Goldie informed him.

"It was just a game, Birdbrain," Angel snapped at her.

"Then why did he attempt to jam my circuits while he loaded number four?" she asked hotly.

Angel gave Striker a real hard look.

"It was *only* a flare," Striker shot back defensively.

Angel's eyes widened as he saw Zar's face become distorted in anger.

"You did not bother to inform me of that," Goldie replied curtly.

"Striker!" Zar bellowed, "you're on report! Red," he barked, only slightly nicer, "no repairs needed. Back out, all of you." He stomped off.

"Hey," Angel called after him. "Don't I get any say in this?"

Zar turned and looked at Angel coldly. "Depends," he replied harshly. "What did you want to say?"

Angel nodded toward Striker. "Don't jump on him. I had it coming."

Zar eyed Angel critically. "Explain."

Angel made a sassy face. "I'm a cocky bastard, right?"

Zar's expression didn't change, but Angel could have sworn he saw a twinkle in the old man's eyes. "Striker," he asked gruffly, "is he?"

Striker studied the ground. "No, sir," he replied flatly.

"Decision stands," Zar barked and started off again.

"What do you think this is," Angel yelled after him, "the fuckin' Air Force? What the hell did you *expect* him to say?"

Zar stopped and turned to face Angel, his expression an icy mask. "You're wrong, Striker. He *is* a cocky bastard. Next time, however, you're grounded." He stared at both of them as he shook his head. "That fighter's got more brains than the both of you put together," he informed them disgustedly.

"I wish you hadn't said that so loud," Angel muttered. "She's gonna gloat for weeks now."

Zar was quietly chuckling as he walked back to his fighter.

"Shit," Striker said softly, looking sheepishly at Angel. "Guess I owe you one."

"Naahh," Angel replied, "but if you got some time later on, maybe you could go over some of them maneuvers you pulled out there."

"Sure," Striker replied with a grin, "if you go over that back flip thing with me."

"Give me some help up here," Dervish called down, oblivious to all that went on. "I found three networks that need rerouting."

"Zar just ordered us back out, Dervish," Angel called up to him. "We'll fix 'em tonight."

"Damn," Dervish mumbled. "I wanted to get some sleep."

Angel slowly strapped himself in and sat gazing pensively at the flight computer. For the life of him he could not figure out how Goldie had known what Striker was doing. He weighed the elation she would feel knowing he had not been able to figure it out against how much he really wanted to know. As they slid into the launch bay his curiosity won the battle with his ego. "Goldie," he asked politely, "how did you know Striker was loading his number four pod?"

Goldie was silent a moment longer than Angel found comfortable. "It did not take me very long to come to the conclusion that you would need all the help you could get. Since I have access to the Guardians' security codes, I requested continuous flight dumps from his fighter. It helped me to stay even."

"You were cheating?"

"All is fair in love and war," Goldie snapped as she floated out of the bay and punched.

"Red, it's you and me now," Zar called to Dervish as they punched back into the training zone.

Angel caught himself holding his breath a few times as the minutes rolled by. Both Zar and Dervish were doing some fairly tricky flying to counter the other's clever maneuvers. They'd been at it close to ten minutes when Dervish's voice broke the silence.

"You win," he said flatly, gliding Love around to fall in by Zar's fighter.

"Why?" Zar yelled at him.

"I'm too tired," Dervish retorted. "Gets real dangerous flying this way."

"You think they call time out in a battle?" Zar snapped.

"I wouldn't stay in a battle for ten fuckin' minutes in manual!" Dervish shot back.

"Manual? That circuitry bothering you *that* much?" Zar asked, almost nicely.

"Yes sir. It is."

"Dump your flight log, Dervish," Zar requested.

Dervish dumped Love's flight log to Zar, then slumped back in the seat, exhausted.

"Why did you not trust me?" Love whimpered to Dervish in an obviously hurt tone of voice.

"If you had pulled on Zar what Goldie pulled on Striker," Dervish told her nicely, "one of us would be dead now."

"Him," Love attempted to assure Dervish.

"Okay, Dervish," Zar called, "take them back in and check out those nodes."

"Thanks," Dervish replied.

Zar sat there a long time after the five fighters had winked out. *Manual*, he thought to himself, after reviewing the dump Love had sent. *He flew like that in manual! Damn, the lad's good.* He tapped his finger against the console. *A few weeks of training and he should peak some. Hmmm; we'll see, little man.*

Dervish was almost asleep by the time Angel landed Goldie and walked over to Love. She lowered the stairs for him and popped the latch on the cabin. "You okay, Dervish?" he asked, as Hawk scrambled up behind him.

"Just tired," Dervish responded with a yawn.

"You could have nailed him if you weren't in manual."

"I don't know," Dervish replied honestly. "He could have locked a few times, but I wouldn't have been hit if he fired on those locks. Probably why he didn't." He paused and let out a puff of air. "I didn't make the same mistake twice, but I made a lot of 'em once."

"He's that good?" Hawk asked.

Dervish nodded. "Hawk, you awake enough to reroute those nodes? I got 'em marked in Goldie."

"Sure. Angel can help."

"I'll just nap here in Love in case you need me," Dervish mumbled as he drifted off to sleep.

Hawk was inside Goldie's cockpit and Angel lay across the stub of a wing, positioned so he could help Hawk, when Nipper called up to them. "Can I come up or will she fire?" he asked, only half kidding.

"Come on up," Hawk replied. "She's catatonic now. I got her main system down."

"You sure?" Nipper questioned as he climbed the stairs. "I don't want her mad at me." He handed Hawk a plate of sandwiches. "Striker's bringing the drinks," he added as he gazed around the cockpit.

"Thanks," Angel said, really meaning it.

Striker handed the drinks up to Nipper. "No way," he chuckled when Angel motioned for him to climb up onto the wing. "Not until I get the invitation from her."

Hawk and Angel took a break to eat and swap a few jokes with the Alderians. They weren't all exactly buddies by the time Nipper and Striker left, but a comfortable sort of truce was in the works.

After finishing Goldie and Gracie, they woke Dervish and started on Love. Dervish joined them as soon as he had wolfed down a sandwich. They had rerouted the automatic and were working on the manual when an ear-piercing siren shattered the silence of the flight deck. Guardians came from every which direction, scrambling to their fighters and somehow began making an orderly takeoff in all the commotion.

"What's up?" Dervish called out as a squad of Guardians raced by.

"Harenden under attack!," one yelled back. "Rudonians."

Dervish looked at Hawk and Angel.

"Why not?" they replied, almost in unison.

As Angel and Hawk ran to their Birds, Dervish requested permission for his squad to scramble. He was told to use launch bays three and seven and given coördinates. The controller never asked him to ID his squad, so he didn't bother. They punched into the far side of the fight, just in time to cover the tails of some outnumbered Guardians that were flanking the battle.

No one would have accused them of exhibiting too much form or grace; still, the Rudonians were not ready for the maneuvers that invariably brought a Rudonian fighter into the range of a Guardian or another Bird. While they were still outnumbered, they had put a real crimp in the Rudonians' numerical advantage by the time another flock of Guardians punched in.

They had fallen in behind two Guardian squads to help with the main skirmish when Zar's voice boomed over the radio. "Dervish, where is the rest of your squad?"

"They didn't show," Dervish shot back.

"A squad flies together or not at all," Zar replied coldly.

"We're kinda outnumbered here, sir," Dervish responded. "Could you chew me out after we get the odds evened out?"

"Zar," a strange voice boomed, "get 'em in here, dammit!"

"I ..." Zar started to reply.

"Objection overruled," the voice interrupted. "Move it!"

As Zar led them screaming toward the fracas, Dervish called to him. "Sorry sir," he said politely. "Didn't mean to cause ..."

"Shut up already," Zar came back, but his voice actually sounded friendly.

✦   ✦   ✦

The flight deck was a madhouse when they finally got permission to land. Repair crews were scurrying about and a few medics could be seen tending the injured. Dervish slumped to the floor next to Love and closed his eyes. Hawk sat beside him, resting his head back against Love.

Angel stumbled over and gazed at the two of them. "Why don't we go get some sleep?" he asked, stifling a yawn.

"We're in enough trouble already," Dervish mumbled. "Better wait to be dismissed."

"This really *is* like the Air Force," Angel lamented as he slumped down next to Hawk.

Zar walked over and looked at the three for a moment. "Come on. Let's get some food before you all fall over."

"I'm too tired to eat," Angel muttered, looking longingly down the hall toward the elevators.

"You were almost too dead to eat," Zar pointed out.

"Dervish watches my tail," Angel replied off-handedly.

"And who watches his tail?" Zar asked.

"Why, you do, sir," Angel replied with a grin.

Zar shook his head. "You're crazy, Angel, and you, Hawk, were improperly labeled."

Hearing his name, Hawk came out of his sleepy daze and looked at Zar blankly.

"Should have been dubbed Shadow Lord," Zar teased him. "Damn, you're hard to keep track of!"

Dervish pondered that for a moment. As they entered the cafeteria, he stopped and looked at Zar. "You noticed that about Hawk too? I thought it was just me."

Zar nodded. "What race are you?" he asked Hawk.

"Descendants of the B Ark," Angel quipped.

"Earth. Jewish. Human, I mean," Hawk said sleepily.

"It's just happened," Dervish commented. "Up until a few days ago he came in loud and clear."

A light went on in Hawk's brain. "Liefwynde," he said flatly.

"Liefwynde?" Zar asked.

"She's an Elf," Hawk explained. "Real upset that I was coming here. She insisted that you folks are evil and play with people's minds; something about making sure you couldn't."

"Looks like she reinvented the Elder stealth spell," Zar chuckled.

As they walked to a table, they couldn't help noticing the scornful looks, hoots and wolf whistles that followed them. "It'd be a lot easier on you lads if you'd put on uniforms and cut your hair," Zar commented as they set down the trays.

"But we'd sure get it when we got home," Dervish informed him.

Zar looked at Dervish oddly and was about to say something when a distinguished looking colonel walked up. Dervish, who had started to sit down, stumbled back to his feet. Angel and Hawk exchanged glances.

The colonel looked the three over critically, then turned to Zar. "So these are Nathan's Fliers. They fly a whole lot better than they look."

"Thank you, sir," Angel snickered, "on both counts."

Dervish looked down; Hawk studied the ceiling. Zar gave Angel a sidelong glance that made him straighten up a bit.

"Why did you take them out?" the colonel asked stiffly.

"They were working on the flight deck, sir," Zar replied casually, noting General Larch approaching. "They scrambled themselves."

"General Larch mentioned that," the colonel replied.

"And I'm not in the habit of making things up," Larch snapped. He turned to look at the bedraggled Fliers. "Which one of you is Dervish?"

"I am, sir," Dervish replied, recognizing the voice; it had been Larch who had overridden Zar's orders and sent them back into the fray.

Larch put out his hand. "Nice flying, lad," he said with a smile. "It was my wingmate you saved with that bizarre maneuver."

"My pleasure, sir," Dervish replied, shaking the man's hand. He was suddenly aware of the quiet around them. He shifted his weight nervously under Larch's hard gaze.

"Tell me, do all Fliers look like you three?" Larch asked pointedly.

"Well, sir," Angel sassed, "actually, most of 'em bathe occasionally."

Zar gave him the evil eye. "There's potential there if they ever grow up," he commented dryly.

The general continued to stare at Dervish. "Do I know your father, lad?"

Dervish shrugged his shoulders. "I'm not sure, sir," he said quietly. "I don't know who my father is."

"He'd be very proud of you," Larch said loudly. "Good day, gentleman," he added as he walked away.

The colonel nodded to them and quickly followed Larch.

They ate in relative silence, then drowsily walked back to their rooms. They slept well into the afternoon.

Nipper was annoyed when Zar told him and Striker they had the day off. "What's all this about anyway?" he demanded. "Those guys sure don't need any training."

Zar gave him a very peeved look. "You seem to be learning a lot from them," he commented caustically.

"What's the real story here? Is Dervish Michelli's kid?" Nipper nailed him.

"Where'd you hear that?" Zar asked, raising an eyebrow.

Nipper paused a moment. "Around. But it would make sense. Why else would he send him here?"

"He has his reasons."

"And General Larch personally stops by to see how he's doing?" Nipper retorted.

"The general was merely thanking him for saving his wingmate," Zar said coldly. "I suggest you take your wealth of misinformation and get lost."

Nipper stormed out. He made his way quickly to Dervish's room and entered without knocking. No one was there. He stood there feeling foolish. Why was he so damn upset that the fool went out without him? Why should he care one way or the other? He did, though, and that bothered him.

Angel and Dervish sat facing each other on Hawk's bed. Hawk lay sprawled on the floor, trying unsuccessfully not to laugh.

"Not funny," Dervish chastised him. "This is serious stuff."

"Sorry," Hawk snickered, "but I keep thinking of how that mind business affects me ... and you two on the bed and all ..."

"Go curl your hair," Angel snapped.

"If we can manage to block ourselves," Dervish tried again, "and still keep in touch with each other, it'd be awesome."

"I know, I know," Hawk chuckled. "Sit on the floor, okay?"

"Horny bastard," Angel snickered.

"Shoot," Dervish teased, "we screwed off the whole day. Think he'd have had enough by now."

"Hey, know what? Love's still got no manual," Hawk reminded them, "and we don't have much more time before old Zar will come calling."

"Yeah. Better get to it," Angel drawled, as they reluctantly headed for the door.

Angel had taken his favorite perch on Love's wing and Hawk sat crosslegged on her nose, each trying to follow Dervish's muttered explanations of what he was doing and why.

"Hey, Shadow! That was some pretty fancy flying this morning," a strange voice called up to them.

Angel whispered, "That's you, Hawk."

Hawk looked down and saw a Guardian standing next to Love; he had a nice sort of smile and a real twinkle in his eye.

Hawk maneuvered around, came down the stairs and held out a hand. "Thanks. I'm usually called Hawk."

"They labeled you wrong," the man replied, shaking Hawk's hand.

Dervish glanced down and smiled. "I like that guy," he told Angel. He caught the man's eye and and gave him a high-sign. "You guys looked pretty sharp yourselves," he called out. "I'm Dervish, he's Angel. What's your handle?"

"They call me Cloud," he said as his mind latched. *Dervish*, he thought; *that's the name Tressel had in his head after talking to Michelli. Hmmm ... could be some interesting stuff going on here.* "I think it refers to raining shit," he added.

"Our kind of guy," Angel called down.

Cloud gave Angel an off-handed salute. "No offense meant," he continued, "but can you guys really get away with dressing like that? And your hair," he said, brushing the tips of Hawk's hair with his hand, "I like it! Man, I haven't even seen a *girl* with hair that long."

"Yeah," Hawk replied, "but we do have to wear something clean if we're heading planetside."

Cloud grinned. "You guys accepting volunteers?" he asked seriously. "There's nine in my squad; they won't miss me."

"Fine with us," Dervish called down, "but Zar might have something unpleasant to say about it."

"I'll talk to him about it," Cloud said. "Now, what are we doing?"

Cloud was lying across Love's nose going over the prints with Hawk when Nipper and Striker walked up. "Here comes trouble with a capital T," Angel muttered in English, noting the Guardians' expressions.

"Dervish!" Nipper yelled. "I want to talk to you."

"We're not deaf," Cloud called down.

"What the hell is *he* doing up there?" Striker muttered.

"Helping my friends," Cloud snapped. "What are *you* doing here?"

"They're in *our* squad," Striker informed him coldly. "I don't recall asking *you* to do *anything*."

Cloud tipped his head to one side and stuck out his tongue. "Phffffft," he commented, as he turned his attention back to the schematics.

Dervish clambered down the stairs hoping to head off an all-out war.

Angel smiled at Cloud. "You really are my kind of guy," he said. "How did you get hoodwinked into this outfit?"

"Short story," Cloud admitted. "I love flying."

Nipper nailed Dervish. "Why did you guys scramble without us?"

Dervish shrugged his shoulders. "I didn't think you really wanted to fly with us," he replied casually. "Figured you'd go out with folks you trusted."

Nipper frowned. "You're real arrogant, you know that?"

"It runs in the family," Hawk commented dryly.

"You children at it again?" Zar barked as he strode up.

"They started it," Cloud shouted down in a whiny voice.

"What in blazes are *you* doing up there?" Zar shouted back.

"Lot of dense folk around here," Angel whispered.

"I'd like to work with them," Cloud replied, slipping down across Love's nose and landing cat-like on the deck. "Could you arrange that, sir?"

"Class is full," Zar told him curtly.

"Only five," Cloud retorted, "if you insist on counting those two."

Zar studied the group. Cloud had somehow broken the barrier and was actually accepted by those crazies. It might make his job easier if they liked someone Alderian. "I'll see what I can do," Zar capitulated.

"You won't be sorry, sir," Cloud replied.

Zar looked at Cloud coldly for a moment, then grinned. "But *you* might be," he informed him. "Remember, you asked for it! All of you, be here, eleven hundred." He turned and walked away; Striker followed him.

Nipper shoved his hands into his pockets, gave Dervish a nasty look and headed off the flight deck.

"I believe you hurt his feelings," Cloud commented.

"Amazing," Angel observed. "Didn't know he *had* any."

Dervish looked at the Alderian PRO-fighter that was sitting uncomfortably close to Love. "Must be Cloud's."

Angel nodded. "Nice guy. Wonder why he was born Alderian."

"Even God can make a mistake," Hawk observed, as Nipper and Striker approached.

Nipper gave him a nasty look.

Zar came over shaking his head. "Babies," he muttered. "You're supposed to be the elite of the elite, and I have to change your diapers. Okay, where's Cloud?"

"Here," Cloud called down from inside his fighter.

"Get your ass down here," Zar ordered.

Cloud exited his fighter and walked toward the group dressed in black jeans and a t-shirt. Zar turned a deep shade of purple. "You're not in uniform!" he shouted.

"Sorry sir," Cloud replied with a grin. "I'll get a blue pair as soon as I can."

"Maybe we ought to get black ones, too," Angel pondered. "Wouldn't have to wash 'em as often."

"You'll definitely be black and blue," Zar snarled, "if you don't get your butts moving. Training zone seven."

All but Nipper scrambled for their fighters. "You're letting him get away with that?" he yelled at Zar.

"If you can't beat 'em," Zar informed him pointedly, "join 'em."

"But ..." Nipper started to protest.

"You can't beat him, Nipper," Zar replied dryly.

17

The Changing Of The Guard

Dervish lay on his bed feeling drained. Between Zar's relentless drilling and his own attempts to play with his Talent, he had pushed himself to the limit. Slowly, under Cloud's tutelage, he had begun to understand how to do things with his mind. It was like getting a new toy, one he couldn't resist playing with. Unfortunately, he was constantly running the batteries down.

Then Zar had come up with another nasty idea. He had paired them off: Cloud and Hawk, Angel and Striker, Dervish and Nipper. Anything you did, you had to do with the other one, from eating to flying. Cloud and Hawk had gotten along from the start. Striker had actually warmed up a bit; he was swapping jokes with Angel the other night. Nipper remained a pain in the butt, and he and Dervish had been going through their maneuvers like a couple of klutzes, Nipper refusing to talk. Things went swiftly downhill from there.

The door opened and Cloud and Hawk slipped in, closing it swiftly behind them. "Angel's keeping Striker occupied. I presume Nipper's off bitching to Zar again," Hawk whispered. "Thought we'd see how you're holding up."

"What's with him, anyway?" Dervish complained. "He's acting like a spoiled brat. It's not like I *asked* to fly with him. Or even *wanted* to."

"That could be the problem," Cloud pointed out. "Alderians aren't known for being humble, and he has a healthier than normal ego."

"Hell, if he won't talk, draw him a picture," Hawk teased.

Dervish lit up. "That's not such a dumb idea, I'll try sending him one; maybe it'll freak him out enough to say something."

"Like, 'get out of my mind, asshole'," Cloud offered.

"Even that'd be an improvement," Dervish replied. "Damn, we're due out in ten minutes. I was gonna get some sleep."

"See ya out there," Hawk called back as they left.

During their first few maneuvers, Dervish tried sending Nipper pictures of his next move. Nipper ignored him.

Maybe it was because of Zar's attitude, or perhaps his own poor performance, but over the next few runs Nipper began to use the pictures enough that he and Dervish didn't once get flagged by the computer as having been killed.

When Zar brought them in for a fifteen minute break, however, Nipper was as sullen as ever. After sulking a while, he confronted Dervish. "I'd appreciate it if you'd stay out of my mind," he stated emphatically.

Dervish thought of several choice retorts, but refrained from verbalizing them. He let out a puff of air and looked at the floor. "Sorry," he mumbled. "I just thought ..."

"You think?" Nipper snapped.

"That is *my* line," Goldie interjected.

Nipper chuckled. "Shit, am I really getting to be that bad?"

Dervish shrugged.

Nipper grimaced.

"Hey, clowns," Zar bellowed. "Get your butts back out there!"

Nipper glanced back at Dervish as he headed to his fighter. Dervish was sure he had seen half a smile on his face.

They punched out to training zone nine and glided to a standstill, waiting for Zar's instructions. Cloud drifted in closer to Hawk and tipped a wing stub in his direction. Angel zig-zagged Goldie toward Striker. Striker waited until Goldie was almost upon him, then flipped his fighter upside down over Goldie.

Striker's voice drifted over the radio. "You're upside down, Angel."

"Hell," Angel replied. "I can't seem to get anything right today." He gracefully flipped Goldie over. "That better?"

"Shall we?" Cloud called to Hawk, rolling his fighter over.

"I would think you lads would have figured out that space has no up or down," Zar informed them dryly.

Hawk dipped Gracie's nose and flipped.

Dervish thought about it a moment, then sent Nipper a picture of a PRO-fighter on a cross grid. He slowly tilted the PRO on the grid and was pleased to see that Nipper was attempting to get his fighter to emulate the action. They almost flipped over in perfect unison.

"Not defined well enough," Nipper called to him. "Can you put numbers on that grid?"

"What are you two doing?" Zar demanded.

"Looking at you sitting upside down," Dervish retorted.

"You're out here to learn how to work together," Zar told them, "not to play!"

"That better?" Dervish asked, defining the grid into radials.

"Let's try it again," Nipper responded, and once more the two attempted a synchronous flip.

"Hey, you *did* it," Hawk called to them.

"Very impressive," Zar informed them. "Are you planning on entertaining the enemy by doing tricks?"

"While they're watching those two," Cloud commented, "we can pick 'em off."

"Wonderful," Zar replied. "Now, stop clowning around and get out there."

✦   ✦   ✦

The simulations had become lot harder since Zar started reprogramming them based on detected weaknesses. They had all lost a few rounds to the computer when Dervish got an idea. He sent Nipper a picture of two fighters, one almost on top of the other, carefully mapped on the radials.

Nipper moved his fighter under Love and attempted to follow every move Dervish projected into his head. As he inched up closer, the simulator saw but one target. It fired;

Dervish went up and Nipper dived down from their starting position. Somehow, trying to track the dual target caused the simulator to lock up, and it took a while to reboot it. Zar grounded the two of them for the rest of the day. They were still laughing when they wandered off the flight deck.

Six hours later, Zar brought the other four in. Tired, but still angry, Angel hung back with Zar as the others staggered off the deck. "What did you ground them for?" he asked seriously. "I thought that was pretty neat, and it really isn't their fault your simulator has a bug in it."

"Ever hear of forbidden fruit?" Zar replied with a chuckle. "They're gonna work on it every chance they get. They might even begin to get along with each other." He winked at Angel. "You did better the last two times. You're protecting your own tail now, instead of relying on your wingmate."

Angel gave Zar a half smile. "Thanks for the walk through. Damn, you're good!"

"So are you," Zar admitted. "Most pilots are crap. Cut and polish 'em, you still have crap. But a very few are real jewels; that's when improvement can be made. Go on," he urged, pointing toward the exit, "they're waiting for you. If one of us isn't yelling pretty soon, they're liable to think something's wrong."

Zar watched as Angel hurried off to join the others. "I must be getting old," he muttered. "I think I'm beginning to like him."

✦　✦　✦

Striker cornered Cloud as he was heading to his room. "I don't know about you," he whispered, "but I'm beginning to really like those guys. We make a real good squad. Okay, so they can't be Guardians without the Talent, but maybe they could stay here and fly with us. Like a troop exchange or something."

"They want to go back," Cloud reminded him. "I don't see how we could change their minds."

"Let me try to talk Zar into a day off," Striker replied. "Take 'em planetside and get their minds blown by a few Alderian girls. Might change their point of view."

"Definitely worth trying," Cloud agreed. "Either way, I could use some of that myself."

✦ ✦ ✦

Hawk rolled over in bed. *Shit*, he thought, *we've been here three weeks. Zar still hasn't given any indication that Dervish is ready for that mission, but I'm sure as hell ready to go home.*

Cloud strolled into his room. "Get up," he said, pulling on Hawk's arm. "Zar posted the schedule. We got the day off."

"Good," Hawk muttered, and rolled over, "I'll go back to sleep."

Cloud wrinkled his nose. "Get your buns up," he insisted. "I want you to meet some friends. Female type friends."

Hawk shook his head to clear the cobwebs. "Fuck," he mumbled, "I don't think I got the energy."

"Well, they probably won't on a first date anyhow," Cloud teased.

"You guys ready?" Striker called from the door. "I want to be out of here before Zar changes his mind."

Nipper met them on the flight deck.

"Where's Dervish?" Angel asked.

"Hey, is he really married?" Nipper questioned.

"Oh, yeah. I forgot about that," Angel replied. "About six weeks ago."

"Well, *he* didn't," Nipper grumbled. "I told him there was no harm in looking, but he still didn't want to go."

"Maybe I ought to go get him," Hawk offered. "Sulking around isn't ..."

"Naw," Nipper cut him off. "I'm staying too. We're gonna install nose sensors. Some feedback on how close we really get them fighters might prove useful."

"Suit yourself," Striker called back, as they boarded the shuttle.

Nipper watched the receding shuttle and stood there, lost in thought. *Things don't add up. Dervish lived with Michelli until he split to become a Flier; he doesn't know who his parents were. And he's married. With a kid on the way. What is Michelli up to? Why hasn't he told Dervish who he is? He probably could pass the Test and become a Guardian; he's good enough, but it's obvious he wants to stay a Flier.* Nothing he could think of made any sense at all. Too many pieces missing to solve the puzzle.

✦ ✦ ✦

Hawk gazed around as they landed, wondering which planet they had arrived at. The sky was a pale turquoise, the air had a fresh snap to it and he didn't see one piece of litter anywhere. The roads had been paved around the numerous trees and brightly colored flowers bloomed everywhere. All the people he saw radiated a general feeling of contentment and pride. He couldn't help but notice that very few were Alderian, but everyone waved and smiled as the Guardians passed.

"Do the Alderians rule these people?" he asked Cloud.

"No one *rules* 'em," Cloud retorted. "People in our galaxy govern themselves."

"They have their own governments?"

"In a way," Cloud replied. "But only to pave the roads and deliver the mail. If the government starts running the lives of its people, we come in and straighten 'em out."

"What if problems arise?"

"If they can't solve 'em, we'll send in the Truth Finders," Cloud replied. "But only as a last resort. Those who go around abusing other people's rights don't live very long. Everyone has weapons and they know how to use 'em."

Striker led Angel in one direction; Cloud headed Hawk in the other. "Come on," he said, "we can talk about this shit any time. We're down here to get the kinks out. I know a few girls that might find you interesting."

"Where are we going?" Hawk asked hesitantly.

"My cousin's place; she has two roommates," Cloud assured him. "Bet they'll go crazy over your hair."

Cloud introduced Hawk to his kin and her two roommates. He then disappeared with his cousin, leaving Hawk to deal with the girls. Hawk was sure of one thing: Cloud had figured right about the hair. Long before evening, the girls dragged him off to a bedroom.

Striker introduced Angel to his girl, and they all went to pick up a friend of hers. Initially, she was not too enthusiastic about entertaining Angel, but with help from the tricks Twink had taught him, he quickly changed her mind. They entertained the girls until morning.

Nathan leaned back in his chair and studied the Furthean Councilman. "I'm sorry, Councilman Rodime," he finally said, "but I can't send the Fliers to protect your country. The Council has refused to renew our contract."

"That's immoral!" Rodime yelled. "Innocent people are being killed by those beastly Rudonians and you want money before you'll help! I thought you *cared* about people and protecting freedom!"

"I won't accept responsibility for your decisions," Nathan informed him quietly. "And, if I remember correctly, you were among those who castigated my Fliers for helping the Ketherians against the poor defenseless Rudonians."

"Well, you didn't have our permission to involve the Fliers in that conflict," Rodime replied hotly. "Their unauthorized attack on the Rudonians was probably what caused this. You have a responsibility to rectify your mistake."

"I have a responsibility to those outlying worlds – like Kethera – that have current contracts," Nathan replied icily. "Besides, if my Fliers are initiating unauthorized attacks on your beloved Rudonians, I don't see why you would want them around anyway. I'm sure if you inform the Rudonians that your countries no longer have a defense contract with my band of ruffians, they will obligingly cut off their attacks."

"They just stepped up the hostilities," Rodime wailed. "My constituents are screaming for the protection they deserve."

"And they are getting the protection they are paying for," Nathan noted. "Freedom isn't a gift. It has to be defended. If they want it, they will have to fight for it themselves."

"So only the rich should be free?" Rodime shrieked. "Only those with money count?"

"Don't twist my words. It tries my patience. Your country seems to have an unlimited budget for social services. Perhaps you should put all those unemployed persons you're paying into an army. You'd have a sizable one." Nathan's face became a stony mask. "Many of the countries we're defending have no money, Rodime. Still, they are in there fighting with us. And they don't have the audacity to tell us how to fight, either."

"I'm only one man, Nathan," Rodime whined. "How can I change the Council's opinion?"

"No one is stopping your country from making its own contract with us," Nathan replied. "And until you're ready to do so, please don't waste any more of my time."

"What kind of a contract are you looking for?" Rodime asked with resigned apprehension.

"I'll have Threenica look over the books and get back to you."

"A rough estimate will do," Rodime countered.

"I don't know how far in the hole we are. I've had to pay my Fliers, buy parts for damaged Birds, ammunition, provide a budget to develop and test new weapons ..."

"That's another thing," Rodime complained. "Why do you have to pay those Fliers so much? And some of my constituents are against funding the development of weapons. I have received a number of petitions against phasor technology."

"Then let them petition the Rudonians to stop using them," Nathan replied coldly. "I've lost a few squads of my Fliers to their phasor equipped fighters. I would be delighted to see them phased out, if you'll excuse the pun."

Threenica opened the door. "Nathan, quick," he said breathlessly; noticing Rodime, he stifled his words. "Ummm, important communication. Needs your attention *now*." He nodded toward the unexpected visitor. "Councilman Rodime," he continued, "please accompany me for some refreshment while Nathan is otherwise occupied."

"What's going on?" Rodime demanded.

"A war," Threenica said sarcastically, "in case you hadn't heard." He led the annoyed Council member out of Nathan's office and down the hall to the cafeteria.

Nathan chuckled as he made his way to the comm room. He paused and looked at the long range receiver that was blinking. *Hmmm. Unusual*, he thought. *Transmissions through Mother are off the short range equipment.* He picked up the communicator, fearing more bad news. "Nathan here," he said apprehensively.

"Nathan, sir," a vaguely familiar voice responded, "I have someone here who wishes to speak with you. Are you alone?"

The voice was formal, but polite, nearly devoid of accent; Nathan's mind raced – *who is this*? "Yes. Threenica and I are the only ones with access to this room." There was a short pause before a new voice came on line.

"Nathan." Michelli's voice was full of concern and sadness. "I just heard about the battle above Serator. How many did we lose?" he asked sympathetically.

"*You* didn't lose any," Nathan reminded him coldly. "*I* lost close to thirty Fliers."

"What happened?" Michelli asked. "They didn't know the Fliers were going to show, did they?"

"No. But we don't have phasors. Until we took out their phasor fighters my boys were sitting ducks."

"What?" Michelli sounded truly astonished. "How can you send them out and not provide them with current weapons? That's a *crock*, Nathan."

"Hey, you and the Rudonians have the only phasor technology, and so far you have refused to sell them. We just recently acquired enough funding to begin development of newer weapons on our own."

There was no response. Nathan had begun to think he had lost the connection when Michelli came back. "I just checked with General Weir. He can have four or five phasor equipped base ships there within twenty-four hours."

"I'll lose another fifty Fliers in twenty-four hours!" Nathan shot back. "It only takes seven hours to punch them in here."

"It takes a while to paint them gray," Michelli stated.

"I don't give a damn *what* color they are. My boys are *dying* out there!"

"But *I* do," Michelli replied. "And you will, too, if the Council finds out you accepted Alderian aid."

"Fuck the Council. I don't care if you have 'Alder Forever' painted on the damn things in fluorescent pink!"

"As soon as the Alderian insignias are sandblasted off," Michelli replied calmly.

"Have it your way. Listen, how are my boys doing? I really need every Flier I have."

"Extremely well," Michelli answered. "They've managed to change a number of hard-nosed opinions concerning the quality and caliber of your Fliers. I doubt Weir would have agreed to send the base ships if I hadn't made it clear that without assistance you'd be forced to call them home."

"Just what are you up to?" Nathan demanded.

"I thought I'd made it quite clear," Michelli replied dryly. "I want Dervish to become a Guardian and take his rightful place among his people."

"Come on. You know he wants no part of that; he's not even Alderian. I had to *order* him to undertake this mission."

"His opinion is slowly changing," Michelli countered.

"Look, keep your ships. Send my boys home *now*."

"I'll inform them of your decision," Michelli replied. "Do try to keep them safe until Dervish returns. He'd be upset to learn they were hurt while he was away."

"I'm sure you'll be the first to offer condolences," Nathan stated bitterly.

"I won't try to convince you that it would bother me," Michelli stated flatly, "but it would. Good luck, Nathan; you'll need it. Even with those ships."

Nathan was grumbling to himself as he returned to inform Threenica he was leaving to talk with his generals. He was even nastier to Councilman Rodime in the brief conversation he granted on the way to the landing field.

✦ ✦ ✦

Hawk and Angel weren't as eager to leave as they had expected they'd be. Nathan's requesting their return on such short notice wasn't a good sign. They'd reluctantly said goodbye to Dervish, Nipper, Striker and Zar, then spent a few minutes looking for Cloud, but they couldn't find him.

As they approached their Birds, Cloud came running up. "Can you guys pilot base ships?"

"Huh?" Hawk replied, a bit confused. "What's going on?"

"General Weir's orders. He sent three phasor-equipped base ships to back up your guys over Serator, and you're supposed to take a few back with you, too," Cloud explained. "If you each pilot one, we could take back five."

Hawk's face lit up. "We? Does that mean you're coming?"

"Hey, someone's got to look after you girls," Cloud teased. "Since Dervish is going off on that mission, I'm sort of volunteering to take his place."

"They're *letting* you?" Angel asked in disbelief.

"Ummm ...they didn't say no," Cloud hedged.

"But what did they say about you coming with us?" Hawk questioned.

"Nothing," Cloud answered. "Well ... I didn't exactly *ask*."

"What *did* you say?"

"They asked if you guys could fly them things," Cloud replied. "I said 'sure, no problem'." Noting their expressions, he continued, "They're real easy to fly. So they said they'd have two Guardians pilot the other ships."

"And?"

"And I said 'great, we can bring back five then'," Cloud grinned. "Nobody said 'no'."

⊲ 18 ⊳

Knowing When To Hold 'em

With the alert siren pounding in his ears, Sparks raced for the comm center. "What the hell's going on?" he demanded.

In the flurry of scrambling Fliers and calls for assistance, his question went unanswered. He scanned the readout, then stared blankly at it for a moment. Five Alderian base ships had punched in above atmosphere.

A familiar voice floated through the room. "Control, this is Angel. Where exactly did you want these things?"

Sparks grabbed the communicator. "You son of a bitch, you could have warned us you were coming in with those things," Sparks yelled.

"What?" Angel drawled, "and let the Rudonians know? I'm sure they monitor our long range communications."

"It's scrambled. You *know* that," Sparks replied hotly.

"Well, ummm ... no point in taking chances."

Sparks was not particularly amused. "Okay, clown. Give those guys some docking instructions, and then you can start explaining just what you happen to be doing with Alderian base ships."

"Sure," Angel drawled. "It's real easy, guys. Just line up with one of the open doors, then glide on in. The outer door will close ..."

"That's quite enough, wise guy," Sparks cut him off. "Was punching in here unannounced Dervish's idea?"

321

"No," Hawk replied quickly. "He's off on that mission. I decided to bring 'em to your base."

"What mission? What are you guys talking about?"

"Ummm, I'll fill you in on that later. Look, do we have permission to land?"

"Who've you got up there with you?" Sparks asked warily. "I don't think base ships are capable of running as droids."

"We've got three Guardians with us," Hawk announced casually. "We'd like to bring 'em down for a look around the base and maybe some dinner before they have to go back."

"Alderians? *Here*? You are aware we're in the middle of a war, aren't you?"

"I think that's why Nathan kind of wanted these things," Angel drawled. "They got phasors."

"Well, now, that's a little different ... hell, for phasors I'll even buy the beer. Sure, land 'em for dinner and maybe you can get them to show us what them things can do," Sparks responded, now sounding considerably more friendly.

"Cloud said he's supposed to hang around and teach us," Angel cut in quickly. "Is that all right?"

"Great," Sparks muttered. "Permission to land granted." He put down the communicator and thought: *mainly so I can get my hands on you for pulling this stunt*! He walked over to the comms officer who was still a bit pale from the experience. "Get in touch with Nathan. Let him know Hawk and Angel are here and they brought five presents."

"What if he doesn't understand the message?"

"Just tell him to get his body over here *now*," Sparks replied. "I think he'll catch on."

Michelli didn't sound pleased. "What did you say?"

"I said, thanks for the help over Serator. Your guys did a terrific job on that one."

"No. Before that."

"Oh. I was just thanking you for the five ships and the loan of one of your Guardians to instruct us in their use," Nathan repeated, glancing at Hawk, Angel and Cloud, who stood by him nervously.

"Which one stayed?" Michelli asked dryly.

"Said his name was going to be mud," Nathan chuckled, "but Hawk called him Cloud."

"Cloud. And would you, perchance, know which squad he was with?" Michelli asked in an irritated tone.

"He was training with my boys, if that helps."

"He wasn't given orders to go, let alone stay. You will inform him he is to return immediately," Michelli replied curtly. "I fear your Fliers' attitudes toward authority are extremely contagious."

Cloud gestured toward the communicator and headed for the door.

"He's leaving the room now," Nathan said. "His response was an extended middle finger. Is that germane?" Nathan watched Cloud stop dead, his hand on the door, eyes wide, with a look of panic on his face.

Michelli was silent for a while. "You're really not very upset by this, are you Nathan?" he finally asked.

"I suppose I should be," Nathan confessed, "but I'm enjoying it far too much."

"I just didn't consider the possibility," Michelli mused. "I never dreamt that a Guardian would actually desert."

"Yet you want ... no, *expect* Dervish to stay *there*," Nathan countered.

Hawk and Angel exchanged glances. Cloud walked back slowly, eyeing Nathan with new respect.

"I'm not at liberty to disclose my reasons at this time," Michelli replied stiffly. "If my suspicions are confirmed, I'll inform you. At that time you may judge whether my intentions are honorable."

"I've never questioned your honor, nor your intentions," Nathan assured him. "It is your methods I find a bit hard to swallow. I've always felt that ordering a Flier to do something he didn't want to do was begging for him to rebel. When I *ask*, however, I'm never refused."

Angel nodded, giving Cloud a thumbs up.

"I don't suppose you could *ask* Cloud to return?" Michelli proposed hopefully. "From the records I just pulled up, he's one of my best."

Cloud's eyes began to sparkle as an embarrassed smile crept across his face. Hawk grinned back at him.

"I could, certainly. But I won't. Let him stay awhile, loosen up a bit. Perhaps he'll get bored with my unruly mob and return of his own volition."

Cloud shook his head left to right.

"I'm not going to hold my breath," Michelli sighed. "What would you do if one of your Fliers pulled this?"

"I'd wish him the best," Nathan answered seriously, "tell him I'd miss him, and to please keep in touch. I'd make sure he knew the door wasn't closed and he was welcome back any time, no questions asked."

"I don't have much choice in this, do I?" Michelli chuckled. "Go on, and tell the lad he may keep that PRO-fighter he took with him. Its phasors may come in handy."

"I believe he wants a Bird."

"All right," Michelli replied slowly. "I'll have a few dropped off for the Bird you give him. "I don't want him getting killed."

"I think he'll be impressed by that," Nathan agreed, looking at the expression on Cloud's face.

"I don't care if he is or he isn't," Michelli stated flatly. "But I really *do* care."

"I'm sure he appreciated hearing that," Nathan answered.

Michelli sighed as he caught Nathan's drift. "I sit with all the aces and you still win the hand. Someone up there must like you," he muttered. "Oh, I'll have those toys delivered by freighter. Lacey's due back in a week or so; I trust her. No point in advertising the fact we're in cahoots."

"Keep in touch," Nathan replied. "If we can ever help, please holler."

"I'll do that," Michelli assured him.

✦   ✦   ✦

Nipper walked into the cafeteria and looked around. He spotted Dervish sitting with Zar and walked over. He sat down and nodded to them both, but remained silent until Zar left.

"What's wrong?" Dervish asked, sensing Nipper's mood.

"Cloud's not coming back," Nipper informed him. "I just heard he requested permission to stay and it was granted."

Dervish looked ecstatic. "My, my," he exclaimed between snickers, "is Michelli gonna be pissed!"

"What will they *do* to him?" Nipper asked hesitantly.

"I don't know," Dervish admitted, not quite sure what Nipper was getting at. "Nathan will probably have a talk with Michelli and attempt to smooth things out."

"No, the Fliers. Can he make it though their Test?"

Dervish stared at Nipper strangely. "Cloud always does what he thinks is right. And the Fliers are a lot more mellow about Alderians now."

"Are you sure he won't get killed?"

"Well, nothing's certain when you're fighting Rudonians, but he's a damn good pilot and Hawk and Angel are with him."

"Not fighting," Nipper said anxiously. "Taking your Test!"

"Test?"

Nipper saw the puzzlement reflected in Dervish's face. "Don't Fliers have to pass a Test?"

"All Nathan tests for is an innate sense of right and wrong, and a willingness to do the right thing even when it isn't convenient or beneficial to yourself."

"No one gets killed while taking the Test?" Nipper asked hesitantly.

Dervish looked at Nipper as if he had stepped off the deep end. "No way!" he exclaimed. "If you're dead, you make a real shitty Flier!"

"But aren't they supposed to risk their life attempting something?"

"No one's expected to do something detrimental to himself. If you don't know how to swim, it's pretty stupid to jump in after a drowning man; the best option is to throw the guy a rope, or go for help. That's what our test is about, to see if you know right from wrong and have the guts and the brains to do the right thing."

"Ours is do or die," Nipper explained reluctantly. "You're sent out by yourself against a fully armed droid base ship. If you call for assist, move, or fire, it will nail you. You have to disarm it with the Talent."

"Bet they lose a lot of good pilots that way," Dervish said disgustedly.

"They teach us that stuff in flight school. No one has to take the Test, but if you don't, you can't be a Guardian."

"No wonder I never wanted to be one," Dervish replied. "That's the stupidest waste of a life I ever heard of!"

"But then how do you know the guy is a good pilot?" Nipper asked defensively.

"Only a Flier can nominate a recruit. If you need more in your squad, you hang around some planet's local defense pilots and see if you spot a good one."

"Makes sense," Nipper admitted. "A trained, seasoned pilot seems like a good place to start."

"Speaking of trained and seasoned," Dervish replied, "we're due out in three minutes. Last one there flies with Zar."

Zar was waiting next to Love when Dervish approached her. "Time has come to fly the real thing, lad," he informed him.

"I will have you know I am real," Love objected. "I have mass, I occupy space, I reside in the same time frame ..."

"That's enough out of you, lassie," Zar snapped. "Damned if I'm going to argue with a fighter."

"That is only because I am correct," she shot back.

"What's the big deal?" Dervish asked. "Love's been doing fine out there with ..."

"The mission you're training for requires you to be proficient with one of ours," Zar replied. He ushered Dervish over to a PRO-fighter and pointed. "Take that one out. Don't scratch it!"

Dervish eyed it disgustedly. "Do I really have to fly that piece of ... *that*?"

"I doubt a Bird would go unnoticed by the Yolluns," Zar replied. "Besides, it won't argue with you."

Dervish looked back at Love, then reluctantly climbed up into the big fighter and stared at the controls. *Fairly straightforward*, he thought, his mind wandering through the circuitry. *And, after all, it only has to get me there and back.*

✦   ✦   ✦

After spending a few days advising the Fliers on the base ship's controls and weaponry, Cloud left with Nathan for Headquarters. Hawk and Angel followed. The first thing Hawk thought of was Liefwynde. Threenica informed him that she had gone with Rusty to visit Killer; they would be returning the next morning or the day after at the latest.

While Threenica tracked down a spare Bird for Cloud, the three of them chatted with Nathan. It was the most casual, yet thorough, debriefing Cloud had ever had.

Hawk and Angel then brought Cloud over to the Fliers' quarters where they found him an empty room.

"We usually don't have our own bathrooms, but Nathan doesn't like naked Fliers 'traipsing down the hall' at headquarters. Something about it not looking dignified if visitors show up," Hawk chuckled.

"Are we stationed here?" Cloud asked, disappointment evident in his voice.

"Just until we've modified your Bird," Hawk informed him. "Then we'll be joining Isslan's squad in the Ulsted galaxy, station nine-twenty-two. Should only be a few days if we really dig in."

Cloud grinned. "Is it going to talk?" he asked hopefully.

"'fraid so," Angel drawled, with a wicked grin.

After stashing their gear, they headed for the repair bay where they worked on Cloud's Bird all night and well past breakfast the next morning. They decided to catch a few hours' sleep before they started making any grave mistakes.

Angel and Cloud headed for the cafeteria to get something to eat while Hawk went to see if Liefwynde had returned. As he approached her room, he heard Rusty's voice. Smiling to himself, he knocked.

"Hawk! Where's Dervish?" Rusty asked, as she opened the door and motioned him inside.

"He should be back in a week or so. Angel and I couldn't go on the mission." He glanced uncertainly at Liefwynde as he sat down on the bed next to her. He looked at Rusty carefully, then grinned broadly. "Hey, I can see some signs of the little fellow!"

Rusty looked at Liefwynde. "I *told* you I was getting fat," she wailed.

"Oh, come on. You're beautiful," Hawk commented quietly.

Rusty blushed. "You always seem to know when I'm in need of reassurance," she giggled. She patted her belly and continued. "I think the two of us need a little nap. You kids be good, now."

"I'll try to be," Hawk quipped as she closed the door.

"Were you?" Liefwynde asked coldly.

Hawk looked at her oddly. "What?"

"Did the two ladies enjoy themselves?"

"I can't deal with this," he stated as he stood up. "You want a faithful companion while you make no commitment at all. Why don't you just buy a dog?"

Liefwynde shot him a scathing glance. "I am an Elf, remember?" she reminded him flatly.

"So, divorce me when I get old and wrinkly," he replied sarcastically.

She softened and looked away. "That is not what I meant," she countered. "I know you want children; I do not think I can have them for you."

Hawk sat back down, put his arms around her and pulled her close. "Dammit, I *love* you," he said. "Doesn't that count for something?"

"It didn't stop you from playing with those Alderian girls," she reminded him.

He let go of her and shook his head. "Did it ever occur to you that I have feelings?" he asked bitterly. "That I might be hurt ... figuring you wanted to wait, to be married first ... then you refused when I asked you? And that maybe I don't like you poking around in my mind, either?"

"We are not a known cross," she said simply. "If I became pregnant, it would have to be tested. Our child must be normal by their standards."

"So I'm normal enough to tease, but not ... you flirt, but you won't let me touch you. There's only so much teasing a guy can take before ..."

She blushed deeply. "I want to, but ... I'm just afraid," she mumbled. "You know genetics. Falling in love is one thing, but getting married and having a child is different."

"Yeah," he said flatly. "It implies a commitment."

"Is that *really* what you want?"

"You can read minds. *You* tell *me*."

"Now, yes, you want that," she replied softly. "But when your memory returns — what will you want then?"

"I'll be the same. I'll just remember why."

She looked at him with a twinkle in her eye. "It takes a lot of time together to make a baby."

"It takes more than time," he said, as he kissed her.

"Oh; yes ... we should plant a seedling today," she replied.

"I thought only Nymphs had to do that."

"Well?"

"Mmmm," he murmured.

✦ ✦ ✦

Isslan ran into the repair bay. "Hey guys, welcome home!" he shouted as he approached.

Hawk looked down from the wingtip of Cloud's bird and waved. "Isslan! What brings you back here?" he called down. "Everyone okay?"

"Great. We just recruited a new Flier, and Nathan wanted to meet him."

Angel poked his head out of the cockpit. "So did we, sort of," he said, pointing at Cloud. "Isslan, meet Cloud; he was our wingmate over at the zoo."

Cloud nodded at Isslan. He had a silly grin on his face which didn't entirely hide his apprehensiveness.

Isslan gave him a thumbs up. "Welcome to the messed up universe. Hope it doesn't scare you into leaving."

Cloud grinned. "Thanks for the warning. I'll leave my night light on."

"You're letting them modify that Bird for you?" Isslan teased. "I thought Alderians had brains."

"There's always an exception," Cloud replied, but he was a lot more at ease.

Isslan climbed up and looked in, shaking his head. "Did you name it yet?"

"Storm," Cloud said jokingly, then looked at the flight computer. "What do you think of that name, 'puter?"

"It's disconnected at the moment," Angel reminded him. "It can't answer."

"We got a new guy named Sundown," Isslan prompted, looking at Hawk. "You ought to meet him; I think you'll get along. He's real shy. Doesn't know much Common, and we're not too good with his language either. Pepper said you were real good with pantomime."

Hawk wrinkled his nose. "You guys are never going to let me live that down, are you?"

"The captain of that Venturian vessel ..." Gracie began.

"I wouldn't mention that if I were you," Hawk interrupted. "Or I'll suddenly remember how you didn't notice ..."

"Never mind," Gracie replied quickly.

Isslan looked at Cloud with a wry grimace. "Are you sure you want yours to behave like that?"

"Isslan?" an unfamiliar voice called out.

"Be right down," Isslan called, as he started down the stairs. "Come on guys, it's Sundown."

"Huh? Me?" Sundown questioned.

"Oh boy, funzies time," Angel muttered. He scrambled down after Isslan.

Cloud slipped over the wingtip and jumped to the deck, while Hawk climbed awkwardly over the cockpit and started down the stairs. He nearly collided with Angel who was almost frozen on the steps.

Angel was staring at Sundown. Almost two meters tall, with extremely long, pale blue hair, handsome by any standard, he gazed back at them with the yellowest eyes that Angel had seen since watching *Village of the Damned*.

Hawk gave Angel a sharp poke in the back and Angel proceeded down, nodding at Sundown. "Wild hair," he said, flicking at a loose strand of the blue stuff. "You wouldn't happen to have some sisters, cousins or ..."

Sundown's hand moved quickly and something flashed in the air. Instantly he was holding a disconcertingly long knife point forward at Angel. His face showed no emotion as he eyed the startled Flier.

Angel put both hands in the air quickly, palms forward. "Sorry," he said loudly on the suddenly silent deck.

The sound of a moving laser positioner broke the silence. "Make one move toward him and I will fire," Goldie threatened.

"Which one of us shouldn't move, Birdbrain?" Angel called to her with obvious affection.

Isslan moved quickly between them, babbling in whatever language Sundown understood.

"What language is that?" Hawk asked softly, continuing down the stairs to stand next to Angel.

"Nice knife," Angel commented, almost to himself, slowly lowering his hands.

Sundown lowered the knife, looking from Goldie to Angel then back at Isslan, who was still attempting to communicate, but wasn't having much luck.

"Does Mother have his language in her data base yet?" Hawk nudged again.

Isslan looked at Hawk and rolled his eyes up. "Threenica's entering what we know of it now. Which isn't very much."

Sundown pointed toward Goldie and then to Angel. "Bird yours?" he asked with a half grin.

"Ummm, yeah," Angel mumbled warily, watching the knife.

Cloud stared wide-eyed at the goings on. He gazed apologetically at Hawk. "I'm glad you don't carry a knife. I hope I didn't offend you when I touched your hair that day."

Hawk smirked. "Naw," he admitted. "Some guys might be a little touchy, but I never saw anyone get *that* upset before."

Sundown's expression mellowed as Isslan finally managed to communicate. He slipped the knife back into his boot and extended his hand. Angel shook it and nodded with a grin.

"Sorry," Sundown said. "Sister ..." he put his hand out about a meter from the ground, "... little."

Angel looked at Isslan. "What was that all about?"

Isslan seemed relieved. "Apparently, in his culture, touching the hair is an invitation to ... for ... ahhh, doing it. I was trying to explain that here we ... well ... touch elsewhere."

Sundown said something, and Isslan grinned. "He wants to know where *we* touch 'em."

"This kid is gonna be dangerous," Cloud mumbled.

Over the next three days, with Isslan's permission, Hawk modified Sundown's Bird so it could attempt to teach him Common. He was running it though a final checkout when Isslan poked his head into the cockpit.

"Sundown around?" Hawk asked quietly.

"No, he's still out with Angel."

"How did you recruit him without understanding the language?" Hawk continued.

"The Rudonians were hassling a star system a couple of light days away from his," Isslan explained. "We managed to hold the sector, but the damage was pretty bad. The base ship was too far out, so I decided to land in what looked like an unoccupied section of his planet; just going to patch up a couple of things and bug out before we were noticed. His planet is on the no-contact list."

"What happened?"

"Seems his world has six nations that are almost always at war. We inadvertently landed in a demilitarized zone."

Cloud looked up from his perch in the Bird's nose, put down the checklist, and glanced quizzically at Isslan. "Always fighting? Probably why they never advanced."

"Could be," Isslan pondered. "Anyhow, we were landing two damaged Birds when a bunch of primitive fighters showed up and started attacking. Sundown came in out of nowhere, attempting to help us. His fighter got hit, but he stayed 'til the rest of my squad punched in and finished off the annoyance. Did some fairly tricky maneuvers up there.

"When we landed he followed us in. He just wanted to get a closer look at the Birds, but since we couldn't communicate we thought he landed 'cause his fighter was damaged. It made for a few strange moments. Then one of your base ships came in response to our call for assist," Isslan said, glancing at Cloud, "having obliterated the Rudonians, and asked if we still needed help."

"One of *mine*?" Cloud asked indignantly.

"You know," Isslan continued, "one of the ones Michelli sent with your Guardians to help protect the frontier."

Cloud scrunched up his face. "One of *theirs*, you mean," he corrected Isslan pointedly. "*Ours* are the five we brought back last week."

Isslan gave Cloud a broad grin. "Okay, one of theirs. Anyway, we were about to tell them we had everything under control, when another bunch of fighters showed up. I couldn't leave the kid there by himself, so we asked the Guardians to beam him aboard. Then we took off. He was real impressed after he got over the shock."

"But why did you keep him?"

"Well, when we beamed him up without his fighter, we sorta made him desert his post," Isslan replied sheepishly. "It turns out you get shot for that in his outfit. It was basically my fault, and I feel real bad about it now, but the problem was it took a while to understand what he was raving about."

"We really ought to go clean his world up, ya know?" Cloud observed. "Probably a lot of bureaucracy. Governments that are always at war drain productivity. It's not healthy."

Hawk and Isslan exchanged glances. "When's Angel bringing him in?" Hawk asked, mostly to change the subject.

"Not sure," Isslan replied. "Its been real hard to get him to land since you loaned him Gracie."

"Well, when he lands, tell him his Bird's ready," Hawk said as he climbed down. "I got to get cleaned up for dinner."

"What's the occasion?" Isslan teased.

"I promised Liefwynde and Rusty I'd take 'em out," Hawk admitted as he started off the deck.

"Why don't we all go?" Cloud called after him. "I'll even bathe!"

"We're leaving around six," Hawk called back, "That only gives you two hours to get the dirt off."

"I'll sandblast it," Cloud shouted, then looked at Isslan. "Come on. They got some great looking girls in this town."

"Didn't take those two very long to corrupt you," Isslan joked. He keyed the communicator in Sundown's Bird and hailed Angel. "You guys ready to land yet? We're all going to town for dinner. If you're clean by six, you both can come."

"Body or mind?" Angel asked.

"Mind? You? I wouldn't even have bothered to ask," Isslan replied.

"We'll be right in," Angel informed him.

The five Fliers actually looked sharp as they escorted Liefwynde and Rusty into one of the finer restaurants in town. The uniforms helped with the lack of reservations.

Sundown seemed to grow more and more uneasy as Isslan translated the menu for him.

"Did anyone tell him he gets paid?" Cloud asked, sensing the reason for the discomfort. Isslan looked a bit awkward, then began talking to Sundown again.

"He's as bad as Dervish," Angel muttered, pointing a thumb at Isslan. He glanced at Rusty and grinned foolishly. "It was almost a year before I found out what Nathan really did. And then it was Sparks that told me."

"He doesn't talk much," Rusty admitted, "but then, *you* don't keep quiet much. It sorta works out in the long run."

While Isslan was talking to him, Sundown glanced at Cloud and gave him a wary smile. "You ... see into mind?" he asked hesitantly.

"Not really," Cloud replied. "I just noted the prices and winced a bit myself." Sundown relaxed noticeably at Isslan's translation.

"Oh, that reminds me, Cloud," Hawk interjected. "Nathan said he put you on the payroll, too."

"These guys are a real wealth of information," Cloud said, grinning at Sundown, "if you happen to have a crowbar to get it out of 'em with."

Sundown looked completely confused. "Huh?"

Isslan began to translate for him as the waiter approached to take their orders.

After they had ordered, Cloud turned to Isslan. "Where are we going to be stationed?" he asked. "Headquarters is nice and all that but ..."

"Borrrrr-ing," Hawk sang out.

"Guess it's back to the frontier. Actually, it's been fun working with you guys ... ummm ... the Guardians," Isslan corrected, when Cloud shot him a nasty look.

Cloud looked at Hawk, then glanced back at Isslan. "How many squads of Guardians were out there with you?"

Isslan looked puzzled. "Someone said they had over seventy-five squads on their space station plus the three base ships. Hmmm ... probably over a hundred. Why?"

"A hundred," Cloud repeated, as he thought a moment, then turned to Rusty and Liefwynde. "Isslan and Hawk didn't seem too keen on the idea, but I really *do* think we ought to go in and clean up Sundown's planet. Between us and those Guardians we could do it easy."

"What's going on there?" Rusty asked.

"Lots of fighting between nations," Cloud replied. "If Sundown is a typical example of their intelligence, they should have achieved space travel a long time ago. Sounds like too much government is sapping their productivity."

"Governments always feed themselves on the lifeblood of the people," Liefwynde agreed.

"Helping clean up the governments would probably help his people a lot," Rusty added.

Isslan looked perplexed. "Do you ladies have even the slightest idea of how Alderians clean up governments?"

"Well, no, not really," Liefwynde answered, "but *any* method that frees a people to advance or fail as they see fit is better than allowing them to be stifled."

Isslan sighed. "We should probably discuss this some other time, okay?"

Cloud glanced disgustedly at the ceiling for a moment and let the issue drop, but not without noting with satisfaction the look that Liefwynde gave Hawk.

After dinner they all headed for the local amusement park famous for intriguing examples of female life. Rusty, Liefwynde and Hawk let the rowdies do some recon on their own. By closing time, even Sundown had found a friend.

✦ ✦ ✦

Isslan's squad returned from their three day leave to find their leader in no better shape. The ten giddy Fliers stumbled sleepily out to their Birds and punched out to the frontier.

Threenica cleared their takeoff and then went in search of Nathan. He found him reviewing the latest contract offer from the Council. "Worth accepting?" he asked hopefully.

"No," Nathan replied, handing it to him, "but it's a lot closer."

Threenica scanned it briefly and tossed it back. "With all the stuff Michelli sent us, we really don't need this."

"Yeah, it's rather nice to be in this position."

"Still," Threenica mused, "why this sudden interest in helping us? I'd like to know what he's up to."

"Oh, I don't know," Nathan pondered. "He's probably not up to much of anything. He likes playing the bad guy, but he's just a softy down inside."

"He has an entire galaxy to defend," Threenica pressed. "And he's got Rudonians up the ass after that stunt he pulled on 'em."

"He wasn't too pleased with them either," Nathan pointed out. "I think it mostly came to a head over the incident with the kids on Erween."

"Isn't he spreading it a bit thin?"

"I asked him that. He seems to think they'll be just fine. Apparently they've acquired some new super-duper defensive system."

"I don't know," Threenica argued. "I've never known him to be generous without a motive. Besides, I'm not too sure about his guys. These reports I'm reviewing about the Guardians he sent us for the frontier ... did you see how they dealt with those Rudonians they took prisoner ..."

"Yes," Nathan chuckled, "but remember, they'd raped half the settlement."

Threenica stared at Nathan. "You mean you *agree* with their methods?" he gasped.

"Well, now," Nathan said, settling back in his chair, his hands behind his neck, "when someone attacks with a weapon, removing the weapon is a logical method of preventing a recurrence."

"But, they ..."

Nathan cut him off. "Rather effective, wouldn't you say? Think about it."

Threenica shivered. "I would prefer not to," he admitted with a cringe, quickly turning his attention to the papers he was carrying. "Oh, Sundown has requested to fly with Angel. That's probably enough for a squad, when Dervish returns."

"Have they picked a lead yet?" Nathan asked.

"I had them cast the customary vote. Angel helped Sundown with his selection, but I overlooked that."

"Sporting of you," Nathan teased.

"Anyhow, I informed Mother that Dervish is squad leader," Threenica continued. "He's also received a lot of votes for promotion. I think he'll get his stripes this round."

"Mostly from the Fliers being protected by those base ships and the ones working with those terrible Guardians, correct?" Nathan asked pointedly.

"Well, yes, now that you mention it," Threenica conceded, "but it's not like he doesn't deserve it. He would have been promoted long ago if they hadn't thought he was Alderian."

"That had very little to do with it after the first few months," Nathan corrected him. "Dervish had a bad habit of expecting everyone to be hostile. He didn't speak unless it was absolutely necessary and he avoided everyone."

"All the Fliers are basically shy; very few of them will seek out a friendship," Threenica countered.

"True, but it was Angel and Hawk that brought him out of his shell; the boys began to see him for himself, instead of the elusive shadow he was pretending to be. Funny. When Dervish proposed them, I wasn't too thrilled, but he sure was set on getting those Earth kids in here."

Threenica nodded, and thought a moment. "Tell me something, how did you feel about Dervish when Sparks first dragged him in here?"

"Let's see," Nathan replied slowly, trying to recreate the moment in his mind. "He was sitting right there in that chair; looked like he was trying to blend in with the walls. I suppose he was scared to death of what I was going to do, but when I just smiled at him, he broke into that big grin of his. Hmmm. Yes, I definitely liked him. I couldn't tell you why, though."

"It's hard not to like him when he smiles like that."

"That it is," Nathan admitted, momentarily lost in thought. "But look, we aren't getting much done standing around reminiscing. Why not run this contract through Mother and come up with a counter. I'll be in the comm center collecting status reports."

"Come on down when you finish," Threenica suggested. "I figured out how that war simulator works."

"Kids," Nathan chuckled as he watched him leave.

19

The Tortoise And The Heir

After seven more grueling days, Zar decided that Dervish was sufficiently competent with the PRO-fighter that plans for the mission could proceed. Zar was requested to report planetside to go over the mission with General Larch.

Zar felt lost in the spacious office that served as Larch's planning center. He sat uneasily in the padded chair across from the general, but he was pleased with himself for what he felt he had accomplished. "I plan on sending him out for the Test this evening. He's one of the best I've ever worked with."

Larch looked up. "He wants to become a Guardian?" he asked with disbelief.

"He didn't say he didn't," Zar replied smugly. "He's pulled that on me enough to get a taste of it back."

"That's a pretty flimsy reason to risk someone's life," Larch reminded him.

"He could easily have passed when he first got here," Zar retorted. "All he lacks is the confidence in his Talent the Test would give him. It'd open the door; make it possible for him to consider the alternative to being a Flier."

"And piss him off royally," Larch said firmly. "I can't take the chance he'll storm off and not do this mission." Larch paused and studied Zar. "Speaking of ruffling his feathers, did you get him to cut his hair? He can't go running around the Yollun headquarters with auburn ringlets down past his shoulders and pass for a Guardian."

"He trimmed it enough to fit it under his cap," Zar replied. "That's as far as he'd go."

"I'll try talking some sense into him," Larch grumbled.

"He said he'd rather be killed by the Yolluns than have Rusty mad at him," Zar said with a smirk.

"Who's Rusty?"

"His wife."

"Mmm. Well, I can appreciate that," Larch nodded. "I have one of those myself."

✦   ✦   ✦

Dervish slunk onto the flight deck. He'd become depressed when he put on the uniform; his mind had become dark with an inexplicable rage, and his stomach had gone sour. It was as if some part of him was trying to alienate itself from the clothes he would have to wear for the next week.

He kept trying to convince himself that his feelings were childish and totally without merit. *After all*, he chided himself, *the Alderians aren't evil, nor even bad. A bit misguided maybe, but their goals are the same as mine and their methods have so far been palatable. They seem harder on their own than on anyone else. Why does it make my skin crawl to be dressed like this?*

"It offends the magic," the little man in his mind replied.

"Huh?" Dervish started; then, realizing he was literally talking to himself, turned his thoughts inward. *Why would it do that?*

"A very old grievance," the man said, "going back centuries."

Was it something the Alderians did that offended it?

"Seems they wiped out the Faeries. Most of 'em anyway."

But they've changed a lot in the last two hundred years.

"The Faeries?"

The Alderians. Shit, now I'm defending them. Wait a minute ... you don't tell yourself things you don't already know. I'm flipping out. I'm really losing it.

"Does that bother you?"

Flipping out? No. I'm getting used to it.

"I was referring to defending the Alderians."

I think so, yes. I'd rather be trying to justify the sick feeling in my stomach, but somehow that wouldn't be right either.

"I'll point that out," the man replied, "but you might end up completely alienating the Magic with that logic."

Nipper waved a hand in front of his face. "Are you there, Dervish?" he asked, somewhat amusedly. "You're standing in the middle of a flight deck, you know."

"Sorry," Dervish mumbled. "I was arguing with myself."

"Who won?" Nipper teased.

"I don't know; I might be losing," Dervish answered honestly, as they walked to the waiting fighters.

Standing next to the fighters for final inspection, they joked with each other and began to laugh. General Larch looked at them coolly. He cleared his throat to get their attention. "Dervish, I can't help but note that you didn't see fit to cut your hair," he said sourly.

"I'll keep it under my cap, sir," Dervish replied.

"If it creeps out from under that cap," Larch informed him dryly, "you had better be ready to talk soprano and kiss your wingmates."

Nipper looked dramatically at Dervish. "It's out again," he said, pointing at Dervish's hair. He spread his arms to the sides. "I'm waiting, darling," he said breathlessly. He doubled up in laughter, sliding down the side of the fighter.

Dervish looked at him wide eyed. "My breath isn't that bad, is it?" he mumbled. "Perhaps I should try ..."

"Grow up! Both of you!" Larch bellowed.

Dervish looked at Nipper, who could not seem to stop laughing, and began laughing too.

Striker about fell over trying to stifle his laughter. That seemed even funnier to him. He completely lost it and began to laugh despite Larch's fierce glare.

"Pre-mission jitters?" Zar asked. "You lads might wish to shape up a bit. This departure is being filmed ... for Michelli."

That revelation seemed to have a moderately sobering effect on the three pilots.

Dervish glided the fighter toward the launch bay and automatically did his pre-flight checkout. As he merged with its circuitry, he felt a strange tingling sensation throughout his body. He pulled his mind back quickly. The tingling slowly ebbed as he locked in the punch coördinates Zar sent. His mind raced through a number of logical reasons for the sudden feelings, but he kept fearing the illogical, unexplained ones.

They punched into an empty sector and switched to local for a last minute briefing.

"We're accompanying General Larch in place of his normal honor guard," Zar informed them. "He'll be attending a formal meeting that Michelli requested with the Yolluns' Defense Ministry. This provides us with the opportunity we need to get Dervish into the presence of their Minister of Defense."

Dervish, still chuckling a bit, quickly bit his lip to silence himself.

"The Yolluns aren't pleased with our presence on their world," Zar continued, "and have been on speaking terms only because they fear we may one day decide to expand from our galaxy and their world is located in the next nearest galaxy.

"Dervish will accompany the general to the meetings; the rest of us will stay with the fighters," Zar informed them. "Don't talk to anyone unless spoken to first; then say as little as possible without being rude. Understood?"

The three of them acknowledged.

✦ ✦ ✦

Reynard escorted the Elder king into the spacious living room where Michelli was seated. Michelli looked up and sighed. "I tried to reach you, Etheren," he said as he rose, "but you had already left."

"I received the message when we punched in," Etheren informed him.

"I'm truly sorry to have raised your hopes, only to discover that we made a mistake," Michelli replied. "Please be seated. Reynard will bring coffee. Or tea, if you'd prefer."

Etheren sat and smiled at Michelli. "It is I who should apologize. You *did* say to come next week, when he got back." He glanced at Reynard. "Coffee would be fine, thank you."

"I feel like such a fool," Michelli admitted. "Everything seemed to fit."

"What have you learned?" Etheren asked eagerly.

"We tracked down the escape vessel," Michelli told him, "and discovered it had landed at the free port where he was raised. And the girl that resembles your sister Ashlaren ... her image is in his head. I'm at a loss to explain it."

"You said you had a film. May I see it?"

"Well, yes, of course. But ... why?" Michelli asked. "We've confirmed that Dervish has elements in his blood that prove he's not pure Elder. Dr. Yarayn wasn't looking for that when he did the original study."

"Although we refused your treaty," Etheren replied, "you never broke your word. I believe you will be honorable with what I must now tell you." He paused and looked at Michelli.

"Considering that you read minds," Michelli chuckled, "I'm flattered that you trust me. It makes me feel better about myself."

Etheren smiled. "True, you have *not* found my son. But you might have found my heir. The child was my sister's; we don't know who the father was. She never told us."

Michelli raised an eyebrow, but he nodded politely.

"The child was so good ... so beautiful," Etheren said reflectively. "Yarenia and I were never blessed with an heir. As our closest kin, we accepted him and named him heir. May I see the film now?"

The antics filmed on the flight deck brought a chuckle to the solemn Elder king. "It's indeed a miracle. He looks exactly like her, down to the auburn ringlets," he said wistfully. "And that smile." He looked at Michelli and shook his head. "I can imagine he's been quite a handful."

"He totally undisciplined a squad of my best Guardians," Michelli griped. "But are you sure? It's hard to tell from ..."

"I've no doubt whatsoever. I'd know that face anywhere," Etheren interrupted. "When will he return? I *must* meet him. So many years have slipped by."

"A few days," Michelli replied. "If you like, I'll notify you the moment he returns."

"I'd rather wait here, if that wouldn't inconvenience you," Etheren stated. "Our people haven't spoken for a long time. Perhaps it's time to correct that."

"I'll have Reynard see to your comfort," Michelli said cordially. "We'd be most honored to consider you our guest for as long as you wish."

✦ ✦ ✦

Tressel sat sideways in the chair, his feet hanging over the edge. He cocked his head to the right to gaze at Michelli. "I can't believe it," he said incredulously. "Dervish even got to Zar. The man was not only civil, he was in good humor!"

Michelli glanced out the window to the black starry sky. "Poor Etheren," he mused. "He's so certain he can scoop the lad up and take him back. I doubt he believes me that Dervish will want nothing to do with being a pampered prince."

"Didn't you tell him he's a Flier?" Tressel asked.

"I even told him about Rusty."

"And?"

"And he's still convinced that he'll leave it all and return to Eldrosin."

Tressel gave Michelli a strange look. "I'd given Etheren credit for brains," he mumbled. "Perhaps it was only because I couldn't read his thoughts too clearly."

"He's very bright," Michelli countered. "It's just that he simply can not conceive that Dervish wouldn't accept the responsibility he was born to."

"*Born* to?" Tressel repeated. His expression went blank for a moment. "Umm, who's Dervish's father?" he asked hesitantly.

"Etheren said his sister wouldn't divulge that."

"Hmmm. You know, I'm a little concerned about Dervish. He was standing out there on the flight deck and I couldn't even read him," Tressel remarked. "His mind was ... off somewhere. Then Nipper walked up to him and *blam*, he was back, just like that. And he was very worried."

"About what?"

"I'm not sure."

"*You*? Not sure?" Michelli teased him.

"No. Very strange. Those thoughts seemed to slip away when I tried to latch onto them," Tressel explained. "All his other thoughts were clear and easy to read."

"Perhaps he didn't want you to read those."

"He didn't know I was there to do the filming," Tressel countered. "I'm very good at that. And another thing: some of those thoughts weren't a part of his physical mind."

Michelli chuckled. "I think perhaps you've been spending too much time around me. Senility may be contagious."

Tressel took his feet off the armrest and put them back on the floor. "I'm really worried, and you're making light of it," he complained. "Zar is planning on giving him the Test. I strongly advise against it."

Michelli looked at Tressel a moment. "I thought you wanted him to be a Guardian," he said dryly.

"I do, but not until I know he won't get killed."

"He certainly has more than enough Talent to pass. Why the sudden doubt?" Michelli wondered.

Tressel fidgeted a bit, realizing that he'd been avoiding the real object of his curiosity. "You said Etheren didn't know who Dervish's father was," he blurted. "Do you?"

Michelli raised an eyebrow. "What are you insinuating?"

"Are *you* his father?" Tressel blurted.

"Answer your own question," Michelli told him. "You heard Dr. Yarayn; how could *I* be his father?"

"A serendipitous cross, perhaps? You and Ashlaren were pretty close ... just about twenty-seven years ago," Tressel responded.

"You're listening to your own rumors," Michelli chuckled. "It'd be nice if everyone would swallow that. It would unite this galaxy forever."

"All right, then. If he's not at least part Alderian," Tressel muttered, "how do you expect him to pass the Test?"

"I've seen him use the Talent. It's different in him, but it's very strong," Michelli countered. "Zar even noted that."

"But he doesn't want to be a Guardian!" Tressel shot back. "That much was obvious in his head."

"Then he won't be given the Test," Michelli replied. "I made that very clear to Larch."

"I'm still worried," Tressel grumbled. "Zar has become as undisciplined under Dervish's guidance as the other three."

Michelli chuckled. "That lad's a real scamp," he mused. "He's due back tomorrow night. That gives Etheren and I two more days to work out the final points on the agreement."

"I can't believe it was his idea," Tressel chuckled. "He must have read the wish for it in your mind."

"Well, I *did* leave my thoughts on the matter lying about."

"Will he go for what we wanted?"

"That and more," Michelli replied. "I'm truly impressed by his willingness to help defend the galaxy. He's agreed to send fifty men immediately and more as needed."

"That *is* impressive," Tressel admitted.

"Our biggest task will be convincing Dervish to accept."

"Well, I don't especially want him to go there," Tressel replied. "But if he just sort of plays Etheren along…"

"I doubt he'll even consider it," Michelli lamented.

"Etheren isn't tying the agreement to Dervish's acceptance, is he?"

"No," Michelli replied slowly. "But I suspect that once he sees for himself how different Dervish is from what he expects him to be, he won't want any more of his people subjected to our … decadence."

"Etheren won't break *this* agreement," Tressel stated. "I've got too much invested in it for him to rain on my parade now."

"How very Alderian of you," Michelli said coldly.

✦ ✦ ✦

Dervish parked the fighter next to Love and let out a sigh of relief. All he had left was a debriefing by the colonel and he'd be on his way home. He joined Nipper and Striker as they headed to the conference room.

Zar met them at the door. "I need to see you lads right after you talk to the colonel," he informed them with a curt smile.

"Knowing Zar," Nipper muttered as they entered the room, "he's probably going to go over all our mistakes."

"Shit," Striker groaned, "*I* thought we did real good."

The colonel asked Nipper and Striker a number of questions, listened to their answers, then excused them. He kept Dervish another couple of hours. He wanted every scrap of information Dervish had gleaned from the mind of the Yollun Minister of Defense. And from any other mind Dervish had peeked into.

Dervish got the feeling that the colonel was stalling for some reason, and it made him uneasy. Finally, he was dismissed. He headed straight for his room, replaced the hated uniform with his jeans and t-shirt, grabbed his bag and headed for the flight deck. Nipper and Striker were already there when he arrived.

"Colonel tell you?" Nipper asked, noting his gear. "We gotta run a sweep before we're out of here."

Dervish groaned. "Guess it's better than a lecture, but dammit, I want to go home!"

"He'll probably get that in while we're out there," Striker lamented.

"We're really short on squads now," Nipper explained. "Michelli just sent a couple hundred of 'em to help the Fliers."

"Really?" Dervish sounded honestly surprised.

"They'll just be working the frontier systems, where they don't know a PRO-fighter from a Bird," Nipper told him. "But it does let your guys have more squads where the action is."

Dervish felt a lot more relaxed in Love. "I've missed ya," he told her as they glided toward the launch bay.

"I was extremely bored," she informed him.

"So was I," he confessed. As he merged with her to do a quick checkout, that odd tingling started to vibrate through his body. "Love, this is really strange. I feel like I ... are my bioreadings normal?" he asked, as the tingling became more intense.

"Abnormal respiration rate, pupils slightly dilated, heart rate up significantly. Are you afraid, Dervish?"

"That's an understatement," he confessed. "I got all tingly when I merged with you."

"I missed you too," she replied softly.

Dervish sighed. He locked in the coördinates Zar sent and decided to wing it. The tingling was strange, but it didn't hurt, and it didn't seem to affect his contact with Love. He took a deep breath while watching the other three fighters wink out, then punched.

"That base ship just scanned me," Love informed him as they winked in. "Alderian ID, type unknown."

"Hey, Nipper, what's that thing?" he asked. Receiving no reply, he looked at the equipment, quickly noting that no other fighter was anywhere within range. "Hey, what's going on?" he muttered. "Where is everybody?"

"It tried to lock on me," Love announced as she activated the automatic weapons system.

The dull monotone of a synthesized voice issued from the radio. "You are about to begin the standard graduating Test for entrance into the Guardians. Your position has been locked in on the phasor weapon system. Any attempt to punch out at this time will result in your destruction."

Dervish about choked as he stared at the radio blankly. "Someone, tell me this is a joke!" he shouted.

"If you move, fire weapons, call for assist, or fail to disarm the testing droid in ten minutes, it will commence firing. If you wish to abort the Test sequence now, raise your shield within the next ten seconds."

What shield? This ain't a PRO-fighter! Bastards! They can't do this to me! He felt his skin grow cold and clammy.

"Abort signal not received. Test commencing."

"Test?" Love questioned.

"Some sadistic jerk gets his jollies by sending a pilot out against a droid base ship. They call it a Test."

"A single fighter cannot disarm a base ship," Love advised.

"Right. The pilot's supposed to use the Talent to disarm the thing. They know I'm not Alderian! What the fuck are they doing this for?"

"It is not scanning us now," she informed him. "Perhaps it will recognize our ID and call this off."

"No, it won't. It was programmed for our ID."

"Why are you so certain?"

"It was in both Zar's and the colonel's heads. I just didn't realize it was *me* they were setting it up for. I didn't ask to be a Guardian!"

"Disarm it, then," Love replied.

"I'm not Alderian. I haven't been to their fucking school. I don't know the first thing about any of this," he grumbled. "Dammit, I don't want to die playing their stupid games! They have no right!"

"I suggest we do something quickly," Love said. "See if you can analyze its weapons system's range and positioning and give me the data. Perhaps I can calculate a blind spot. If there is one, maybe we can do a stalled hop to the blind spot before it can react. From there we should be able to punch," she assured him, locking in the coördinates for home.

He noted the coördinates and gave her half a smile. "My sentiments exactly. If we get out of this, I'll *never* come back."

"Actually, yes, it would be very satisfying to turn that droid ship into space junk," Love replied matter-of-factly.

"Hmm," Dervish muttered. "I didn't know you ... " *That's just what I was thinking,* he realized. *Love picked up on my thoughts? It's never gone both ways before.* He reached out his mind and slowly began to merge with the droid.

He shivered as he felt the tingling increase. *Shit, this is a lousy time to have the Talent get mad at me,* he thought. *I may be dead no matter what I do.*

He thought it odd that it was so easy to merge with the droid's computer. He quickly analyzed the entire weapons system. Although he was practically vibrating from the intense tingling, he wasn't getting tired. He relaxed a bit. *Well,* he thought, *maybe it won't be that hard to pass this little test after all. Space junk, huh? That might be possible. It'd really frost Michelli to blow up his little toy. Okay, let's see here. The upper phasors can be rotated almost 360 degrees. Now, a few degrees of downward tilt ... then, bypass the angular interlock ... now, broaden the beam width ...*

✦ ✦ ✦

Nipper punched in and glided to a stop next to Zar and Striker. "Where's Dervish?" he asked after a few seconds. "I don't see Love anywhere."

"He's busy at the moment," Zar said smugly.

"What?"

"He's taking his final," Zar replied.

"You can't do that!" Nipper shouted. "He didn't ask to be a Guardian!"

"What are you so upset about?" Zar asked. "*You* took the Test with no problem."

"But I *wanted* to. I was trained for it, dammit!" he shouted. "You're risking his life for nothing! Where is he?"

"You can't go out there," Zar said. "The droid would nail you as you punched in."

"Well, I can't sit here and do nothing," Nipper exploded. "That's my wingmate you're trying to kill!"

"He can't be your wingmate until he passes the Test," Zar informed him dryly.

"Asshole!" Nipper yelled. "He's not pure Alderian! No one's ever passed the Test who's not full Alderian! Where is he?"

"You're out of order, Nipper," Zar barked. "Shape up *now*, or you're grounded."

"Cram it!" Nipper retorted. He moved his fighter out and punched.

Striker sat in silence for a moment. "Nipper's right, Zar," he finally said. "You can ground me too if you want, but I'll never fly with you again. Ever!" He glided forward and punched.

Zar sat, staring at empty space. *What is it about Dervish that binds people to him so strongly? Cloud leaves to watch over Dervish's wingmates. These two clowns are ready to get themselves blown up to rescue him from something they both accomplished. And now, to top it off, I'm beginning to doubt my own judgement. I'd better go get those nitwits before someone really gets hurt*, he concluded.

The radio was filled with shouting voices when Zar punched in. The colonel was yelling at Nipper to dock, Nipper was responding with profanity in four languages, and Striker was editorializing on the proper way to run an organization. All the while, the communications officer was trying to dock a few other squads that were coming off sweeps.

The Emergency Interrupt signal brought the channel to a dead silence, followed by the shocked voice of the comms officer. "I've got a large energy burst in test zone three!"

"Is that where Dervish is?" Nipper shouted.

"Or ... was," the man said, frantically issuing commands to the test ship. "The droid isn't responding. Neither is Dervish ..." he continued, as both Nipper and Striker winked out.

"He got it?" Zar asked quickly.

"I don't know," the officer replied. "Still trying to contact the droid and your test candidate."

"What's going on?" the colonel demanded.

"Problem out at the test zone," Zar replied. "I'll be right back."

"You're going *nowhere* until I get a full explanation for the actions of your squad!" the colonel informed him pointedly.

"They were upset when they found out that Dervish was being tested. Now, something just exploded out there. I got to go!" Zar punched, concern for Dervish outweighing his fear of the colonel's rage.

Nipper and Striker punched in with shields raised, not too sure what to expect. "Dervish!" Nipper yelled, looking at the bits of junk floating aimlessly past him.

"Ummm ... where's the droid?" Striker asked, checking the readouts.

"Floating past you," Dervish responded, moving Love into tracking range.

"You okay?" Nipper shot back, relief obvious in his voice.

Dervish laughed. "Fine, now. Need to change pants though."

"You're supposed to disarm it, not blow it up," Striker said, somewhat awestruck, "How did you *do* that?"

"Eight fighters approaching," Love informed them.

"Probably want to see what's going on out here," Nipper opined.

"Rudonians," Love stated, activating her weapon systems. "They are trying for lock." She dropped rapidly to avoid the phasor fire that sent Striker's fighter reeling.

"Striker!" Dervish yelled, as he checked the readouts. "Shit, two phasor and six short range. Nipper?"

Striker didn't answer. His fighter continued to swirl off into the distance.

Nipper put in a call for assistance as he deftly maneuvered to keep from being locked on. "Same reading here," he called back. "Got to keep 'em off Striker 'til assist arrives."

Zar punched in, raised shield, and joined the cat and mouse game. Dervish sent a picture to Nipper, who quickly dived in under Love. They formed one target over the short range fighters while Zar entertained the phasor fighters. As the fighters locked on them, Dervish peeled left, Nipper right, and they both set off a load of sparklers.

The weapons system computers went into dynamic halt for a moment. The Rudonian pilots stared in amazed disbelief for just that millisecond Zar needed to take out a phasor fighter. "Good show!" he called as he came around to engage the other phasor fighter.

Two squads of Alderians punched in and swarmed into the fray. Just as Zar got lock on the fighter, the Rudonian fighters dropped their beacons to acknowledge surrender. Zar dropped lock in response to the surrender.

"Dammit, Zar, *fire*," Dervish yelled as the Rudonian fighter shot forward and blasted Zar. Fragments of his fighter drifted off in all directions. The Rudonian continued forward, attempting a punch. Dervish's mind screamed out, locking into its flight computer. He overrode the coördinates set by its pilot and substituted a new set. The fighter winked out. Scraps flew everywhere as it winked back in, trying to occupy the same space as another Rudonian fighter.

Dervish swooped Love in, quickly locking on one of the five remaining Rudonian fighters.

"Dervish," Nipper yelled, "they surrendered. Leave 'em be."

"So had that other slimeball!" Dervish yelled back.

"We've got lock on 'em," another Guardian asserted. "They're staying right here 'til the base ship arrives to tow 'em in."

"They killed Zar!" Dervish yelled back, not dropping lock.

"They killed a lot of folk," the Guardian replied flatly. "Unlike them, we don't blow anyone up once they've surrendered."

"We'd better get Striker," Nipper said, as he took off in the direction Striker's fighter had gone.

Dervish sat there looking into the mind of each Rudonian pilot, hoping to find an excuse to blow him up. None of them, however, appeared willing to follow the example set by their fragmented comrade. He dropped lock and dived after Nipper.

✦   ✦   ✦

Striker had regained consciousness by the time they towed his fighter back to the station. Neither Nipper nor Dervish mentioned Zar when they told him what had happened.

Dervish waited on the flight deck as Nipper accompanied Striker to sick bay. He fidgeted a while, realizing for the first time why he had fired on that Rudonian fighter when it had signaled surrender to him. Heretofore he had always doubted his actions, figuring that he had simply been angry about Hawk, but now he knew differently. Something inside him had *known* that the surrendered Rudonian pilot had intended to blow him up; he had the same feeling when he yelled at Zar to fire. At least now he was relieved to know that he hadn't fired on a genuinely surrendered pilot.

Removing the Alderian ID flag from Love was fairly straightforward. That was fortunate; Dervish had trouble concentrating. This was all Michelli's fault, he rationalized: if that bastard hadn't told Zar to test him, Zar would still be alive.

When Dervish was nearly finished extracting the flag, Nipper poked his head into Love's cockpit . "Striker's gonna be fine. It'll be a week or so before he can fly again, but all in all he was pretty lucky. If his shield hadn't been up, he'd be history."

Dervish looked up at Nipper. "Shit, and I was ready to kill Zar for testing me. It seems so stupid now."

"You leaving?" Nipper asked hesitantly.

"Yeah. We all do pretty much the same thing, but you guys only have one galaxy to protect. We have to cover half the universe."

"Need any help?" Nipper asked.

"Sure," Dervish replied, as he handed Nipper the ID flag. "Hold this for me."

"Mmmm ... you were supposed to stop by Michelli's before you leave, right? Guess without this, you're gonna need an escort, huh?"

"I'd appreciate that," Dervish replied with a wink.

Nipper nodded as he headed down Love's stairs and walked across the bay to his fighter. He requested permission for them to launch.

"What's up?" the communications officer asked.

"Escort service," Nipper responded. "Dervish is supposed to see Michelli before he heads home and he's already removed the ID flag."

"Permission to launch granted," the officer responded.

The two fighters winked in above Michelli's estate. Dervish hailed and Michelli responded within a few minutes.

"Dervish, please land those fighters. I have someone here who wants to meet you," Michelli informed him.

"No way," Dervish responded. "I got the information for you. And in case you haven't heard, I passed your stupid Test. Your test droid is now space junk. And one more thing ..."

"Dervish," Michelli cut in. "Please land. I can explain it all over dinner."

"I don't want to play any more," Dervish shot back. "Your little game cost Zar his life and nearly killed Striker. You didn't win a Guardian; *we* gained two Fliers!"

"Dervish!" Michelli yelled as the two fighters winked out. He shook his head in disgust.

"I understand now what you were trying to tell me," Etheren admitted. "We do have a problem with that one."

20

Rose Is A Rose Is A Rose

Dervish leaned back in his chair studying Nathan intently. "He didn't order Nipper back?" He scrunched up his face and lowered his eyes to the floor. "That's about as hard to believe as him not knowing Zar was going to set up that test."

"His exact words were 'have him keep an eye on Dervish for me'," Nathan said, trying to catch his eye. "He made it clear that his instructions had been to test you only if you expressed a wish to be a Guardian. You can't hold him responsible for Zar disobeying orders."

Dervish gave him a perverse grin. "Hey, why not?"

"I do understand how you feel," Nathan replied, shaking his head, "but he's only asking for a few hours of your time. There are some things he wishes to talk to you about."

"I gave him over a month of my time. I don't want to go back. Ever!"

"He didn't want me to tell you this, but he's learned who your mother was," Nathan admitted slowly. He paused a while, trying to read Dervish's mixed expression. "Your uncle was there, waiting to meet you."

Dervish looked up quickly.

"Your mother was Elder," Nathan explained.

"Elder? What's Elder? Who's my father? Where's my mother?"

"I believe the Elder are thought to be distant cousins of the Elves, common ancestry or something; I'm not quite certain. Your uncle isn't sure who your father is. It's a rather long story," Nathan hedged. "Your uncle wanted to tell you in person."

"He's free to come here," Dervish countered, "but I'm *not* going back."

Nathan sighed. "It's not quite as simple as all that. Are you familiar with the planet Eldrosin?

"Nope."

"Well, my boy ... or should I say Your Highness ..." Nathan chuckled, "it is in the Alderian galaxy, and inhabited by those of Elder blood. They have had little to do with other peoples for centuries. Probably why you haven't heard of them."

"Highness? What are you getting at?"

"Your uncle Etheren is their king," Nathan said quickly. "You are the heir apparent. He would like you to at least visit your future kingdom."

Dervish sat frozen in disbelief. "You're joking," he finally hedged. Nathan shook his head. Dervish stuck out his tongue. "No way, unh-uh. I'm no king," he stated firmly. "I'm a Flier!" He looked apprehensively at Nathan. "I still am, aren't I?"

"Of course," Nathan assured him. "Matter of fact, I already took the liberty of telling him that you considering a change of residence was highly unlikely. All he's requesting now is that you visit. That's what Michelli had in mind when you and Nipper took off."

Dervish smiled at Nathan. "We're fighting a war. No time for social calls." He got up and headed for the door. "Does Rusty know I'm back yet?"

Nathan gave him a wink. "No," he replied softly. "I wasn't going to have Threenica wake her at this hour."

"Be prepared for a scream," Dervish called back wickedly as he disappeared out the door. "King, my ass ..."

Nathan chuckled as he opened the door to Threenica's office. "Looks as though both of the Guardians will be staying with us permanently," he said with a smile.

"I'll keep my eyes open for a possible test for them," Threenica replied. "I have a couple things in mind, but let's see what falls into place over the next couple of months."

"I'm not too concerned about them," Nathan informed him. "Michelli assured me they had unsmudged records before Dervish took them under his wing."

"If Dervish likes someone, they do seem to fall under his spell," Threenica observed. "If Michelli kept him around much longer, he'd have all his Guardians flying in gray."

"I'm sure Michelli is very aware of that now," Nathan replied. "He made mention of something of that sort. He referred to it as a cultural exchange, however."

"How did Dervish take the news?" Threenica asked.

"He didn't seem overjoyed. I believe Etheren will have a hard time convincing him to come home."

"I suppose you didn't push it much; you do look pleased," Threenica observed. "Michelli will be livid when he hears."

"I don't suppose he will find it as amusing as I do," Nathan agreed, "but I really can't make Dervish do anything he doesn't want to do."

"Is Dervish even considering a visit?"

"He's with Rusty now," Nathan said with a grin. "I seriously doubt he's even thinking."

Threenica blushed. "Nathan, you know what I meant! Sometimes I think you're becoming a dirty old man."

"Becoming?" Nathan said in mock indignation. "I'll have you know that I'm fully accredited. Lechery is an art, you know."

"Then I must be the Lecher's Apprentice," Threenica spoofed. "I'm anxiously awaiting my chance to do some research."

"Hmmm. We appear to be all out of available subjects," Nathan noted. "Perhaps you should hire a receptionist."

"Can we really afford that luxury?"

"Hey, we have enough found money to run this outfit; since the Council has finally agreed to our terms on the contact, why don't we use their money to pay our weapons development team and hire someone to help with mundane tasks. And your continuing education."

"My, my, Nathan, you really *are* in a good mood."

"I'd love to have seen the expression on Michelli's face when Dervish punched out," Nathan chuckled.

"I'll bet he was as green as his uniforms," Threenica noted, "though he didn't sound *all* that upset."

"But he really wants me to send Dervish back."

"What has you so convinced that Michelli cares all that much about Dervish one way or the other?" Threenica asked hesitatingly, but seriously. "It doesn't seem at all logical to me."

"He went to a lot of trouble to track him down," Nathan mused. "I wish I had a better idea of what is really going on. Still too many pieces to this puzzle to see where they all fit."

"Why not invite King Etheren here?" Threenica offered. "Perhaps something will come up that will tell us which pieces to start with."

"Not a bad idea," Nathan replied. "I'll invite him first thing in the morning. Michelli, too, for that matter."

"I'll be down with Mother if you need me."

"Way past my bedtime," Nathan chuckled. "I'll be asleep."

Dervish tiptoed across the room and lay down on the bed next to Rusty. He stared numbly at the ceiling for a while, trying to put it all together. It was just too bizarre for words. He finally convinced himself that Michelli had simply made a big mistake that would become obvious real soon; then they would all go away and leave him alone.

Content with that feigned reality, he sent his mind drifting through Rusty's. He painted a beautiful forest; soft green moss grew down toward a babbling brook and tiny purple flowers dotted the landscape. He placed her beneath a twisted old tree, then painted himself there also. She reached out to him, so he wrapped his arms around her and gave her a big kiss.

She opened her eyes and looked at him sleepily. "Dervish! I was just dreaming about you. Boy, have I missed you," she whispered as she returned the embrace.

Much better than a scream, he thought. It was hours before they got to talking.

He brushed over the training and mission, concentrating more on the antics he and Nipper pulled. He told her about the Test, but not about the battle that followed. He didn't want her to know that Zar got killed; she'd just worry more

about *him*. She giggled when he told her what he and Nipper
pulled off when they left.

"Poor Michelli," she mused. "It looks like he lost a round."

"I don't know. When we got here, Nathan cornered me."

"I can't believe he'd be mad at you," she reflected.

"He wasn't mad. He started telling me Michelli found out
who my mother was and that my uncle had been down there
waiting to meet me."

"Really? That's neat."

"No, it's not," he mumbled. "This guy seems to be the king
of some world and I'm supposed to be his heir. Even Nathan
thinks I should go back and talk to the guy."

"Don't you want to meet your mother?"

"Would you want to meet someone who abandoned you?"

"Maybe just to spit on 'em," she confessed. "But didn't your
uncle offer any explanation as to what happened?"

"Don't call him my uncle," Dervish snapped. "He claims to
be my uncle, but I can't accept that. Not now, anyway."

"Okay, fine," she sighed. "Did the great pretender offer up
an explanation?"

He gave her a nasty look. "Nathan said the jerk wanted to
tell me in person."

"Maybe we *should* meet him. See what he has to say. We
can always tell him he's barking up the wrong tree."

"I don't *want* to meet him," he said firmly.

"Why?"

"I don't *know* why," he lamented.

"Dervish," she chided, "you're being a bit unreasonable. You
should at least give the man a chance to explain."

"Now you're sounding like Michelli," he said hotly.

"Well, what's wrong with Michelli?" she challenged. "He's a
warm, sensitive man. He's very fond of you, too!"

"If you're so damn fond of him, why didn't you marry *him*
instead?" he yelled.

Rusty just stared at him as he threw on his clothes and
started for the door. "Dervish, cut it out. Come back here!"

"Maybe I don't *want* to," he snapped, and slammed the door.
He stomped down the hall and made his way outside, his
thoughts turbulent and dark. He had almost never raised his

voice to anyone before; now he had gone and yelled at Rusty. He wanted desperately to go back and apologize, but he feared that he'd just blow up again until he sorted out what he was going to do. He eventually found himself at the landing field. He climbed into Love and sat a while, thinking. "Remember the coördinates for that system I told you to remember?" he finally asked.

"Which system?" Love asked.

"Angel and I ended up there before we took out that base ship, remember?"

"That one, yes."

"Lock 'em in and let's go," he said.

"Logging takeoff to Mother," Love replied.

"Glad you're with it," he commented dryly, "'cause I'm sure coming apart."

✦ ✦ ✦

They winked in a bit close for comfort to one of the system's planets. "Forgot that planets revolve. Shit, we could have ended up in the middle of that one had we been a bit earlier," he muttered. He began to recheck the system to see if it was what he had once thought. "Yep, it's almost exactly what I plugged into that celestial mechanics program." Something bothered him just a little; then, the obvious hit him broadside. He sat motionless, his mind a swirl of questions without answers.

"Dervish, are you all right?" Love asked.

"The possibility that this place would actually exist is remote, but not impossible," he rambled, "but for me to have *found* it ... the odds are staggering."

"Do you wish me to compute the probability of such an occurrence?"

"No, no ... it's ... it's okay. How's it look?"

"I have locked orbit and completed initial surveillance," Love reported. "Breathable atmosphere, small animals, no sign of civilization or even intelligent sentients."

"Can we land?"

"I see no reason not to," Love replied, gliding down through the atmosphere and skimming over a large body of water, "providing we find dry land to set down on."

They continued to drift across the planet until the water turned to beaches, the beaches changed to hills, and those in turn became a forest. The forest thinned out into a meadow. There Dervish landed. He walked around a while, perhaps enjoying the tranquil beauty, perhaps looking for signs of stinky bear. He finally returned and sat down beside Love. He watched the small creatures scurrying about and listened to the chattering of the birds.

✦   ✦   ✦

Quilbraugh lay snoozing in the soft moss growing within a circle of trees. Something tugged at the corner of his mind and he opened his eyes. He looked about; seeing nothing but the toadstools that were growing around the circle, he quieted his mind and drifted back into the flow of the Magic.

He awoke with a start. "Bah. I can't be believin' me luck," he grumbled. "I no sooner be ditchin' them pesky cyclers than someone be invadin' me meadow."

He stretched, then slowly got up. "I best be gettin' rid of the pest before it be makin' itself at home," he told the toadstools, as if they might be interested. He gathered his will, moved his hand through the air, and sent sparkling wavy lines drifting out toward the meadow.

✦   ✦   ✦

Dervish became aware of tiny lines in the air that seemed to have a life of their own. "Love, what are those line things?"

"What are you talking about?" Love responded.

"Those wiggly colored line patterns in the air. They're all around us now."

"I do not detect the presence of anything in the air. Are you sure that you are not simply perceiving reflections?"

"I don't think so. I don't see anything that would reflect ..."

"Seein' the lines, are ya, sprout?" a strange but friendly voice inquired from behind him.

Dervish jumped and turned his head quickly. A delicately built man about his own height stood next to him. "Whoa, I didn't hear you coming," he told the man. "I didn't even think anyone else was here."

"Hmmm," Quilbraugh muttered, eyeing Dervish closely. "What *did* y'be thinkin' then?" he asked almost musically, sitting down next to Dervish. *I best be dustin' him good*, he thought, *if he be seein' the Magic*.

"Wild," Dervish said absently, watching the patterns begin to reform and shimmer with transparent colors. "Are you doing that?" he asked, pointing at the wiggling lines.

"And didn't your good mother be teachin' ya it's not polite to be answerin' a question with a question?" Quilbraugh chided, adding a bit more Magic to the mix.

"I never met my mother," Dervish told him flatly. "Love didn't detect any higher life forms, so I landed. I didn't mean to disturb you."

Quilbraugh looked at Dervish intently. For a moment, Dervish felt like he was swimming; his body felt light and his thoughts became disjointed. That old strange tingly feeling returned; it screamed through him, and yet seemed to clear his mind. He shook his head a bit and looked at Quilbraugh warily.

Quilbraugh's face showed a great deal of surprise. *This one be somethin' special to the Magic*, he thought. "Who be your Master, sprout?" he asked goodnaturedly.

"What?"

"Who be teachin' ya?"

"Teaching me what?" Dervish asked bewilderedly.

"Ahhh. Well, that be explainin' it *all* then," Quilbraugh muttered delightedly.

"Explaining what?"

"Why you be here, Mad Wand," Quilbraugh replied with a wink. "I be called Quilbraugh."

"Mad Wand? I'm Dervish," came the baffled response. "How does what explain why I'm here? I thought I came here to think things through. By myself. But I'm more confused now than when I landed."

"In the dark," Quilbraugh corrected, weaving the sparkling strands tighter around Dervish.

"Huh?"

"Not confused, just not enough knowledge to be proceedin'," Quilbraugh continued. "There be a big difference."

"There doesn't seem to be," Dervish lamented. "My thoughts keep going around in circles."

"That be because y'be avoidin' a most obvious conclusion," Quilbraugh informed him.

"What are you ... we ... talking about?" Dervish asked.

"*You*, me young sprout," Quilbraugh chuckled. "And some thoughts that be bothersome to ya."

Dervish looked down and picked at the grass.

"So 'tis that bad, now, is it?" Quilbraugh said softly. "Well, perhaps y'might be tellin' old Quilbraugh all about it."

"I think I've done enough damage," Dervish replied. "I land in your meadow, disturb your afternoon, and I really don't understand you at all. It was nice meeting you Quilbraugh, but I'd really better be going." He started to get up, but the little man motioned for him to be seated, and somehow he felt compelled to do so.

"Not so fast, sprout," Quilbraugh said firmly. *The Magic be sendin' y'here to learn*, he thought. *And learn y'will, whether y'be likin' it or not.* "Y'be runnin' away again. Isn't it time y'be seein' an unpleasantness through? How old might y'be?"

"Around twenty-five," Dervish replied. "I don't really know for sure."

"That be years, I take it. My, y'be just a wee sprout at that," Quilbraugh chuckled. "Perhaps there be hope. What be on your mind when y'be comin' here?" he asked firmly.

Dervish sighed. He didn't understand why, but suddenly he wanted to talk about everything. "I was abandoned as a baby. Sorta raised myself. I joined the Fliers around five years ago. I just got married, we have a kid on the way, and now out of nowhere comes this guy who says he's my uncle, and he's the Elder king, and ..."

"... and he be intrudin' on the life y'finally put together," Quilbraugh said, reading Dervish's mind. "Real nasty of 'im I be thinkin'. Where the hell he be twenty-five years ago?"

"Right! That's exactly what I was thinking," Dervish agreed. "But no one else seems to see it that way. They all say I ought to go and meet him."

"He be chained up somewhere? For child abuse, maybe?"

"No," Dervish replied quizzically.

"Well then, if he be so hot on seein' ya, why can't he just be comin' t'look ya up himself?"

"Nathan said that I'm this guy's heir," Dervish admitted, "and it's not proper to make him come to see me."

"Who be Nathan?"

"He sorta runs the Fliers."

"Oh yes," Quilbraugh said, "that little group y'be joinin'."

"It's not so little. We really do a ..."

"Never mind," Quilbraugh interrupted, his calculating mind revelling in the possibility of playing the ultimate prank on the stuffy Elders. "The Elder king, y'say. Well, well. And o'course, y'not be wishin' to get involved with royalty. That be involvin' too much responsibility and not enough fun."

"It isn't really fun getting shot at, either," Dervish said defensively, "but, I love flying, and it's keeping folk safe and letting them be free to do what they want. That's what the Fliers do."

"And kings just be sittin' around and lookin' impressive," Quilbraugh offered. "A lot like gods. If they don't be protectin' and coddlin' their people, their people be hatin' them. And if they do be protectin' and coddlin' them, the people be turnin' into pawns instead of players. No, a king can never win. My advice is to be stayin' out of the king business altogether."

"That's the way I see it," Dervish agreed. "What difference could a king make anyway?"

"Kings be makin' no difference at all, I be thinkin'. It be a real waste of time," Quilbraugh commented. "Y'never be meetin' a good king, I be wagerin'."

"Yeah, I have," Dervish admitted. "But then, he's the only king I know."

"And what might this guy be doin' that's so good?"

"He's changed his people a lot," Dervish offered. "The Alderians aren't the bad guys they used to be."

Quilbraugh choked. *Those barbaric cutthroats nearly be wipin' us out*, he thought. "Alderians? That, sprout, be open to debate."

Dervish looked at Quilbraugh sternly. "No, it's not," he said firmly. "Maybe Alderians weren't so nice a long time ago, but the ones *I* know are good."

"And this king be changin' them?"

"He must have," Dervish pondered. "People don't generally change on their own."

Quilbraugh considered that a long moment. *There be a bit of truth in that; perhaps I be holdin' the grudge too long.* "This Alderian; y'think he be better than you?"

"No. Why?"

"Then y' could be a good king if y'be wantin' to."

"But I don't want to."

"As I be sayin'," Quilbraugh needled him, "too much work. Not enough play."

"But I don't know the first thing about being a king!" Dervish argued.

"'Tis not all that hard. I'm sure that Nathan fellow would be glad to be givin' y'some pointers," Quilbraugh informed him, "And I might even take a mind to be helpin' out. If you be acceptin', that is."

"What do you know about being a king?"

Quilbraugh cleared his throat. "A significant amount," he replied candidly. "If y'not be dazzlin' 'em with brilliance, y'be bafflin' 'em with parlor tricks."

"Parlor tricks?"

"Like this," Quilbraugh said as he sent his thoughts swiftly into Dervish's mind. "Picture a flower."

Dervish tried frantically to close down his mind and pull in his thoughts.

"Stop *fightin'* me, sprout!" Quilbraugh demanded. "You'll not be seein' how 'tis done."

Dervish felt a tingling streaming through his body, pouring toward the picture of a flower Quilbraugh had placed there. *Might as well go along with this*, he thought, *but that flower needs some modification.* He changed its color from dark red to lavender and made the petals more delicate. Satisfied, he looked at Quilbraugh.

"Now," Quilbraugh instructed, "y'just be sendin' it to your hand." Quilbraugh manipulated Dervish's thoughts, helping him create the proper patterns within the flow of energy in his mind. Then Dervish began to send the picture toward his hand.

"No!" Quilbraugh rasped. "Not through you. *From* you." He pushed a few more thoughts around, and suddenly ✳𝔭𝔬𝔬𝔣✳ Dervish sat there holding the flower that moments ago had existed only in his mind.

Dervish looked at it in utter amazement. "Wow!" was all he managed to get out.

"Cheap trick," Quilbraugh chuckled. "And easy. Really be impressin' the ladies, though."

Dervish looked at Quilbraugh with awe. "Could you teach *me* this kind of stuff?"

Quilbraugh narrowed his eyes and studied Dervish. "I could be teachin' me apprentice," he offered. *If that's what the Magic be wantin', it'll be keepin' the sprout workin' at it*, he thought.

"What does an apprentice do?"

"He'd be doin' exactly what he's told," Quilbraugh pointed out. "And not be questionin' his Master."

"How can someone learn if they don't ask questions?"

"'Tis definitely a nuisance y'd be," Quilbraugh continued, "but a very talented one." He wriggled his nose and scratched his chin.

"What would I have to do?" Dervish pressed.

"Y'd have to be trustin' me," Quilbraugh shot back. "I can't be teachin' ya a bloody thing if y'be blockin' your mind!"

Dervish sighed. "Sorry; it's gotten to be a natural reflex."

"Okay," Quilbraugh said, shaking Dervish's hand, "I accept ya as me apprentice. Now, y'must be goin' back and meetin' your uncle."

"But I thought ... *why?*"

"Because I be wantin' to see the Elders' faces when you refuse to be their king," Quilbraugh chuckled.

"How will you get there?"

Quilbraugh unrolled a star chart that moments ago was not in his hands. "Y'll be pointin' it out to me."

Dervish stared at the chart a moment before taking it gingerly. He quickly pointed out Fliers' headquarters and the Alderian galaxy. "I really don't know which planet it is," he explained, "only that it's somewhere in that part of the galaxy."

"That be narrowin' it down a bit," Quilbraugh pondered. "I'll be findin' it." He got up and started into the forest. "Matter of fact, I'll probably be waitin' there for ya," he called back.

"You forgot your ..." Dervish called out, as he watched the parchment disappear from his hands, " ... chart. Well, maybe not."

Dervish got up and walked slowly back to Love. *Real weird*, he thought. *I could have imagined it all, but this flower sure is real. Rusty will like it.* Thinking of Rusty made him wince.

"Love," he said as he set coördinates for home, "I thought you said there was no sign of intelligent life on this planet."

"Yes, that is correct," she responded.

"What do you call the person I was talking to, then?"

"What person? You were sitting out there talking to yourself."

Dervish let out a low whistle. "I think I finally lost it."

"Lost what?" Love questioned.

"My sanity."

"Sanity is the state of mind acceptable to the masses," Love reminded him. "Perhaps losing it is a good thing."

Dervish chuckled. "I like your logic, Love," he told her as he punched.

✦ ✦ ✦

He entered Rusty's room as silently as he could. She was lying across the bed, sleeping, her arms wrapped around the pillow. He came and sat down next to her and gently shook her. She looked up at him, hurt and anger reflected in her eyes.

He held out the flower. She took it and laid it on the bed with a definitely hostile motion. He bit his lip and pictured another flower. He made each petal a different pastel color and set sparkles in them. He thought hard about the patterns Quilbraugh had placed in his mind. The tingling rushed through him, sounding almost like the wind. He sent the flower to his hand and *POOF* it was there. He looked at it with sheer delight as he handed it to her.

Rusty's mouth dropped open. She stared at the flower, then Dervish. She reached up, took the flower and gave him a kiss. He wrapped his arms around her and held her close.

Quilbraugh had at least been right about that; it surely did impress the lady.

✦　✦　✦

Nathan sat in the cafeteria worshipping his morning coffee. He looked up and noticed Dervish, his arm around Rusty, walking toward him. *Dervish certainly looks chipper this morning*, he thought. *Maybe all he needed was ... oh dear, I really am a dirty old man.* He smiled at them as he got up to pull out Rusty's chair.

"Morning, kids," he said, nodding at Dervish. "The rest of your squad is on its way here, Captain."

"My squad? *Captain*?" Dervish stammered. "You mean ..."

"Yeah," Nathan muttered, "You got promoted. 'Course the vote was held right after Michelli's base ships arrived," he chuckled, "and you were a definite hero at the time."

Dervish just stood there with his mouth open, his face aglow and his eyes sparkling.

Nathan smiled. *Tell him he's royalty and he growls; tell him he made captain and it's like he was handed the world. He's definitely a Flier through and through.* "Don't just stand there," he teased. "Go get your lady some breakfast."

Dervish nodded and walked off in the general direction of the food.

"Watch out for the walls," Nathan called after him.

Rusty began giggling. "The last time he looked like that was the first time he kissed me," she confided. "Though he lit up a little last night when he poofed a flower."

Nathan raised an eyebrow. "Poofed a flower?"

Rusty nodded. "Like, poof! and it was in his hand. Every petal is a different color, and it sparkles!"

"Oh," Nathan replied, chiding himself for having his mind in the gutter. "I was never any good at sleight of hand."

Dervish returned and set the tray on the table. "We've decided to go see my uncle. Would it be all right if I took my squad with?"

"Fine with me," Nathan replied. "I'll inform Michelli so arrangements can be made."

"Ummm, which planet is it?" Dervish asked.

"I'll find that out too," Nathan assured him, then glanced at Rusty. "Are you feeling well enough to travel?"

"Sure," she replied with a grin, "I've gotten used to feeling green."

"Besides, it's Michelli's favorite color," Dervish quipped.

21

And Yet Again

Watching the six fighters settle down in formation brought a smile to Reynard. He quickly masked his emotions, noting Michelli's icy stare. They waited in silence until they saw Dervish helping Rusty down out of Love.

Michelli only raised an eyebrow, but Reynard let out a stream of language that was obviously not meant for ears that could understand it. "Lad," he barked sharply, "a lady with child should not be schlepped about in a fighter!"

His genuine concern touched Rusty deeply. "It was my idea," she confessed, wrapping an arm around Dervish. "He just can't say no to me."

Reynard puffed himself up while taking Rusty's free arm. "It's into the house with you, milady," he said politely, but firmly. "Your wiles will not work with me. There's a nip in the air and I'll not have you catching cold."

Rusty gave Dervish a half smile. "See you inside," she called back, as she was marched off by a determined Reynard.

Michelli watched them walk off with an expression somewhere between amusement and annoyance. "He missed his calling," he noted dryly. "He should have been a nanny." He abruptly turned his attention to the six Fliers. He stared hard at Nipper and Cloud, who returned his gaze without flinching. "I'm proud of you lads. Not *pleased*, mind you," he admitted with a wink, "but I can always hold out hope that you'll reconsider."

"I wouldn't hold my breath if I were you," Angel drawled. "I'd kinda hate to lose ya that way."

"I've often wondered why I liked you," Michelli stated tartly.

"It's his charming personality and manners," Dervish observed. "Wins folks over every time."

Michelli eyed Dervish; he noted the addition on his sleeve, and smiled. "Congratulations, Captain," he said warmly. "We will certainly have to celebrate your promotion, not to mention the fact that you have worn your uniform. Oh, by the way ... someone named Quilbraugh arrived yesterday. Said he was a friend of yours."

"Ahhh ... kind of, I guess. I just met him. But he sorta talked me into coming back here."

"Actually," Michelli informed him, "he's a charming fellow. I just couldn't imagine where you'd meet a Faerie."

"Fairy?" Dervish made a funny face. "He didn't hit on me or anything."

Michelli did a double take, then started laughing. "No," he said. "Faeries are a race, lad."

"Oh."

Still chuckling, Michelli started back toward the house. "Well, come on lads. No point spending the evening out here. Rusty will start to worry if we don't join her soon."

"Quilbraugh hasn't been any trouble, has he?" Dervish asked, falling in next to Michelli.

"Quite the contrary," Michelli replied. "He's been helpful as well as entertaining." He glanced at Dervish and chuckled. "You know," he observed, "you really *did* look better in green. It matches your eyes."

King Etheren wished to make some preparations, and requested they delay their arrival until the following morning. The Fliers were a bit skittish, especially the former Guardians, but Michelli made them all feel at home. By evening, both Cloud and Nipper had felt pangs of guilt for deserting their king — not enough to return, but enough to realize that their loyalty would always be divided.

Reynard showed them to their rooms. Only Rusty seemed to have somehow crept under the old man's skin; to her, he was as warm as a spring breeze. To the rest of them, he was a midwinter blizzard.

Just as Dervish was about to get into bed, there was a knock on the door. Rusty pouted as he got up and went to the door. "Yeah?" he muttered.

"I need to talk with you privately," Michelli said softly.

"Now?"

"I'm really sorry, but it's important."

"Aw, crap," he said, looking wistfully at Rusty. She nodded, so he yielded. "All right; hang on while I get dressed."

Dervish didn't think Michelli looked sorry enough as they walked down the hall to the library. He put on his best pout as he slumped into Michelli's favorite chair. "What's up?" he asked hesitatingly.

Michelli looked at Dervish and sighed. "I was hoping that this conversation could have been held some other time. Unfortunately, it's now or never."

Dervish's expression turned to concern. "What's wrong?"

Michelli thought a while, trying to decide where to begin. "Let me start with the facts. You're not the first to pass the Test without being pure Alderian."

Dervish looked puzzled.

"No, let me try this again." Michelli poured himself a brandy and walked to the window, staring off into the night. After a moment, he turned back to Dervish. "There's no heir to the Alderian throne," he said quietly, "and I'll never produce one."

Dervish looked at him strangely. "Uh ... girls? I mean ..."

"I'm half Elf," Michelli interrupted. "If I were to father a child with elven characteristics, this entire galaxy could fall apart. I can't risk all that I've worked for. On the other hand, with your mother being an Elder, those features would be expected."

"What can ... how does ... ?" Dervish stammered. He was too shocked to comprehend what Michelli was getting at.

"Just listen," Michelli replied. "Your mother died at the hands of her captors. How she saved you nobody knows, but she took with her the identity of your father."

Dervish had turned a pasty white; he felt numb all over. Guilt and sorrow competed for his emotional state. "I was hating her for dumping me," he mumbled. "Who killed her? Why? What happened?"

"It is a complicated story," Michelli explained. "It was almost twenty-six years ago, five years before I took the throne. Had I been king, it wouldn't have happened. But I wasn't. My father pulled back the Guardians because the Elders refused to sign a treaty, leaving their planetary system unprotected. The Rudonians had made an agreement with Eldrosin's sister planet, Terawren, and expressed an interest in coming to terms with the Elders. Your uncle wasn't very nice to them either."

"So? What does that have to do with my mother?"

"Your mother was Etheren's sister. She was also the Elder ambassador to Terawren. I assume that's where she met your father, since the Elders didn't allow visitors. You were both kidnapped from their embassy."

"Weren't we protected? I mean how ... why would someone kidnap us?"

"Over twenty men died trying to protect you. You and your mother were taken in an attempt to force your uncle's hand. But he didn't budge. The Rudonians denied any knowledge of the kidnapping, of course, but offered to negotiate with the terrorists for your release. Your uncle told them not to bother. The terrorists stated they killed your mother, and once again made their demands, threatening to do the same to you. Etheren still ignored them."

"He just let them kill my mother? What an asshole!"

"It was the hardest thing he ever had to do, Dervish," Michelli said quietly. "You can never capitulate — or even negotiate — with terrorists. No one would be safe, especially those you love."

"So, ya tell 'em anything, get your people back. Then to hell with 'em."

"No. Then they go slaughter all the children in a village, or blow up a hospital. If they get to you once, they will keep trying. If you ignore them, they realize that form of behavior won't achieve their goals. They change tactics."

"But ..."

Michelli gave Dervish a hard look. "There are no buts about it," he interrupted firmly. "If Tressel hadn't intervened and the Rudonians had captured Rusty, would you have ordered the Fliers to surrender?"

"Surrender?" Dervish stared numbly for a long time. "No ... I think I would have wanted to kill every last one of 'em," he finally mumbled.

Michelli raised an eyebrow. "Children too?" he asked.

"I don't know," Dervish admitted reluctantly. "I think I'd flip out."

"That would create a bitterness between peoples that could never be healed," Michelli reminded him. "Not until the entire race of Rudonians and all those races that they rule were wiped from the universe. The killing would go on and on. It is far better to nip it in the bud."

"What do you mean?"

"Hostages must be considered victims of war; that's the only way the taking of hostages becomes useless to terrorists. Look at it this way," Michelli pointed out, "if the Rudonians had blasted your headquarters and Rusty had been killed, you'd deal with it a lot more realistically."

"I doubt it," Dervish responded bitterly, "but yeah, I see your point. I'd go out of my mind, but I'd probably stop before I killed babies."

Michelli's expression was blank. "It was a very difficult decision for Etheren. He's carried the guilt all these years; that's why he wanted to explain it to you himself."

"Why did *you* tell me, then?"

"I wished you to understand that there's probably no one alive that knows who your father is. Considering this, I'd like to acknowledge you as my heir," Michelli said quietly. "It'd be logical; we saw each other fairly often, your mother and I. My father made it very clear I wasn't to see her, and her father gave her the same lecture. It didn't *stop* us, but it did slow us down a bit. As I told you, the Alderians didn't have a good relationship with the Elders at the time."

Dervish looked at Michelli, his eyes reflecting the vast flux of emotions racing through him.

"We became friends, Dervish," Michelli continued. "I gave her rides in my fighter and she taught me how to cloak my mind. It became very difficult for me to see her. Perhaps, if your father hadn't stolen her heart, we would have eventually gotten approval."

"Is that why you kept me here?" Dervish asked.

Michelli took a deep breath, and looked away for a few moments. Finally he turned his pensive gaze back on Dervish. "Possibly," he said quietly, "although, if so, I didn't realize it. Remember, it'd been twenty some years since I'd seen your mother, and you kept that stupid cap over your hair all the time. Reynard pointed it out after you'd been here a few weeks. You did look a lot like her, but then you had the Talent. We both dismissed it until we learned you weren't pure Alderian."

"But why me?"

"I suppose I still love your mother. I really don't care who your biological father was."

Dervish shook his head slowly. "Why not appoint one of your generals. They're real good and ..."

"And the galaxy will break apart into little factions, each wanting their favorite to rule. Blood can't be argued with."

"I'm honored, really I am," Dervish admitted, "but I don't have any Alderian blood."

"I hate to spoil your evening, but you do have some. It's really immaterial though. If I say you're my son," Michelli chuckled, "no one's going to give you a blood test."

"I ... I ... don't know what to say. I'm not ... I mean ... I'm a Flier ... and ..."

"The black sheep of two families," Michelli finished for him.

"But my uncle ..." Dervish started to protest.

"I'll approach him on the subject," Michelli assured him. "Now, be a good lad and get yourself off to bed. I have a lot of work to finish before we leave tomorrow."

"But ... I'm no king."

"Run along."

"I don't want ..."

"Good night, son."

"Night," Dervish muttered as he wandered back down the hall.

This is real weird, he thought. *I'm going to have a hard time convincing 'em I don't want any part of this shit.* He stopped as he opened the door and looked at Rusty's questioning face. "I think I've been snookered. Again," he lamented.

✦ ✦ ✦

Quilbraugh made his way silently into the moonlit garden. He paused to see if anything or anybody was watching or listening. Satisfied, he picked up a stick and began to draw strange patterns in the ground.

Hawk's voice startled him. "What are you doing?"

"Whoa!" Quilbraugh yelped as he turned. Recognizing Hawk, he visibly relaxed. "I didn't hear you approachin'," he said, admiring his handiwork. "I truly must be gettin' old." He walked over to the closest bench and sat down. "Since I be puttin' meself out on a limb for the sprout, I really ought t'be knowin' a bit more about 'im. I should be gettin' an answer soon."

The patterns began to glitter and reform. Quilbraugh looked at it and a smile crept over his face.

"I like it," Hawk said, "but why did you make that particular shape?"

"The truth of it is, the Magic picked the shape. Do you know what it means?"

"Yeah. It's the Star of David."

"Bah. 'Tis the Intersectin' Triangles, sprout!" Quilbraugh sputtered. "The first Triangle be representin' Happiness, Health, and Love; the second be Wisdom, Imagination, and Courage. The points of each be closely aligned with its neighbor. If y'be losin' one of the three, the other two be deterioratin'." He looked at Hawk a moment and grinned. "Some folks be havin' the audacity to be substitutin' Intelligence for Wisdom or Imagination. Or, and 'tis even a worse thing, they be sayin' Love is all y' need. Not a one of the six can exist without its complement on the other Triangle."

Hawk looked at Quilbraugh oddly. "I don't get it. Why would the Magic make that shape just because you asked it about Dervish?"

Quilbraugh stared at the ground as the glimmering shape faded away. "It be tellin' me he's in balance, he be carryin' its will."

"What does that mean?" Hawk asked with a trace of concern.

"It be intendin' for him to be accomplishin' something," Quilbraugh muttered. "We'll just have to be stickin' around to find out what it be havin' in mind."

"But how can it expect him to do something if he doesn't know what it is?"

"He'll be doin' it all right," Quilbraugh replied while lighting his pipe. "I be thinkin' he might not be too eager ... but he'll be doin' it. In the color of Magic they be formin' to follow him. Soon it'll be but one group that be protectin' the Universe."

Hawk sniffed the air. "That smells like tobacco," he observed as he got up to leave, "so the only explanation is that you're crazy!"

Quilbraugh watched Hawk walk off toward the Villa and sighed. He took a few more puffs on his pipe and glanced up at the sky. "So, I be crazy," he mumbled.

Don't Let Out The Magic Smoke
continues with
Book II: Candles In The Rain

For those of you who are interested in such things: This manuscript was written on an Amiga 3000 with a 25 MHz 68030 processor and 32 MB of 32-bit memory using UEdit by Rick Stiles. Typesetting was done on the Amiga using PageStream by Grasshopper LLC. The primary typeface is New Century Schoolbook

V5

Made in the USA
Monee, IL
04 December 2020